THE VINTAGE BOOK
OF LOVE STORIES

Helen Byatt graduated from Cambridge University in
1982. She has worked as a reviewer and critic, as well as
in arts administration at the Arts Council of Great
Britain, and currently at the South Bank Centre in
London. She has two young children.

THE VINTAGE BOOK OF LOVE STORIES

Edited by Helen Byatt

V

VINTAGE

Published by Vintage 1997

2 4 6 8 10 9 7 5 3 1

First published in Great Britain as
The Chatto Book of Love Stories by
Chatto & Windus Ltd, 1994

Vintage
Random House, 20 Vauxhall Bridge Road,
London SW1V 2SA

Random House Australia (Pty) Limited
20 Alfred Street, Milsons Point, Sydney
New South Wales 2061, Australia

Random House New Zealand Limited
18 Poland Road, Glenfield,
Auckland 10, New Zealand

Random House South Africa (Pty) Limited
Endulini, 5A Jubilee Road, Parktown 2193, South Africa

Random House UK Limited Reg. No. 954009

A CIP catalogue record for this book
is available from the British Library

ISBN 0 09 970251 7

Papers used by Random House UK Ltd are natural, recyclable products made from wood grown in sustainable forests. The manufacturing processes conform to the environmental regulations of the country of origin

Printed and bound in Great Britain by
Cox & Wyman, Reading, Berkshire

Contents

Sylvia Townsend Warner   1
A Love Match

Elizabeth Taylor   27
Good-Bye, Good-Bye

Robert Louis Stevenson   43
The Sire de Malétroit's Door

Bernard Malamud   68
The First Seven Years

Aldous Huxley   81
Happily Ever After

Peter Taylor   125
Reservations

Bobbie Ann Mason   158
Hunktown

Alice Munro   182
Fits

V. S. Pritchett   212
Blind Love

A. S. Byatt   263
Precipice-Encurled

Virginia Woolf   295
The Legacy

Ivan Klima 304
The Tightrope Walkers

Antonio Tabucchi 336
Cinema

Angela Carter 357
Puss-in-Boots

Introduction

'Love is desire sustained by unfulfilment' says the randy cat in Angela Carter's 'Puss-in-Boots'. Love is not easily pinned down; like mercury it shines but will not hold a clear form. Once grasped it has gone. Indeed, Love has a propensity to slip through one's fingers and this makes it dangerous because mercury, of course, is poisonous.

It is both a curse and a blessing that there turns out to be no such thing as a simple love story. There is no crystallised essence of love lying between these pages. Instead, love is as various as the people who experience it. The stories in this collection approach love as formal courtship; as the celebration of ancient fertility rights; as sexual embarrassment; as loss or a complete impossibility. I have not chosen them to provide a complete or even particularly coherent representation of love in all its particular forms. Any anthology must contain a strong element of personal choice and I have selected the stories here because none of them is quite straightforward. As a result, none is self-satisfied.

There is one other guiding hand shaping this collection. The stories here are all from the Chatto backlist and represent 150 years of one literary publisher's choice of writers. Of course, not all the writers on the Chatto list write short stories, including many of the newest generation; nevertheless the Chatto backlist offers enormous wealth. Spanning the Atlantic as well as reaching well into Europe it contains some of the most significant short-story writers over the last 150 years—V. S. Pritchett, Alice Munro, Peter Taylor and Angela Carter. By necessity the choice has been slightly retrospective; the new cutting edge of Chatto writing is still being cut, after all.

It is dangerous to make generalisations about such a distinguished and varied group of writers but I think there are common approaches amongst them. Perhaps it is just an inevitable ingredient of good writing, but these writers never plump for an obvious view (which is just as well because one of love's common bedfellows is sentimentality). Whether the writers here are brashly rebellious or darkly complex there is often something disturbing in what they offer. Recurrently love is bittersweet, and even at its most comic and raucous it can be blackly shocking (one pair of lovers literally make love over a corpse). In some of the more serious stories love's nature is dark and bottomless whilst others use love to defy social acceptability or the limits of narrative. Love is at odds with order.

Of course, there is a longstanding tradition of writing about love and some of the stories here use fairly traditional forms to question the notion of formulaic love. Both Robert Louis Stevenson and Bernard Malamud are represented by different forms of courtly story. Stevenson's 'The Sire de Malétroit's Door' is a kind of unromantic pre-Raphaelite's medieval Romance; courtly concerns verge into a comedy of social manners. In the midst of the formal courtship dance the heroine notices the hero's somewhat ostentatious shoes and smirks to one side, a gesture at odds with the extenuating circumstances they also happen to be in at the time. The moral tone that comes through the language of courtship is less about honour than it is about male pride. More modern relations between men and women, (in the form of a kind of banter where each lover vies for position), intrude into this formal tale and unsettle it.

'The First Seven Years' has perfect manners at its heart. Again it is a traditional format expounding the values of constancy and love above material well-being and wealth. The shoemaker is the epitome of the committed and patient lover who is lucky enough to have an open, full-faced vision of love. 'She knows who I am and what is in my heart' he boasts, a knowledge characters in other stories find extremely hard to come by. Yet the modern world intrudes on this clear view. There is a dilemma at the centre of this story a bit like the problem some people have with the concept of God—if God is good how can He permit such suffering? How can the shoemaker see love with such purity when he is the same man as the one who has been through the concentration camps? Shining optimism or dogged sentimentality? Make of it what you will.

The contrasts may not be as shocking in the English stories which place love as a parallel to, rather than part of, social convention, but they are no less complicated. Like Malamud, Elizabeth Taylor's version of love is permanent and constant. It is offered with such conviction that in many ways 'Goodbye, Good-bye' is the saddest story told here. It is the kind of short story that comes nearest to how Pritchett defines one, as something 'that tells only one thing, and that, intensely'. 'Good-bye, Good-bye' releases one of those intense and tightly focused moments—a glimpse of a tear in an eye—which creates an architectural structure to contain the love between two people. The rest of the story bombards this adulterous love and it survives only tenuously as this hidden moment. Love escapes social convention in principle; it is not so obvious it does in practice.

There are more outrageous versions of illicit love than

adultery, though there is something about the calmness of the English short story that can make anything acceptable. If Nabokov's great scoop was to make paedophilia seem understandably pleasurable, Sylvia Townsend Warner's is to make incest so unquestioningly natural that it can be assimilated entirely into English country life. It is such a quiet act of rebellion. The love in 'A Love Match' is quite private, walled off like an English country garden, but its foundations are very strong and they are dug into ground more deep and frightening than the easy suitability of the title suggests. Love is neither safe nor sacred. Sounds of violent bombardment echo through the story as memories, as malicious people, as destruction. Social acceptability is, after all, out on the attack.

The consequences of a love affair that does not fit socially are no less dire in Virginia Woolf's 'The Legacy'. Passion is very private and allied to violent death whilst conventional middle-class marriage is a passive state of not being fully alive. Sylvia Townsend Warner and Virginia Woolf both suggest that real love is hidden (a code for their own homosexuality?) and that love which belongs to social convention is superficial and second best.

Peter Taylor's irreverence for social form is a pure piece of comic relief. I've included 'Reservations' for its sheer slapstick quality and because it is about the embarrassment of love. There is something ridiculous about the pyjamas and négligés worn by the newly-weds in this story that allies sexual embarrassment with the clothing of social requirement. The newly-weds would be better off free of destructive social concerns just as they would basically find things less hindered naked. Taylor takes the comedy of manners a step further. His suggestion that true knowledge rather than social cladding lies at the bare core of love is founded on a desire to believe this rather than a firm belief that it is so: 'As they gazed deep into each other's eyes, they believed they had got all that off their chests once and for all. There was nothing in the world to come between them now.' Love, it seems, is not quite to be trusted.

The sexual embarrassment in Huxley's 'Happily Ever After' belongs to the tacit English habit of criticising the elevation of mind over body but which nevertheless writes very politely about sexual attraction. Huxley is more bold on this subject than his contemporary E. M. Forster. If he does not quite feel in the right place and time to write rudely about sex he is grotesquely wicked instead. He is cruelly dismissive of any teetering higher notions of love but he is not a cynic. 'Happily Ever After' satisfyingly, if facetiously, falls out right, built as it is on physical love.

Taylor and Huxley hint that naked, raw knowledge lies at the heart of love and I've included a group of stories in this collection that confront head on what might be meant by such knowledge. Pat answers are not provided. These are open-ended and questioning stories which draw the reader into their darker centres where exploring the intimacy between people is dangerous and sometimes intensely frightening. At first glance V. S. Pritchett's story 'Blind Love' appears neatly framed. It is a kind of formal courtship dance: two people meet, fall in love, argue, make declarations and settle. But their steps are paced out on the brim of an abyss. The lovers' knowledge of each other is part of original sin, they bite the apple and descend into a sightless intimate world that is more than sensuous exploration. The lovers risk drowning in it but it is only the depth of their exploration which allows Mrs Johnson to surface feeling 'gaudy' with love. ('Mrs Johnson', only Pritchett can be so formal and so wild at the same time.)

Alice Munro's story 'Fits' is the most shatteringly violent one here and it is an indication of her skill that she can build such a strong love story around a bloody and unexplained suicide. (It is all encapsulated in the pun in the title.) As a small town gossips about this horrifying event the relationship between husband and wife remains unspoken and blankly private. The metaphorical backdrop of this story consists of vast expanses of blank cold snow. It is hard to see any route into such self-contained privacy. Getting close to another person is not quite getting there; however well you know and anticipate them they will always remain other—to love someone is to recognise their complete separateness. The husband here loves his wife despite what he cannot know about her, it is dangerous because there might be something unpleasant at her core, but his trust is complete. It is this completeness that makes the story so strong.

Bobby Ann Mason is also interested in what love cannot reach or touch. With a lighter touch she explores the parts of the loved one that escape the grasp of the lover, or is it just the bits her heroine does not like about her husband? Joann loves Cody the way she sees him, not the way he sees himself (and who can blame her—his insistence on squeezing himself into trousers that are too tight is an embarrassing moment of self-deception). The misfit between what Joann sees and Cody's own perception of himself is partly comic but mostly bleak because it is clear Joann *has* to take him as he is, pathetic vanity included. It is Joann's persistence in doing this that makes the story about love rather than loss.

Other writers explore love as a literary idea examining the gap between its actual and fictional existence. A. S. Byatt's 'Precipice-Encurled' is primarily about the nature of narrative but its centre-piece clearly focuses on the nature of the lovers' gaze. In 'Precipice-Encurled' it is also a moment which alludes to many other written about meetings of eyes (and there are plenty of examples in this collection)—'Love had blossomed, or struck, like lightning, like a hawk, as it was clearly seen to do in novels and poems'. This intense, moving moment strings and twists itself into the rest of the story, at once the passionately private experience that can only exist between two people and the public, fictional depiction of it.

The lover in Tabucchi's story is a master of dramatic artifice. The subject is the same as Elizabeth Taylor's; 'Cinema' laments a past affair, but this time it really is over. The story only hints at past love, its existence is outside the current narrative. Tabucchi writes instead a mimic of what has been. These second-hand emotions are constructed around a film set forcing the love here to be acted out rather than felt. 'Cinema' warns against nostalgia for love lost and our inability to let lost lovers go, but it is also about the privacy of love between two people. What is available to the reader is clearly a fiction, the parallel reality is kept at a distance, safeguarded.

I have included Ivan Klima's 'The Tightrope Walkers' because it is a kind of abstract and mysterious discussion about the idea of love which never comes to a prosaic definition. It keeps the reader suspended, floating. Klima presents a glistening, ecstatic picture of love as a necessary ideal and balances it finely with its dark absence. The narrator aspires to the full life love gives, longs for it, but does not really have the stomach for it. Rising to its shining heights runs too great a risk of falling into the darkness of death. Love is a vision here created by the writer, dangerously. It slips out of his grasp and falls away, out of sight.

In many of these stories then, love lies somewhere just beyond our reach, it is an idea, a private thing, or an emotion not quite obtained. Such intangible love is not for Angela Carter, though this does not mean what she grabs is simple. 'Puss-in-Boots' is a joyous celebration of love and fiction rather than an exponent of their joint difficulties. Rebellious and bold, I've included her story because it is so unashamedly about sex.

Besides obviously being an adaptation, 'Puss-in-Boots' reson-
ates with a long line of love stories—princesses in towers,
renaissance comedy, Beaumarchais. This comedy of disguises
steps a love dance which is based on deception and which fires
a warning against sentimental or over formalised expressions
of love (particularly by men after one thing). 'Puss-in-Boots'
celebrates bawdiness; a bawdiness which its female characters
do not fall victim to but practise equally. The eroticism here
is that of 'The Miller's Tale'—the formal lover's eye-to-eye
gaze is quickly passed over for a quick bit of bodily gratification. There are no romantic sentiments here, just selfish *joie
de vivre*. Yet Carter's story is the only one here which bears
fruit —a litter of kittens and human children. This is a product-
ive and positive union which does not just praise lust but
celebrates fertility. 'Puss-in-Boots' is quick with life.

Perhaps it is the life-force in a love story that makes it one.
Love never lies clearly defined but inert, it rushes on through
dark and light.

Helen Byatt
May 1993

Sylvia Townsend Warner
A Love Match

It was Mr Pilkington who brought the Tizards to Hallowby.
He met them, a quiet couple, at Carnac, where he had gone
for a schoolmasterly Easter holiday to look at the monoliths.
After two or three meetings at a café, they invited him to their
rented chalet. It was a cold, wet afternoon and a fire of pine
cones crackled on the hearth. 'We collect them on our walks,'
said Miss Tizard. 'It's an economy. And it gives us an object.'
The words, and the formal composure of her manner, made
her seem like a Frenchwoman. Afterwards, he learned that the
Tizards were a Channel Island family and had spent their
childhood in Jersey. The ancestry that surfaced in Miss Tizard's
brisk gait and erect carriage, brown skin and compact sentences,
did not show in her brother. His fair hair, his red face, his
indecisive remarks, his diffident movements—as though with
the rest of his body he were apologising for his stiff leg—were
entirely English. He ought not, thought Mr Pilkington, to be
hanging about in France. He'd done more than enough for
France already. For this was in 1923 and Mr Pilkington, with
every intention of preserving a historian's impartiality, was
nevertheless infected by the current mood of disliking the
French.

The weather continued cold and wet; there was a sameness
about the granite avenues. Mr Pilkington's mind became increasingly engaged with the possibility, the desirability, the

positive duty of saving that nice fellow Tizard from wasting his days in exile. He plied him with hints, with suggestions, with tactful inquiries. Beyond discovering that money was not the obstacle to return, he got no further. Tizard, poor fellow, must be under his sister's thumb. Yet it was from the sister that he got his first plain answer. 'Justin would mope if he had nothing to do.' Mr Pilkington stopped himself from commenting on the collection of pine cones as an adequate lifework. As though she had read his thought, she went on, 'There is a difference between idling in a foreign country and being an idler in your own.' At that moment Tizard limped into the room with crayfish bristling from his shopping basket. 'It's begun,' he said ruefully. '*La Jeune France* has arrived. I've just seen two young men in pink trousers with daisy chains round their necks, riding through the town on donkeys.' Mr Pilkington asked if this was a circus. Miss Tizard explained that it was the new generation, and would make Carnac a bedlam till the summer's end. 'Of course, there's a certain amount of that sort of thing in England, too,' observed Mr Pilkington. 'But only in the South. It doesn't trouble us at Hallowby.' As he spoke, he was conscious of playing a good card; then the immensity of the trump he held broke upon him. He was too excited to speak. Inviting them to dine at his hotel on the following night, he went away.

By next evening, more of *La Jeune France* had arrived, and was mustered outside the hotel extemporising a bullfight ballet in honour of St Cornély, patron saint of cattle and of the parish church. Watching Tizard's look of stoically endured embarrassment Mr Pilkington announced that he had had a blow; the man who had almost promised to become curator of the Beelby Military Museum had written to say he couldn't take up the post. 'He didn't say why. But I know why. Hallowby is too quiet for him.'

'But I thought Hallowby had blast furnaces and strikes and all that sort of thing,' said Tizard.

'That is Hallowby juxta Mare,' replied Mr Pilkington. 'We are Old Hallowby. Very quiet; quite old, too. The school was founded in 1623. We shall be having our modest tercentenary this summer. That is why I am so put out by Dalsover's not taking up the curatorship. I hoped to have the museum all in order. It would have been something to visit, if it rains during the Celebrations.' He allowed a pause.

Tizard, staring at the toothpicks, inquired, 'Is it a wet climate?'

But Mr Pilkington was the headmaster of a minor public school, a position of command. As if the pause had not taken place, raising his voice above the bullfight he told how fifty years earlier Davenport Beelby, a rich man's sickly son, during a lesson on the Battle of Minden awoke to military glory and began to collect regimental buttons. Buttons, badges, pikes, muskets and bayonets, shakos and helmets, despatches, newspaper cuttings, stones from European battlefields, sand from desert campaigns—his foolish collection grew into the life-work of a devoted eccentric and, as such collections sometimes do, became valuable and authoritative, though never properly catalogued. Two years ago he had died, bequeathing the collection to his old school, with a fund sufficient for upkeep and the salary of a curator.

'I wish you'd consider coming as our curator,' said Mr Pilkington. 'I'm sure you would find it congenial. Beelby wanted an Army man. Three mornings a week would be quite enough.'

Tizard shifted his gaze from the toothpicks to the mustard jar. 'I am not an Army man,' he said. 'I just fought. Not the same thing, you know.'

Miss Tizard exclaimed, 'No! Not at all,' and changed the subject.

But later that evening she said to her brother, 'Once we were there, we shouldn't see much of him. It's a possibility.'

'Do you want to go home, Celia?'

'I think it's time we did. We were both of us born for a sober, conventional, taxpaying life, and if—'

'*Voici Noël!*' sang the passing voices. '*Voici Noël! Voici Noël, petits enfants!*'

She composed her twitching hands and folded them on her lap. 'We were young rowdies once,' he said placatingly.

A fortnight later, they were Mr Pilkington's guests at Hallowby. A list of empty houses had been compiled by Miss Robson, the secretary. All were variously suitable; each in turn was inspected by Miss Tizard and rejected. Mr Pilkington felt piqued that his offer of a post should dance attendance on the aspect of a larder or the presence of decorative tiles. Miss Tizard was a disappointment to him; he had relied on her support. Now it was the half-hearted Tizard who seemed inclined to root, while she flitted from one eligible residence to another, appearing, as he remarked to the secretary, to expect impossibilities. Yet when she settled as categorically as a queen bee the house she chose had really nothing to be said for it. A square, squat mid-Victorian box, Newton Lodge was one of the ugliest houses in Hallowby; though a high surrounding wall with a green door in it hid the totality of its ugliness from passers-by, its hulking chimneys proclaimed what was below. It was not even well situated. It stood in a deteriorating part of the town, and was at some distance from the school buildings and the former gymnasium—Victorian also—which had been assigned to the Beelby Collection. But the house having been chosen, the curatorship was bestowed and the move made. Justin Tizard, rescued from wasting his days in exile—though too late for the tercentenary celebrations—began his duties as curator by destroying a quantity of cobwebs and sending for a window-cleaner.

All through the summer holidays he worked on, sorting things into heaps, subdividing the heaps into lesser heaps. Beelby's executors must have given carte-blanche to the packers, who had acted on the principle of filling up with anything that came handy, and the unpackers had done little more than tumble things out and scatter them with notices saying 'DO NOT DISTURB'. The largest heap consisted of objects he could not account for, but unaccountably it lessened, till the day came when he could look round on tidiness. Ambition seized him. Tidiness is not enough; no one looks twice at tidiness. There must also be parade and ostentation. He bought stands, display cases, dummies for the best uniforms. Noticing a decayed wooden horse in the saddler's shop, he bought that, too; trapped, with its worser side to the wall and with a cavalry dummy astride, it made a splendid appearance. He combed plumes, shook out bearskins, polished holsters and gunstocks, oiled the demi-culverin, sieved the desert sand. At this stage, his sister came and polished with him, mended, refurbished, sewed on loose buttons. Of the two, she had more feeling for the exhibits themselves, for the discolouring glory and blood-shed they represented. It was the housewife's side that appealed to him. Sometimes, hearing him break into the whistle of a contented mind, she would look up from her work and stare at him with the unbelief of thankfulness.

Early in the autumn term, Mr Pilkington made time to visit the museum. He did not expect much and came prepared with speeches of congratulation and encouragement. They died on his lips when he saw the transformation. Instead, he asked how much the display cases had cost, and the dummies, and the horse, and how much of the upkeep fund remained after all this expenditure. He could not find fault; there was no reason to do so. He was pleased to see Tizard so well established as master in his own house. Perhaps he was also pleased that there was no reason to find fault. Though outwardly unchanged, the Tizard of Carnac appeared to have been charged with new contents—with something obstinately reckless beneath the easy-going manner, with watchfulness beneath the diffidence. But this, reflected Mr Pilkington, might well be accounted for by the startling innovations in the museum. He stayed longer than he meant, and only after leaving remembered that he had omitted to say how glad he was that Tizard had accepted the curatorship. This must be put right; he did not want to discourage the young man who had worked so hard and so efficiently, and also he must get into the way of remembering that Tizard was in fact a young man—under thirty. Somehow, one did not think of him as a young man.

Justin Tizard, newly a captain in an infantry regiment, came on leave after the battle of the Somme. His sister met the train at Victoria. There were some pigeons strutting on the platform and he was watching them when a strange woman in black came up to him, touched his shoulder, and said, 'Justin!' It was as though Celia were claiming a piece of lost luggage, he thought. She had a taxi waiting, and they drove to her flat. She asked about his health, about his journey; then she congratulated him on his captaincy. 'Practical reasons,' he said. 'My habit of not getting killed. They were bound to notice it sooner or later.' After this, they fell silent. He looked out of the window at the streets so clean and the people so busy with their own affairs. 'That's a new Bovril poster, isn't it?' he inquired. Her answer was so slow in coming that he didn't really take in whether it was yes or no.

Her flat was new, anyway. She had only been in it since their mother's remarriage. It was up a great many flights of stairs, and she spoke of moving to somewhere with a lift, now that Tim's legacy had made a rich woman of her. The room smelled of polish and flowers. There was a light-coloured rug on the floor and above this was the blackness of Celia's skirts. She was wearing black for her fiancé. The news of his death had come to her in this same room, while she was still sorting books and hanging pictures. Looking round the room, still not looking at Celia, he saw Tim's photograph on her desk. She saw his glance, and hers followed it. 'Poor Tim!' they said, both speaking at once, the timbre of their voices relating them. 'They say he was killed instantaneously,' she went on. 'I hope it's true—though I suppose they always say that.'

'I'm sure it is,' he replied. He knew that Tim had been blown to pieces. Compassion made it possible to look at her. Dressed in black, possessing these new surroundings, she seemed mature and dignified beyond her actual three years' seniority. For the first time in his life he saw her not as a sister but as an individual. But he could not see her steadily for long. There was a blur on his sight, a broth of mud and flame and frantic unknown faces and writhing entrails. When she showed him to his bedroom she stepped over mud that heaved with the bodies of men submerged in it. She had drawn the curtains. There was a bed with sheets turned back, and a bedside lamp shed a serene, unblinking light on the pillows. 'Bed!' he exclaimed, and heard the spontaneity die in his voice. 'Wonderful to see a bed!'

'And this is the bathroom. I've got everything planned. First of all, you must have a bath, lie and soak in it. And then put on these pyjamas and the dressing gown, and we will have supper.'

Left to himself, he was violently sick. Shaking with fatigue, he sat in a hot scented bath and cleaned his knees with scrupulous care, like a child. Outside was the noise of London.

The pyjamas were silk, the dressing gown was quilted and wrapped him round like a caress. In the sitting-room was Celia, still a stranger, though now a stranger without a hat. There was a table sparkling with silver and crystal, smoked salmon, a bottle of champagne. It was all as she had planned it for Tim—Oh, poor Celia!

They discussed their mother's remarriage. It had been decided on with great suddenness, and appeared inexplicable. Though they refrained from saying much, their comments implied that her only reason for marrying a meat king from the Argentine was to get away from England and the war. 'There he was, at eleven in the morning, with a carnation—a foot shorter than she,' said Celia, describing the return from the registry office.

'In that case, he must be four foot three.'

'He is exactly four foot three. I stole up and measured him.'

Spoken in her imperturbable voice, this declaration struck him as immensely funny, as funny as a nursery joke. They laughed hilariously, and after this their evening went almost naturally.

Turning back after his unadorned, brotherly 'Good night, Celia,' he exclaimed, 'But where are you sleeping?'

'In here.' Before he could demur she went on, 'The sofa fits me. It would be far too short for you.'

He told her how balmily he had slept, one night behind the lines, with his head on a bag of nails.

'Exactly! That is why tonight you are going to sleep properly. In a bed.'

She heard him get into bed, heard the lamp switched off. Almost immediately she heard his breathing lengthen into slumber. Then, a few minutes later, he began to talk in his sleep.

Perhaps a scruple—the dishonourableness of being an eavesdropper, a Peeping Tom—perhaps mere craven terror, made her try not to listen. She began to read, and when she found that impossible she repeated poems she had learned at school, and when that failed she polished the silver cigarette box. But Justin's voice was raised, and the partition wall was thin, and the ghastly confidences went on and on. She could not escape them. She was dragged, a raw recruit, into battle.

In the morning she thought she would not be able to look him in the face. But he was cheerful, and so was she. She had got off from the canteen, she explained, while he was on leave; they had nothing to do but enjoy themselves. They decided to have some new experiences, so they went up the Monument. If he wants to throw himself off, she thought, I won't stop him. They looked down on London; on the curve of the Thames, the shipping, the busy lighters. They essayed how many City churches they could identify by their spires. They talked about Pepys. She would be surprised, Justin said, how many chaps carried a copy of the *Diary*, and she asked if bullets also glanced off Pepys carried in a breast pocket. So they made conversation quite successfully. And afterwards, when they had decided to go for a walk down Whitechapel High Street and lunch off winkles at a stall, many people glanced at them with kindness and sentimentality, and an old woman patted Celia's back, saying, 'God bless you, dearie! Isn't it lovely to have him home?'

Whitechapel was a good idea. The throng of people carried some of the weight of self-consciousness for them; the wind blowing up-river and the hooting of ships' sirens made them feel they were in some foreign port of call, taking a stroll till it was time to re-embark. He was less aware that she had grown strange to him, and she was momentarily able to forget the appalling stranger who had raved in her bed all night.

They dined at a restaurant, and went on to a music hall. That night he took longer to fall asleep. She had allowed herself a thread of hope, when he began to talk again. Three Justins competed, thrusting each other aside: a cold, attentive observer, a debased child, a devil bragging in hell. At intervals they were banished by a recognisable Justin interminably muttering to himself, 'Here's a sword for Toad, here's a sword for Rat, here's a sword for Mole, here's a sword for Badger.' The reiteration from that bible of their childhood would stick on the word, 'Rat'. 'Got you!' And he was off again.

The next day they went to the Zoo. The Zoo was not so efficacious as Whitechapel. It was feeling the pinch, the animals looked shabby and dejected, many cages were empty. Two sleepless nights had made Celia's feet swell. It was pain to walk, pain to stand. She wondered how much longer she could keep it up, this 'God bless you, dearie' pretence of a lovely leave. The day accumulated its hours like a windlass. The load grew heavier; the windlass baulked under it, but wound on. He went to bed with the usual 'Good night, Celia'. As usual, she undressed and put on that derision of a nightdress, and wrapped herself in an eiderdown and lay down to wait under the smiling gaze of Tim's photograph. She felt herself growing icy cold, couldn't remember if she had wound her watch, couldn't remember what diversion she had planned for the morrow, was walking over Richmond Bridge in a snowstorm, when she noticed he had begun again. *She noticed*. It had come to that. Two nights of a vicarious endurance of what was being endured, had been endured, would continue to be endured by a cancelled generation, had so exhausted her that now she felt neither horror nor despair, merely a bitter acquiescence. Justin went on with his Hail Devil Rosary, and in France the guns went on and on, and the mud dried into dust and slumped back into mud again. People went down to Kent to listen to the noise of the guns: the people in Kent said that they had grown used to it, didn't hear it any longer. The icy cold sensation bored into her midriff, nailed her down in sleep.

Some outcry, some exclamation (she could not afterwards remember what it was), woke her. Before she knew what she was doing she was in the next room, trying to waken the man who lay so rigidly in her bed, who, if she could awaken him, would be Justin, her brother Justin. 'Oh, poor Justin, my poor Justin!' Throwing herself on the bed, she clasped him in her arms, lifted his head to lie against her breast, kissed his chattering lips. 'There, there!' She felt him relax, waken, drag her towards him. They rushed into the escape of love like winter-starved cattle rushing into a spring pasture.

When light came into the room, they drew a little apart and looked at each other.

'Now we've done it,' he said; and hearing the new note in his voice she replied, 'A good thing, don't you think?'

Their release left them no option. After a few hours they were not even astonished. They were mated for life, that was all—for a matter of days, so they made the most of it. At the end of his leave they parted in exaltation, he convinced that he was going off to be killed, she that she would bear his child, to which she would devote the remainder of her existence.

A little later she knew she was not pregnant.

Early in the new year Justin, still panoplied in this legendary and by now rather ludicrous charmed life, was made a major. In April, he was wounded in the leg. 'Nothing to worry about,' he wrote; 'just a few splinters. I am in bed, as peaceful as a pincushion.' Later, she heard that he had been moved to a hospital on the outskirts of London. One of the splinters had escaped notice, and gas gangrene had developed in the wound.

I shall be a peg leg, he thought. It's not decent for a peg leg to make love; even to his sister. He was ravaged with fret and behaving with perfect decorum when Celia was shown

in—dressed all in leaf green, walking like an empress, smelling delicious. For a moment the leaf-green Celia was almost
as much of a stranger as the Celia all in black had been. When
she kissed him, he discovered that she was shaking from head
to foot. 'There, there,' he said, patting her. Still holding his
hand, she addressed herself to charming Nurse Painter. Nurse
Painter was in favour of sisters. They weren't so much trouble,
didn't upset a patient, as sweethearts or wives did—and you
didn't have to be hanging round all the time, ready to shoo
them off. When Celia came next day, Nurse Painter congratulated her on having done the Major no end of good. There had
been a lot of pus; she liked to see a lot of pus.

They continued to give satisfaction; when Justin left hospital
with a knee that would always be stiff and from time to time
cause him pain, Nurse Painter's approval went with them. A
sister was just what he wanted—there would be no silly excitement; and as Miss Tizard was a trifle older than the Major,
there would be a restraining hand if called for. If Nurse Painter
had known what lay beneath this satisfactory arrangement, it
is probable that her approval would not have been seriously
withdrawn. The war looked like going on for ever; the best
you could hope for was a stalemate. Potatoes were unobtain-
able, honesty was no more, it was hate and muddle wherever
you looked. If a gentleman and lady could pluck up heart
enough to love and be happy—well, good luck to them!

Justin and Celia went to Oxfordshire, where they compared
the dragonflies on the Windrush with the dragonflies on the
Evenlode. Later, they went to France.

Beauty cannot be suborned. Never again did Justin see Celia
quivering with beauty as she had done on the day she came to
him in hospital. But he went on thinking she had a charming
face and the most entertaining eyebrows in the world. Loving

each other criminally and sincerely, they took pains to live together happily and to safeguard their happiness from injuries of their own infliction or from outside. It would have been difficult for them to be anything but inconspicuous, or to be taken for anything but a brother and sister—the kind of brother and sister of whom one says, 'It will be rather hard for her when he marries'. Their relationship, so conveniently obvious to the public eye, was equally convenient in private life, for it made them unusually intuitive about each other's feelings. Brought up to the same standard of behaviour, using the same vocabulary, they felt no need to impress each other and were not likely to be taken aback by each other's likes and dislikes. Even the fact of remembering the same foxed copy of *The Swiss Family Robinson* with the tear across the picture of the boa constrictor was a reassuring bond. During the first years in France they felt they would like to have a child—or for the sake of the other's happiness ought to have a child— and discussed the possibilities of a child put out to nurse, learning French as its native speech, and then being adopted as a postwar orphan, since it was now too late for it to be a war orphan. But however the child was dated, it would be almost certain to declare its inheritance of Grandfather Tizard's nose, and as a fruitful incest is thought even worse of than a barren one, they sensibly gave up the idea; though regretting it.

Oddly enough, after settling in Hallowby they regretted it no longer. They had a home in England, a standing and things to do. Justin had the Beelby Museum; Celia had a household. In Hallowby it was not possible to stroll out to a restaurant or to bring home puddings from the pastry cook, fillets of veal netted into bolsters by the butcher. Celia had to cook serious-ly, and soon found that if she was to cook meals worth eating she must go shopping too. This was just what was needed for their peace and quiet, since to be seen daily shopping saved a great deal of repetitious explanation that she and Justin could not afford to keep a servant in the house but must be content with Mrs Mugthwaite coming in three afternoons a week, and a jobbing gardener on Fridays. True, it exposed her to a certain amount of condolence and amazement from the school wives, but as they, like Mrs Mugthwaite, came only in the afternoons, she could bear with it. Soon they came more sparingly; for, as Justin pointed out, poverty is the sturdiest of all shelters, since people feel it to be rather sad and soon don't think about it, whereas her first intention of explaining that ever since her Aunt Dinah had wakened in the middle of the night to see an angered cook standing over her with a meat hatchet she had been nervous of servants sleeping under the same roof would only provoke gossip, surmise and insistent recommendations of cooks without passions. Justin was more long-sighted than Celia. She always knew what to do or say at the moment. He could look ahead, foresee dangers, and take steps to dodge them.

They did not see as much of Mr Pilkington as they had apprehended, and members of the staff were in no hurry to take up with another of Pilkington's Pets. Celia grew alarmed; if you make no friends, you become odd. She decided that they must occasionally go to church, though not too often or too enthusiastically, as it would then become odd that they did not take the Sacrament. No doubt a great many vicious church attenders took the Sacrament, and the rubric only forbids it to 'open and notorious evil-livers', which they had every intention of not being; but she could see a scruple of honour at work in Justin, so she did not labour this argument. There was a nice, stuffy pitch-pine St Cuthbert's near by, and at judicious intervals they went there for evensong—thereby renewing another bond of childhood: the pleasure of hurrying home on a cold evening to eat baked potatoes hot from the oven. How

old Mr Gillespie divined from Justin's church demeanour that
he was a whist player was a mystery never solved. But he
divined it. He had barely saved Celia's umbrella from being
blown inside out, remarking, 'You're newcomers, aren't you?
You don't know the east wind at this corner,' before he was
saying to Justin, 'You don't play whist, by any chance?' But
probably he would have asked this of anyone not demonstrably
a raving maniac, for since Colin Colbeck's death he, Miss
Colbeck and Canon Pendarves were desperate for a fourth
player. Canon Pendarves gave dinner parties, with a little
music afterwards. Celia, driven into performance and remembering how Becky Sharp had wooed Lady Steyne by singing
the religious songs of Mozart, sat down at the piano and played
'The Carmen's Whistle', one of the few things she reliably
knew by heart. This audacious antiquarianism delighted the
Canon, who kept her at his side for the rest of the evening,
relating how he had once tried to get up a performance of
Tallis's forty-part motet.

The Tizards were no longer odd. Their new friends were all
considerably older than they; the middle-aged had more conscience about the war and were readier to make friends with a
disabled major and his devoted maiden sister. In time, members of the staff overlooked their prejudice against Pilkington
Pets and found the Tizard couple agreeable, if slightly boring.

Returning from their sober junketings Justin and Celia, safe
within their brick wall, cast off their weeds of middle age,
laughed, chattered and kissed with an intensified delight in
their scandalous immunity from blame. They were a model
couple, the most respectable couple in Hallowby, treading
hand in hand the thornless path to fogydom. They began to
give small dinner parties themselves. They set up a pug and a
white cat. During their fifth summer in Hallowby they gave an
evening party in the Beelby Museum. This dashing even

almost carried them too far. It was such a success that they were begged to make an annual thing of it; and Celia was so gay, and her dress so fashionable, that she was within an inch of being thought a dangerous woman. Another party being expected of them, another had to be given. But this was a very different set-out: a children-and-parents party with a puppet show, held in St Cuthbert's Church Room, with Canon Pendarves speaking on behalf of the Save the Children Fund and a collection taken at the door. The collection was a master stroke. It put the Tizards back in their place as junior fogies— where Justin, for his part, was thankful to be. He had got there a trifle prematurely, perhaps, being in his mid-thirties, but it was where he intended to end his days.

He was fond of gardening, and had taken to gardening seriously, having an analysis made of the Newton Lodge soil— too acid, as he suspected—buying phosphates and potash and lime and kainite, treating different plots with different mixtures and noting the results in a book. He could not dig, but he limpingly mowed and rolled the lawn, trained climbing roses and staked delphiniums. Within the shelter of the wall, delphiniums did magnificently. Every year he added new varieties and when the original border could be lengthened no further a parallel bed was dug, with a grass walk in between. Every summer evening he walked there, watching the various blues file off, some to darkness, some to pallor, as the growing dusk took possession of them, while the white cat flitted about his steps like a moth. Because one must not be wholly selfish, from time to time he would invite a pair of chosen children to tea, cut each of them a long delphinium lance (cutting only those which were going over, however) and set them to play jousting matches on the lawn. Most of them did no more than thwack, but the two little Semples, the children of the school chaplain, fought with system, husbanding their strokes and aiming at each other's faces. Even when they had outgrown jousting they still came to Newton Lodge, hunting snails, borrowing books, helping him weigh out basic slag, addressing him as 'Justin'.

'Mary is just the age our child would have been,' remarked Celia after one of these visits. Seeing him start at the words, she went on, 'When you went back to be killed, and I was quite sure I would have a baby.'

'I wouldn't stand being called Justin—if she were.'

'You might have to. They're Bright Young Things from the cradle on, nowadays.'

By now the vogue for being a Bright Young Thing had reached even to Hallowby, its ankles growing rather muddied and muscular on the way. It was not like Celia to prefer an inferior article, and Justin wondered to see her tolerance of this anglicisation of the *Jeune France* when the original movement had so exasperated her. He hoped she wasn't mellowing; mellowness is not the food of love. A quite contrary process, however, was at work in Celia. At Carnac, even when accepting Pilkington as a way out of it, the exaltation of living in defiance of social prohibitions and the absorbing manoeuvres of seeming to live in compliance with them had been stimulus enough; she had had no mercy for less serious rebels. But during the last few years the sense of sinking month by month into the acquiescence of Hallowby, eating its wholesome lotus like cabbage, conforming with the inattentiveness of habit— and aware that if she overlooked a conformity the omission would be redressed by the general conviction that Justin Tizard, though in no way exciting, was always so nice and had a sister who devoted her life to him, so nice for them both, etc. etc.—had begun to pall, and the sight of any rebellion, however puerile, however clumsy, roused up her partisanship. Since she could not shock Hallowby to its foundations, she liked to see these young creatures trying to, and wished them luck. From time to time she even made approaches to them, solicited their trust, indicated that she was ranged on their side. They accepted, confided, condescended—and dropped her.

When one is thus put back in one's place, one finds one has grown out of it, and is a misfit. Celia became conscious how greatly she disliked Hallowby society. The school people nauseated her with their cautious culture and breezy heartiness. The indigenous inhabitants were more bearable, because they were less pretentious; but they bored her. The Church, from visiting bishops down to Salvation Army cornet players, she loathed for its hypocrisy. Only in Hallowby's shabbiest quarter—in Edna Road, Gladstone Terrace and Gas Lane— could she find anyone to love. Mr Newby the fishmonger in his malodorous den; old Mrs Foe among her sallowing cabbages and bruised apples; Mr Raby, the grocer, who couldn't afford to buy new stock because he hadn't the heart to call in the money his poorer customers owed him, and so had none but the poorest customers—these people were good. Probably it was only by their goodness that they survived and had not cut their throats in despair long ago. Celia began to shop in Gas Lane. It was not a success. Much as she might love Mr Newby she loved Justin better, and when a dried haddock gave him food poisoning she had to remove her custom—since the cat wouldn't touch Newby's fish anyhow. These disheartening experiences made her dislike respectable Hallowby even more. She wanted to cast it off, as someone tossing in fever wants to cast off a blanket.

The depression began. The increase of Mr Raby's customers drove him out of business: he went bankrupt and closed the shop. Groups of unemployed men from Hallowby juxta Mare appeared in Gas Lane and Edna Road and sang at street

corners—for misfortune always resorts to poor neighbour-
hoods for succour. People began to worry about their invest-
ments and to cut down subscriptions to such examples of
conspicuous waste as the Chamber Music Society. Experts on
nutrition wrote to the daily papers, pointing out the wasteful-
ness of frying, and explaining how, by buying cheaper cuts of
meat and cooking them much longer, the mothers of families
on the dole would be able to provide wholesome adequate
meals. Celia's uneasy goodwill and smouldering resentment
found their outlet. As impetuously as she had flung herself into
Justin's bed, she flung herself into relief work at Hallowby
juxta Mare. Being totally inexperienced in relief work she
exploded there like a nova. Her schemes were so outrageous
that people in authority didn't think them worth contesting
even; she was left to learn by experience, and made the most
of this valuable permission. One of her early outrages was to
put on a revue composed and performed by local talent. Local
talent ran to the impromptu, and when it became known what
scarification of local reputations could be expected, everyone
wanted to hear what might be said of everyone else and Celia
was able to raise the price of admission, which had been
sixpence, to as much as half a guinea for the best seats. Her
doings became a joke; you never knew what that woman
wouldn't be up to next. Hadn't she persuaded Wilson & Beck
to take on men they had turned off, because now, when half
the factory stood idle, was the moment to give it a spring
cleaning? Celia worked herself to the bone, and probably did
a considerable amount of good, but her great service to Hallowby juxta Mare was that she made the unemployed interested in their plight instead of dulled by it, so that helpers came
to her from the unemployed themselves. If she was not so
deeply impressed by their goodness as she had been by the
idealised goodness of Mr Newby and Mrs Foe, she was

impressed by their arguments; she became political, and by 1936 she was marching in Communist demonstrations, singing:

> Twenty-five years of hunger and war
> And they call it a glorious Jubilee.

Inland Hallowby was also looking forward to the Jubilee. The school was rehearsing a curtailed version of Purcell's *King Arthur*, with Mary Semple, now home from her finishing school, coming on in a chariot to sing 'Fairest Isle'. There was to be folk dancing by Scouts and Guides, a tea for the old people, a fancy-dress procession; and to mark the occasion Mr Harvey, JP, one of the school governors, had presented the Beelby Museum with a pair of buckskin breeches worn by the Duke of Wellington on the field of Talavera. 'I shall be expected to make a speech about them,' groaned Justin. 'I think I shall hire a deputy and go away for the day.'

Celia jumped at this. 'We'll both go away. Not just for the day but for a fornight. We'll go to Jersey, because you must attend the Jubilee celebrations on your native island—a family obligation. Representative of one of the oldest families. And if we find the same sort of fuss going on there, we can nip over to France in the Escudiers' boat and be quit of the whole thing. It's foolproof, it's perfect. The only thing needed to make it perfectly perfect is to make it a month. Justin, it's the answer.' She felt indeed that it was the answer. For some time now, Justin had seemed distrait and out of humour. Afraid he was unwell, she told herself he was stale and knew that he had been neglected. An escapade would put all right. Talavera had not been fought in vain. But she couldn't get him to consent. She was still persuading when the first letter arrived. It was typed and had been posted in Hallowby. It was unsigned, and began, 'Hag.'

Reading what followed, Celia tried to hold on to her first impression that the writer was some person in Hallowby juxta Mare. 'You think you're sitting pretty, don't you? You think no one has found you out.' She had made many enemies there; this must come from one of them. Several times she had been accused of misappropriating funds. Yes, that was it: '. . . and keep such a tight hold on him.' But why *him*? It was as though two letters lay on the flimsy page—the letter she was bent on reading and the letter that lay beneath and glared through it. It was a letter about her relations with Justin that she tore into bits and dropped in the wastepaper basket as he came down to breakfast.

She could hardly contain her impatience to get the bits out again, stick them on a backing sheet, make sure. Nothing is ever quite what it first was; the letter was viler, but it was also feebler. It struck her as amateurish.

The letter that came two days later was equally vile but better composed; the writer must be getting his or her hand in. A third was positively elegant. Vexatiously, there was no hint of a demand for hush money. Had there been, Celia could have called in the police, who would have set those ritual springes into which blackmailers—at any rate, blackmailers one reads of in newspapers—walk so artlessly. But the letters did not blackmail, did not even threaten. They stated that what the writer knew was common knowledge. After two letters, one on the heels of the other, which taunted Celia with being ugly, ageing and sexually ridiculous—letters that ripped through her self-control and made her cry with mortification—the writer returned to the theme of common knowledge and concluded with an 'It may interest you to hear that the following know all about your loathsome performances' and a list of half a dozen Hallowby names. Further letters laconically listed more names. From the outset, Celia had decided to keep all this to herself, and still held to the decision; but she hoped she wouldn't begin to talk in her sleep. There was less chance of this, as by now she was sleeping scarcely at all.

It was a Sunday morning and she and Justin were spraying roses for greenfly when Justin said, 'Puss, what are you concealing?' She syringed Mme Alfred Carrière so violently that the jet bowed the rose, went beyond it, and deluged a robin. Justin took the syringe out of her hand and repeated the question.

Looking at him, she saw his face was drawn with woe. 'No, no, it's nothing like that,' she exclaimed. 'I'm perfectly well. It's just that some poison-pen imbecile . . .'

When he had read through the letters, he said thoughtfully, 'I'd like to wring that little bitch's neck.'

'Yes, it is some woman or other, isn't it? I felt sure of that.'

'Some woman or other? It's Mary Semple.'

'That pretty little Mary Semple?'

'That pretty little Mary Semple. Give me the letters. I'll soon settle her.' He looked at his watch. 'No, I can't settle her yet. She'll still be in church.'

'But I don't understand why.'

'You do, really.'

'Justin! Have you been carrying on with Mary Semple?'

'No, I wouldn't say that. She's got white eyelashes. But ever since she came home Mary Semple has been doing all she could to carry on with me. There I was in the Beelby, you see, like a bull at the stake. No one comes near the place now; I was at her mercy. And in she tripped, and talked about the old days, telling me her little troubles, showing me poems, pitying me for my hard lot. I tried to cool her down, I tried to taper it off. But she was bent on rape, and one morning I lost all patience, told her she bored me and that if she came again I'd empty the fire bucket over her. She wept and wailed, and I paid no attention, and when there was silence I looked cautiously round and she was gone. And a day or so after'—he looked at the mended letter—'yes, a couple of days after, she sat her down to take it out of you.'

'But, Justin—how did she know about us?'

'No fire without smoke, I suppose. I dare say she overheard her parents cheering each other along the way with Christian surmises. Anyhow, children nowadays are brought up on that sort of useful knowledge.'

'No fire without smoke,' she repeated. 'And what about those lists?'

'Put in to make your flesh creep, most likely. Even if they do know, they weren't informed at a public meeting. Respectable individuals are too wary about libel and slander to raise their respectable voices individually. It's like that motet Pendarves used to talk about, when he could never manage to get them all there at once. Extraordinary ambitions people have! Fancy wanting to hear forty singers simultaneously yelling different tunes.'

'It can be done. There was a performance at Newcastle—he was dead by then. But, Justin—'

'That will do, Celia. I am now going off to settle Mary Semple.'

'How will you manage to see her alone?'

'I shall enter her father's dwelling. Mary will manage the rest.'

The savagery of these last words frightened her. She had not heard that note in his voice since he cried out in his sleep. She watched him limp from the room as though she were watching an incalculable stranger. A moment later he reappeared, took her hand, and kissed it. 'Don't worry, Puss. If need be, we'll fly the country.'

Whatever danger might lie ahead, it was the thought of the

danger escaped that made her tremble. If she had gone on concealing those letters—and she had considered it her right and duty to do so—a wedge would have been driven between her and Justin, bruising the tissue of their love, invisibly fissuring them, as a wedge of ice does in the living tree. And thus a scandal about their incest would have found them without any spontaneity of reaction and distracted by the discovery of how long she had been arrogating to herself a thing that concerned them both. 'Here and now,' she exclaimed, 'I give up being an elder sister who knows best.' Justin, on his way to the Semples', was muttering to himself, 'Damn and blast it, why couldn't she have told me sooner? If she had it would all be over by now.' It did not occur to him to blame himself for a lack of openness. This did not occur to Celia, either. It was Justin's constancy that mattered, not his fidelity—which was his own business.

When he reappeared, washed and brushed and ready for lunch, and told her there would be no more billets-doux from Mary, it was with merely tactical curiosity that she asked, 'Did you have to bribe her?' And as he did not answer at once, she went on to ask, 'Would you like potted shrimps or mulligatawny? There's both.'

They did not have to fly the country. Mary Semple disposed of the rest of her feelings by quarrelling with everyone in the cast of *King Arthur* and singing 'Fairest Isle' with such venom that her hearers felt their blood run cold, and afterwards remarked that stage fright had made her sing out of tune. The people listed by Mary as cognisant showed no more interest in the Tizards than before. The tradesmen continued to deliver. Not a cold shoulder was turned. But on that Sunday morning the balance between Justin and Celia had shifted, and never returned to its former adjustment. Both of them were aware of this, so neither of them referred to it, though at first Celia's abdication made her rather insistent that Justin should know best, make decisions, assert his authority. Justin asserted his authority by knowing what decisions could be postponed till the moment when there was no need to make them at all. Though he did not dislike responsibility, he was not going to be a slave to it. Celia's abdication also released elements in her character which till then had been penned back by her habit of common sense and efficiency. She became slightly frivolous, forgetful and timid. She read novels before lunch, abandoned all social conscience about bores, mislaid bills, took second helpings of risotto and mashed potatoes and began to put on weight. She lost her aplomb as a driver and had one or two small accidents. She discovered the delights of needing to be taken away for pick-me-up holidays. Mrs Mugthwaite, observing all this, knew it was the Change, and felt sorry for poor Mr Tizard; the Change wasn't a thing that a brother should be expected to deal with. From time to time, Justin and Celia discussed leaving Hallowby and going to live somewhere away from the east-coast climate and the east wind at the corner by St Cuthbert's, but they put off moving, because the two animals had grown old, were set in their ways, and would be happier dying in their own home. The pug died just before the Munich crisis, the cat lived on into the war.

So did Mr Pilkington, who died from overwork two months before the first air raid on Hallowby juxta Mare justified his insistence on constructing an air-raid shelter under the school playing fields. This first raid was concentrated on the iron-works, and did considerable damage. All next day, inland Hallowby heard the growl of demolition explosives. In the second raid, the defences were better organised. The enemy bombers were driven off their target before they could finish their mission. Two were brought down out to sea. A third, twisting inland, jettisoned its remaining bombs on and around

Hallowby. One dropped in Gas Lane, another just across the road from Newton Lodge. The blast brought down the roof and dislodged a chimney stack. The rescue workers, turning the light of their torches here and there, noting the usual disparities between the havocked and the unharmed, the fire-place blown out, the portrait smiling above it, followed the trail of bricks and rubble upstairs and into a bedroom whose door slanted from its hinges. A cold air met them; looking up, they saw the sky. The floor was deep in rubble; bits of broken masonry, clots of brickwork, stood up from it like rocks on a beach. A dark bulk crouched on the hearth, and was part of the chimney stack, and a torrent of slates had fallen on the bed, crushing the two bodies that lay there.

The wavering torchlights wandered over the spectacle. There was a silence. Then young Foe spoke out. 'He must have come in to comfort her. That's my opinion.' The others concurred. Silently, they disentangled Justin and Celia, and wrapped them in separate tarpaulin sheets. No word of what they had found got out. Foe's hypothesis was accepted by the coroner and became truth.

Elizabeth Taylor
Good-Bye, Good-Bye

On his last evening in England he broke two promises—one, that he would dine with his brother, and another, older promise made to a woman whom he loved. When he and Catherine had tried, years before, to put an end to this impermissible love for one another the best they could decide was to give it no nourishment and let it wither if it would. 'No messages,' she had said when they parted, 'no letters.' His letters had always incapacitated her: on days when she received them, she moved slowly at her work, possessed by his words, deaf to any others, from husband or children or friends. 'I don't want to know how you are getting on,' she told him, 'or to think of you in any particular place. You might die: you might marry. I never want to know. I want you to stop, here, for ever.' (*Then, there*, an autumn night, a railway station.) As his train moved off he saw that her face had a look of utter perplexity, as if the meaning of her future were beyond her comprehension. The look had stayed in his mind and was in his imagination this evening as he walked from the bus stop in the village and out on the sea-road towards the house.

This house, which she rented each summer for the children's holidays, was where they had sometimes been together. The recklessness, the deceit which, in London, they suppressed, they had indulged here, as if a different sort of behaviour were allowed at the seaside. Returning to her husband, who had no part in those holidays, she would at once feel so mortified and so uneasily ashamed, that their few meetings were humiliating to them both and full of recriminations and despair; and it was after such a summer that they had parted—for ever, both had believed.

The road under the sea-wall was sheltered. Inland, sheep cropped the salt-marshes where he and Catherine had walked in the evening when the children were in bed. When it was dark, they would kiss and say good-bye, then kiss again. He would walk back to the village along this sea-road and she would tiptoe into the house, so that the children's nurse would not be wakened or discover how late she had stayed out.

Memories agitated him as he walked along the road. The landscape seemed to have awaited him, to have kept itself unchanged to pain him now with a great sense of strangeness. He had no hopes for this visit, no vestige of confidence in it, knew that it was mistakenly made and fraught with all perils— her anger, her grief, her embarrassment. In him, love could not be reawakened, for it had not slept. He did not know what risk faced her; how she had dealt with her sadness, or laid him away in his absence. He was compelled to find out, to discover if he were quick or dead in her mind, and to see if the look—the perplexed expression—had hardened on her face, or vanished. But as he came round a bend in the road and saw the chimneys of the house and the beginning of the garden, he was so appalled by his venture that he walked more slowly and longed to turn back. He thought: 'She will be changed, look different, wear new clothes I have never seen, the children will be older, and, oh God,' he prayed, his heart swerving at the sudden idea, 'let there be no more! Let her not have had more children! Let her not have filled her life that way!'

He stopped in the road and listened for children's voices in the garden but in the still evening the bleating of sheep was the only sound. High up on the orchard trees red apples shone in the sun. An old net sagged across the tennis-lawn. The gabled, hideous house with its verandas and balconies came into view. At the open windows, faded curtains flapped over the newly cleaned tennis-shoes bleaching on sills and sandy swim-suits and towels hung out to dry. The house, which looked as if it had been burst asunder, and left with all its doors ajar, had a vacant—though only lately vacant—appearance.

In the conservatory-porch a tabby cat was sleeping on a shelf among flower-pots and tennis racquets. A book lying open had all its pages arched up in the sun and a bunch of wild flowers were dying on a ledge. He pressed the bell and away at the back of the house heard it ringing. The heat under the dusty panes made him feel faint and he stepped back from it, away from the door. As he did so, a girl leaned from an upstairs window and called down to him. 'Do you want mother?'

Hit by the irony of the words, the shock of seeing Catherine's eyes looking down at him, he could not answer her at once. Her daughter did not wait for his reply. 'She's on the beach. They're all there. I'm just going, too. One moment!' She moved from sight, he heard her running downstairs, then she came to the door.

'You are Sarah?' he said.

'Yes.'

'Oh, Catherine's eyes, those eyes!' he thought. 'The miracle, but the enormity, that they should come again; clearer, more beautiful'—he would not think it. 'You don't remember me. I am Peter Lord.'

'I remember the name. I remember *you* now. I had only forgotten. You came here once and helped us with a picnic on the beach; lit a fire, do you remember that? It's what they are all doing at this moment. I was waiting for a friend.' She hesitated, looked towards the gate. 'But they didn't come.'

' "They" because she will not say "he" ', Peter thought. 'The embarrassments of the English language!' She was bright with some disappointment.

'Shall we go down together and find them?' she asked; then, in the patronising tone young people use when they try to carry on conversations with their elders on equal terms, she asked: 'Let me see, you went abroad, didn't you? Wasn't it South America?'

'South Africa.'

'I always get those two muddled. And now you have come back home again?'

'For a short time. I am off in the morning.'

'Oh, what a pity; but mother *will* be pleased that you came to say good-bye.'

They crossed the road and climbed the bank to the top of the sea-wall. There they paused. The tide was out and the wet sand far down the beach reflected a pink light from the sun, which was going down in an explosive, Turneresque brilliance above the sand-hillocks. Farther along, they could see figures busily bringing driftwood to a fire and two children at the sea's edge were digging in the sand.

Seeing Peter and Sarah on the skyline, one of the group waved, then turned away again.

'He thinks you are my friend,' Sarah said. She wore Catherine's anxious look. 'That's Chris. Do you remember Chris? He is fifteen—nearly two years younger than me.'

'Yes, I remember him.' Peter was feeling tired now, rather puffed by keeping up with her across a stretch of hot white sand in which his feet sank at every step. This sand, seldom washed by the sea, was full of dried seaweed and bits of old newspapers. Clumps of spiky reed grew in it and sea-poppies and thistles.

'Who are all those other children?' he asked. He stopped and took off his shoes and socks, rolled his trousers above his ankles. 'A fine sight,' he thought crossly. 'Completely ridiculous.'

'Our friends,' said Sarah, turning and waiting for him.

He could see Catherine. She was apart from the others and was bending over a picnic-basket. When Sarah called to her, she turned and, still kneeling in the sand, looked up towards them, her arm shading her eyes. The incredulous look was on her face as if it had never left it and at the sight of the agitation she could not hide from her children and their friends, he realised the full cruelty of his treachery. She took his hand, and recovered enough to hide shock beneath a show of superficial surprise, glossing over the grotesque situation with an hostessy condescension.

'Are you on leave?' Her voice indicated his role of old friend of the family.

'No, my father died. I had to come over in a hurry.'

'I am sorry. Graham will be sad when he hears that.'

'So I am to be her husband's comrade, too!' he thought.

As if she were in her drawing-room she invited him to sit down, but before he could do so, the younger children had run up from the sea and stood on either side of their mother, staring in curiosity at him and awaiting an explanation.

They were all variations of her, her four sons and daughters and these two, a boy and a girl, with their unguarded, childish gaze, were more like her than the other two whose defined features were brightly masked to preserve the secrets of adolescence.

'Lucy, this is Mr Lord. He gave you your Fairy-Tale book that you love so much.'

'Yes, I do.'

'And this is Ricky.'

'What did you give *me*?' the boy asked.

'I'm sure I don't know. Perhaps you were to share the book.'

'No, it is only mine,' Lucy said certainly.

'He gave you lots of things,' said Catherine.

'More than me?'

'No, Lucy, I am sure not.'

'I think *I* only had the book.'

'This isn't a nice conversation. You should think of other things than what you are given. Go and help Chris to find some firewood. You can't enjoy the fire and the supper if you do nothing to help.'

The children wandered off, but back to the edge of the sea. They left a vacuum. She had tried to fill it with what he disliked and had always thought of as 'fussing with the children'— the children whom he had half-loved, for having her likeness, and half-resented, for not being his, for taking her attention from him and forbidding their life together.

'They've grown,' he said.

'Yes, of course.'

She put her hand deep in the sand, burying it in coolness. He watched her, remembering how once long ago she had done that and he had made a tunnel with his own hand and clasped hers and they had sat in silence, their fingers entwined beneath the sand. Such far-off lovers' games seemed utterly sad now, utterly forlorn, dead, their meaning brushed away like dust.

'Why did you come?' she whispered, her eyes fixed on the young ones building their fire; but fearing his answer, she caught her breath and called to her son. 'Chris, darling, bring the others over to meet Mr Lord.'

They came over, polite and estranged, willing to be kind. Chris hadn't remembered, but now he did. He introduced his friends, the same bright, polite boys and girls as himself. The

boys called him 'Sir,' the girls smiled warmly and encouraging-
ly. 'You are quite welcome, don't feel out of it—the fun, the
lovely evening—just because you are old,' their smiles said.

They diminished Catherine. They were all taller. She
seemed to Peter now to be set apart as 'mother', their voices
were protective to her, undemanding. (Once they had clam-
oured for her attention, claimed every second. 'Look at me,
mummy! Look at me!') They had set her firmly in her present
role and, instinctively, they made her part quite clear to Peter.

They returned to the fire. Chris was peeling sticks and
sharpening the ends so that they could hold sausages over the
fire to cook.

'What about the children?' Sarah asked. 'How long are you
staying, Mother?'

This was Catherine's dilemma which she had been pon-
dering as she sat there with her hand buried in the sand.

'They can stay up,' she said. 'We will all stay. It will be a
special treat for the little ones and they can sleep late in the
morning. You others shall have a party on your own another
night.'

She looked away from Sarah and her voice was gentle, for
she knew that *this* could not be Sarah's special night, that the
girl was desperate with disappointment. 'This evening is nothing,' Catherine tried to imply. 'There will be so many others
for you.'

'We always like it better if you are here,' Sarah said. 'I was
wondering about the children.' She dreaded that her mother
should feel old or left out, and she often was alone on these
long holidays. Peter's presence lightened the load of responsibility she felt towards her. For an hour or two, Catherine had
someone of her own and Sarah could let go of her, could turn
back to her own secrets, aloof, in love.

'Has she a confidante among the other girls?' Catherine

wondered. Remembering her own girlhood she did not hope to be confided in herself; the very last, she knew—even if first to know, before Sarah sometimes, yet still the last of all to be told.

If she had taken Lucy and Ricky home to bed, Peter would have gone with her. Then they would be alone and nothing could prevent him from talking to her. To stay where she was not much wanted and to endure an evening of social exchanges before the children—painful though it must be—would be less menacing than that.

She turned to the picnic-basket, put a loaf of bread on a board and began to cut it into slices. 'You haven't changed much,' she said. 'Are you happy in South Africa and is the work interesting? How is your brother?'

'I had no intention of coming here, but suddenly, this morning, it seemed so unreasonable, so falsely dramatic—our promise.'

'No, sensible.'

'I'm sorry I gave no warning.'

'You could have telephoned,' she said lightly, her back turned to him.

'You would have said "No".'

She wrapped the slices of bread in a napkin and put them back in the hamper. 'Being needlessly busy,' he thought. 'Fussing with the children, anything to exclude me.'

'You *would* have said "No", wouldn't you?'

'Yes, of course.'

'You haven't changed either,' he said at last, dutifully.

She was smoothing her hair, thinking, 'I don't know what I look like.' She wished that she could glance in a mirror, or that she had done so before she had left the house.

In her brown hair, some strands, coarser than the others, were silver. Fine lines crossed her forehead, and deeper ones curved from the corners of her eyes.

'Graham all right?' he asked.

'Yes, very well. Very busy. He gets tired.'

'And bloody cross, I bet,' Peter thought. He imagined the tetchy, pompous little man, returning from the city, briefcase full of documents and stomach full of bile.

'And is he as rich as ever?' he asked.

'I've noticed no difference,' Catherine said angrily. 'Have *you* prospered? You always had such money-troubles.'

'Father's dying should help.'

He had always refused to see Graham as anything but a monstrous begetter of money and children, and showed himself up in contrast—the bachelor beyond the gates, without home or family, whose schemes came to nothing as his love-making came to nothing, neither bearing fruit. His insistence on her wealth was partly from a feeling that she had shared too much with her husband and he could not bear her to share any more, not even anxieties about money.

'They are nice children,' he said, looking on the sunnier side of her marriage. 'A great credit to you.'

'Thank you.' Her eyes filled with tears and at that moment Sarah, standing by the fire, turned and looked curiously at her, then at Peter.

The fire was burning high and the young people moved about it continually as if performing some ceremony. As the sun went down, shadows fell across the beach from the sea-wall, cooling the sand quickly. Catherine spread out a rug for Peter to sit on and then sat down herself on a corner of it, as far from him as she could.

'Come by the fire,' Chris shouted to her.

'It is too smoky for her,' said Sarah.

'Not on the other side.'

'It blows about.'

Catherine had not asked her the one question she had

dreaded—'He didn't come then?'—and so in turn she would protect her mother. She, Sarah, no longer prayed for him to come, for her thoughts of him were angry now. Absorbed in this anger, she asked only that no one should speak of him. Waiting for him and the gradual loss of hope had been destructive, and a corrosive indignation worked on her love; it became non-love, then nothing.

'Is that Ronnie coming?' Chris asked, mopping his eyes with a handkerchief, waving away smoke.

A figure in the dusk appeared on the sea-wall, then a dog followed and flew down through the sand, crashed over the stretch of loose shingle to the wet, runnelled sands where the children worked, murmuring and intent, over their digging. Lucy cried out as the dog bounded towards her and a man's voice—nothing like Ronnie's—called the dog back.

Sarah was glad that she had not moved forward to wave or made any mistake. Standing quite still by the fire, she had kept her patience; but all the carefully tended hatred had vanished in those few seconds, love had come hurrying back with hope and forgiving. 'It is worse for her now,' Catherine thought, and she felt hostility towards men. 'As it is worse for me.'

The man and the dog disappeared. Lucy and Ricky, disturbed into realisation of the darkness falling, began to trail up from the sea. The water between the hard ribs of sand felt cold to their bare feet and they came up to the bonfire and stood watching it, at the fringe of their elders and betters who laughed and danced and waved their speared sausages in the air to cool.

'Let them cook their own,' said Catherine, and Chris handed the little ones two sticks and fixed on the sausages for them. They stood by the fire holding the sticks waveringly over the flames. Once, Ricky's nervousness broke into a laugh, his serious expression disintegrated into excited pleasure. 'It will never cook like that,' Chris said. 'Keep it to the hot part of the fire.' He sighed affectedly and murmured, 'Pesky kids' to one of the girls, who said haughtily: '*I* think they're sweet.'

'They're all yours, then,' said lordly Chris.

'I never had anything like this when I was young,' Peter said. 'I didn't even know any girls.'

The children had their feast and Catherine and Peter sat and watched them; even, Catherine thought, in Peter's case, sat in judgment on them—'as if he were their father and jealous of their youth, saying "*I* didn't have this or do that when *I* was a boy; but was made to do such and such, and go without etcetera, and be grateful for nothing. And look at me . . ." If he were their father, that is how he would be, if he had not come back to me this evening, I should never have thought such a thing of him. How I loved you, my darling, darling. The passion of tears, the groping bewilderment of being without you, the rhythm of long boredom and abrupt grief, that I endured because of you; then my prayers, my prayers especially that Sarah shall have a happier time, and a more fortunate love.'

The children brought them sausages wrapped in bread. The young girls were attentive to Catherine. 'I *adore* your jersey,' one said, and Catherine would not conceal her pleasure. 'But it's so old. It's Chris's, really.'

'Then you shouldn't let him have it back,' the girl said. '*He* couldn't look so nice in it.'

'All right!' said Chris. 'You may cook your own sausages now. Didn't you know that the whole family wear my old cast-offs?'

'Not I,' said Sarah.

'Not I,' said Lucy.

Peter had glanced at the jersey in annoyance. He was beginning, Catherine knew, to harden against Chris, identifying him

with his father, comparing himself and his own lost oppor-
tunities with the boy and the life lying before him. When
Chris brought sausages, said 'For you, sir,' he refused to eat.

'Then coffee,' Catherine suggested, beginning to unscrew a
flask.

'Oh, dear, it is so cold,' Lucy cried, and she flung herself
against Catherine's thighs, burrowing under her arm.

'Steady, my love, I can't pour out,' Catherine said, and she
held the flask and the cup high out of reach and for the first
time looked truly at Peter and laughed.

'Come to me, then,' he said, and he lifted Lucy away and
held her to him. She lolled against him, her salty, sticky hair
touching his cheek. 'That isn't good for you,' he said, taking
the half-eaten sausage, which was pink inside, uncooked, and
throwing it away across the sand.

'Fishes will eat it,' Ricky said. 'When the tide comes up.'

'Coffee!' Catherine called out and they came over to fetch
it, then went back to gather round the dying fire. The girls
began to sing, one of their school songs, which the boys did
not know and Chris said: 'What a filthy row.'

'Did you read that fairy book to me when I was in bed?'
Lucy asked Peter drowsily.

'I don't know.'

'Yes, you did.'

'Do you remember then?'

'No, Mummy told me.'

Then Catherine had talked of him! He had often wanted to
talk to someone about *her*, to say her name. In Africa, he had
nicknamed a little native girl—his servant's child—'Catherine', for the sake of saying the name occasionally. 'Good
morning, Catherine' or 'What a pretty frock, Catherine!' The
child could not understand English. He might, he had sometimes thought, have said anything, out loud, bold and clear. 'I

cannot forget you, Catherine, and my life is useless without you.'

Lucy had crawled inside his jacket for warmth, he rubbed her cold, sandy legs, held her bare feet, and once kissed her forehead. Catherine sipped her coffee, looking away from this display of tenderness, thinking: 'A barren evening. Nothing said; nothing felt, but pain. The wheel starting to creak again, starting to revolve in agony.'

'If any . . . regrets . . . have arisen from my visit,' Peter said, trying to speak obscurely, above Lucy's head in two senses, 'I couldn't blame myself more or detest my own egotism.'

'There is no need to say anything,' she said hurriedly. 'No need at all. I would rather you didn't.'

'Are you . . .?'

'No,' she interrupted him, afraid of what Lucy might hear. 'Am I what?' she wondered. 'I am in love with you still. In love, certainly. And there isn't a way out and never will be now.'

Her eyes might say this without Lucy knowing, and she turned to him so that before he went away he could be a witness to her constancy; but their situation was changed now; the observant eyes of the children were on them, Sarah's, the other girls, and Chris, brusque and guarded, goodness knew what thoughts *he* had about her.

'I shall soon have to go,' Peter said and as he glanced at his watch, Lucy pushed herself closer to him, almost asleep.

Singing together now, the girls and boys were beginning to pack up—one of the girls turned cartwheels, and Sarah suddenly spun round, her bell-like skirt flying out.

'Are you staying at the pub?' Catherine asked.

'No, I am catching the last bus, then the last train.'

'The last train,' Lucy murmured cosily, as if there were no such thing save in a story he was telling her.

Catherine shivered.

'Are you sure you won't write to me?' Peter asked her, as quietly as he could. 'Or let me write to you?'

'Quite sure.'

'She will,' said Lucy. 'She writes to Sarah and Chris every day when they are at school.'

'Then there wouldn't be time for me,' said Peter.

Catherine packed the basket wishing that she might pack up the evening, too, and all that it had brought to the light, but it lay untidily about them. The children ran to and fro, clearing up, exhilarated by the darkness and the sound of the sea, the tide coming up across the sands, one wave unrolling under the spray of the next. The boys took the baskets and the girls looked the beach over, as if it were a room in some home of their own which they wished to leave tidy until they returned.

'Who will remember the evening?' Catherine wondered. 'Perhaps only he and I, and Sarah.' Little Ricky had attached himself to the others as they left the beach. He walked beside Sarah, clinging to her skirt. Peter had Lucy on his back, his shoes dangling by their laces round his neck as he walked unsteadily on the cold, loose sand.

'We live only once,' he said.

'Of course,' said Lucy, awake now and laughing. She wriggled her sandy feet, trying to force them into the pockets of his jacket.

'Lucy, sit still or walk,' her mother said sharply.

A little surprised, she sat still for a bit and then, when she could see the house, the lights going on as the others went indoors, she slipped down and ran away from Peter, down the bank and across the lane.

Catherine and Peter sat down just below the sea-wall and put on their shoes.

'Will you forgive me?' he asked.

'I might have done the same.'

'There is far too much to say for us to begin talking.'

'And no time,' she said. She fastened her sandals, then looked up at the sky, as if she were scanning it anxiously for some weather-sign, but he knew that she was waiting for tears to recede, her head high, breath held. If he kissed her, she would fail, would break, weep, betray herself to the children. 'To have thought of her so long, imagined, dreamed, called that child "Catherine" for her sake, started at the sight of her name printed in a book, pretended her voice to myself, called her in my sleep, and now sit close to her and it is almost over.' He stood up and took her hand, helping her to her feet.

In the lane the children were trying one another's bicycles, the lamp light swung over the road and hedges. Lucy was crying and Sarah attempted to comfort her, but impatiently. 'The same old story,' she told her mother. 'Stayed up too late.'

'Yes, she did.'

'I didn't undo my sand-castle,' Lucy roared.

'Hush, dear. It doesn't matter.'

'I like to undo it. You know I like to undo it and now the sea will get it.'

'It doesn't matter.'

'Don't *say* it doesn't matter.'

'Peter, do borrow Chris's bicycle. You can leave it at the pub and he can fetch it tomorrow.'

'I like the walk.'

'I am not leaving her like that,' he thought, 'not bicycling off up the road with a mob of adolescents.'

'Good-bye, and thank you for the picnic,' the children began to say, coming one after another to shake hands with Catherine.

'You should have *reminded* me,' shrieked Lucy, at the end of her tether.

'Oh, Christ . . .' said Chris.

'Chris, I won't have that,' said Catherine.

'Good-bye, and thank you so much.'

'I hope you will come again.'

'Good-bye, good-bye,' Chris shouted.

They swung on to their bicycles and began to ride away, turning often to wave.

'Good-bye, Fanny! Good-bye, Sue!' Chris shouted.

The voices came back, as the lights bobbed along the lane. 'Good-bye, Sarah! Good-bye, Chris!'

Sarah called once, then she shook hands with Peter and turned towards the house, gathering up Ricky, who was swinging on the gate as if hypnotised, too tired to make the next step.

'Good-bye, Catherine, or I shall miss the bus.'

'Yes. Good-bye, Peter.'

'Take care of yourself. And *you* take care of her,' he said to Chris with bright jocularity, as he began to walk away down the road.

'What, my dear old mum?' Chris said, and flung his arm across her shoulder so that she staggered slightly. Then, hearing a faint cry in the distance he rushed from her into the middle of the road and shouted again, his hands cupped to his mouth. 'Good-bye, Good-bye.'

Robert Louis Stevenson
The Sire de Malétroit's Door

Denis de Beaulieu was not yet two-and-twenty, but he counted himself a grown man, and a very accomplished cavalier into the bargain. Lads were early formed in that rough, warfaring epoch; and when one has been in a pitched battle and a dozen raids, has killed one's man in an honourable fashion, and knows a thing or two of strategy and mankind, a certain swagger in the gait is surely to be pardoned. He had put up his horse with due care, and supped with due deliberation; and then, in a very agreeable frame of mind, went out to pay a visit in the grey of the evening. It was not a very wise proceeding on the young man's part. He would have done better to remain beside the fire or go decently to bed. For the town was full of the troops of Burgundy and England under a mixed command; and though Denis was there on safe-conduct, his safe-conduct was like to serve him little on a chance encounter.

It was September, 1429; the weather had fallen sharp; a flighty piping wind, laden with showers, beat about the township; and the dead leaves ran riot along the streets. Here and there a window was already lighted up; and the noise of men-at-arms making merry over supper within, came forth in fits and was swallowed up and carried away by the wind. The night fell swiftly; the flag of England, fluttering on the spire-top, grew ever fainter and fainter against the flying clouds—a black speck like a swallow in the tumultuous, leaden chaos of the sky. As the night fell the wind rose and began to hoot under archways and roar amid the tree-tops in the valley below the town.

Denis de Beaulieu walked fast and was soon knocking at his friend's door; but though he promised himself to stay only a little while and make an early return, his welcome was so pleasant, and he found so much to delay him, that it was already long past midnight before he said good-bye upon the threshold. The wind had fallen again in the meanwhile; the night was as black as the grave; not a star, nor a glimmer of moonshine, slipped through the canopy of cloud. Denis was ill-acquainted with the intricate lanes of Chateau Landon; even by daylight he had found some trouble in picking his way; and in this absolute darkness he soon lost it altogether. He was certain of one thing only—to keep mounting the hill; for his friend's house lay at the lower end, or tail, of Chateau Landon, while the inn was up at the head, under the great church spire. With this clue to go upon he stumbled and groped forward, now breathing more freely in open places where there was a good slice of sky overhead, now feeling along the wall in stifling closes. It is an eerie and mysterious position to be thus submerged in opaque blackness in an almost unknown town. The silence is terrifying in its possibilities. The touch of cold window bars to the exploring hand startles the man like the touch of a toad; the inequalities of the pavement shake his heart into his mouth; a piece of denser darkness threatens an ambuscade or a chasm in the pathway; and where the air is brighter, the houses put on strange and bewildering appearances, as if to lead him farther from his way. For Denis, who had to regain his inn without attracting notice, there was real danger as well as mere discomfort in the walk; and he went warily and boldly at once, and at every corner paused to make an observation.

He had been for some time threading a lane so narrow that he could touch a wall with either hand, when it began to open out and go sharply downward. Plainly this lay no longer in the direction of his inn; but the hope of a little more light tempted him forward to reconnoitre. The lane ended in a terrace with a bartisan wall, which gave an outlook between high houses, as out of an embrasure, into the valley lying dark and formless several hundred feet below. Denis looked down, and could discern a few tree-tops waving and a single speck of brightness where the river ran across a weir. The weather was clearing up, and the sky had lightened, so as to show the outline of the heavier clouds and the dark margin of the hills. By the uncertain glimmer, the house on his left hand should be a place of some pretensions; it was surmounted by several pinnacles and turret-tops; the round stern of a chapel, with a fringe of flying buttresses, projected boldly from the main block; and the door was sheltered under a deep porch carved with figures and overhung by two long gargoyles. The windows of the chapel gleamed through their intricate tracery with a light as of many tapers, and threw out the buttresses and the peaked roof in a more intense blackness against the sky. It was plainly the hotel of some great family of the neighbourhood; and as it reminded Denis of a town house of his own at Bourges, he stood for some time gazing up at it and mentally gauging the skill of the architects and the consideration of the two families.

There seemed to be no issue to the terrace but the lane by which he had reached it; he could only retrace his steps, but he had gained some notion of his whereabouts, and hoped by this means to hit the main thoroughfare and speedily regain the inn. He was reckoning without that chapter of accidents which was to make this night memorable above all others in his career; for he had not gone back above a hundred yards before he saw a light coming to meet him, and heard loud voices speaking together in the echoing of the lane. It was a party of men-at-arms going the night round with torches. Denis assured himself that they had all been making free with the wine-bowl, and were in no mood to be particular about safe-conducts or the niceties of chivalrous war. It was as like as not that they would kill him like a dog and leave him where he fell. The situation was inspiriting but nervous. Their own torches would conceal him from sight, he reflected; and he hoped that they would drown the noise of his footsteps with their own empty voices. If he were but fleet and silent, he might evade their notice altogether.

Unfortunately, as he turned to beat a retreat, his foot rolled upon a pebble; he fell against the wall with an ejaculation, and his sword rang loudly on the stones. Two or three voices demanded who went there—some in French, some in English; but Denis made no reply and ran the faster down the lane. Once upon the terrace, he paused to look back. They still kept calling after him, and just then began to double the pace in pursuit, with a considerable clank of armour, and great tossing of the torchlight to and fro in the narrow jaws of the passage.

Denis cast a look around and darted into the porch. There he might escape observation, or—if that were too much to expect—was in a capital posture whether for parley or defence. So thinking, he drew his sword and tried to set his back against the door. To his surprise, it yielded behind his weight; and though he turned in a moment, continued to swing back on oiled and noiseless hinges, until it stood wide open on a black interior. When things fall out opportunely for the person concerned, he is not apt to be critical about the how or why, his own immediate personal convenience seeming a sufficient reason for the strangest oddities and revolutions in our sublunary things; and so Denis, without a moment's hesitation, stepped within and partly closed the door behind him to conceal his place of refuge. Nothing was further from his thoughts than to close it altogether; but for some inexplicable reason—perhaps by a spring or a weight—the ponderous mass of oak whipped itself out of his fingers and clanked to, with a formidable rumble and a noise like the falling of an automatic bar.

The round, at that very moment, debouched upon the terrace and proceeded to summon him with shouts and curses. He heard them ferreting in the dark corners; and the stock of a lance even rattled along the outer surface of the door behind which he stood; but these gentlemen were in too high a humour to be long delayed, and soon made off down a corkscrew pathway which had escaped Denis's observation, and passed out of sight and hearing along the battlements of the town.

Denis breathed again. He gave them a few minutes' grace for fear of accidents, and then groped about for some means of opening the door and slipping forth again. The inner surface was quite smooth, not a handle, not a moulding, not a projection of any sort. He got his finger-nails round the edges and pulled, but the mass was immovable. He shook it, it was as firm as a rock. Denis de Beaulieu frowned and gave vent to a little noiseless whistle. What ailed the door? he wondered. Why was it open? How came it to shut so easily and so effectually after him? There was something obscure and underhand about all this, that was little to the young man's fancy. It looked like a snare; and yet who would suppose a snare in such a quiet by-street and in a house of so prosperous and even noble an exterior? And yet—snare or no snare, intentionally or unintentionally—here he was, prettily trapped; and for the life

of him he could see no way out of it again. The darkness began
to weigh upon him. He gave ear; all was silent without, but
within and close by he seemed to catch a faint sighing, a faint
sobbing rustle, a little stealthy creak—as though many persons
were at his side, holding themselves quite still, and governing
even their respiration with the extreme of slyness. The idea
went to his vitals with a shock, and he faced about suddenly as
if to defend his life. Then, for the first time, he became aware
of a light about the level of his eyes and at some distance in the
interior of the house—a vertical thread of light, widening
towards the bottom, such as might escape between two wings
of arras over a doorway. To see anything was a relief to Denis;
it was like a piece of solid ground to a man labouring in a
morass; his mind seized upon it with avidity; and he stood
staring at it and trying to piece together some logical concep-
tion of his surroundings. Plainly there was a flight of steps
ascending from his own level to that of this illuminated doorway; and indeed he thought he could make out another
thread of light, as fine as a needle and as faint as phosphores-
cence, which might very well be reflected along the polished
wood of a handrail. Since he had begun to suspect that he was
not alone, his heart had continued to beat with smothering
violence, and an intolerable desire for action of any sort had
possessed itself of his spirit. He was in deadly peril, he believed.
What could be more natural than to mount the staircase, lift
the curtain, and confront his difficulty at once? At least he
would be dealing with something tangible; at least he would
be no longer in the dark. He stepped slowly forward with
outstretched hands, until his foot struck the bottom step; then
he rapidly scaled the stairs, stood for a moment to compose his
expression, lifted the arras and went in.

He found himself in a large apartment of polished stone.
There were three doors; one on each of three sides; all similar-

ly curtained with tapestry. The fourth side was occupied by
two large windows and a great stone chimney-piece, carved
with the arms of the Malétroits. Denis recognised the bearings,
and was gratified to find himself in such good hands. The room
was strongly illuminated; but it contained little furniture except a heavy table and a chair or two, the hearth was innocent
of fire, and the pavement was but sparsely strewn with rushes
clearly many days old.

On a high chair beside the chimney, and directly facing
Denis as he entered, sat a little old gentleman in a fur tippet.
He sat with his legs crossed and his hands folded, and a cup of
spiced wine stood by his elbow on a bracket on the wall. His
countenance had a strongly masculine cast; not properly
human, but such as we see in the bull, the goat, or the
domestic boar; something equivocal and wheedling, something greedy, brutal, and dangerous. The upper lip was inordin-
ately full, as though swollen by a blow or a toothache; and
the smile, the peaked eyebrows, and the small, strong eyes
were quaintly and almost comically evil in expression. Beautiful white hair hung straight all round his head, like a saint's,
and fell in a single curl upon the tippet. His beard and moustache were the pink of venerable sweetness. Age, probably in
consequence of inordinate precautions, had left no mark upon
his hands; and the Malétroit hand was famous. It would be
difficult to imagine anything at once so fleshy and so delicate
in design; the taper, sensual fingers were like those of one of
Leonardo's women; the fork of the thumb made a dimpled
protuberance when closed; the nails were perfectly shaped,
and of a dead, surprising whiteness. It rendered his aspect tenfold
more redoubtable, that a man with hands like these should
keep them devoutly folded in his lap like a virgin martyr—that
a man with so intense and startling an expression of face should
sit patiently on his seat and contemplate people with an

unwinking stare, like a god, or a god's statue. His quiescence seemed ironical and treacherous, it fitted so poorly with his looks.

Such was Alain, Sire de Malétroit.

Denis and he looked silently at each other for a second or two.

'Pray step in,' said the Sire de Malétroit. 'I have been expecting you all the evening.'

He had not risen, but he accompanied his words with a smile and a slight but courteous inclination of the head. Partly from the smile, partly from the strange musical murmur with which the Sire prefaced his observation, Denis felt a strong shudder of disgust go through his marrow. And what with disgust and honest confusion of mind, he could scarcely get words together in reply.

'I fear,' he said, 'that this is a double accident. I am not the person you suppose me. It seems you were looking for a visit; but for my part, nothing was further from my thoughts—nothing could be more contrary to my wishes—than this intrusion.'

'Well, well,' replied the old gentleman indulgently, 'here you are, which is the main point. Seat yourself, my friend, and put yourself entirely at your ease. We shall arrange our little affairs presently.'

Denis perceived that the matter was still complicated with some misconception, and he hastened to continue his explanations.

'Your door . . .' he began.

'About my door?' asked the other, raising his peaked eyebrows. 'A little piece of ingenuity.' And he shrugged his shoulders. 'A hospitable fancy! By your own account, you were not desirous of making my acquaintance. We old people look for such reluctance now and then; and when it touches our honour, we cast about until we find some way of over-coming it. You arrive uninvited, but believe me, very welcome.'

'You persist in error, sir,' said Denis. 'There can be no question between you and me. I am a stranger in this country-side. My name is Denis, damoiseau de Beaulieu. If you see me in your house, it is only—'

'My young friend,' interrupted the other, 'you will permit me to have my own ideas on that subject. They probably differ from yours at the present moment,' he added with a leer, 'but time will show which of us is in the right.'

Denis was convinced he had to do with a lunatic. He seated himself with a shrug, content to wait the upshot; and a pause ensued, during which he thought he could distinguish a hurried gabbling as of prayer from behind the arras immediately opposite him. Sometimes there seemed to be but one person engaged, sometimes two; and the vehemence of the voice, low as it was, seemed to indicate either great haste or an agony of spirit. It occurred to him that this piece of tapestry covered the entrance to the chapel he had noticed from without.

The old gentleman meanwhile surveyed Denis from head to foot with a smile, and from time to time emitted little noises like a bird or a mouse, which seemed to indicate a high degree of satisfaction. This state of matters became rapidly insupportable; and Denis, to put an end to it, remarked politely that the wind had gone down.

The old gentleman fell into a fit of silent laughter, so prolonged and violent that he became quite red in the face. Denis got upon his feet at once, and put on his hat with a flourish.

'Sir,' he said, 'if you are in your wits, you have affronted me grossly. If you are out of them, I flatter myself I can find better

employment for my brains than to talk with lunatics. My
conscience is clear; you have made a fool of me from the first
moment; you have refused to hear my explanations; and now
there is no power under God will make me stay here any
longer; and if I cannot make my way out in a more decent
fashion, I will hack your door in pieces with my sword.'

The Sire de Malétroit raised his right hand and wagged it at
Denis with the fore and little fingers extended.

'My dear nephew,' he said, 'sit down.'

'Nephew!' retorted Denis, 'you lie in your throat;' and he
snapped his fingers in his face.

'Sit down, you rogue!' cried the old gentlemen, in a sudden
harsh voice, like the barking of a dog. 'Do you fancy,' he went
on, 'that when I had made my little contrivance for the door I
had stopped short with that? If you prefer to be bound hand
and foot till your bones ache, rise and try to go away. If you
choose to remain a free young buck, agreeably conversing
with an old gentleman—why, sit where you are in peace, and
God be with you.'

'Do you mean I am a prisoner?' demanded Denis.

'I state the facts,' replied the other. 'I would rather leave the
conclusion to yourself.'

Denis sat down again. Externally he managed to keep pretty
calm; but within, he was now boiling with anger, now chilled
with apprehension. He no longer felt convinced that he was
dealing with a madman. And if the old gentleman was sane,
what, in God's name; had he to look for? What absurd or
tragical adventure had befallen him? What countenance was he
to assume?

While he was thus unpleasantly reflecting, the arras that
overhung the chapel door was raised, and a tall priest in his
robes came forth and, giving a long, keen stare at Denis, said
something in an undertone to Sire de Malétroit.

'She is in a better frame of spirit?' asked the latter.

'She is more resigned, messire,' replied the priest.

'Now the Lord help her, she is hard to please!' sneered the old gentleman. 'A likely stripling—not ill-born—and of her own choosing, too? Why, what more would the jade have?'

'The situation is not usual for a young damsel,' said the other, 'and somewhat trying to her blushes.'

'She should have thought of that before she began the dance. It was none of my choosing, God knows that: but since she is in it, by our Lady, she shall carry it to the end.' And then addressing Denis, 'Monsieur de Beaulieu,' he asked, 'may I present you to my niece? She has been waiting your arrival, I may say, with even greater impatience than myself.'

Denis had resigned himself with a good grace—all he desired was to know the worst of it as speedily as possible; so he rose at once, and bowed in acquiescence. The Sire de Malétroit followed his example and limped, with the assistance of the chaplain's arm, towards the chapel door. The priest pulled aside the arras, and all three entered. The building had considerable architectural pretensions. A light groining sprang from six stout columns, and hung down in two rich pendants from the centre of the vault. The place terminated behind the altar in a round end, embossed and honeycombed with a superfluity of ornament in relief, and pierced by many little windows shaped like stars, trefoils, or wheels. These windows were imperfectly glazed, so that the night air circulated freely in the chapel. The tapers, of which there must have been half a hundred burning on the altar, were unmercifully blown about; and the light went through many different phases of brilliancy and semi-eclipse. On the steps in front of the altar knelt a young girl richly attired as a bride. A chill settled over Denis as he observed her costume; he fought with desperate energy against the conclusion that was thrust upon his mind; it could not—it should not—be as he feared.

'Blanche,' said the Sire, in his most flute-like tones, 'I have brought a friend to see you, my little girl; turn round and give him your pretty hand. It is good to be devout; but it is necessary to be polite, my niece.'

The girl rose to her feet and turned towards the new comers. She moved all of a piece; and shame and exhaustion were expressed in every line of her fresh young body; and she held her head down and kept her eyes upon the pavement, as she came slowly forward. In the course of her advance, her eyes fell upon Denis de Beaulieu's feet—feet of which he was justly vain, be it remarked, and wore in the most elegant accoutrement even while travelling. She paused—started, as if his yellow boots had conveyed some shocking meaning—and glanced suddenly up into the wearer's countenance. Their eyes met; shame gave place to horror and terror in her looks; the blood left her lips; with a piercing scream she covered her face with her hands and sank upon the chapel floor.

'That is not the man!' she cried. 'My uncle, that is not the man!'

The Sire de Malétroit chirped agreeably. 'Of course not,' he said; 'I expected as much. It was so unfortunate you could not remember his name.'

'Indeed,' she cried, 'indeed, I have never seen this person till this moment—I have never so much as set eyes upon him—I never wish to see him again. Sir,' she said, turning to Denis, 'if you are a gentleman, you will bear me out. Have I ever seen you—have you ever seen me—before this accursed hour?'

'To speak for myself, I have never had that pleasure,' answered the young man. 'This is the first time, messire, that I have met with your engaging niece.'

The old gentleman shrugged his shoulders.

'I am distressed to hear it,' he said. 'But it is never too late to begin. I had little more acquaintance with my own late lady ere I married her; which proves,' he added with a grimace, 'that these impromptu marriages may often produce an excellent understanding in the long run. As the bridegroom is to have a voice in the matter, I will give him two hours to make up for lost time before we proceed with the ceremony.' And he turned towards the door, followed by the clergyman.

The girl was on her feet in a moment. 'My uncle, you cannot be in earnest,' she said. 'I declare before God I will stab myself rather than be forced on that young man. The heart rises at it; God forbid such marriages; you dishonour your white hair. Oh, my uncle, pity me! There is not a woman in all the world but would prefer death to such a nuptial. Is it possible,' she added, faltering, 'is it possible that you do not believe me—that you still think this'—and she pointed at Denis with a tremor of anger and contempt—'that you still think *this* to be the man?'

'Frankly,' said the old gentleman, pausing on the threshold, 'I do. But let me explain to you once for all, Blanche de Malétroit, my way of thinking about this affair. When you took it into your head to dishonour my family and the name that I have borne, in peace and war, for more than three-score years, you forfeited, not only the right to question my designs, but that of looking me in the face. If your father had been alive, he would have spat on you and turned you out of doors. His was the hand of iron. You may bless your God you have only to deal with the hand of velvet, mademoiselle. It was my duty to get you married without delay. Out of pure goodwill, I have tried to find your own gallant for you. And I believe I have succeeded. But before God and all the holy angels, Blanche de Malétroit, if I have not, I care not one jackstraw. So let me recommend you to be polite to our young friend; for upon my word, your next groom may be less appetising.'

And with that he went out, with the chaplain at his heels; and the arras fell behind the pair.

The girl turned upon Denis with flashing eyes.

'And what, sir,' she demanded, 'may be the meaning of all this?'

'God knows,' returned Denis gloomily. 'I am a prisoner in this house, which seems full of mad people. More I know not; and nothing do I understand.'

'And pray how came you here?' she asked.

He told her as briefly as he could. 'For the rest,' he added, 'perhaps you will follow my example, and tell me the answer to all these riddles, and what, in God's name, is like to be the end of it.'

She stood silent for a little, and he could see her lips tremble and her tearless eyes burn with a feverish lustre. Then she pressed her forehead in both hands.

'Alas, how my head aches!' she said wearily—'to say nothing of my poor heart! But it is due to you to know my story, unmaidenly as it must seem. I am called Blanche de Malétroit; I have been without father or mother for—oh! for as long as I can recollect, and indeed I have been most unhappy all my life. Three months ago a young captain began to stand near me every day in church. I could see that I pleased him; I am much to blame, but I was to glad that anyone should love me; and when he passed me a letter, I took it home with me and read it with great pleasure. Since that time he has written many. He was so anxious to speak with me, poor fellow! and kept asking me to leave the door open some evening that we might have two words upon the stair. For he knew how much my uncle trusted me.' She gave something like a sob at that, and it was a moment before she could go on. 'My uncle is a hard man, but he is very shrewd,' she said at last. 'He has performed many feats in war, and was a great person at court, and much trusted by Queen Isabeau in old days. How he came to suspect me I cannot tell; but it is hard to keep anything from his knowledge; and this morning, as we came from mass, he took my hand in his, forced it open, and read my little billet, walking by my side all the while. When he had finished, he gave it back to me with great politeness. It contained another request to have the door left open; and this has been the ruin of us all. My uncle kept me strictly in my room until evening, and then ordered me to dress myself as you see me—a hard mockery for a young girl, do you not think so? I suppose, when he could not prevail with me to tell him the young captain's name, he must have laid a trap for him: into which, alas! you have fallen in the anger of God. I looked for much confusion; for how could I tell whether he was willing to take me for his wife on these sharp terms? He might have been trifling with me from the first; or I might have made myself too cheap in his eyes. But truly I had not looked for such a shameful punishment as this! I could not think that God would let a girl be so disgraced before a young man. And now I have told you all; and I can scarcely hope that you will not despise me.'

Denis made her a respectful inclination.

'Madam,' he said, 'you have honoured me by your confidence. It remains for me to prove that I am not unworthy of the honour. Is Messire de Malétroit at hand?'

'I believe he is writing in the salle without,' she answered.

'May I lead you thither, madam?' asked Denis, offering his hand with his most courtly bearing.

She accepted it; and the pair passed out of the chapel, Blanche in a very drooping and shamefast condition, but Denis strutting and ruffling in the consciousness of a mission, and the boyish certainty of accomplishing it with honour.

The Sire de Malétroit rose to meet them with an ironical obeisance.

'Sir,' said Denis with the grandest possible air, 'I believe I am to have some say in the matter of this marriage; and let me tell you at once, I will be no party to forcing the inclination of this young lady. Had it been freely offered to me, I should have been proud to accept her hand, for I perceive she is as good as she is beautiful; but as things are, I have now the honour, messire, of refusing.'

Blanche looked at him with gratitude in her eyes; but the old gentleman only smiled and smiled, until his smile grew positively sickening to Denis.

'I am afraid,' he said, 'Monsieur de Beaulieu, that you do not perfectly understand the choice I have to offer you. Follow me, I beseech you, to this window.' And he led the way to one of the large windows which stood open on the night. 'You observe,' he went on, 'there is an iron ring in the upper masonry, and reeved through that, a very efficacious rope. Now, mark my words; if you should find your disinclination to my niece's person insurmountable, I shall have you hanged out of this window before sunrise. I shall only proceed to such an extremity with the greatest regret, you may believe me. For it is not at all your death that I desire, but my niece's establishment in life. At the same time, it must come to that if you prove obstinate. Your family, Monsieur de Beaulieu, is very well in its way; but if you sprang from Charlemagne, you should not refuse the hand of a Malétroit with impunity— not if she had been as common as the Paris road—not if she were as hideous as the gargoyle over my door. Neither my niece nor you, nor my own private feelings, move me at all in this matter. The honour of my house has been compromised; I believe you to be the guilty person; at least you are now in the secret; and you can hardly wonder if I request you to wipe out the strain. If you will not, your blood be on your own head! It will be no great satisfaction to me to have your interesting relics kicking their heels in the breeze below my windows; but half a loaf is better than no bread, and if I cannot cure the dishonour, I shall at least stop the scandal.'

There was a pause.

'I believe there are other ways of settling such imbroglios among gentlemen,' said Denis. 'You wear a sword, and I hear you have used it with distinction.'

The Sire de Malétroit made a signal to the chaplain, who crossed the room with long silent strides and raised the arras over the third of the three doors. It was only a moment before he let it fall again; but Denis had time to see a dusky passage full of armed men.

'When I was a little younger, I should have been delighted to honour you, Monsieur de Beaulieu,' said Sire Alain; 'but I am now too old. Faithful retainers are the sinews of age, and I must employ the strength I have. This is one of the hardest things to swallow as a man grows up in years; but with a little patience, even this becomes habitual. You and the lady seem to prefer the salle for what remains of your two hours; and as I have no desire to cross your preference, I shall resign it to your use with all the pleasure in the world. No haste!' he added, holding up his hand, as he saw a dangerous look come into Denis de Beaulieu's face. 'If your mind revolts against hanging, it will be time enough two hours hence to throw yourself out of the window or upon the pikes of my retainers. Two hours of life are always two hours. A great many things may turn up in even as little a while as that. And, besides, if I understand her appearance, my niece has still something to say to you. You will not disfigure your last hours by a want of politeness to a lady?'

Denis looked at Blanche, and she made him an imploring gesture.

It is likely that the old gentleman was hugely pleased at this symptom of an understanding; for he smiled on both, and added sweetly: 'If you will give me your word of honour, Monsieur de Beaulieu, to wait my return at the end of the two hours before attempting anything desperate, I shall withdraw my retainers, and let you speak in greater privacy with mademoiselle.'

Denis again glanced at the girl, who seemed to beseech him to agree.

'I give you my word of honour,' he said.

Messire de Malétroit bowed, and proceeded to limp about the apartment, clearing his throat the while with that odd musical chirp which had already grown so irritating in the ears of Denis de Beaulieu. He first possessed himself of some papers which lay upon the table; then he went to the mouth of the passage and appeared to give an order to the men behind the arras; and lastly he hobbled out through the door by which Denis had come in, turning upon the threshold to address a last smiling bow to the young couple, and followed by the chaplain with a hand-lamp.

No sooner were they alone than Blanche advanced towards Denis with her hands extended. Her face was flushed and excited, and her eyes shone with tears.

'You shall not die!' she cried, 'you shall marry me after all.'

'You seem to think, madam,' replied Denis, 'that I stand much in fear of death.'

'Oh no, no,' she said, 'I see you are no poltroon. It is for my own sake—I could not bear to have you slain for such a scruple.'

'I am afraid,' returned Denis, 'that you underrate the difficulty, madam. What you may be too generous to refuse, I may
be too proud to accept. In a moment of noble feeling towards
me, you forgot what you perhaps owe to others.'

He had the decency to keep his eyes upon the floor as he
said this, and after he had finished, so as not to spy upon
her confusion. She stood silent for a moment, then walked
suddenly away, and falling on her uncle's chair, fairly burst
out sobbing. Denis was in the acme of embarrassment. He
looked round, as if to seek for inspiration, and seeing a stool,
plumped down upon it for something to do. There he sat,
playing with the guard of his rapier, and wishing himself
dead a thousand times over, and buried in the nastiest kitchen-
heap in France. His eyes wandered round the apartment,
but found nothing to arrest them. There were such wide
spaces between the furniture, the light fell so badly and cheer-
lessly over all, the dark outside air looked in so coldly through
the windows, that he thought he had never seen a church
so vast, nor a tomb so melancholy. The regular sobs of Blanche de Malétroit measured out the time like the ticking of a
clock. He read the device upon the shield over and over again,
until his eyes became obscured; he stared into shadowy corners until he imagined they were swarming with horrible
animals; and every now and again he awoke with a start, to
remember that his last two hours were running, and death was
on the march.

Oftener and oftener, as the time went on, did his glance
settle on the girl herself. Her face was bowed forward and
covered with her hands, and she was shaken at intervals by
the convulsive hiccup of grief. Even thus she was not an
unpleasant object to dwell upon, so plump and yet so fine,
with a warm brown skin, and the most beautiful hair, Denis
thought, in the whole world of womankind. Her hands were

like her uncle's; but they were more in place at the end of her young arms, and looked infinitely soft and caressing. He remembered how her blue eyes had shone upon him, full of anger, pity, and innocence. And the more he dwelt on her perfections, the uglier death looked, and the more deeply was he smitten with penitence at her continued tears. Now he felt that no man could have the courage to leave a world which contained so beautiful a creature; and now he would have given forty minutes of his last hour to have unsaid his cruel speech.

Suddenly a hoarse and ragged peal of cockcrow rose to their ears from the dark valley below the windows. And this shattering noise in the silence of all around was like a light in a dark place, and shook them both out of their reflections.

'Alas, can I do nothing to help you?' she said, looking up.

'Madam,' replied Denis, with a fine irrelevancy, 'if I have said anything to wound you, believe me, it was for your own sake and not for mine.'

She thanked him with a tearful look.

'I feel your position cruelly,' he went on. 'The world has been bitter hard on you. Your uncle is a disgrace to mankind. Believe me, madam, there is no young gentleman in all France but would be glad of my opportunity to die in doing you a momentary service.'

'I know already that you can be very brave and generous,' she answered. 'What I *want* to know is whether I can serve you—now or afterwards,' she added, with a quaver.

'Most certainly,' he answered with a smile. 'Let me sit beside you as if I were a friend, instead of a foolish intruder; try to forget how awkwardly we are placed to one another; make my last moments go pleasantly; and you will do me the chief service possible.'

'You are very gallant,' she added, with a yet deeper sadness . . . 'very gallant . . . and it somehow pains me. But draw
nearer, if you please; and if you find anything to say to me, you
will at least make certain of a very friendly listener. Ah!
Monsieur de Beaulieu,' she broke forth—'ah! Monsieur de
Beaulieu, how can I look you in the face?' And she fell to
weeping again with a renewed effusion.

'Madam,' said Denis, taking her hand in both of his, 'reflect
on the little time I have before me, and the great bitterness into
which I am cast by the sight of your distress. Spare me, in my
last moments, the spectacle of what I cannot cure even with
the sacrifice of my life.'

'I am very selfish,' answered Blanche. 'I will be braver,
Monsieur de Beaulieu, for your sake. But think if I can do you
no kindness in the future—if you have no friends to whom I
could carry your adieux. Charge me as heavily as you can;
every burden will lighten, by so little, the invaluable gratitude
I owe you. Put it in my power to do something more for you
than weep.'

'My mother is married again, and has a young family to care
for. My brother Guichard will inherit my fiefs; and if I am not
in error, that will content him amply for my death. Life is a
little vapour that passeth away, as we are told by those in holy
orders. When a man is in a fair way and sees all life open in front
of him, he seems to himself to make a very important figure in
the world. His horse whinnies to him; the trumpets blow and
the girls look out of window as he rides into town before his
company; he receives many assurances of trust and regard—
sometimes by express in a letter—sometimes face to face, with
persons of great consequence falling on his neck. It is not
wonderful if his head is turned for a time. But once he is dead,
were he as brave as Hercules or as wise as Solomon, he is soon
forgotten. It is not ten years since my father fell, with many

other knights around him, in a very fierce encounter, and I do not think that any one of them, nor so much as the name of the fight, is now remembered. No, no, madam, the nearer you come to it, you see that death is a dark and dusty corner, where a man gets into his tomb and has the door shut after him till the judgment day. I have few friends just now, and once I am dead I shall have none.'

'Ah, Monsieur de Beaulieu!' she exclaimed, 'you forget Blanche de Malétroit.'

'You have a sweet nature, madam, and you are pleased to estimate a little service far beyond its worth.'

'It is not that,' she answered. 'You mistake me if you think I am so easily touched by my own concerns. I say so, because you are the noblest man I have ever met; because I recognise in you a spirit that would have made even a common person famous in the land.'

'And yet here I die in a mouse-trap—with no more noise about it than my own squeaking,' answered he.

A look of pain crossed her face, and she was silent for a little while. Then a light came into her eyes, and with a smile she spoke again.

'I cannot have my champion think meanly of himself. Anyone who gives his life for another will be met in Paradise by all the heralds and angels of the Lord God. And you have no such cause to hang your head. For . . . Pray, do you think me beautiful?' she asked, with a deep flush.

'Indeed, madam, I do,' he said.

'I am glad of that,' she answered heartily. 'Do you think there are many men in France who have been asked in marriage by a beautiful maiden—with her own lips—and who have refused her to her face? I know you men would half despise such a triumph; but believe me, we women know more of what is precious in love. There is nothing that should set a person higher in his own esteem; and we women would prize nothing more dearly.'

'You are very good,' he said; 'but you cannot make me forget that I was asked in pity and not for love.'

'I am not so sure of that,' she replied, holding down her head. 'Hear me to an end, Monsieur de Beaulieu. I know how you must despise me; I feel you are right to do so; I am too poor a creature to occupy one thought of your mind, although, alas! you must die for me this morning. But when I asked you to marry me, indeed, and indeed, it was because I respected and admired you, and loved you with my whole soul, from the very moment that you took my part against my uncle. If you had seen yourself, and how noble you looked, you would pity rather than despise me. And now,' she went on, hurriedly checking him with her hand, 'although I have laid aside all reserve and told you so much, remember that I know your sentiments towards me already. I would not, believe me, being nobly born, weary you with importunities into consent. I too have a pride of my own: and I declare before the holy mother of God, if you should now go back from your word already given, I would no more marry you than I would marry my uncle's groom.'

Denis smiled a little bitterly.

'It is a small love,' he said, 'that shies at a little pride.'

She made no answer, although she probably had her own thoughts.

'Come hither to the window,' he said, with a sigh. 'Here is the dawn.'

And indeed the dawn was already beginning. The hollow of the sky was full of essential daylight, colourless and clean; and the valley underneath was flooded with a grey reflection. A few thin vapours clung in the coves of the forest or lay along the winding course of the river. The scene disengaged a surprising effect of stillness, which was hardly interrupted when the cocks began once more to crow among the steadings. Perhaps the same fellow who had made so horrid a clangour in the darkness not half-an-hour before, now sent up the merriest cheer to greet the coming day. A little wind went bustling and eddying among the tree-tops underneath the windows. And still the daylight kept flooding insensibly out of the east, which was soon to grow incandescent and cast up that red-hot cannon-ball, the rising sun.

Denis looked out over all this with a bit of a shiver. He had taken her hand, and retained it in his almost unconsciously.

'Has the day begun already?' she said; and then, illogically enough: 'the night has been so long! Alas! what shall we say to my uncle when he returns?'

'What you will,' said Denis, and he pressed her fingers in his. She was silent.

'Blanche,' he said, with a swift, uncertain, passionate utterance, 'you have seen whether I fear death. You must know well enough that I would as gladly leap out of that window into the empty air as lay a finger on you without your free and full consent. But if you care for me at all do not let me lose my life in a misapprehension; for I love you better than the whole world; and though I will die for you blithely, it would be like all the joys of Paradise to live on and spend my life in your service.'

As he stopped speaking, a bell began to ring loudly in the interior of the house; and a clatter of armour in the corridor showed that the retainers were returning to their post, and the two hours were at an end.

'After all that you have heard?' she whispered, leaning towards him with her lips and eyes.

'I have heard nothing,' he replied.

'The captain's name was Florimond de Champdivers,' she said in his ear.

'I did not hear it,' he answered, taking her supple body in his arms and covering her wet face with kisses.

A melodious chirping was audible behind, followed by a beautiful chuckle, and the voice of Messire de Malétroit wished his new nephew a good morning.

Bernard Malamud
The First Seven Years

Feld, the shoemaker, was annoyed that his helper, Sobel, was so insensitive to his reverie that he wouldn't for a minute cease his fanatic pounding at the other bench. He gave him a look, but Sobel's bald head was bent over the last as he worked, and he didn't notice. The shoemaker shrugged and continued to peer through the partly frosted window at the nearsighted haze of falling February snow. Neither the shifting white blur outside, nor the sudden deep remembrance of the snowy Polish village where he had wasted his youth, could turn his thoughts from Max the college boy (a constant visitor in the mind since early that morning when Feld saw him trudging through the snowdrifts on his way to school), whom he so much respected because of the sacrifices he had made throughout the years—in winter or direst heat—to further his education. An old wish returned to haunt the shoemaker: that he had had a son instead of a daughter, but this blew away in the snow, for Feld, if anything, was a practical man. Yet he could not help but contrast the diligence of the boy, who was a peddler's son, with Miriam's unconcern for an education. True, she was always with a book in her hand, yet when the opportunity arose for a college education, she had said no she would rather find a job. He had begged her to go, pointing out how many fathers could not afford to send their children to college, but she said she wanted to be independent. As for education, what was it, she asked, but books, which Sobel, who diligently read the classics, would as usual advise her on. Her answer greatly grieved her father.

A figure emerged from the snow and the door opened. At the counter the man withdrew from a wet paper bag a pair of battered shoes for repair. Who he was the shoemaker for a moment had no idea, then his heart trembled as he realised, before he had thoroughly discerned the face, that Max himself was standing there, embarrassedly explaining what he wanted done to his old shoes. Though Feld listened eagerly, he couldn't hear a word, for the opportunity that had burst upon him was deafening.

He couldn't exactly recall when the thought had occurred to him, because it was clear he had more than once considered suggesting to the boy that he go out with Miriam. But he had not dared speak, for if Max said no, how would he face him again? Or suppose Miriam, who harped so often on independence, blew up in anger and shouted at him for his meddling? Still, the chance was too good to let by: all it meant was an introduction. They might long ago have become friends had they happened to meet somewhere, therefore was it not his duty—an obligation—to bring them together, nothing more, a harmless connivance to replace an accidental encounter in the subway, let's say, or a mutual friend's introduction in the street? Just let him once see and talk to her and he would for sure be interested. As for Miriam, what possible harm for a working girl in an office, who met only loudmouthed salesmen and illiterate shipping clerks, to make the acquaintance of a fine scholarly boy? Maybe he would awaken in her a desire to go to college; if not—the shoemaker's mind at last came to grips with the truth—let her marry an educated man and live a better life.

When Max finished describing what he wanted done to his shoes, Feld marked them, both with enormous holes in the soles which he pretended not to notice, with large white-chalk X's and the rubber heels, thinned to the nails, he marked with O's, though it troubled him he might have mixed up the letters. Max inquired the price, and the shoemaker cleared his throat and asked the boy, above Sobel's insistent hammering, would he please step through the side door there into the hall. Though surprised, Max did as the shoemaker requested, and Feld went in after him. For a minute they were both silent, because Sobel had stopped banging, and it seemed they understood neither was to say anything until the noise began again. When it did, loudly, the shoemaker quickly told Max why he had asked to talk to him.

'Ever since you went to high school,' he said, in the dimly lit hallway, 'I watched you in the morning go to the subway to school, and I said always to myself, this is a fine boy that he wants so much an education.'

'Thanks,' Max said, nervously alert. He was tall and grotesquely thin, with sharply cut features, particularly a beak-like nose. He was wearing a loose, long, slushy overcoat that hung down to his ankles, looking like a rug draped over his bony shoulders, and a soggy old brown hat, as battered as the shoes he had brought in.

'I am a businessman,' the shoemaker abruptly said to conceal his embarrassment, 'so I will explain you right away why I talk to you. I have a girl, my daughter Miriam—she is nineteen—a very nice girl and also so pretty that everybody looks on her when she passes by in the street. She is smart, always with a book, and I thought to myself that a boy like you, an educated boy—I thought maybe you will be interested sometime to meet a girl like this.' He laughed a bit when he had finished and was tempted to say more but had the good sense not to.

Max stared down like a hawk. For an uncomfortable second he was silent, then he asked, 'Did you say nineteen?'

'Yes.'

'Would it be all right to inquire if you have a picture of her?'

'Just a minute.' The shoemaker went into the store and hastily returned with a snapshot that Max held up to the light.

'She's all right,' he said.

Feld waited.

'And is she sensible—not the flighty kind?'

'She is very sensible.'

After another short pause, Max said it was okay with him if he met her.

'Here is my telephone,' said the shoemaker, hurriedly handing him a slip of paper. 'Call her up. She comes home from work six o'clock.'

Max folded the paper and tucked it away into his worn leather wallet.

'About the shoes,' he said. 'How much did you say they will cost me?'

'Don't worry about the price.'

'I just like to have an idea.'

'A dollar—dollar fifty. A dollar fifty,' the shoemaker said.

At once he felt bad, for he usually charged $2.25 for this kind of job. Either he should have asked the regular price or done the work for nothing.

Later, as he entered the store, he was startled by a violent clanging and looked up to see Sobel pounding upon the naked last. It broke, the iron striking the floor and jumping with a thump against the wall, but before the enraged shoemaker could cry out, the assistant had torn his hat and coat off the hook and rushed out into the snow.

So Feld, who had looked forward to anticipating how it would go with his daughter and Max, instead had a great worry on his mind. Without his temperamental helper he was a lost man, especially as it was years now since he had carried the store alone. The shoemaker had for an age suffered from a heart condition that threatened collapse if he dared exert himself. Five years ago, after an attack, it had appeared as though he would have either to sacrifice his business on the auction block and live on a pittance thereafter, or put himself at the mercy of some unscrupulous employee who would in the end probably ruin him. But just at the moment of his darkest despair, this Polish refugee, Sobel, had appeared one night out of the street and begged for work. He was a stocky man, poorly dressed, with a bald head that had once been blond, a severely plain face, and soft blue eyes prone to tears over the sad books he read, a young man but old—no one would have guessed thirty. Though he confessed he knew nothing of shoemaking, he said he was apt and would work for very little if Feld taught him the trade. Thinking that with, after all, a landsman, he would have less to fear than from a complete stranger, Feld took him on and within six weeks the refugee rebuilt as good a shoe as he, and not long thereafter expertly ran the business for the thoroughly relieved shoemaker.

Feld could trust him with anything and did, frequently going home after an hour or two at the store, leaving all the money in the till, knowing Sobel would guard every cent of it. The amazing thing was that he demanded so little. His wants were few; in money he wasn't interested—in nothing but books, it seemed—which he one by one lent to Miriam, together with his profuse, queer written comments, manufactured during his lonely rooming house evenings, thick pads of commentary which the shoemaker peered at and twitched his shoulders over as his daughter, from her fourteenth year, read page by sanctified page, as if the word of God were inscribed on them. To protect Sobel, Feld himself had to see that he received more than he asked for. Yet his conscience bothered him for not insisting that the assistant accept a better wage than he was getting, though Feld had honestly told him he could earn a handsome salary if he worked elsewhere, or maybe opened a place of his own. But the assistant answered, somewhat ungraciously, that he was not interested in going elsewhere, and though Feld frequently asked himself, What keeps him here? why does he stay? he finally answered it that the man, no doubt because of his terrible experiences as a refugee, was afraid of the world.

After the incident with the broken last, angered by Sobel's behaviour, the shoemaker decided to let him stew for a week in the rooming house, although his own strength was taxed dangerously and the business suffered. However, after several sharp nagging warnings from both his wife and daughter, he went finally in search of Sobel, as he had once before, quite recently, when over some fancied slight—Feld had merely asked him not to give Miriam so many books to read because her eyes were strained and red—the assistant had left the place in a huff, an incident which, as usual, came to nothing, for he had returned after the shoemaker had talked to him, and taken his seat at the bench. But this time, after Feld had plodded through the snow to Sobel's house—he had thought of sending Miriam but the idea became repugnant to him—the burly landlady at the door informed him in a nasal voice that Sobel was not at home, and though Feld knew this was a nasty lie, for where had the refugee to go? still for some reason he was not completely sure of—it may have been the cold and his fatigue—he decided not to insist on seeing him. Instead he went home and hired a new helper.

Thus he settled the matter, though not entirely to his satisfaction, for he had much more to do than before, and so, for example, could no longer lie late in bed mornings because he had to get up to open the store for the new assistant, a speechless, dark man with an irritating rasp as he worked, whom he would not trust with the key as he had Sobel. Furthermore, this one, though able to do a fair repair job, knew nothing of grades of leather or prices, so Feld had to make his own purchases; and every night at closing time it was necessary to count the money in the till and lock up. However, he was not dissatisfied, for he lived much in his thoughts of Max and Miriam. The college boy had called her, and they had arranged a meeting for this coming Friday night. The shoe-maker would personally have preferred Saturday, which he felt would make it a date of the first magnitude, but he learned Friday was Miriam's choice, so he said nothing. The day of the week did not matter. What mattered was the aftermath. Would they like each other and want to be friends? He sighed at all the time that would have to go by before he knew for sure. Often he was tempted to talk to Miriam about the boy, to ask whether she thought she would like his type—he had told her only that he considered Max a nice boy and had suggested he call her—but the one time he tried she snapped at him— justly—how should she know?

At last Friday came. Feld was not feeling particularly well so he stayed in bed, and Mrs Feld thought it better to remain in the bedroom with him when Max called. Miriam received the boy, and her parents could hear their voices, his throaty one, as they talked. Just before leaving, Miriam brought Max to the bedroom door and he stood there a minute, a tall, slightly hunched figure wearing a thick, droopy suit, and apparently at ease as he greeted the shoemaker and his wife, which was surely a good sign. And Miriam, although she had worked all day, looked fresh and pretty. She was a large-framed girl with a well-shaped body, and she had a fine open face and soft hair. They made, Feld thought, a first-class couple.

Miriam returned after 11:30. Her mother was already asleep,

but the shoemaker got out of bed and after locating his bath-
robe went into the kitchen, where Miriam, to his surprise, sat
at the table, reading.

'So where did you go?' Feld asked pleasantly.

'For a walk,' she said, not looking up.

'I advised him,' Feld said, clearing his throat, 'he shouldn't
spend so much money.'

'I didn't care.'

The shoemaker boiled up some water for tea and sat down
at the table with a cupful and a thick slice of lemon.

'So how,' he sighed after a sip, 'did you enjoy?'

'It was all right.'

He was silent. She must have sensed his disappointment, for
she added, 'You can't really tell much the first time.'

'You will see him again?'

Turning a page, she said that Max had asked for another
date.

'For when?'

'Saturday.'

'So what did you say?'

'What did I say?' she asked, delaying for a moment—'I said
yes.'

Afterwards she inquired about Sobel, and Feld, without
exactly knowing why, said the assistant had got another job.
Miriam said nothing more and went on reading. The shoemaker's conscience did not trouble him; he was satisfied with
the Saturday date.

During the week, by placing here and there a deft question,
he managed to get from Miriam some information about Max.
It surprised him to learn that the boy was not studying to be
either a doctor or lawyer but was taking a business course leading to a degree in accountancy. Feld was a little disappointed
because he thought of accountants as bookkeepers and would

have preferred 'a higher profession'. However, it was not long before he had investigated the subject and discovered that Certified Public Accountants were highly respected people, so he was thoroughly content as Saturday approached. But because Saturday was a busy day, he was much in the store and therefore did not see Max when he came to call for Miriam. From his wife he learned there had been nothing especially revealing about their greeting. Max had rung the bell and Miriam had got her coat and left with him—nothing more. Feld did not probe, for his wife was not particularly observant. Instead, he waited up for Miriam with a newspaper on his lap, which he scarcely looked at so lost was he in thinking of the future. He awoke to find her in the room with him, tiredly removing her hat. Greeting her, he was suddenly inexplicably afraid to ask anything about the evening. But since she volunteered nothing he was at last forced to inquire how she had enjoyed herself. Miriam began something noncommittal, but apparently changed her mind, for she said after a minute, 'I was bored.'

When Feld had sufficiently recovered from his anguished disappointment to ask why, she answered without hesitation, 'Because he's nothing more than a materialist.'

'What means this word?'

'He has no soul. He's only interested in things.'

He considered her statement for a long time, then asked, 'Will you see him again?'

'He didn't ask.'

'Suppose he will ask you?'

'I won't see him.'

He did not argue; however, as the days went by he hoped increasingly she would change her mind. He wished the boy would telephone, because he was sure there was more to him than Miriam, with her inexperienced eye, could discern. But

Max didn't call. As a matter of fact he took a different route to school, no longer passing the shoemaker's store, and Feld was deeply hurt.

Then one afternoon Max came in and asked for his shoes. The shoemaker took them down from the shelf where he had placed them, apart from the other pairs. He had done the work himself and the soles and heels were well built and firm. The shoes had been highly polished and somehow looked better than new. Max's Adam's apple went up once when he saw them, and his eyes had little lights in them.

'How much?' he asked, without directly looking at the shoemaker.

'Like I told you before,' Feld answered sadly. 'One dollar fifty cents.'

Max handed him two crumpled bills and received in return a newly minted silver half dollar.

He left. Miriam had not been mentioned. That night the shoemaker discovered that his new assistant had been all the while stealing from him, and he suffered a heart attack.

Though the attack was very mild, he lay in bed for three weeks. Miriam spoke of going for Sobel, but sick as he was Feld rose in wrath against the idea. Yet in his heart he knew there was no other way, and the first weary day back in the shop thoroughly convinced him, so that night after supper he dragged himself to Sobel's rooming house.

He toiled up the stairs, though he knew it was bad for him, and at the top knocked at the door. Sobel opened it and the shoemaker entered. The room was a small, poor one, with a single window facing the street. It contained a narrow cot, a low table, and several stacks of books piled haphazardly around on the floor along the wall, which made him think how queer Sobel was, to be uneducated and read so much. He had once asked him, Sobel, why you read so much? and the assistant could not answer him. Did you ever study in a college someplace? he had asked, but Sobel shook his head. He read, he said, to know. But to know what, the shoemaker demanded, and to know, why? Sobel never explained, which proved he read so much because he was queer.

Feld sat down to recover his breath. The assistant was resting on his bed with his heavy back to the wall. His shirt and trousers were clean, and his stubby fingers, away from the shoemaker's bench, were strangely pallid. His face was thin and pale, as if he had been shut in this room since the day he had bolted from the store.

'So when you will come back to work?' Feld asked him.

To his surprise, Sobel burst out, 'Never.'

Jumping up, he strode over to the window that looked out upon the miserable street. 'Why should I come back?' he cried.

'I will raise your wages.'

'Who cares for your wages!'

The shoemaker, knowing he didn't care, was at a loss what else to say.

'What do you want from me, Sobel?'

'Nothing.'

'I always treated you like you was my son.'

Sobel vehemently denied it. 'So why you look for strange boys in the street they should go out with Miriam? Why you don't think of me?'

The shoemaker's hands and feet turned freezing cold. His voice became so hoarse he couldn't speak. At last he cleared his throat and croaked, 'So what has my daughter got to do with a shoemaker thirty-five years old who works for me?'

'Why do you think I worked so long for you?' Sobel cried out. 'For the stingy wages I sacrificed five years of my life so you could have to eat and drink and where to sleep?'

'Then for what?' shouted the shoemaker.

'For Miriam,' he blurted—'for her.'

The shoemaker, after a time, managed to say, 'I pay wages in cash, Sobel,' and lapsed into silence. Though he was seething with excitement, his mind was coldly clear, and he had to admit to himself he had sensed all along that Sobel felt this way. He had never so much as thought it consciously, but he had felt it and was afraid.

'Miriam knows?' he muttered hoarsely.

'She knows.'

'You told her?'

'No.'

'Then how does she know?'

'How does she know?' Sobel said. 'Because she knows. She knows who I am and what is in my heart.'

Feld had a sudden insight. In some devious way, with his books and commentary, Sobel had given Miriam to understand that he loved her. The shoemaker felt a terrible anger at him for his deceit.

'Sobel, you are crazy,' he said bitterly. 'She will never marry a man so old and ugly like you.'

Sobel turned black with rage. He cursed the shoemaker, but then, though he trembled to hold it in, his eyes filled with tears and he broke into deep sobs. With his back to Feld, he stood at the window, fists clenched, and his shoulders shook with his choked sobbing.

Watching him, the shoemaker's anger diminished. His teeth were on edge with pity for the man, and his eyes grew moist. How strange and sad that a refugee, a grown man, bald and old with his miseries, who had by the skin of his teeth escaped Hitler's incinerators, should fall in love, when he had got to America, with a girl less than half his age. Day after day, for five years he had sat at his bench, cutting and hammering away, waiting for the girl to become a woman, unable to ease his heart with speech, knowing no protest but desperation.

'Ugly I didn't mean,' he said half aloud.

Then he realised that what he had called ugly was not Sobel but Miriam's life if she married him. He felt for his daughter a strange and gripping sorrow, as if she were already Sobel's bride, the wife, after all, of a shoemaker, and had in her life no more than her mother had had. And all his dreams for her—why he had slaved and destroyed his heart with anxiety and labour—all these dreams of a better life were dead.

The room was quiet. Sobel was standing by the window reading, and it was curious that when he read he looked young.

'She is only nineteen,' Feld said brokenly. 'This is too young yet to get married. Don't ask her for two years more, till she is twenty-one, then you can talk to her.'

Sobel didn't answer. Feld rose and left. He went slowly down the stairs but once outside, though it was an icy night and the crisp falling snow whitened the street, he walked with a stronger stride.

But the next morning, when the shoemaker arrived, heavy-hearted, to open the store, he saw he needn't have come, for his assistant was already seated at the last, pounding leather for his love.

Aldous Huxley
Happily Ever After

At the best of times it is a long way from Chicago to Blaybury in Wiltshire, but war has fixed between them a great gulf. In the circumstances, therefore, it seemed an act of singular devotion on the part of Peter Jacobsen to have come all the way from the Middle West, in the fourth year of war, on a visit to his old friend Petherton, when the project entailed a single-handed struggle with two Great Powers over the question of passports and the risk, when they had been obtained, of perishing miserably by the way, a victim of frightfulness.

At the expense of much time and more trouble Jacobsen had at last arrived; the gulf between Chicago and Blaybury was spanned. In the hall of Petherton's house a scene of welcome was being enacted under the dim gaze of six or seven brown family portraits by unknown masters of the eighteenth and nineteenth centuries.

Old Alfred Petherton, a grey shawl over his shoulders—for he had to be careful, even in June, of draughts and colds—was shaking his guest's hand with interminable cordiality.

'My dear boy,' he kept repeating, 'it *is* a pleasure to see you. My dear boy . . .'

Jacobsen limply abandoned his forearm and waited in patience.

'I can never be grateful enough,' Mr Petherton went on—
'never grateful enough to you for having taken all this endless
trouble to come and see an old decrepit man—for that's what
I am now, that's what I am, believe me.'

'Oh, I assure you . . .' said Jacobsen, with vague deprecation.
'Le vieux crétin qui pleurniche,' he said to himself. French was
a wonderfully expressive language, to be sure.

'My digestion and my heart have got much worse since I saw
you last. But I think I must have told you about that in my
letters.'

'You did indeed, and I was most grieved to hear it.'

'Grieved'—what a curious flavour that word had! Like
somebody's tea which used to recall the most delicious blends
of forty years ago. But it was decidedly the *mot juste*. It had the
right obituary note about it.

'Yes,' Mr Petherton continued, 'my palpitations are very
bad now. Aren't they, Marjorie?' He appealed to his daughter
who was standing beside him.

'Father's palpitations are very bad,' she replied dutifully.

It was as though they were talking about some precious
heirloom long and lovingly cherished.

'And my digestion . . . This physical infirmity makes all
mental activity so difficult. All the same, I manage to do a little
useful work. We'll discuss that later, though. You must be
feeling tired and dusty after your journey down. I'll guide you
to your room. Marjorie, will you get someone to take up his
luggage?'

'I can take it myself,' said Jacobsen, and he picked up a small
Gladstone-bag that had been deposited by the door.

'Is that all?' Mr Petherton asked.

'Yes, that's all.'

As one living the life of reason, Jacobsen objected to owning
things. One so easily became the slave of things and not their

master. He liked to be free; he checked his possessive instincts and limited his possessions to the strictly essential. He was as much or as little at home at Blaybury or Pekin. He could have explained all this if he liked. But in the present case it wasn't worth taking the trouble.

'This is your humble chamber,' said Mr Petherton, throwing open the door of what was, indeed, a very handsome spare-room, bright with chintzes and cut flowers and silver candle-sticks. 'A poor thing, but your own.'

Courtly grace! Dear old man! Apt quotation! Jacobsen un-packed his bag and arranged its contents neatly and method-ically in the various drawers and shelves of the wardrobe.

It was a good many years now since Jacobsen had come in the course of his grand educational tour to Oxford. He spent a couple of years there, for he liked the place, and its inhabitants were a source of unfailing amusement to him.

A Norwegian, born in the Argentine, educated in the United States, in France, and in Germany; a man with no nationality and no prejudices, enormously old in experience, he found something very new and fresh and entertaining about his fellow-students with their comic public-school traditions and fabulous ignorance of the world. He had quietly watched them doing their little antics, feeling all the time that a row of bars separated them from himself, and that he ought, after each particularly amusing trick, to offer them a bun or a handful of peanuts. In the intervals of sight-seeing in this strange and delightful Jardin des Plantes he read Greats, and it was through Aristotle that he had come into contact with Alfred Petherton, fellow and tutor of his college.

The name of Petherton is a respectable one in the academic world. You will find it on the title-page of such meritorious, if not exactly brilliant, books as *Plato's Predecessors, Three Scottish*

Meta-physicians, Introduction to the Study of Ethics, Essays in Neo-Idealism. Some of his works are published in cheap editions as text-books.

One of those curious inexplicable friendships that often link the most unlikely people had sprung up between tutor and pupil, and had lasted unbroken for upwards of twenty years. Petherton felt a fatherly affection for the younger man, together with a father's pride, now that Jacobsen was a man of world-wide reputation, in having, as he supposed, spiritually begotten him. And now Jacobsen had travelled three or four thousand miles across a world at war just to see the old man. Petherton was profoundly touched.

'Did you see any submarines on the way over?' Marjorie asked, as she and Jacobsen were strolling together in the garden after breakfast the next day.

'I didn't notice any; but then I am very unobservant about these things.'

There was a pause. At last, 'I suppose there is a great deal of war-work being done in America now?' said Marjorie.

Jacobsen supposed so; and there floated across his mind a vision of massed bands, of orators with megaphones, of patriotic sky-signs, of streets made perilous by the organised highway robbery of Red Cross collectors. He was too lazy to describe it all; besides, she wouldn't see the point of it.

'I should like to be able to do some war-work,' Marjorie explained apologetically. 'But I have to look after father, and there's the housekeeping, so I really haven't the time.'

Jacobsen thought he detected a formula for the benefit of strangers. She evidently wanted to make things right about herself in people's minds. Her remark about the housekeeping made Jacobsen think of the late Mrs Petherton, her mother; she had been a good-looking, painfully sprightly woman with a hankering to shine in University society at Oxford. One quickly learned that she was related to bishops and country families; a hunter of ecclesiastical lions and a snob. He felt glad she was dead.

'Won't it be awful when there's no war-work,' he said. 'People will have nothing to do or think about when peace comes.'

'I shall be glad. Housekeeping will be so much easier.'

'True. There are consolations.'

Marjorie looked at him suspiciously; she didn't like being laughed at. What an undistinguished-looking little man he was! Short, stoutish, with waxed brown moustaches and a forehead that incipient baldness had made interminably high. He looked like the sort of man to whom one says: 'Thank you, I'll take it in notes with a pound's worth of silver.' There were pouches under his eyes and pouches under his chin, and you could never guess from his expression what he was thinking about. She was glad that she was taller than he and could look down on him.

Mr Petherton appeared from the house, his grey shawl over his shoulders and the crackling expanse of *The Times* between his hands.

'Good morrow,' he cried.

To the Shakespearean heartiness of this greeting Marjorie returned her most icily modern 'Morning'. Her father always said 'Good morrow' instead of 'Good morning', and the fact irritated her with unfailing regularity every day of her life.

'There's a most interesting account,' said Mr Petherton, 'by a young pilot of an air fight in today's paper,' and as they walked up and down the gravel path he read the article, which was a column and a half in length.

Marjorie made no attempt to disguise her boredom, and

occupied herself by reading something on the other side of the page, craning her neck round to see.

'Very interesting,' said Jacobsen when it was finished.

Mr Petherton had turned over and was now looking at the Court Circular page.

'I see,' he said, 'there's someone called Beryl Camberley-Belcher going to be married. Do you know if that's any relation of the Howard Camberley-Belchers, Marjorie?'

'I've no idea who the Howard Camberley-Belchers are,' Marjorie answered rather sharply.

'Oh, I thought you did. Let me see. Howard Camberley-Belcher was at college with me. And he had a brother called James—or was it William?—and a sister who married one of the Riders, or at any rate some relation of the Riders; for I know the Camberley-Belchers and the Riders used to fit in somewhere. Dear me, I'm afraid my memory for names is going.'

Marjorie went indoors to prepare the day's domestic campaign with the cook. When that was over she retired to her sitting-room and unlocked her very private desk. She must write to Guy this morning. Marjorie had known Guy Lambourne for years and years, almost as long as she could remember. The Lambournes were old family friends of the Pethertons: indeed they were, distantly, connections; they 'fitted in somewhere', as Mr Petherton would say—somewhere, about a couple of generations back. Marjorie was two years younger than Guy; they were both only children; circumstances had naturally thrown them a great deal together. Then Guy's father had died, and not long afterwards his mother, and at the age of seventeen Guy had actually come to live with the Pethertons, for the old man was his guardian. And now they were engaged; had been, more or less, from the first year of the war.

Marjorie took pen, ink, and paper. 'DEAR GUY,' she began—
('*We* aren't sentimental,' she had once remarked, with a mixture of contempt and secret envy, to a friend who had confided
that she and her fiancé never began with anything less than
Darling.)—'I am longing for another of your letters . . .' She
went through the usual litany of longing. 'It was father's
birthday yesterday; he is sixty-five. I cannot bear to think that
some day you and I will be as old as that. Aunt Ellen sent him a
Stilton cheese—a useful war-time present. How boring housekeeping is. By dint of thinking about cheeses my mind is
rapidly turning into one—a Gruyère; where there isn't cheese
there are just holes, full of vacuum . . .'

She didn't really mind housekeeping so much. She took it
for granted, and did it just because it was there to be done.
Guy, on the contrary, never took anything for granted; she
made these demonstrations for his benefit.

'I read Keats's letters, as you suggested, and thought them *too*
beautiful . . .'

At the end of a page of rapture she paused and bit her pen.
What was there to say next? It seemed absurd one should have
to write letters about the books one had been reading. But
there was nothing else to write about; nothing ever happened.
After all, what had happened in her life? Her mother dying
when she was sixteen; then the excitement of Guy coming to
live with them; then the war, but that hadn't meant much to
her; then Guy falling in love, and their getting engaged. That
was really all. She wished she could write about her feelings in
an accurate, complicated way, like people in novels; but when
she came to think about it, she didn't seem to have any feelings
to describe.

She looked at Guy's last letter from France. 'Sometimes,'
he had written, 'I am tortured by an intense physical desire
for you. I can think of nothing but your beauty, your young,

strong body. I hate that; I have to struggle to repress it. Do you forgive me?' It rather thrilled her that he should feel like that about her: he had always been so cold, so reserved, so much opposed to sentimentality—to the kisses and endearments she would, perhaps, secretly have liked. But he had seemed so right when he said, 'We must love like rational beings, with our minds, not with our hands and lips.' All the same . . .

She dipped her pen in the ink and began to write again. 'I know the feelings you spoke of in your letter. Sometimes I long for you in the same way. I dreamt the other night I was holding you in my arms, and woke up hugging the pillow.' She looked at what she had written. It was too awful, too vulgar! She would have to scratch it out. But no, she would leave it in spite of everything, just to see what he would think about it. She finished the letter quickly, sealed and stamped it, and rang for the maid to take it to the post. When the servant had gone, she shut up her desk with a bang. Bang—the letter had gone, irrevocably.

She picked up a large book lying on the table and began to read. It was the first volume of the *Decline and Fall*. Guy had said she must read Gibbon; she wouldn't be educated till she had read Gibbon. And so yesterday she had gone to her father in his library to get the book.

'Gibbon,' Mr Petherton had said, 'certainly, my dear. How delightful it is to look at these grand old books again. One always finds something new every time.'

Marjorie gave him to understand that she had never read it. She felt rather proud of her ignorance.

Mr Petherton handed the first of eleven volumes to her. 'A great book,' he murmured—'an essential book. It fills the gap between your classical history and your mediaeval stuff.'

'Your' classical history, Marjorie repeated to herself, 'your' classical history indeed! Her father had an irritating way of taking it for granted that she knew everything, that classical history was as much hers as his. Only a day or two before he had turned to her at luncheon with, 'Do you remember, dear child, whether it was Pomponazzi who denied the personal immortality of the soul, or else that queer fellow, Laurentius Valla? It's gone out of my head for the moment.' Marjorie had quite lost her temper at the question—much to the innocent bewilderment of her poor father.

She had set to work with energy on the Gibbon; her book-marker registered the fact that she had got through one hundred and twenty-three pages yesterday. Marjorie started reading. After two pages she stopped. She looked at the number of pages still remaining to be read—and this was only the first volume. She felt like a wasp sitting down to eat a vegetable marrow. Gibbon's bulk was not perceptibly diminished by her first bite. It was too long. She shut the book and went out for a walk. Passing the Whites' house, she saw her friend, Beatrice White that was, sitting on the lawn with her two babies. Beatrice hailed her, and she turned in.

'Pat a cake, pat a cake,' she said. At the age of ten months, baby John had already learnt the art of patting cakes. He slapped the outstretched hand offered him, and his face, round and smooth and pink like an enormous peach, beamed with pleasure.

'Isn't he a darling!' Marjorie exclaimed. 'You know, I'm sure he's grown since last I saw him, which was on Tuesday.'

'He put on eleven ounces last week,' Beatrice affirmed.

'How wonderful! His hair's coming on splendidly . . .'

It was Sunday the next day. Jacobsen appeared at breakfast in the neatest of black suits. He looked, Marjorie thought, more than ever like a cashier. She longed to tell him to hurry up or he'd miss the 8.53 for the second time this week and the manager would be annoyed. Marjorie herself was, rather consciously, not in Sunday best.

'What is the name of the Vicar?' Jacobsen inquired, as he helped himself to bacon.

'Trubshaw. Luke Trubshaw, I believe.'

'Does he preach well?'

'He didn't when I used to hear him. But I don't often go to church now, so I don't know what he's like these days.'

'Why don't you go to church?' Jacobsen inquired, with a silkiness of tone which veiled the crude outlines of his leading question.

Marjorie was painfully conscious of blushing. She was filled with rage against Jacobsen. 'Because,' she said firmly, 'I don't think it necessary to give expression to my religious feelings by making a lot of'—she hesitated a moment—'a lot of meaningless gestures with a crowd of other people.'

'You used to go,' said Jacobsen.

'When I was a child and hadn't thought about these things.'

Jacobsen was silent, and concealed a smile in his coffee-cup. Really, he said to himself, there ought to be religious conscription for women—and for most men, too. It was grotesque the way these people thought they could stand by themselves—the fools, when there was the infinite authority of organised religion to support their ridiculous feebleness.

'Does Lambourne go to church?' he asked maliciously, and with an air of perfect naïveté and good faith.

Marjorie coloured again, and a fresh wave of hatred surged up within her. Even as she had said the words she had wondered whether Jacobsen would notice that the phrase 'meaningless gestures' didn't ring very much like one of her own coinages. 'Gesture'—that was one of Guy's words, like 'incredible', 'exacerbate', 'impinge', 'sinister'. Of course all her present views about religion had come from Guy. She looked Jacobsen straight in the face and replied:

'Yes, I think he goes to church pretty regularly. But I really don't know: his religion has nothing to do with me.'

Jacobsen was lost in delight and admiration.

Punctually at twenty minutes to eleven he set out for church. From where she was sitting in the summer-house Marjorie watched him as he crossed the garden, incredibly absurd and incongruous in his black clothes among the blazing flowers and the young emerald of the trees. Now he was hidden behind the sweet-briar hedge, all except the hard black melon of his bowler hat, which she could see bobbing along between the topmost sprays.

She went on with her letter to Guy. '. . . What a strange man Mr Jacobsen is. I suppose he is very clever, but I can't get very much out of him. We had an argument about religion at breakfast this morning; I rather scored off him. He has now gone off to church all by himself;—I really couldn't face the prospect of going with him—I hope he'll enjoy old Mr Trubshaw's preaching!'

Jacobsen did enjoy Mr Trubshaw's preaching enormously. He always made a point, in whatever part of Christendom he happened to be, of attending divine service. He had the greatest admiration of churches as institutions. In their solidity and unchangeableness he saw one of the few hopes for humanity. Further, he derived great pleasure from comparing the Church as an institution—splendid, powerful, eternal—with the childish imbecility of its representatives. How delightful it was to sit in the herded congregation and listen to the sincere outpourings of an intellect only a little less limited than that of an Australian aboriginal! How restful to feel oneself a member of a flock, guided by a good shepherd—himself a sheep! Then there was the scientific interest (he went to church as student of anthropology, as a Freudian psychologist) and the philosophic amusement of counting the undistributed middles and tabulating historically the exploded fallacies in the parson's discourse.

Today Mr Trubshaw preached a topical sermon about the Irish situation. His was the gospel of the *Morning Post*, slightly tempered by Christianity. It was our duty, he said, to pray for the Irish first of all, and if that had no effect upon recruiting, why, then, we must conscribe them as zealously as we had prayed before.

Jacobsen leaned back in his pew with a sigh of contentment. A connoisseur, he recognised that this was the right stuff.

'Well,' said Mr Petherton over the Sunday beef at lunch, 'how did you like our dear Vicar?'

'He was splendid,' said Jacobsen, with grave enthusiasm. 'One of the best sermons I've ever heard.'

'Indeed? I shall really have to go and hear him again. It must be nearly ten years since I listened to him.'

'He's inimitable.'

Marjorie looked at Jacobsen carefully. He seemed to be perfectly serious. She was more than ever puzzled by the man.

The days went slipping by, hot blue days that passed like a flash almost without one's noticing them, cold grey days, seeming interminable and without number, and about which one spoke with a sense of justified grievance, for the season was supposed to be summer. There was fighting going on in France—terrific battles, to judge from the headlines in *The Times*; but, after all, one day's paper was very much like another's. Marjorie read them dutifully, but didn't honestly take in very much; at least she forgot about things very soon. She couldn't keep count with the battles of Ypres, and when somebody told her that she ought to go and see the photographs of the *Vindictive*, she smiled vaguely and said Yes, without remembering precisely what the *Vindictive* was—a ship, she supposed.

Guy was in France, to be sure, but he was an Intelligence Officer now, so that she was hardly anxious about him at all. Clergymen used to say that the war was bringing us all back to a sense of the fundamental realities of life. She supposed it was true: Guy's enforced absences were a pain to her, and the difficulties of housekeeping continually increased and multiplied.

Mr Petherton took a more intelligent interest in the war than did his daughter. He prided himself on being able to see the thing as a whole, on taking an historical, God's-eye view of it all. He talked about it at meal-times, insisting that the world must be made safe for democracy. Between meals he sat in the library working at his monumental *History of Morals*. To his dinner-table disquisitions Marjorie would listen more or less attentively, Jacobsen with an unfailing, bright, intelligent politeness. Jacobsen himself rarely volunteered a remark about the war; it was taken for granted that he thought about it in the same way as all other right-thinking folk. Between meals he worked in his room or discussed the morals of the Italian Renaissance with his host. Marjorie could write to Guy that nothing was happening, and that but for his absence and the weather interfering so much with tennis, she would be perfectly happy.

Into the midst of this placidity there fell, delightful bolt from the blue, the announcement that Guy was getting leave at the end of July. 'DARLING,' Marjorie wrote, 'I am so excited to think that you will be with me in such a little—such a long, long time.' Indeed, she was so excited and delighted that she realised with a touch of remorse how comparatively little she had thought of him when there seemed no chance of seeing him, how dim a figure in absence he was. A week later she heard that George White had arranged to get leave at the same time so as to see Guy. She was glad; George was a charming boy, and Guy was so fond of him. The Whites were their nearest neighbours, and ever since Guy had come to live at Blaybury he had seen a great deal of young George.

'We shall be a most festive party,' said Mr Petherton. 'Roger will be coming to us just at the same time as Guy.'

'I'd quite forgotten Uncle Roger,' said Marjorie. 'Of course, his holidays begin then, don't they?'

The Reverend Roger was Alfred Petherton's brother and a master at one of our most glorious public schools. Marjorie hardly agreed with her father in thinking that his presence would add anything to the 'festiveness' of the party. It was a pity he should be coming at this particular moment. However, we all have our little cross to bear.

Mr Petherton was feeling playful. 'We must bring down,' he said, 'the choicest Falernian, bottled when Gladstone was consul, for the occasion. We must prepare wreaths and unguents and hire a flute player and a couple of dancing girls . . .'

He spent the rest of the meal in quoting Horace, Catullus, the Greek Anthology, Petronius, and Sidonius Apollinaris. Marjorie's knowledge of the dead languages was decidedly limited. Her thoughts were elsewhere, and it was only dimly and as it were through a mist that she heard her father murmuring—whether merely to himself or with the hope of eliciting an answer from somebody, she hardly knew—'Let me see: how does that epigram go?—that one about the different kinds of fish and the garlands of roses, by Meleager, or is it Poseidippus? . . .'

II

Guy and Jacobsen were walking in the Dutch garden, an incongruous couple. On Guy military servitude had left no outwardly visible mark; out of uniform, he still looked like a tall, untidy undergraduate; he stooped and drooped as much as ever; his hair was still bushy and, to judge by the dim expression of his face, he had not yet learnt to think imperially. His khaki always looked like a disguise, like the most absurd fancy dress. Jacobsen trotted beside him, short, fattish, very sleek, and correct. They talked in a desultory way about things indifferent. Guy, anxious for a little intellectual exercise after so many months of discipline, had been trying to inveigle his companion into a philosophical discussion. Jacobsen consistently eluded his efforts; he was too lazy to talk seriously; there was no profit that he could see to be got out of this young man's opinions, and he had not the faintest desire to make a disciple. He preferred, therefore, to discuss the war and the weather. It irritated him that people should want to trespass on the domain of thought—people who had no right to live anywhere but on the vegetative plane of mere existence. He wished they would simply be content to *be* or *do*, not try, so hopelessly, to think, when only one in a million can think with the least profit to himself or anyone else.

Out of the corner of his eye he looked at the dark, sensitive face of his companion; he ought to have gone into business at eighteen, was Jacobsen's verdict. It was bad for him to think; he wasn't strong enough.

A great sound of barking broke upon the calm of the garden. Looking up, the two strollers saw George White running across the green turf of the croquet lawn with a huge fawn-coloured dog bounding along at his side.

'Morning,' he shouted. He was hatless and out of breath. 'I

was taking Bella for a run, and thought I'd look in and see how you all were.'

'What a lovely dog!' Jacobsen exclaimed.

'An old English mastiff—our one aboriginal dog. She has a pedigree going straight back to Edward the Confessor.'

Jacobsen began a lively conversation with George on the virtues and short-comings of dogs. Bella smelt his calves and then lifted up her gentle black eyes to look at him. She seemed satisfied.

He looked at them for a little; they were too much absorbed in their doggy conversation to pay attention to him. He made a gesture as though he had suddenly remembered something, gave a little grunt, and with a very preoccupied expression on his face turned to go towards the house. His elaborate piece of by-play escaped the notice of the intended spectators; Guy saw that it had, and felt more miserable and angry and jealous than ever. They would think he had slunk off because he wasn't wanted—which was quite true—instead of believing that he had something very important to do, which was what he had intended they should believe.

A cloud of self-doubt settled upon him. Was his mind, after all, worthless, and the little things he had written—rubbish, not potential genius as he had hoped? Jacobsen was right in preferring George's company. George was perfect, physically, a splendid creature; what could he himself claim?

'I'm second-rate,' he thought—'second-rate, physically, morally, mentally. Jacobsen is quite right.'

The best he could hope to be was a pedestrian literary man with quiet tastes.

NO, no, no! He clenched his hands and, as though to register his resolve before the universe, he said, aloud:

'I will do it; I will be first-rate, I will.'

He was covered with confusion on seeing a gardener pop

up, surprised from behind a bank of rose-bushes. Talking to himself—the man must have thought him mad!

He hurried on across the lawn, entered the house, and ran upstairs to his room. There was not a second to lose; he must begin at once. He would write something—something that would last, solid, hard, shining . . .

'Damn them all! I will do it, I can . . .'

There were writing materials and a table in his room. He selected a pen—with a Relief nib he would be able to go on for hours without getting tired—and a large square sheet of writing-paper.

> 'HATCH HOUSE,
> BLAYBURY,
> WILTS.
>
> Station: Cogham, 3 miles; Nobes
> Monacorum, 4½ miles'

Stupid of people to have their stationery printed in red, when black or blue is so much nicer! He inked over the letters.

He held up the paper to the light; there was a watermark, 'Pimlico Bond'. What an admirable name for the hero of a novel! Pimlico Bond . . .

> *There's be-eef in the la-arder*
> *And du-ucks in the pond;*
> *Crying dilly dilly, dilly dilly . . .*

He bit the end of his pen. 'What I want to get,' he said to himself, 'is something very hard, very external. Intense emotion, but one will somehow have got outside it.' He made a movement of hands, arms, and shoulders, tightening his muscles in an effort to express to himself physically that hardness and tightness and firmness of style after which he was struggling.

He began to draw on his virgin paper. A woman, naked, one arm lifted over her head, so that it pulled up her breast by that wonderful curving muscle that comes down from the shoulder. The inner surface of the thighs, remember, is slightly concave. The feet, seen from the front, are always a difficulty.

It would never do to leave that about. What would the servants think? He turned the nipples into eyes, drew heavy lines for nose, mouth, and chin, slopped on the ink thick; it made a passable face now—though an acute observer might have detected the original nudity. He tore it up into very small pieces.

A crescendo booming filled the house. It was the gong. He looked at his watch. Lunch-time, and he had done nothing. O God! . . .

III

It was dinner-time on the last evening of Guy's leave. The uncovered mahogany table was like a pool of brown unruffled water within whose depths flowers and the glinting shapes of glass and silver hung dimly reflected. Mr Petherton sat at the head of the board, flanked by his brother Roger and Jacobsen. Youth, in the persons of Marjorie, Guy, and George White, had collected at the other end. They had reached the stage of dessert.

'This is excellent port,' said Roger, sleek and glossy like a well-fed black cob under his silken clerical waistcoat. He was a strong, thick-set man of about fifty, with a red neck as thick as his head. His hair was cropped with military closeness; he liked to set a good example to the boys, some of whom showed distressing 'aesthetic' tendencies and wore their hair long.

'I'm glad you like it. I mayn't touch it myself, of course. Have another glass.' Alfred Petherton's face wore an expression of dyspeptic melancholy. He was wishing he hadn't taken quite so much of that duck.

'Thank you, I will.' Roger took the decanter with a smile of satisfaction. 'The tired schoolmaster is worthy of his second glass. White, you look rather pale; I think you must have another.' Roger had a hearty, jocular manner, calculated to prove to his pupils that he was not one of the slimy sort of parsons, not a Creeping Jesus.

There was an absorbing conversation going on at the youthful end of the table. Secretly irritated at having been thus interrupted in the middle of it, White turned round and smiled vaguely at Roger.

'Oh, thank you, sir,' he said, and pushed his glass forward to be filled. The 'sir' slipped out unawares; it was, after all, such a little while since he had been a schoolboy under Roger's dominion.

'One is lucky,' Roger went on seriously, 'to get any port wine at all now. I'm thankful to say I bought ten dozen from my old college some years ago to lay down; otherwise I don't know what I should do. My wine merchant tells me he couldn't let me have a single bottle. Indeed, he offered to buy some off me, if I'd sell. But I wasn't having any. A bottle in the cellar is worth ten shillings in the pocket these days. I always say that port has become a necessity now one gets so little meat. Lambourne! you are another of our brave defenders; you deserve a second glass.'

'No, thanks,' said Guy, hardly looking up. 'I've had enough.' He went on talking to Marjorie—about the different views of life held by the French and the Russians.

Roger helped himself to cherries. 'One has to select them carefully,' he remarked for the benefit of the unwillingly listening George. 'There is nothing that gives you such stomachaches as unripe cherries.'

'I expect you're glad, Mr Petherton, that holidays have begun at last?' said Jacobsen.

'Glad? I should think so. One is utterly dead beat at the end of the summer term. Isn't one, White?'

White had taken the opportunity to turn back again and listen to Guy's conversation; recalled, like a dog who has started off on a forbidden scent, he obediently assented that one did get tired at the end of the summer term.

'I suppose,' said Jacobsen, 'you still teach the same old things—Caesar, Latin verses, Greek grammar, and the rest? We Americans can hardly believe that all that still goes on.'

'Thank goodness,' said Roger, 'we still hammer a little solid stuff into them. But there's been a great deal of fuss lately about new curriculums and so forth. They do a lot of science now and things of that kind, but I don't believe the children learn anything at all. It's pure waste of time.'

'So is all education, I dare say,' said Jacobsen lightly.

'Not if you teach them discipline. That's what's wanted—discipline. Most of these little boys need plenty of beating, and they don't get enough now. Besides, if you can't hammer knowledge in at their heads, you can at least beat a little in at their tails.'

'You're very ferocious, Roger,' said Mr Petherton, smiling. He was feeling better; the duck was settling down.

'No, it's the vital thing. The best thing the war has brought us is discipline. The country had got slack and wanted tightening up.' Roger's face glowed with zeal.

From the other end of the table Guy's voice could be heard saying, 'Do you know César Franck's "Dieu s'avance à travers la lande"? It's one of the finest bits of religious music I know.'

Mr Petherton's face lighted up; he leaned forward. 'No,' he said, throwing his answer unexpectedly into the midst of the young people's conversation. 'I don't know it; but do you know this? Wait a minute.' He knitted his brows, and his lips moved as though he were trying to recapture a formula. 'Ah, I've got it. Now, can you tell me this? The name of what famous piece of religious music do I utter when I order an old carpenter, once a Liberal but now a renegade to Conservatism, to make a hive for bees?'

Guy gave it up; his guardian beamed delightedly.

'Hoary Tory, oh, Judas! Make a bee-house,' he said. 'Do you see? Oratorio *Judas Maccabeus*.'

Guy could have wished that this bit of flotsam from Mr Petherton's sportive youth had not been thus washed up at his feet. He felt that he had been peeping indecently close into 'the dark backward and abysm of time'.

'That was a good one,' Mr Petherton chuckled. 'I must see if I can think of some more.'

Roger, who was not easily to be turned away from his favourite topic, waited till this irrelevant spark of levity had quite expired, and continued: 'It's a remarkable and noticeable fact that you never seem to get discipline combined with the teaching of science or modern languages. Who ever heard of a science master having a good house at a school? Scientists' houses are always bad.'

'How very strange!' said Jacobsen.

'Strange, but a fact. It seems to me a great mistake to give them houses at all if they can't keep discipline. And then there's the question of religion. Some of these men never come to chapel except when they're on duty. And then, I ask you, what happens when they prepare their boys for Confirmation?

Why, I've known boys come to me who were supposed to have been prepared by one or other of these men, and, on asking them, I've found that they know nothing whatever about the most solemn facts of the Eucharist.—May I have some more of those excellent cherries please, White?—Of course, I do my best in such cases to tell the boys what I feel personally about these solemn things. But there generally isn't the time; one's life is so crowded; and so they go into Confirmation with only the very haziest knowledge of what it's all about. You see how absurd it is to let anyone but the classical men have anything to do with the boys' lives.'

'Shake it well, dear,' Mr Petherton was saying to his daughter, who had come with his medicine.

'What is that stuff?' asked Roger.

'Oh, it's merely my peptones. I can hardly digest at all without it, you know.'

'You have all my sympathies. My poor colleague, Flexner, suffers from chronic colitis. I can't imagine how he goes on with his work.'

'No, indeed. I find I can do nothing strenuous.'

Roger turned and seized once more on the unhappy George. 'White,' he said, 'let this be a lesson to you. Take care of your inside; it's the secret of a happy old age.'

Guy looked up quickly. 'Don't worry about his old age,' he said in a strange harsh voice, very different from the gentle, elaborately modulated tone in which he generally spoke. 'He won't have an old age. His chances against surviving are about fourteen to three if the war goes on another year.'

'Come,' said Roger, 'don't let's be pessimistic.'

'But I'm not. I assure you, I'm giving you a most rosy view of George's chance of reaching old age.'

It was felt that Guy's remarks had been in poor taste. There was a silence; eyes floated vaguely and uneasily, trying not to encounter one another. Roger cracked a nut loudly. When he had sufficiently relished the situation, Jacobsen changed the subject by remarking:

'That was a fine bit of work by our destroyers this morning, wasn't it?'

'It did one good to read about it,' said Mr Petherton. 'Quite the Nelson touch.'

Roger raised his glass. 'Nelson!' he said, and emptied it at a gulp. 'What a man! I am trying to persuade the Headmaster to make Trafalgar Day a holiday. It is the best way of reminding boys of things of that sort.'

'A curiously untypical Englishman to be a national hero, isn't he?' said Jacobsen. 'So emotional and lacking in Britannic phlegm.'

The Reverend Roger looked grave. 'There's one thing I've never been able to understand about Nelson, and that is, how a man who was so much the soul of honour and of patriotism could have been—er—immoral with Lady Hamilton. I know people say that it was the custom of the age, that these things meant nothing then, and so forth; but all the same, I repeat, I cannot understand how a man who was so intensely a patriotic Englishman could have done such a thing.'

'I fail to see what patriotism has got to do with it,' said Guy.

Roger fixed him with his most pedagogic look and said slowly and gravely, 'Then I am sorry for you. I shouldn't have thought it was necessary to tell an Englishman that purity of morals is a national tradition: you especially, a public-school man.'

'Let us go and have a hundred up at billiards,' said Mr Petherton. 'Roger, will you come? And you, George, and Guy?'

'I'm so incredibly bad,' Guy insisted, 'I'd really rather not.'

'So am I,' said Jacobsen.

'Then, Marjorie, you must make the fourth.'

The billiard players trooped out; Guy and Jacobsen were left alone, brooding over the wreckage of dinner. There was a long silence. The two men sat smoking, Guy sitting in a sagging, crumpled attitude, like a half-empty sack abandoned on a chair, Jacobsen very upright and serene.

'Do you find you can suffer fools gladly?' asked Guy abruptly.

'Perfectly gladly.'

'I wish I could. The Reverend Roger has a tendency to make my blood boil.'

'But such a good soul,' Jacobsen insisted.

'I dare say, but a monster all the same.'

'You should take him more calmly. I make a point of never letting myself be moved by external things. I stick to my writing and thinking. Truth is beauty, beauty is truth, and so forth: after all, they're the only things of solid value.' Jacobsen looked at the young man with a smile as he said these words. There is no doubt, he said to himself, that that boy ought to have gone into business; what a mistake this higher education is, to be sure.

'Of course, they're the only things,' Guy burst out passionately. 'You can afford to say so because you had the luck to be born twenty years before I was, and with five thousand miles of good deep water between you and Europe. Here am I, called upon to devote my life, in a very different way from which you devote yours to truth and beauty—to devote my life to—well, what? I'm not quite sure, but I preserve a touching faith that it is good. And you tell me to ignore external circumstances. Come and live in Flanders a little and try . . .' He launched forth into a tirade about agony and death and blood and putrefaction.

'What is one to do?' he concluded despairingly. 'What the

devil is right? I had meant to spend my life writing and thinking, trying to create something beautiful or discover something true. But oughtn't one, after all, if one survives, to give up everything else and try to make this hideous den of a world a little more habitable.'

'I think you can take it that a world which has let itself be dragooned into this criminal folly is pretty hopeless. Follow your inclinations; or, better, go into a bank and make a lot of money.'

Guy burst out laughing, rather too loudly. 'Admirable, admirable!' he said. 'To return to our old topic of fools: frankly, Jacobsen, I cannot imagine why you should elect to pass your time with my dear old guardian. He's a charming old man, but one must admit—' He waved his hand.

'One must live somewhere,' said Jacobsen. 'I find your guardian a most interesting man to be with.—Oh, do look at that dog!' On the hearth-rug Marjorie's little Pekingese, Confucius, was preparing to lie down and go to sleep. He went assiduously through the solemn farce of scratching the floor, under the impression, no doubt, that he was making a comfortable nest to lie in. He turned round and round, scratching earnestly and methodically. Then he lay down, curled himself up in a ball, and was asleep in the twinkling of an eye.

'Isn't that too wonderfully human!' exclaimed Jacobsen delightedly. Guy thought he could see now why Jacobsen enjoyed living with Mr Petherton. The old man was so wonderfully human.

Later in the evening, when the billiards was over and Mr Petherton had duly commented on the anachronism of introducing the game into Antony and Cleopatra, Guy and Marjorie went for a stroll in the garden. The moon had risen above the trees and lit up the front of the house with its bright pale light that could not wake the sleeping colours of the world.

'Moonlight is the proper architectural light,' said Guy, as they stood looking at the house. The white light and the hard black shadows brought out all the elegance of its Georgian symmetry.

'Look, here's the ghost of a rose.' Marjorie touched a big cool flower, which one guessed rather than saw to be red, a faint equivocal lunar crimson. 'And, oh, smell the tobacco-plant flowers. Aren't they delicious!'

'I always think there's something very mysterious about perfume drifting through the dark like this. It seems to come from some perfectly different immaterial world, peopled by unembodied sensations, phantom passions. Think of the spiritual effect of incense in a dark church. One isn't surprised that people have believed in the existence of the soul.'

They walked on in silence. Sometimes, accidentally, his hand would brush against hers in the movement of their march. Guy felt an intolerable emotion of expectancy, akin to fear. It made him feel almost physically sick.

'Do you remember,' he said abruptly, 'that summer holiday our families spent together in Wales? It must have been nineteen four or five. I was ten and you were eight or thereabouts.'

'Of course I remember,' cried Marjorie. 'Everything. There was that funny little toy railway from the slate quarries.'

'And do you remember our gold-mine? All those tons of yellow ironstone we collected and hoarded in a cave, fully believing they were nuggets. How incredibly remote it seems!'

'And you had a wonderful process by which you tested whether the stuff was real gold or not. It all passed triumphantly as genuine, I remember!'

'Having that secret together first made us friends, I believe.'

'I dare say,' said Marjorie. 'Fourteen years ago—what a time!

And you began educating me even then: all that stuff you told me about gold-mining, for instance.'

'Fourteen years,' Guy repeated reflectively, 'and I shall be going out again tomorrow . . .'

'Don't speak about it. I am so miserable when you're away.' She genuinely forgot what a delightful summer she had had, except for the shortage of tennis.

'We must make this the happiest hour of our lives. Perhaps it may be the last we shall be together.' Guy looked up at the moon, and he perceived, with a sudden start, that it was a sphere islanded in an endless night, not a flat disk stuck on a wall not so very far away. It filled him with an infinite dreariness; he felt too insignificant to live at all.

'Guy, you mustn't talk like that,' said Marjorie appealingly.

'We've got twelve hours,' said Guy in a meditative voice, 'but that's only clock-work time. You can give an hour the quality of everlastingness, and spend years which are as though they had never been. We get our immortality here and now; it's a question of quality, not of quantity. I don't look forward to golden harps or anything of that sort. I know that when I am dead, I shall be dead; there isn't any afterwards. If I'm killed, my immortality will be in your memory. Perhaps, too, somebody will read the things I've written, and in his mind I shall survive, feebly and partially. But in your mind I shall survive intact and whole.'

'But I'm sure we shall go on living after death. It can't be the end.' Marjorie was conscious that she had heard those words before. Where? Oh yes, it was earnest Evangeline who had spoken them at the school debating society.

'I wouldn't count on it,' Guy replied, with a little laugh. 'You may get such a disappointment when you die.' Then in an altered voice, 'I don't want to die. I hate and fear death. But probably I shan't be killed after all. All the same . . .' His voice

faded out. They stepped into a tunnel of impenetrable darkness
between two tall hornbeam hedges. He had become nothing
but a voice, and now that had ceased; he had disappeared. The
voice began again, low, quick, monotonous, a little breathless.
'I remember once reading a poem by one of the old Provençal
troubadours, telling how God had once granted him supreme
happiness; for the night before he was to set out for the
Crusade, it had been granted him to hold his lady in his
arms—all the short eternal night through. Ains que j'aille oltre
mer: when I was going beyond sea.' The voice stopped again.
They were standing at the very mouth of the hornbeam alley,
looking out from that close-pent river of shadow upon an
ocean of pale moonlight.

'How still it is.' They did not speak; they hardly breathed.
They became saturated with the quiet.

Marjorie broke the silence. 'Do you want me as much as all
that, Guy?' All through that long, speechless minute she had
been trying to say the words, repeating them over to herself,
longing to say them aloud, but paralysed, unable to. And at last
she had spoken them, impersonally, as though through the
mouth of someone else. She heard them very distinctly, and
was amazed at the matter-of-factness of the tone.

Guy's answer took the form of a question. 'Well, suppose I
were killed now,' he said, 'should I ever have really lived?'

They had stepped out of the cavernous alley into the moonlight. She could see him clearly now, and there was something
so drooping and dejected and pathetic about him, he seemed
so much of a great, overgrown child that a wave of passionate
pitifulness rushed through her, reinforcing other emotions less
maternal. She longed to take him in her arms, stroke his hair,
lullaby him, baby-fashion, to sleep upon her breast. And Guy,
on his side, desired nothing better than to give his fatigues and
sensibilities to her maternal care, to have his eyes kissed fast,

and sleep to her soothing. In his relations with women—but his experience in this direction was deplorably small—he had, unconsciously at first but afterwards with a realisation of what he was doing, played this child part. In moments of self-analysis he laughed at himself for acting the 'child stunt', as he called it. Here he was—he hadn't noticed it yet—doing it again, drooping, dejected, wholly pathetic, feeble . . .

Marjorie was carried away by her emotion. She would give herself to her lover, would take possession of her helpless, pitiable child. She put her arms round his neck, lifted her face to his kisses, whispered something tender and inaudible.

Guy drew her towards him and began kissing the soft, warm mouth. He touched the bare arm that encircled his neck; the flesh was resilient under his fingers; he felt a desire to pinch it and tear it.

It had been just like this with that little slut Minnie. Just the same—all horrible lust. He remembered a curious physiological fact out of Havelock Ellis. He shuddered as though he had touched something disgusting, and pushed her away.

'No, no, no. It's horrible; it's odious. Drunk with moonlight and sentimentalising about death . . . Why not just say with Biblical frankness, Lie with me—Lie with me?'

That this love, which was to have been so marvellous and new and beautiful, should end libidinously and bestially like the affair, never remembered without a shiver of shame, with Minnie (the vulgarity of her!)—filled him with horror.

Marjorie burst into tears and ran away, wounded and trembling, into the solitude of the hornbeam shadow. 'Go away, go away,' she sobbed, with such intensity of command that Guy, moved by an immediate remorse and the sight of tears to stop her and ask forgiveness, was constrained to let her go her ways.

A cool, impersonal calm had succeeded almost immediately to his outburst. Critically, he examined what he had done, and judged it, not without a certain feeling of satisfaction, to be the greatest 'floater' of his life. But at least the thing was done and couldn't be undone. He took the weak-willed man's delight in the irrevocability of action. He walked up and down the lawn smoking a cigarette and thinking, clearly and quietly—remembering the past, questioning the future. When the cigarette was finished he went into the house.

He entered the smoking-room to hear Roger saying, '. . . It's the poor who are having the good time now. Plenty to eat, plenty of money, and no taxes to pay. No taxes—that's the sickening thing. Look at Alfred's gardener, for instance. He gets twenty-five or thirty bob a week and an uncommon good house. He's married, but only has one child. A man like that is uncommonly well off. He ought to be paying income-tax; he can perfectly well afford it.'

Mr Petherton was listening somnolently, Jacobsen with his usual keen, intelligent politeness; George was playing with the blue Persian kitten.

It had been arranged that George should stay the night, because it was such a bore having to walk that mile and a bit home again in the dark. Guy took him up to his room and sat down on the bed for a final cigarette, while George was undressing. It was the hour of confidence—that rather perilous moment when fatigue has relaxed the fibres of the mind, making it ready and ripe for sentiment.

'It depresses me so much,' said Guy, 'to think that you're only twenty and that I'm just on twenty-four. You will be young and sprightly when the war ends; I shall be an old antique man.'

'Not so old as all that,' George answered, pulling off his shirt. His skin was very white, face, neck, and hands seeming dark brown by comparison; there was a sharply demarcated highwater mark of sunburn at throat and wrist.

'It horrifies me to think of the time one is wasting in this bloody war, growing stupider and grosser every day, achieving nothing at all. It will be five, six—God knows how many—years cut clean out of one's life. You'll have the world before you when it's all over, but I shall have spent my best time.'

'Of course, it doesn't make so much difference to me,' said George through a foam of tooth-brushing; 'I'm not capable of doing anything of any particular value. It's really all the same whether I lead a blameless life broking stocks or spend my time getting killed. But for you, I agree, it's too bloody . . .'

Guy smoked on in silence, his mind filled with a languid resentment against circumstance. George put on his pyjamas and crept under the sheet; he had to curl himself up into a ball, because Guy was lying across the end of the bed, and he couldn't put his feet down.

'I suppose,' said Guy at last, meditatively—'I suppose the only consolations are, after all, women and wine. I shall really have to resort to them. Only women are mostly so fearfully boring and wine is so expensive now.'

'But not all women!' George, it was evident, was waiting to get a confidence off his chest.

'I gather you've found the exceptions.'

George poured forth. He had just spent six months at Chelsea—six dreary months on the barrack square; but there had been lucid intervals between the drills and the special courses, which he had filled with many notable voyages of discovery among unknown worlds. And chiefly, Columbus to his own soul, he had discovered all those psychological intricacies and potentialities, which only the passions bring to light. *Nosce teipsum*, it has been commanded; and a judicious cultivation of the passions is one of the surest roads to self-knowledge. To George, at barely twenty, it was all so amazingly new and exciting, and Guy listened to the story of his adventures with admiration and a touch of envy. He regretted the dismal and cloistered chastity—broken only once, and how sordidly! Wouldn't he have learnt much more, he wondered—have been a more real and better human being if he had had George's experiences? He would have profited by them more than George could ever hope to do. There was the risk of George's getting involved in a mere foolish expense of spirit in a waste of shame. He might not be sufficiently an individual to remain himself in spite of his surroundings; his hand would be coloured by the dye he worked in. Guy felt sure that he himself would have run no risk; he would have come, seen, conquered, and returned intact and still himself, but enriched by the spoils of a new knowledge. Had he been wrong after all? Had life in the cloister of his own philosophy been wholly unprofitable?

He looked at George. It was not surprising that the ladies favoured him, glorious ephebus that he was.

'With a face and figure like mine,' he reflected, 'I shouldn't have been able to lead his life, even if I'd wanted to.' He laughed inwardly.

'You really must meet her,' George was saying enthusiastically.

Guy smiled. 'No, I really mustn't. Let me give you a bit of perfectly good advice. Never attempt to share your joys with anyone else. People will sympathise with pain, but not with pleasure. Good night, George.'

He bent over the pillow and kissed the smiling face that was as smooth as a child's to his lips.

Guy lay awake for a long time, and his eyes were dry and aching before sleep finally came upon him. He spent those dark interminable hours thinking—thinking hard, intensely, painfully. No sooner had he left George's room than a feeling of intense unhappiness took hold of him. 'Distorted with misery,' that was how he described himself; he loved to coin such phrases, for he felt the artist's need to express as well as to feel and think. Distorted with misery, he went to bed; distorted with misery, he lay and thought and thought. He had, positively, a sense of physical distortion: his guts were twisted, he had a hunched back, his legs were withered . . .

He had the right to be miserable. He was going back to France tomorrow, he had trampled on his mistress's love, and he was beginning to doubt himself, to wonder whether his whole life hadn't been one ludicrous folly.

He reviewed his life, like a man about to die. Born in another age, he would, he supposed, have been religious. He had got over religion early, like the measles—at nine a Low Churchman, at twelve a Broad Churchman, and at fourteen an Agnostic—but he still retained the temperament of a religious man. Intellectually he was a Voltairian, emotionally a Bunyanite. To have arrived at this formula was, he felt, a distinct advance in self-knowledge. And what a fool he had been with Marjorie! The priggishness of his attitude—making her read Wordsworth when she didn't want to. Intellectual love—his phrases weren't always a blessing; how hopelessly he had deceived himself with words! And now this evening the crowning outrage, when he had behaved to her like a hysterical anchorite dealing with a temptation. His body tingled, at the recollection, with shame.

An idea occurred to him; he would go and see her, tiptoe downstairs to her room, kneel by her bed, ask for her forgiveness. He lay quite still imagining the whole scene. He even went so far as to get out of bed, open the door, which made a noise in the process like a peacock's scream, quite unnerving him, and creep to the head of the stairs. He stood there a long time, his feet growing colder and colder, and then decided that the adventure was really too sordidly like the episode at the

beginning of Tolstoy's *Resurrection*. The door screamed again
as he returned; he lay in bed, trying to persuade himself that
his self-control had been admirable and at the same time
cursing his absence of courage in not carrying out what he had
intended.

He remembered a lecture he had given Marjorie once on the
subject of Sacred and Profane Love. Poor girl, how had she
listened in patience? He could see her attending with such a
serious expression on her face that she looked quite ugly. She
looked so beautiful when she was laughing or happy; at the
Whites, for instance, three nights ago, when George and
she had danced after dinner and he had sat, secretly envious,
reading a book in the corner of the room and looking superior.
He wouldn't learn to dance, but always wished he could. It
was a barbarous, aphrodisiacal occupation, he said, and he
preferred to spend his time and energies in reading. Salvationist
again! What a much wiser person George had proved himself
than he. He had no prejudices, no theoretical views about the
conduct of life; he just lived, admirably, naturally, as the spirit
or the flesh moved him. If only he could live his life again, if
only he could abolish this evening's monstrous stupidity . . .

Marjorie also lay awake. She too felt herself distorted with
misery. How odiously cruel he had been, and how much she
longed to forgive him! Perhaps he would come in the dark,
when all the house was asleep, tiptoeing into the room very
quietly to kneel by her bed and ask to be forgiven. Would he
come, she wondered? She stared into the blackness above her
and about her, willing him to come, commanding him—angry
and wretched because he was so slow in coming, because he
didn't come at all. They were both of them asleep before two.

Seven hours of sleep make a surprising difference to the state
of mind. Guy, who thought he was distorted for life, woke to
find himself healthily normal. Marjorie's angers and despairs

had subsided. The hour they had together between breakfast and Guy's departure was filled with almost trivial conversation. Guy was determined to say something about last night's incident. But it was only at the very last moment, when the dog-cart was actually at the door, that he managed to bring out some stammered repentance for what had happened last night.

'Don't think about it,' Marjorie had told him. So they had kissed and parted, and their relations were precisely the same as they had been before Guy came on leave.

George was sent out a week or two later, and a month after that they heard at Blaybury that he had lost a leg—fortunately below the knee.

'Poor boy!' said Mr Petherton. 'I must really write a line to his mother at once.'

Jacobsen made no comment, but it was a surprise to him to find how much he had been moved by the news. George White had lost a leg; he couldn't get the thought out of his head. But only below the knee; he might be called lucky. Lucky—things are deplorably relative, he reflected. One thanks God because He has thought fit to deprive one of His creatures of a limb.

'Neither delighteth He in any man's legs,' eh? Nous avons changé tout cela.

George had lost a leg. There would be no more of that Olympian speed and strength and beauty. Jacobsen conjured up before his memory a vision of the boy running with his great fawn-coloured dog across green expanses of grass. How glorious he had looked, his fine brown hair blowing like fire in the wind of his own speed, his cheeks flushed, his eyes very bright. And how easily he ran, with long, bounding strides, looking down at the dog that jumped and barked at his side!

He had had a perfection, and now it was spoilt. Instead of a leg he had a stump. *Moignon*, the French called it; there was the right repulsive sound about *moignon* which was lacking in 'stump'. Soignons le moignon en l'oignant d'oignons.

Often, at night before he went to sleep, he couldn't help thinking of George and the war and all the millions of *moignons* there must be in the world. He had a dream one night of slimy red knobbles, large polyp-like things, growing as he looked at them, swelling between his hands—*moignons*, in fact.

George was well enough in the late autumn to come home. He had learnt to hop along on his crutches very skilfully, and his preposterous donkey-drawn bath-chair soon became a familiar object in the lanes of the neighbourhood. It was a grand sight to behold when George rattled past at the trot, leaning forward like a young Phoebus in his chariot and urging his unwilling beast with voice and crutch. He drove over to Blaybury almost every day; Marjorie and he had endless talks about life and love and Guy and other absorbing topics. With Jacobsen he played piquet and discussed a thousand subjects. He was always gay and happy—that was what especially lacerated Jacobsen's heart with pity.

IV

The Christmas holidays had begun, and the Reverend Roger was back again at Blaybury. He was sitting at the writing-table in the drawing-room, engaged, at the moment, in biting the end of his pen and scratching his head. His face wore an expression of perplexity; one would have said that he was in the throes of literary composition. Which indeed he was: 'Beloved ward of Alfred Petherton . . .' he said aloud. 'Beloved ward . . .' He shook his head doubtfully.

The door opened and Jacobsen came into the room. Roger turned round at once.

'Have you heard the grievous news?' he said.

'No. What?'

'Poor Guy is dead. We got the telegram half an hour ago.'

'Good God!' said Jacobsen in an agonised voice which seemed to show that he had been startled out of the calm belonging to one who leads the life of reason. He had been conscious ever since George's mutilation that his defences were growing weaker; external circumstance was steadily encroaching upon him. Now it had broken in and, for the moment, he was at its mercy. Guy dead . . . He pulled himself together sufficiently to say, after a pause, 'Well, I suppose it was only to be expected sooner or later. Poor boy.'

'Yes, it's terrible, isn't it?' said Roger, shaking his head. 'I am just writing out an announcement to send to *The Times*. One can hardly say "the beloved ward of Alfred Petherton," can one? It doesn't sound quite right; and yet one would like somehow to give public expression to the deep affection Alfred felt for him. "Beloved ward"—no, decidedly it won't do.'

'You'll have to get round it somehow,' said Jacobsen. Roger's presence somehow made a return to the life of reason easier.

'Poor Alfred,' the other went on. 'You've no idea how hardly he takes it. He feels as though he had given a son.'

'What a waste it is!' Jacobsen exclaimed. He was altogether too deeply moved.

'I have done my best to console Alfred. One must always bear in mind for what Cause he died.'

'All those potentialities destroyed. He was an able fellow, was Guy.' Jacobsen was speaking more to himself than to his companion, but Roger took up the suggestion.

'Yes, he certainly was that. Alfred thought he was very promising. It is for his sake I am particularly sorry. I never got on very well with the boy myself. He was too eccentric for my taste. There's such a thing as being too clever, isn't there? It's rather inhuman. He used to do most remarkable Greek iambics for me when he was a boy. I dare say he was a very good fellow under all that cleverness and queerness. It's all very distressing, very grievous.'

'How was he killed?'

'Died of wounds yesterday morning. Do you think it would be a good thing to put in some quotation at the end of the announcement in the paper? Something like, "Dulce et Decorum", or "Sed Miles, sed Pro Patria", or "Per Ardua ad Astra"?'

'It hardly seems essential,' said Jacobsen.

'Perhaps not.' Roger's lips moved silently; he was counting. 'Forty-two words. I suppose that counts as eight lines. Poor Marjorie! I hope she won't feel it too bitterly. Alfred told me they were unofficially engaged.'

'So I gathered.'

'I am afraid I shall have to break the news to her. Alfred is too much upset to be able to do anything himself. It will be a most painful task. Poor girl! I suppose as a matter of fact they would not have been able to marry for some time, as Guy had next to no money. These early marriages are very rash. Let me see: eight times three shillings is one pound four, isn't it? I suppose they take cheques all right?'

'How old was he?' asked Jacobsen.

'Twenty-four and a few months.'

Jacobsen was walking restlessly up and down the room. 'Just reaching maturity! One is thankful these days to have one's own work and thoughts to take the mind off these horrors.'

'It's terrible, isn't it?—terrible. So many of my pupils have been killed now that I can hardly keep count of the number.'

There was a tapping at the French window; it was Marjorie

asking to be let in. She had been cutting holly and ivy for the Christmas decorations, and carried a basket full of dark, shining leaves.

Jacobsen unbolted the big window and Marjorie came in, flushed with the cold and smiling. Jacobsen had never seen her looking so handsome: she was superb, radiant, like Iphigenia coming in her wedding garments to the sacrifice.

'The holly is very poor this year,' she remarked. 'I am afraid we shan't make much of a show with our Christmas decorations.'

Jacobsen took the opportunity of slipping out through the French window. Although it was unpleasantly cold, he walked up and down the flagged paths of the Dutch garden, hatless and overcoatless, for quite a long time.

Marjorie moved about the drawing-room fixing sprigs of holly round the picture frames. Her uncle watched her, hesitating to speak; he was feeling enormously uncomfortable.

'I am afraid,' he said at last, 'that your father's very upset this morning.' His voice was husky; he made an explosive noise to clear his throat.

'Is it his palpitations?' Marjorie asked coolly; her father's infirmities did not cause her much anxiety.

'No, no.' Roger realised that his opening gambit had been a mistake. 'No It is—er a more mental affliction, and one which, I fear, will touch you closely too. Marjorie, you must be strong and courageous; we have just heard that Guy is dead.'

'Guy dead?' She couldn't believe it; she had hardly envisaged the possibility; besides he was on the Staff. 'Oh, Uncle Roger, it isn't true.'

'I am afraid there is no doubt. The War Office telegram came just after you had gone out for the holly.'

Marjorie sat down on the sofa and hid her face in her hands.

Guy dead; she would never see him again, never see him again, never; she began to cry.

Roger approached and stood, with his hand on her shoulder, in the attitude of a thought-reader. To those overwhelmed by sorrow the touch of a friendly hand is often comforting. They have fallen into an abyss, and the touching hand serves to remind them that life and God and human sympathy still exist, however bottomless the gulf of grief may seem. On Marjorie's shoulder her uncle's hand rested with a damp, heavy warmth that was peculiarly unpleasant.

'Dear child, it is very grievous, I know; but you must try and be strong and bear it bravely. We all have our cross to bear. We shall be celebrating the Birth of Christ in two days' time; remember with what patience He received the cup of agony. And then remember for what Cause Guy has given his life. He has died a hero's death, a martyr's death, witnessing to Heaven against the powers of evil.' Roger was unconsciously slipping into the words of his last sermon in the school chapel. 'You should feel pride in his death as well as sorrow. There, there, poor child.' He patted her shoulder two or three times. 'Perhaps it would be kinder to leave you now.'

For some time after her uncle's departure Marjorie sat motionless in the same position, her body bent forward, her face in her hands. She kept on repeating the words, 'Never again,' and the sound of them filled her with despair and made her cry. They seemed to open up such a dreary grey infinite vista—'never again'. They were as a spell evoking tears.

She got up at last and began walking aimlessly about the room. She paused in front of a little old black-framed mirror that hung near the window and looked at her reflection in the glass. She had expected somehow to look different, to have changed. She was surprised to find her face entirely unaltered: grave, melancholy perhaps, but still the same face she had looked at when she was doing her hair this morning. A curious idea entered her head; she wondered whether she would be able to smile now, at this dreadful moment. She moved the muscles of her face and was overwhelmed with shame at the sight of the mirthless grin that mocked her from the glass. What a beast she was! She burst into tears and threw herself again on the sofa, burying her face in a cushion. The door opened, and by the noise of shuffling and tapping Marjorie recognised the approach of George White on his crutches. She did not look up. At the sight of the abject figure on the sofa, George halted, uncertain what he should do. Should he quietly go away again, or should he stay and try to say something comforting? The sight of her lying there gave him almost physical pain. He decided to stay.

He approached the sofa and stood over her, suspended on his crutches. Still she did not lift her head, but pressed her face deeper into the smothering blindness of the cushion, as though to shut out from her consciousness all the external world. George looked down at her in silence. The little delicate tendrils of hair on the nape of her neck were exquisitely beautiful.

'I was told about it,' he said at last, 'just now, as I came in. It's too awful. I think I cared for Guy more than for almost anyone in the world. We both did, didn't we?'

She began sobbing again. George was overcome with remorse, feeling that he had somehow hurt her, somehow added to her pain by what he had said. 'Poor child, poor child,' he said, almost aloud. She was a year older than he, but she seemed so helplessly and pathetically young now that she was crying.

Standing up for long tired him, and he lowered himself, slowly and painfully, into the sofa beside her. She looked up at last and began drying her eyes.

'I'm so wretched, George, so specially wretched because I feel I didn't act rightly towards darling Guy. There were times, you know, when I wondered whether it wasn't all a great mistake, our being engaged. Sometimes I felt I almost hated him. I'd been feeling so odious about him these last weeks. And now comes this, and it makes me realise how awful I've been towards him.' She found it a relief to confide and confess; George was so sympathetic, he would understand. 'I've been a beast.'

Her voice broke, and it was as though something had broken in George's head. He was overwhelmed with pity; he couldn't bear it that she should suffer.

'You mustn't distress yourself unnecessarily, Marjorie dear,' he begged her, stroking the back of her hand with his large hard palm. 'Don't.'

Marjorie went on remorselessly. 'When Uncle Roger told me just now, do you know what I did? I said to myself, Do I really care? I couldn't make out. I looked in the glass to see if I could tell from my face. Then I suddenly thought I'd see whether I could laugh, and I did. And that made me feel how detestable I was, and I started crying again. Oh, I have been a beast, George, haven't I?'

She burst into a passion of tears and hid her face once more in the friendly cushion. George couldn't bear it at all. He laid his hand on her shoulder and bent forward, close to her, till his face almost touched her hair. 'Don't,' he cried. 'Don't, Marjorie. You mustn't torment yourself like this. I know you loved Guy; we both loved him. He would have wanted us to be happy and brave and to go on with life—not make his death a source of hopeless despair.' There was a silence, broken only by the agonising sound of sobbing. 'Marjorie, darling, you mustn't cry.'

'There, I'm not,' said Marjorie through her tears. 'I'll try to stop. Guy wouldn't have wanted us to cry for him. You're right; he would have wanted us to live for him—worthily, in his splendid way.'

'We who knew him and loved him must make our lives a memorial of him.' In ordinary circumstances George would have died rather than make a remark like that. But in speaking of the dead, people forget themselves and conform to the peculiar obituary convention of thought and language. Spontaneously, unconsciously, George had conformed.

Marjorie wiped her eyes. 'Thank you, George. You know so well what darling Guy would have liked. You've made me feel stronger to bear it. But, all the same, I do feel odious for what I thought about him sometimes. I didn't love him enough. And now it's too late. I shall never see him again.' The spell of that 'never' worked again: Marjorie sobbed despairingly.

George's distress knew no bounds. He put his arm round Marjorie's shoulders and kissed her hair. 'Don't cry, Marjorie. Everybody feels like that sometimes, even towards the people they love most. You really mustn't make yourself miserable.'

Once more she lifted her face and looked at him with a heart-breaking, tearful smile. 'You have been too sweet to me, George. I don't know what I should have done without you.'

'Poor darling!' said George. 'I can't bear to see you unhappy.' Their faces were close to one another, and it seemed natural that at this point their lips should meet in a long kiss. 'We'll remember only the splendid, glorious things about Guy,' he went on—'what a wonderful person he was, and how much we loved him.' He kissed her again.

'Perhaps our darling Guy is with us here even now,' said Marjorie, with a look of ecstasy on her face.

'Perhaps he is,' George echoed.

It was at this point that a heavy footstep was heard and a

hand rattled at the door. Marjorie and George moved a little farther apart. The intruder was Roger, who bustled in, rubbing his hands with an air of conscious heartiness, studiously pretending that nothing untoward had occurred. It is our English tradition that we should conceal our emotions. 'Well, well,' he said. 'I think we had better be going in to luncheon. The bell has gone.'

Peter Taylor
Reservations

It was arranged, of all things, that the bride and groom should
make their escape from the country club through the little
boys' locker room! But this was very reasonable, really. At
nine o'clock on a night in January, the exit from the little
boys' locker room to the swimming-pool terrace was the exit
least likely to be congested. It was the exit also most likely
to be overlooked by mischievous members of the wedding
party. Every precaution had to be taken! No one was to be
trusted!

In the lounge of the women's locker room, the bride got
out of her gown in exactly thirty seconds. (She had taken an
hour, more or less, to get into it.) She pushed the wedding
dress into the hands of one of the club's maids and from the
hands of another accepted the tweed travelling suit—puce-
brown tweed trimmed with black velvet. Because it was imperative that no suspicion of her departure be roused among
the guests, the bride was not attended by her mother or by
her maid of honour. Her mother and all the bridal attend-
ants remained upstairs at the party, where there was dancing, and where waiters moved about balancing trays of
stemmed glasses. At two minutes to nine, the bride ran on
tiptoe along a service passageway that connected most of
the rooms on the ground floor. She was accompanied now
by the elder of the two maids who had assisted in the change

from white satin to tweed. This woman was one of the club's veteran maids, a large, rather middle-aged person who, though she dyed her hair a lemon yellow and rouged her cheeks excessively, was known for her stalwart character and her incorruptibility. In the passageway, the bride chattered nervously to this companion who had been assigned to her. She told how she had written her name in the club's brides' book as 'Franny Crowell', having forgotten momentarily that she was now Mrs Miles Miller. The maid was not a very responsive sort, and said nothing. But this didn't bother Franny; she went on to say, sometimes laughing while she spoke, that somehow she could not shake off the feeling that it was a pity and a shame to be slipping away from a party given in your own honour.

In one hand the maid held the key to a door down the passageway that would let the bride into the little boys' locker room. In the other hand she carried a pair of fur-trimmed galoshes. As they approached the locked door, the maid interrupted Franny's chatter: 'Your father said tell you your fur coat's in the car, with your corsage pinned to it. He said be careful you don't sit on it.' Simultaneously the maid held out the galoshes, giving them a little shake that indicated Franny should take them.

'What are those?' Franny chirped. 'They're not mine.'

'No, they're not yours, Mrs Miller,' said the maid, still pressing them on her.

'Well, I don't believe I'll want them,' Franny said politely.

'Yes, your mother said so. It's snowing outside now—a nasty, wet snow, Mrs Miller.'

'But they're not mine, and they're not Mother's either . . . How long has it been snowing?' She hoped to change the subject.

'Two hours off and on, Mrs Miller. Ever since you got here

from the church. It's not sticking, but there'll be slush under-foot.'

'Well, whose are they?'

'Your mother snitched them from one of the guests—out of the cloakroom. She told me, "Something borrowed".'

Franny burst into laughter and took the galoshes. But she resolved not to put on the ugly things until after Miles had seen her and got the effect of her outfit.

While the maid fitted the key into the lock, Franny stood with her eyes lifted to the low basement ceiling. She heard the sound of the dancing overhead, and she speculated about which of the dancers upstairs these boots might belong to and thought of the pleasure it was sure to give some child-hood friend of hers, or possibly some aunt or some woman friend of her parents, to learn that *she* had provided the bride with the one item that had been overlooked—the something borrowed.

Presently the door before her stood open. But Franny's eyes and thoughts were still directed towards the ceiling. 'There you are,' said the maid, obviously provoked by the bride's inattention.

Franny lowered her eyes. She looked at the woman beside her with a startled expression. Then she glanced briefly into the shadows of the unlighted locker room. And in the next moment she was clutching frantically at the starched sleeve of the maid's uniform. 'But he is not here!' she exclaimed. Her tone was accusing; she eyed the maid suspiciously. Then, as if on further reflection, she spoke in a bewailing whisper: 'He isn't hee-er!' According to the plan, he was to have been admitted to the little boys' locker room through a door from the adjoining men's locker room. But had he ever intended to be there? *He was gone! Of course he was! How else would it be?* Already Franny was thinking of what kind of poison she would administer to herself, of how she would manage to obtain the poison, of how she would look when they found her.

'What do you mean "not here"?' said the maid, jerking her sleeve free.

Franny smiled coolly. She knew how she must carry it off. 'Maybe I'll stay on for the party, after all,' she said.

'What do you mean "not here"?' the maid repeated. 'He's standing there before your eyes.'

Franny looked again, and of course there her bridegroom stood. 'I didn't see him, it's so dark,' she stammered.

But, instead of going to the bridegroom, suddenly the bride threw her arms about the woman with the lemon-yellow hair who had delivered her to him. This trustworthy woman had been known to Franny during most of her young life, but she was by no means a favourite of Franny's. And almost certainly Franny had never been a favourite of the woman's, either . . . But still it seemed the thing to do. Somehow it was like embracing the whole wedding party or even the whole club membership, or possibly just simply her own mother. And, no doubt, in that moment this woman forgave Franny many an old score—forgave a little girl's criticism of sandwiches served toasted when they had been ordered untoasted, complaints about a bathing suit's not having been hung out to dry, and many another complaint besides. At any rate, the woman responded and returned the warm embrace. Then for an instant the two of them smiled at each other through the general mist of tears.

'Goodbye, little Miss "Franny Crowell",' the woman said.

'Goodbye, Bernice,' said Franny, 'and thanks for everything.' Yes, the woman's name was Bernice. What a bother it had always been, trying to remember it, but now it had come out without Franny's having to try to think of it even.

Bernice took several steps backwards, as if quitting a royal presence. At a respectful distance she turned her back, and in her white gum-soled shoes she retreated silently down the long service passageway.

While waiting for the bride to come through the doorway to him, the bridegroom had literally stood dangling his little narrow-brimmed hat, shifting it from one hand to the other. He did not know what to make of that blank look she had given him at first, didn't know what to make of her saying 'He is not here', didn't know what to make of her throwing herself into the arms of the hired help instead of into his own . . . The embrace perhaps he understood better than the look. But anyway, she had come to him at last, which was what he wanted most in the world at the moment. Presently he had seated her on one of the rough wooden benches in the locker room and, on his knees before her, he was struggling to push her feet into the borrowed galoshes. Franny had held on to the galoshes through both her embraces, and as soon as she had handed them to Miles and was seated on the bench, she began to chatter again—about the galoshes now, about how her mother had positively stolen 'the ugly things' from somebody upstairs.

It wasn't easy getting the galoshes on. They were a near-perfect fit, but Franny seemed incapable of being any help. Her little ankles had gone limp, like an absent-minded child's. But finally Miles managed to force both galoshes on. He zipped them up neatly, and then lifted his face to Franny and smiled. Franny extended one of her tiny gloved hands to him, as if she were going to pull him to his feet. Miles seized it, but he remained on one knee before her, pressing the hand firmly between the two of his. While he knelt there, Franny made a vague gesture with her free hand, a gesture that indicated the whole of the dark locker room. 'I've never been in here before, Miles,' she said.

'Neither have I, you know,' Miles said playfully.

'Oh,' Franny breathed, thoughtfully. 'No, you probably haven't, have you.'

Now she felt she understood . . . *That* was why she had not been able to see him there at first. She had never *imagined* him there. It was because Miles Miller was not one of the local boys she had grown up with, wasn't one of that familiar group from whose number she had always assumed she would some day accept a husband. He was better than any of *those*, of course; he was her own, beloved, blue-eyed, black-haired, fascinating Miles Miller, whom she had recognised the first moment she ever saw him as the best-looking man she had ever laid eyes on (or ever would), as the man she must have for *hers*—and the very same Miles, of course, that at least half a dozen other girls of her year had thought they must have for *theirs*. Moreover, he was the young man who doesn't turn up in *every*body's year: the young bachelor from out of town, brought in from a distant region by one of the big corporations to fill a place in its local office, a young man without any local history of teenage romances to annoy and perhaps worry the bride. And in Miles's case the circumstances were enhanced still further. He was an only child, and his parents had died while he was still in college. For his bride there would be no parents or brothers and sisters to be visited and adjusted to, and, since he had lived always on the West Coast and gone to Stanford, no prep-school friends, not even—at such a distance—a college roommate to be won over. Once they were married, Franny's family would be *their* family, her friends *their* friends. Besides all this, her Miles was at once the most modest and most self-assured human being imaginable. With one gentle look—gentle and yet reasonable and terribly penetrating—he could make her aware of the utter absurdity of something she said or did, and make her simultaneously aware of how little such absurdities mattered to someone who loved you.

Franny bent forward and kissed her husband gently on his smiling lips. He came up beside her on the bench, no longer smiling, and took Franny in his arms. For Franny it was as it had always been before—every time he had ever held her in his tender, confident way. It was as though she possessed at last, or was about to possess at last, what she had always wanted above everything else and had never dreamed she wanted—or, that is, never dreamed she wanted in quite the same way she wanted everything else. That was what seemed so incredible to her about it: *this* desire and *this* happiness differed only in degree from the other longings and other satisfactions one experienced. There was nothing at all unreal about it. And somehow the most miraculous part was that the man she was going to marry was not the man she had ever imagined herself marrying. On the contrary, he was the frightening stranger of her girlish daydreams—the dark, handsome man she was always going to meet on a train coming home from boarding school at Christmas or during the summer at Lake Michigan. In her daydreams she sometimes even bore that man a child, but there had always had to be a barrier to their marrying. The man was already married (perhaps to an invalid!), or he was a Jew, he was a Catholic—a French Canadian—or he was the foreign agent of a country committed to the destruction of her own country, or (when she was still younger) there was insanity or even a strain of Negro blood in his family! Yet the stranger had turned up after all—after she had almost forgotten him—and there was no barrier.

Still holding Franny close to him, Miles got to his feet and for a moment lifted his bride completely off the floor. 'Franny, oh, "little Miss Franny," let's go!' he said. Franny laughed aloud. And to Miles she sounded for all the world like a delighted little girl of four or five. 'Let's be on our way,' he said, still holding her there. 'Let's get out of here.'

'Carry me to the car, Miles,' she whispered.

'I will,' he said. 'You bet I will. Not this way, though. I'll set you down and get a good hold and then we'll dash.'

But just as Franny's feet touched the floor, there came a great rattling sound from over towards the door to the terrace. Franny gave a little shriek that came out almost 'Aha!' And then, in a quiet voice, in a tone of utter resignation, she said, 'They've found us'. She meant, of course, that the mischief-makers had found them. 'We'll *never* get away.'

'No, they haven't, darlng,' Miles said impatiently.

Franny turned away from him. At the far end of the room she saw a man's figure silhouetted against the glass door to the terrace. She realised at once that the man must be one of the club's waiters. It was he, she surmised, who had let Miles in from the men's locker room. He had been present all the while, and actually he was now holding the terrace door a little way open. The rattling noise had, plainly, come from the long venetian blind on that door. But the source of the rattling no longer interested Franny; she was too angry with Miles for not having told her they weren't alone.

Suddenly her impulse was to turn back and deliver Miles a slap across the face. His inference that the waiter's presence hadn't mattered was insulting both to herself and to this man who had so faithfully performed the duties assigned him. But before she could turn or speak, Miles had seized her by the hand and the waiter had thrown open the door. Hand in hand, the bride and groom ran the length of the little boys' locker room. In the excitement of the moment, Miles had forgotten that he was going to carry Franny to the car. It was well for him that he had. Franny consented to let him hold her hand only in order to keep from embarrassing the waiter. Halfway to the door she made out just which of the club's waiters he was, and she could easily have called him by name. But instead she dropped her eyes, and she kept them lowered even when Miles paused in the doorway to slip a bill into the hand at the end of the white sleeve. In her pique with Miles, she wondered if the bill was of as large a denomination as it ought to be.

Outside, they ran along the edge of the gaping swimming pool and on in the direction of the tennis courts. Beyond the courts, Miles's new car was hidden. The wet snow was falling heavily, and it was beginning to stick now. It seemed to Franny that the snow might fill the empty swimming pool before the night was over. They went through the gate into the area of the tennis courts. From there Franny glanced back once at the lighted windows of the low, sprawling clubhouse. Through the snow it seemed miles away. They ran across the courts and through the white shrubbery. Neither of them spoke until they were in the car. By then their rendezvous in the locker room seemed like something that happened too long ago to mention. As Miles was helping her into her coat, and she was carefully protecting the big white orchid that she knew her father had pinned on the coat with his own hands, Franny said, 'What are we going to do, Miles? I'm terrified. I hate snow. We can't get even as far as Bardstown tonight.'

'Of course we can't, honey,' he said. He had switched on the car lights and was starting the motor. 'We'll have to stay here in town tonight. I telephoned the hotel a while ago. We'll have to stay there.'

They had planned to spend the first night at Bardstown, which in good weather was only a few hours away, down in Kentucky, and where there was an attractive old inn. They had planned to make it to Natchez by the second night, and to be at the Gulf Coast by the third. Franny's father had urged them to fly down, or to take a train. But they were able to think only of what fun it would be to have their own car once they got to Biloxi. It had been silly of them, they acknowledged now, driving into town through the snow, but they did have the satisfaction of knowing that all planes would be grounded on such a night, anyway. And to both of them the idea of spending their wedding night in a Pullman berth seemed grotesque.

It took Miles three quarters of an hour to get them through the snow and the traffic to the downtown hotel where he had managed to make reservations. Along the way, he apologised to Franny for putting them up at this particular hotel—the hotel, that is, where he had himself been living during the past year and a half. 'As luck would have it,' he explained, 'there are two big conventions in town this week. I was lucky to find a room anywhere at all. I hope you don't mind too much.'

'Why in the world should I mind?' Franny laughed. 'We're a bona fide married couple now.'

Yet the moment she had passed through the revolving door into the marble-pillared lobby of the hotel, Franny rested a gloved hand on the sleeve of Miles's overcoat and said, 'I *do* feel a little funny about it, after all.'

'I was afraid you might feel funny about it,' Miles said. They stood there a moment waiting for the boy with their luggage to follow them through the revolving door, and Miles began to apologise all over again. 'The other hotels were all full up,' he said. 'It's only because I happen to hit it off so well with Bill Carlisle that I was able to get a room here. It wasn't easy for him even; he's just the assistant manager. Your father, or almost any of the guys in the wedding, might have found us something better. But it seemed worse, somehow, to have any

of them—even your father—know exactly where we're spending the night, since we can't get out of town. I guessed you
would feel the same way about it.'

But Franny was not listening to Miles. She had become
aware that she was the only woman in the lobby, and the
mention of the assistant manager's name had further distracted
her. Bill Carlisle had been invited to the wedding—she recalled addressing his invitation—but he had not been invited
to the reception and supper dance. As for her own acquaintance with him, it was very slight. She had known him for a
long time, however, and she knew that he knew just about
everyone that she did. She interrupted Miles's apologies to say,
'Do we have to see Bill Collier?'

'Who?' asked Miles.

'You know—the assistant manager.'

'Of course we don't, darling,' he said. 'We don't even have
register. That's all set.'

The boy with their luggage had joined them now. Another
boy had appeared with their key and was beckoning them to
follow him to the elevator. As they crossed the lobby, Franny
began laughing to herself. Miles noticed, and asked what was
funny.

'I was wondering,' she said, 'do you think he'll have put us
in your room?'

'Will who have?'

'You know, your friend Bill—the assistant manager.'

'At least it won't be that,' said Miles. 'There was someone
waiting to take it over when I got the last of my possessions
out this morning.'

'What a shame,' Franny whispered. 'It would have been
kind of interesting, and no one but Bill Cook need ever have
known.'

'Bill Carlisle's his name,' Miles said rather petulantly.

Then he added, 'He's a pretty nice fellow, in case you don't know.'

'Certainly he is,' Franny said with a wink. 'I've known him for years.'

Franny stepped into the elevator, followed by Miles. Then the boy with the luggage got in, then the one with the key. Franny observed that both the boys were mature men, and the key boy was even bald-headed. They kept their heads bowed, very courteously, not even looking up when presently they had occasion to speak to each other.

'Where's Jack?' the luggage boy asked quietly.

'He's coming,' said the key boy.

'Who's Jack?' Franny asked Miles.

Thinking the question directed to him, the luggage boy replied, 'He's the elevator boy.' As he spoke, he glanced up at Franny. Probably he thought it was demanded of him. Unlike the key boy, he had a heavy head of hair, as dark and thick as Miles's own, and the face he lifted was youthful, almost handsome even, with a broad jaw and black, rather cruel eyes that seemed brimming with energy. As soon as he looked up he realised his mistake and bent his head again. But he had reminded Franny of someone—someone she didn't like. Or *did* like. Which was it? She couldn't think who it was, and felt vaguely that she didn't want to. And what would Jack, the elevator operator, be like, she wondered, when he turned up? Somehow she was sure he would be a redhead. Presently he would come running; he would hop into the elevator, close the door, push the button, and there she would be, locked in the elevator with Miles and with the three men in their dark-green livery and with the heap of luggage, and the elevator would shoot them up to their floor and stop with a sickening little bounce. She wished Miles would *say* something!

'Jack seems to have gotten lost,' Miles said. Franny burst out laughing.

Immediately, Jack appeared, as if from nowhere. He was a Negro boy, but with light skin and a reddish tint to his hair.

Franny was conscious of Jack's arrival, and conscious of the colour of his hair, but at the same time her real attention had been caught by a figure out in the lobby. It was the figure of a woman, and she was moving swiftly across the lobby towards this elevator, making her way between the heavier figures of the conventioners in their tweed overcoats and grey fedoras. (Most of them, it seemed to Franny, were smoking cigars, the way conventioners were supposed to.) The woman was wearing a navy-blue topcoat and hat, and carried an oversize hand-bag. 'Wait!' Franny said to the elevator boy.

'What do you mean, "Wait"?' Miles asked.

'Don't you see who that is trying to catch us?' Franny said, rising on her toes.

'I see who it is, but you don't know her, and I can promise you I don't either.'

One of the hotel boys snorted, but he cut it off so short Franny couldn't tell for sure which of them it was. She suspected the bald-headed one.

'It's Bernice! The maid from the club!' Franny tried to recall whether she had forgotten anything essential. No, the woman must have an urgent message for her. Her father or her mother had been taken ill, or there had been some disaster at the club—a fire perhaps. She remembered distinctly having left a cigarette burning in the women's lounge.

'It's no such thing,' Miles was saying. 'Let's go, Jack!'

The woman was close enough now for Franny to see it was not Bernice. The long stride and the yellow hair sticking out from under the hat had deceived her. But she should have known, shouldn't she, that Bernice could not have worn such heels.

The elevator door was closing right in the woman's face, and even if the woman wasn't Bernice, this was more than Franny could bear. 'Stop it!' she commanded, utterly outraged by the ungallant behaviour of these men. 'There's room for another person, easily!'

The boys looked at Miles. 'Let the lady in,' Miles thundered.

Jack slid the door open. But the woman hesitated. With a swift glance she seemed to have taken in every aspect of the situation—that it was a bride and groom she was intruding upon, that the bride had insisted upon holding the car for her, that the groom had protested. She now signalled Jack to go on without her, but with Miles's thundering command still in his ears Jack made no move to do so. Miles kept silent. And so did Franny, who in a last-minute glance as swift as the woman's had taken in *her* total situation—that she was middle-aged prostitute late for an engagement. There was but one solution to the awful silence and to the irresolution of the elevator boy. The woman stepped into the elevator and abruptly turned her back to the other passengers.

As the car shot upward, Jack asked with easy nonchalance, 'Your floor, please?'

Again there was silence. Finally Miles said, 'What's our floor?'

The key boy looked up, showing his full face for the first time—eyes set close together, a small, puffy nose, ears flat against the bald head. Franny thought it the stupidest, most brutal face she had ever set eyes on. '*Your* floor is eight, Mr Miller,' he said, barely opening his swollen lips when he spoke.

After a moment Jack repeated, 'Your floor, please?'

The woman now turned her face towards the elevator boy so that Franny saw her profile. Her face was plain—neither homely nor otherwise, really—and seemed devoid of expression. Only the fact that she had turned her face towards him showed that she knew the boy expected an answer from her. It occurred to Franny that in her agitation this poor creature had forgotten what floor she was going to. At last, and as if with great effort, she did speak. 'Seven for me,' she said.

With a long, bony forefinger Jack stabbed the seventh-floor button. The elevator stopped almost at once, and the door slid open. The woman stepped out into the hallway, where there was a broad mirror facing her between two metal cigarette urns. Instead of turning to left or right she stopped here just outside the elevator, and for one instant her pale eyes met Franny's in the glass. Then the door closed quietly between them.

Franny had not been aware of a bouncing sensation when the elevator stopped at that floor. But when it stopped at the floor above, the sensation so upset her equilibrium that she felt positively faint. Her two feet in their fur-trimmed galoshes seemed chilled to numbness. She felt that if she tried to take one step down the hallway in the direction of the bridal chamber her knees might buckle underneath her. She wondered how she would ever manage it.

To Miles Miller, his bride had seemed not herself at all, from the time they met in the shadows of the locker room at the country club until at last they were alone in the hotel room. But her confusion and nervousness were very understandable, he reasoned, in view of the upsetting change in their plans. And once they were alone in the room, she was indeed very much herself again. She was once again the vivacious, unaffected, ingenuous little being he had decided to marry after talking to her for five minutes during an intermission at a big debut party last year. From the beginning, Miles had felt that he appreciated her special brand of innocence and even artlessness as no one else ever before had. One thing he had determined when he left college and entered upon his career in business was that he would not be the sort—the type—to marry the boss's daughter and further his career that way. He detested that type. He extended this pledge to himself even to include the daughters of prominent and influential men who might indirectly help him in his career. He extended it even to cover all the debutantes he had ever met or would ever meet. He had had no definite ideas about where he *would* find his wife, except one idea that was so childish he laughed at it himself: He had thought of meeting a perfectly unspoiled girl while vacationing in an unspoiled countryside—perhaps in the highland South, perhaps even somewhere in Europe. He had thought particularly of Switzerland. But when thinking more realistically, Miles told himself simply that he would not marry for the sake of his business or social advancement. His marriage and his family life must be something altogether apart from his career.

And then, in his twenty-sixth year, he had met Franny Crowell and had had a wonderful insight. Franny was, in a most important sense, as beautifully innocent and provincial as any little mountain girl might have been. She delighted in her surroundings, accepted her relation to them without question, and would be content to remain where she was and as she was for the rest of her life. She had been practically nowhere away from home. For two years she went to boarding school in Virginia but hated dormitory life and thought it silly of girls to go East to college when they could be so much more comfortable staying at home. She had herself attended the local city university for two years and had relished meeting different kinds of people from her own home town. True, she had spent most of her summers at a resort on Lake Michigan, but even there most of her companions had been the same people she went to school with at home during the winter. Miles Miller recognised in Franny Crowell the flaxen-haired mountain girl of his childish imaginings. Her outward appearance might deceive the world but never him. She arranged her golden-brown hair always in the very latest, most sophisticated fashions. Last summer she had even let the beauty parlour put a blond streak in her hair. She plucked her eyebrows, even pencilled them. The shade of her lipstick paled or darkened according to whatever was newest. But Miles perceived that all of this was as innocent and natural in his Franny as plaiting flaxen pigtails might have been.

Miles and Franny had agreed in advance that they should each have only one glass of champagne at the club on their wedding night. But among the bags that they had had brought into the hotel was Miles's genuine Gucci liquor case—a present from the men at his office. Packed with ice in the plastic compartment of the elaborate leather case were two bottles of champagne of a somewhat earlier and better year than that offered the guests by the bride's father. And into Franny's make-up bag she had managed to fit two of their very own champagne glasses. Together they had thought of everything.

In their hotel room, they spent the first half hour making toasts. They drank to Betty Manville's debut ball, where they had met, drank to their first date, to their first kiss, to the night he first proposed, to the night she accepted, to the night of the announcement party. Each toast had to be followed by a kiss. Each kiss inspired and motivated another reminiscence. Finally, they turned to toasting people whom they associated with events of their courtship. Since Franny was a talented and tireless mimic, Miles encouraged her to 'do' each of these people. She 'did' Betty Manville's mother, her own father, and then one of her bridesmaids, who had once upon a time imagined *she* was going to have Miles Miller for herself. This last was the funniest of all to Miles. He was seated on the side of the bed, leaning on one elbow, and when he had witnessed

Franny's version of that poor, misguided girl, he set his champagne glass on the floor and fell back on the bed in a spasm of laughter. He threshed about, still laughing aloud, and all the while wiping tears from his eyes and begging Franny to stop.

When Franny promised to stop, Miles got control of himself and sat up in the centre of the bed. Wiping his eyes with his handkerchief, he looked up again and found Franny sitting on the side of the bed with her thumb pressed against her nose so hard that her little nose was flattened on her face. Her eyes were squinted up and her mouth, which was normally small and tight, was stretched and spread into a wide ribbon across her face. 'You know who this is?' she asked, barely moving her lips.

'I'm glad to say I don't,' Miles said, as if offended by her ugliness.

'Oh, you do,' Franny insisted.

'I don't, and it's not very attractive.'

'Of course it's not attractive,' said Franny, keeping the thumb pressed against her nose. 'It's that bald-headed bellboy, the one with the key.'

'What's wrong with him?' Miles said, swinging his feet around to the other side of the bed and thus momentarily turning his back to Franny.

'You don't have to turn your back,' Franny said. 'See, it's still only me.'

Miles looked around and smiled apologetically. Franny's face was her own again, and she was looking down at her hands very seriously. 'Weren't all three of those bellboys grotesque?' she said.

'I don't think so,' Miles said. 'They're perfectly normal-looking human beings. I see them every day.'

'Normal-looking!' Franny exclaimed, lifting her eyes to his. 'How can you say so? The bald-headed one was really monstrous. And the one with the mop of hair had a really mad look in his eyes. And that pale Negro boy with the kinky red hair! How blind you are to people, Miles. You don't really *see* them.'

'Maybe not,' said Miles, meaning to dismiss the subject, since Franny seemed so emotional about it. Turning now, he let himself fall across the bed towards her, and again he took one of her hands between the two of his. But before he could speak the endearment he intended, something else occurred to him that he felt must be said first. It was in defence of his vision, or—he couldn't define it—in defence of something even more specially his own that had been disparaged. 'Anyway,' he said, 'you must admit that not one of those bellhops was half as weird-looking as that painted-up creature you had your hug fest with when we were leaving the club. After the elevator ride, I don't have to tell you what *she* looked like.' Though they had been in the room for more than half an hour, this was the first reference either of them had made to the woman in the elevator.

Franny withdrew her hand and stood up.

Miles said, 'We're not going to quarrel about something so silly on our wedding night, are we?'

Franny was silent for a moment. Her eyes moved about the room as if taking it in for the first time. Then she bent over and kissed Miles on the top of his head. 'We aren't *ever* going to quarrel again, are we, Miles?'

'Never,' he said. He reached out a hand, but she pulled away. 'Come back,' he said in a whisper.

'Not until I've slipped into something more—more right.' She smiled vaguely.

Miles lay with his head propped on one hand and watched her go to her little overnight bag and take out the folds of lace and peach silk that were her négligé and gown. Suddenly he leaped from the bed with outstretched arms. But the bride dashed through the open doorway to the bathroom and closed the door.

Miles had long since changed into his blue silk pajamas with the white monogram on the pocket when he saw the first turning and twisting of the doorknob. When Franny failed to appear at once—that is, when the knob ceased its twisting and the bathroom door didn't open—his vexation showed itself momentarily in one little horizontal crease in his smooth forehead. But the moment was so brief that even his eyes didn't reflect it, and soon a sly little smile came to his lips . . . He would give her a signal that all was ready and waiting, and at the same time give her motivation and courage. Stepping over to the dresser he uncorked the second bottle of champagne. He managed it very expertly, taking satisfaction in his expertness. The pop was loud enough for Franny to hear and comprehend, yet there was not one bubble of wasteful overflow. The tiny golden bubbles came just to the mouth of the champagne bottle and no farther. Miles had not even taken the precaution of having the two glasses handy. He was expert and he was confident of his expertness.

He watched the first bubbles appear and then shot a glance across the room at the doorknob. It was turning again. He stepped over to where the two glasses were, on the bedside table, filled them, and then returned the bottle to its ice. Still no Franny. But the doorknob was now turning back and forth rather rapidly. Miles watched it as if hypnotised. Finally he uttered a tentative 'Franny?' There was no response except in the acceleration of the knob's turning. 'Franny?' he repeated, striding towards the door. 'What's the matter?' Still no answer. The turning was frenzied now. 'Franny, do you hear me? What are you doing?'

'Of course I hear you!' Franny exclaimed through the door. 'I'm trying to get out of here, you fool!'

Miles seized the knob and gave it a forceful twist.

'That's not going to help,' said Franny, resentful of the over-powering yank to the knob she had been holding on to.

'The thing must be locked,' Miles said, astonished. 'Why did you lock it?'

Franny was silent. Then said, '*I* didn't lock it.'

'Well, *I* didn't,' Miles laughed. 'Anyway, try unlocking it.'

'Do you think I haven't already?'

'What kind of lock is it? Is there a key?'

'No. It's one of those damned little eggs you turn.'

'But why on earth would you have locked it?'

'If I did it, Miles, I did it without thinking.'

Miles was now trying to see the bolt through the crack of the door. 'But why would you?' he said absently.

'Why would I what?'

'Lock it without thinking.'

'All decent people lock bathroom doors,' she said with conviction.

'We didn't at our house,' Miles said. He could definitely see the bolt through the crack. 'My father used to throw away the key to the bathroom door as soon as we moved into a place.'

'Don't start on your father *now*, Miles.'

'My father was all right.'

'Who said he wasn't? *Do* something, Miles, for God's sake.'

'There's nothing to do but call the desk and have them take down the door.'

Franny, who had for a moment been leaning against the rim of the washbowl, now straightened and grasped the doorknob again. 'Miles, you *wouldn't!*'

'Don't go to pieces, Franny.'

'You'd let them send up those three stooges—'

Miles burst into laughter.

'How coarse you are, Miles,' Franny said, her voice deepening.

'Oh, honey, there's a regular maintenance crew, and—'

'Maybe so,' she broke in, her voice climbing the scale till it was much higher than Miles had ever heard it before. 'But don't you know, Miles, that Bill Carlisle would certainly know about it? Oh, God, everybody in this town would know about it before tomorrow morning!'

'In God's name, Franny, what do you propose I do?'

'What kind of man are you, Miles? Take the door down yourself. You've been living in this hotel so long you depend on them for everything. You seem to think the world's just one big hotel and that you call in the maintenance crew for any and every thing.'

'OK, Franny, I'll try,' Miles said amiably. 'But have you ever tried taking down a locked door?'

'Why did you have to bring me to this dump?' Franny wailed.

'And why did you have to lock the door?' he countered.

Now they were both silent as Miles went to the closet door where his Valpak hung, and dug out a small gold pocketknife. His first effort to remove the pin in the upper door hinge was fruitless. The pin wouldn't budge. Neither would the pin in the lower hinge. He decided he needed a hammer to drive the knife blade upwards against the heads of the pins, and he was just turning to go and fetch his shoe for that purpose when Franny spoke again.

'Miles,' she began, speaking very slowly and in a tone so grave that it stopped him, 'do you remember that night at Cousin Jane Thompson's party?'

He listened, waiting for her to continue. Then he realised she expected some response from him. 'Yes, Franny,' he said.

'That night at Cousin Jane's,' she now went on in the same sepulchral tone, 'when you said Sue Maynard's date was drunk and that she asked you to take her home.' Sue Maynard was the bridesmaid who had thought *she* would have Miles for herself. Miles had been a stag at the party that night.

'Yes, I remember.'

'You were lying.'

'In a way, Franny—'

'In the worst way,' she said flatly. 'You thought I would think it was just Sue's lie and that you didn't know better, or that you knew better but were too honourable to give her away.'

'Maybe.'

'That's how you *thought* I would think. But I knew even that night, Miles Miller, that you engineered it all. Her date was Puss Knowlton, and you had no trouble giving *him* the shove. And don't you think I know it's more than just necking that Sue Maynard goes in for? . . . And, Miles, the night last summer, *after* we were engaged, when you couldn't come for dinner at our house with Daddy's Aunt Caroline because of the report you had to write up—you didn't have any report to write up, Miles. You went some place out on the South Side with a little creature named Becky Louise Johnson.'

By the time Franny had finished, Miles had silently crossed the room to the bedside table and downed one of the two waiting glassfuls of champagne. He had listened intently to what she said, and the more he heard the more intent he had become on getting that damned door down. In his liquor case he found a bottle opener that he decided would work better than his knife. He returned to the door with his shoe and the bottle opener, and in no time he had the top pin out of its hinge.

'Miles—' Franny began again, still in the same tone.

'Shut up, Franny!' Miles said, and at once began hammering at the lower pin. It offered a little more resistance than the other, but was soon dislodged. The door was still firmly in place, however. Twice Miles jabbed the bottle opener into the crack on the hinge side, as though he might prise the door open. Then he laughed aloud at himself.

Franny heard him laugh, of course. 'Is it funny? Is it really funny to you, Miles?' she said.

'Try giving it a push from in there, on the hinge side of the door,' said Miles. Franny pushed. The door creaked, but that was all.

'Miles,' Franny began once again, in a whisper now, and he could tell that she was leaning against the door and speaking into the crack. 'I've thought of something else I've never confronted you with.'

Miles felt the blood rush to his face. Suddenly he banged on the door with his fist. 'Will you shut up, you little bitch! You know, I'm not above socking you in earnest if ever I get you out of there!'

'You would sock me just one time, Miles Miller.'

'It would be the second time. Don't you forget that,' he said.

They were really at it now, for he was reminding her of an occasion two days after their announcement party when he had found her kissing a college kid whose name he did not even know. He had struck her with his open hand on the back of her neck—not while she was kissing the kid but afterwards, as he pushed her along the terrace there at the Polo Club. He had had too much to drink that night, and that was what saved them. Franny could claim that he had deserted her in favour of the bar. She also claimed that she had not really been kissing the boy and added that, anyway, he was an old, old, old friend and therefore meant nothing to her. They hardly spoke to each other during the week following, though of course they con-

tinued going about together. And until now they had neither
of them ever referred to the incident, as if by mutual agree-
ment.

'You're no gentleman, Miles,' Franny pronounced, carefully
keeping away from the door now. 'As Daddy said of you to
start with, you have all the outward signs of a gentleman but
that's no evidence you're one inside.'

'I've already settled your father's hash, Franny.'

'You mean he's settled yours.'

It was an unfortunate word—'settled'. And both of them
were aware of it immediately. It quieted both of them for some
time. It referred to another incident that was assumed to be
closed. Franny's father had apparently suspected Miles of being
a fortune hunter, and before the engagement was announced
he had asked Miles frankly what kind of 'settlement' he expected. Miles had stormed out of the house, and was recon-
ciled with Mr Crowell only after having it hammered home to
him by Franny that what her father had done was merely the
conventional, old-fashioned thing for a man in Mr Crowell's
position to do. Miles had finally accepted Franny's explanation, but only a few weeks ago he had had another stormy
session over a similar matter. This time it was with both the
bride's parents. At that very late date he had learned about
certain letters of inquiry that had been sent out concerning his
'background'. The letters had been written to various family
friends and relatives of the Crowells who had lived for many
years in Santa Barbara and Laguna Beach. When Miles learned
of these letters through a remark of Franny's, it was many
months after the letters had been written and replied to. The
revelation sent Miles into a rage. He was in such a state that
Franny feared he might do real violence to her father, or even
to her mother, who had actually written the letters.

She had let the cat out of the bag inadvertently. She and he were just going out to a movie one night. Franny had come down to the living-room already wearing her coat and even with her gloves on, but Miles had wanted to linger and talk awhile. Before she came down, he had wandered about the room studying some family photographs taken thirty years before. These 'portraits', in their upright frames on the mantel-shelf and on the various tables, had reminded him of pictures in his own family's living-room when he was growing up. He commenced talking to Franny about how his mother always placed the same pictures on the same tables and bureaux no matter where they were living, and then he went on to speak, as he had on several previous occasions, of how restless his father had been after he left the service. (Miles's father had been a West Point graduate and had remained in the army until he had his first heart attack, just a few months before Pearl Harbor.) And now, as Miles had already done several times before, he began listing for Franny the towns they had lived in during and after the war. Franny, who was impatient to get on to the movie, didn't listen very carefully. When Miles hesitated, trying to think of which town it was he had omitted from his list, Franny absent-mindedly supplied 'Palo Alto'. But it was not Palo Alto he was trying to think of; it was San Jose.

'Palo Alto?' said Miles. 'How did you know we ever lived in Palo Alto?'

'You've told me all this before,' she answered.

But he had not told her about the spring in Palo Alto! It was then that his parents had quarrelled so endlessly, though he—and probably they—had never known just why. At any rate, he was always careful to leave Palo Alto out of his catalogue of towns. And he was not content now until he had wrung a confession of the whole business of the letters of inquiry out of Franny. Once she had confessed, he insisted upon taking the matter up with her parents that very night; he insisted upon *seeing* the letters. For a time, Mrs Crowell maintained that she had already thrown away the letters. But at last she broke down. She went upstairs and returned with the packet of letters, all of which Miles read, sitting there in the family circle. He had known there couldn't be anything really bad in them, because just as there was nothing very good that could be said of his parents, there was nothing very bad, either. The worst the letters said of them was that they were 'rootless people and apparently of restricted means'. Miles found he could not even resent one lady's description of his mother as a 'harmless little woman—pleasant enough—with a vague Southern background'. The letters repeated each other with phrases like 'thoroughly nice' and 'well bred' and 'well behaved'. The sole reference to Palo Alto was 'I think they lived at Palo Alto for a time. John's sister Laura met them there. She thought Major Miller very handsome. He had a small black mustache, if I recall.'

The memory of all this and of the 'settlement' episode occupied Miles's mind as he crossed the hotel room and picked up the glass of champagne that he had poured for Franny. The champagne had gone flat already, but he relished its flatness. He sipped it slowly, as if tasting in each sip a different unpleasant incident or aspect of their courtship and engagement—tasting all they had not tasted and toasted with the first bottle. Suddenly he put down the glass, leaving still a sip or two in the bottom, and stepped quickly over to the bathroom door. 'Franny,' he said, 'it has just occurred to me! It wasn't your father's idea to talk about a settlement with me. You put him up to it! It was you who thought I might be after your family's money! If it had been your father's idea, he wouldn't have been so meek and mild when I called his hand. And, by God, you put your mother up to writing those letters, or she never would have given in and shown them to me.'

He waited for Franny's denial, but none came. 'And, Franny,' he went on after a moment, 'there's one more thing I know that you didn't know I knew. Your father went down to my office and asked about the likelihood of my staying on here or being transferred.'

'I knew he did that, Miles.'

'Darn right you knew it. You put him up to that, too. You didn't even want to take a chance on my moving you away from here.' But before he had finished his last sentence, Miles heard the water running full force into the bathtub. 'Franny, I'm not finished!' he shouted. 'What are you doing?'

'If you don't get this door down within ten minutes'—she was speaking through the crack again—'and get it down without having Bill Carlisle up here to witness it, I'm going to drown myself in the damned bathtub.'

As a matter of fact, she had begun running the water to drown out Miles's accusations, but as she spoke she became convinced that suicide really had been her original intention.

'Yes,' Miles boomed, 'you drown yourself in the bathtub and I'll jump out our eighth-floor window! Romeo and Juliet, that's us!'

Franny shut off the water. She opened her mouth to reply, but no words came. She burst into tears. And the poor little bride could not herself have said whether her tears were brought on by the heavy irony and sarcasm of her groom or by the thought of her dear Miles and her dear self lying dead in their caskets with their love yet unfulfilled.

Almost at once Miles began pleading with her not to cry. But it seemed that his every word brought increased volume to the wailing beyond the bathroom door. It was as if she had decided she could more effectively drown out the sound of his voice with tears than with the rush of bath water.

But actually it wasn't the sound of her bridegroom's voice alone that she wished not to hear. There was the sound of another voice—other voices. She had first become aware of the other voices during one of her and Miles's silences. Which silence she couldn't have said, because for some time afterwards she tried to believe that she had only imagined hearing the other voices, or at least imagined that they sounded as near to her as they did. Finally, though, the persistence of the voices drew her attention to the fact of the other door. The other door, she finally acknowledged, must certainly lead into an adjoining room. And the voices—a man's and a woman's— came to her from that room. And now the ever-increasing volume of her own wailing was meant to conceal from herself that the woman's voice was addressing her directly through that door.

'Honey, I think we can help you.' The offer was unmistakable.

'No, you can't, no, you can't!' Franny wailed.

'The gentleman in here thinks he is pretty good with locks.'

'No, no, please don't come in here,' Franny begged, too frightened, too perplexed for more tears now.

'Franny, what's going on?' Miles seemed on the verge of tears himself. 'Darling, I'll get a doctor, you'll be all right!'

'Miles, there's another door.'

'Yes?'

'And there's someone over there. Oh, Miles, make them go away.'

'Keep your head, Franny. What do they want?'

'It's a woman. She says there's a man in there who can get me out of here.'

'You do want to get out, don't you, Franny?' It was as though he were speaking to someone on a window ledge.

'Not that way, I don't,' said Franny. Now she was

whispering through the door crack. 'Miles, their voices sound familiar!'

'Now, Franny, cut it out!' scolded Miles, and Franny understood his full meaning. For a moment she listened to the other voices. From the start the man's voice had been no more than a low mumbling. He didn't want his voice recognised! The woman spoke more distinctly. Franny could hear them now discussing the problem. Presently the man said something and laughed. And the woman said, 'Hush, the kid will hear you.' Somehow this gave Franny courage. She stepped over to the other door and said bravely, '*Will* you help me?'

Hearing her, Miles gave a sigh of relief. Then he said, 'Ask them to let me come around into their room—and help.'

'Will you let my—my husband come around into your room?'

She heard them deliberating. The man was opposed. Finally, the woman said, 'No. He can come and meet you outside our hall door if we get this one open.'

She repeated this to Miles.

'Tell them OK,' he commanded.

'OK,' said Franny softly.

Now the man and woman were at the door. The man was still mumbling. 'Is there a latch on your side?' the woman asked.

'Yes,' said Franny. 'A little sort of knob.'

'Tell her to turn it,' the man muttered.

'Turn it,' said the woman.

Franny turned it. It moved easily. 'I have,' she said. She watched the big doorknob revolving, but the door didn't open. There was more discussion on the other side of the door.

'It's locked with a key,' said the woman to Franny. 'But that's how he's going to make hisself useful.' Franny's deliverer was hard at work. She couldn't tell whether it was a skeleton key or some makeshift instrument he was using. Presently, she heard the click of the lock and heard the man say, 'That's got it.'

'Miles!' Franny called out. But Miles didn't answer. He was already waiting at their neighbours' hall door. There was the sound of footsteps hurriedly retreating, and then the door opened. The room itself was in darkness, but in the light from the bathroom Franny could see the man's figure outlined on the bed. The sheet was pulled up over his face. Franny looked at the woman. She was fully dressed, though barefoot, and she stood smiling at the ridiculous sight in the bed and probably at the memory of the male figure's racing across the room and jumping into the bed and pulling the sheet over its head.

'You're an angel,' Franny said, without having known she was going to say it.

The woman acknowledged the compliment only by allowing the smile to fade from her lips. 'He'll get up from there and try to open the other door for you in a minute,' she said.

Franny gave her a grateful smile, and then she turned and walked with perfect poise toward the hall door. Her peach négligé was floor-length and its little train of lace swept gracefully along the dark carpet. When her hand was on the doorknob, she turned and said simply, 'Good night'. She might have been at home, turning to say a casual good night to her mother.

In the hallway, Miles had waited, fully expecting to have to carry his bride back to their room in his arms. When she appeared he was stunned by her radiance and self-possession. He had never seen her so beautiful. And Franny was equally stunned by Miles's manly beauty as he stood before her in his blue silk pajamas. For a moment they stood there beaming at one another. Finally, Miles slipped his arm gently about his bride's waist and hurried her off to their room.

They found their bathroom door standing half open, and the door beyond it tightly closed. The two heavy pins still lay on the floor, but Miles quickly slipped them into the hinges. The door was now in perfect working order. Miles stood a moment gazing into the bright bathroom where Franny's clothes were heaped in one corner like a child's. 'Well,' he said at last, 'that fellow worked fast.'

'Miles,' said Franny, also looking into the bathroom but with her eyes focused on the door opposite, 'did you see who it was?'

'What do you mean?'

'The woman over there—she was the woman on the elevator.'

'Franny, Franny! . . . She got off at the seventh floor! How could you forget?'

'And the man—'Franny began.

'Franny, Franny, Franny,' Miles interrupted, already having left her side to fetch the champagne glasses and refill them. 'The man in that room is one of the conventioners from out of town. You never heard his voice or saw him before in your life.'

She had been going to say that the man in the bed was Bill Carlisle. But she saw it was useless. And she knew she would never say it now. Miles came towards her slowly with the two glasses filled to the brim. They sipped their champagne, looking at one another over the glasses. In their hearts, both of them were glad they had said all the things that they said through the door. As they gazed deep into each other's eyes, they believed that they had got all of that off their chests once and for all. There was nothing in the world to come between them now. They believed, really and truly, that neither of them would ever deceive or mistrust the other again. Silently they were toasting their own bliss and happiness, confident that it would never again be shadowed by the irrelevances of the different circumstances of their upbringings or by the possibly impure and selfish motives that had helped to bring them together.

Bobbie Ann Mason
Hunktown

Joann noticed that her daughter Patty had started parting her hair on the left, so that it fell over the right side of her forehead, hiding the scar from her recent car accident.

'That scar doesn't show, Mom,' said Patty, when she caught Joann looking. Patty had the baby on her hip, and her little girl, Kristi, was on the floor, fooling with the cat.

'Where's Cody?' Patty asked.

'Gone to Nashville. He got tired of waiting for that big shot he met in Paducah to follow up on his word, so he's gone down with Will Ed and them to make a record album on his own.' Joann's husband, Cody Swann, was going to make a record album. She could hardly believe it. Cody had always wanted to make a record album.

'Is it one of those deals where you pay the studio?' Patty asked suspiciously.

'He pays five hundred dollars for the studio, and then he gets ten percent after they sell the first thousand.'

'That's a rip-off,' said Patty. 'Don't he know that? I saw that on "Sixty Minutes".'

'Well, he got tired of waiting to be discovered. You know how he is.'

The baby, Rodney, started to cry, and Patty stuck a pacifier in his mouth. She said, 'The thing is, will they distribute the record? Them companies get rich making records for every little two-bit band that can hitchhike to Nashville. And then they don't distribute the records.'

'Cody says he can sell them to all his fans around here.'

'He could sell them at the store,' Patty said. She worked at a discount chain store.

'He took off this morning in that van with the muffler dragging. He had it wired up underneath and tied with a rope to the door handle on the passenger side.'

'That sounds just like Cody. For God's sake, Kristi, what are you doing to that cat?'

Kristi had the cat upside down between her knees. 'I'm counting her milkers. She's got four milkers.'

'That's a tomcat, hon,' said Joann gently.

Joann was taking her daughter shopping. Patty, who had gotten a ride to Joann's, was depending on her mother for transportation until the insurance money came through on her car. She had totalled it when she ran into a blue Buick, driven by an old woman on her way to a white sale in town. Patty's head had smashed against the steering wheel, and her face had been so bruised that for a while it resembled a ripe persimmon blackened by frost.

With the children in the back seat, Joann drove Patty around town on her errands. Patty didn't fasten her seat belt. She had had two wrecks before she was eighteen, but this latest accident was not her fault. Cody said Patty's middle name was Trouble. In high school, she became pregnant and had to get married, but a hay bale fell on her and caused a miscarriage. After that, she had two babies, but then she got divorced. Patty had a habit of flirting with Cody and teasing her mother for marrying such a good-looking man. Cody had grown up in a section of town known as Hunktown because so many handsome guys used to live there. That part of town—a couple of streets between Kroger's and the high school—was still known as Hunktown. The public housing project and the new health clinic were there now. Recently, a revival of pride in Hunktown had developed, as though it had been designated a historic area, and Cody had a Hunktown T-shirt. He wore cowboy outfits, and he hung his hats in a row on the scalloped trim of the china cabinet that Joann had antiqued.

Joann had known Cody since high school, but they had married only three years ago. After eighteen years of marriage to Joe Murphy, Joann found herself without a man—one of those women whose husbands suddenly leave them for someone younger. Last year, Phil Donahue had a show on that theme, and Joann remembered Phil saying something ironic like 'It looks like you've got to keep tap-dancing in your négligé or the son of a gun is going to leave you.' Joann was too indignant to sit around and feel sorry for herself. After filing for divorce, she got a new hairdo and new clothes and went out on weekends with some women. One night, she went to a place across the county line that sold liquor. Cody Swann was there, playing a fancy red electric guitar and singing about fickle women and trucks and heartache. At intermission, they reminisced about high school. Cody was divorced, and he had two grown children. Joann had two teenagers still living at home, and Patty had already left. In retrospect, Joann realised how impulsive their marriage had been, but she had been happy with Cody until he got laid off from his job, four months ago. He'd worked at the Crosbee plant, which manufactured electrical parts. Now he was drinking too much, but he assured Joann he couldn't possibly become an alcoholic on beer. Their situation was awkward, because she had a good job at the post office, and she knew he didn't like to depend on her. He had thrown himself into rehearsing for his album with his friends Will Ed and L. J. and Jimmy. 'What we really need is a studio,' Cody kept saying impatiently. They had been playing at county fairs and civic events around western Kentucky off and on for years. Every year, Cody played at the International Banana Festival, in Fulton, and recently he had played for the Wal-Mart grand opening and got a free toaster.

'Being out of work makes you lose your self-respect,' Cody had told Joann matter-of-factly. 'But I ain't going to let that happen to me. I've been fooling around too much. It's time to get serious about my singing.'

'I don't want you to get your hopes up too much and then get disappointed,' Joann said.

'Can't you imagine me with a television series? You could be on it with me. We'd play like we were Porter Wagoner and Dolly Parton. You could wear a big wig and balloons in your blouse.'

'I can just see me—Miss Astor, in my plough shoes!' Joann said, squealing with laughter at the idea, playing along with Cody's dream.

'Do you care if we drive out to that truck patch and pick a few turnip greens before I take you home?' Joann asked Patty. 'It's on the way.'

'You're the driver. Beggars can't be choosers.' Patty rummaged around on the floor under the bucket seat and found Rodney's pacifier, peppered with tobacco and dirt. She wiped it on her jeans and jammed it into the baby's mouth.

On the CB, a woman suddenly said, 'Hey, Tomcat, you lost something back here. Come in, Tomcat. Over.' A spurt of static followed. The woman said, 'Tomcat, it looks like a big old sack of feed. You better get in reverse.'

'She's trying to get something started with those cute guys in that green pickup we passed,' Patty said.

'Everybody's on the make,' Joann said uneasily. She knew what that was like.

At the truck patch, Patty stood there awkwardly in her high heels, like a scarecrow planted in the dirt.

'Let me show you how to pick turnips greens,' Joann said. 'Gather them like this. Just break them off part way down the stem, and clutch them in your hand till you get a big wad. Then pack them down in the sack.'

'They're fuzzy, and they sting my hands. Is this a turnip green or a weed?' Patty held up a leaf.

'That's mustard. Go ahead and pick it. Mustard's good.' Joann flicked the greens off expertly. 'Don't get down into the stalk,' she said. 'And they wilt down when they're cooked, so pack them real good.'

Kristi was looking for bugs, and Rodney was asleep in the car. Joann bent over, grabbing the greens. Some of the turnips were large enough to pull, their bulbs showing above ground like lavender pomanders. The okra plants in a row next to the turnip patch were as tall as corn, with yellow blossoms like roses. Where the blossoms had shrivelled, the new okras thrust their points skyward. Joann felt the bright dizziness of the Indian-summer day, and she remembered many times when nothing had seemed important except picking turnip greens. She and Cody had lived on her parents' farm since her father died, two years before, but they had let it go. Cody wasn't a farmer. The field where her father used to grow turnips was wild now, spotted with burdock and thistles, and Cody was away in Nashville, seeking fame.

At a shed on the edge of the patch, Joann paid for the turnip greens and bought half a bushel of sweet potatoes from a black man in overalls, who was selling them from the back end of a pickup truck. The man measured the sweet potatoes in a half-bushel basket, then transferred them to grocery sacks. When he packed the sweet potatoes in the basket, he placed them so that their curves fit into one another, filling up the spaces. The man's carefulness was like Cody's when he was taping, recording a song over and over again. But Cody had tilled the garden last week in such a hurry that it looked as though cows had trampled the ground.

The man was saying, 'When you get home with these, lay them in a basket and don't stir them. The sweet will settle in them, but if you disturb them, it will go away. Use them off the top. Don't root around in them.'

'I'll put them in the basement,' Joann said, as he set the sacks into her trunk. She said to Patty, who was concentrating on a hangnail, 'Sweet potatoes are hard to keep. They mold on you.'

That evening, Joann discovered one of Cody's tapes that she had not heard before. On the tape, he sang 'There Stands the Glass,' a Webb Pierce song that made her cry, the way Cody sang it so convincingly. When Cody sang 'The Wild Side of Life' on the tape, Joann recalled Kitty Wells's answer to that song. 'It wasn't God who made honky-tonk angels,' Kitty Wells had insisted, blaming unfaithful men for every woman's heartbreak. Joann admired the way Kitty Wells sang the song so matter-of-factly, transcending her pain. A man wrote that song, Cody had told her. Joann wondered if he was being unfaithful in Nashville. She regarded the idea in a detached way, the way she would look at a cabbage at Kroger's.

Now Cody was singing an unfamiliar song. Joann rewound the tape and listened.

> I was born in a place they call Hunktown,
> Good-lookin's my middle name—

The song startled her. He had been talking about writing his own material, and he had started throwing around terms like 'backup vocals' and 'sound mixing.' In this song, he sang along with himself to get a multiple-voice effect. The song was a lonesome tune about being a misfit. It sounded strangely insincere.

When Cody returned from Nashville, his voice bubbled along enthusiastically, like a toilet tank that ran until the handle was jiggled. He had been drinking. Joann had missed him, but she realised she hadn't missed his hat. It was the one with the pheasant feathers. He hung it on the china cabinet again. Cody was happy. In Nashville, he had eaten surf-and-turf, toured the Ryman Auditorium, and met a guy who had once been a sideman for Ernest Tubb.

'And here's the best part,' said Cody, smacking Joann on the lips again. She got a taste of his mint-flavoured snuff. 'We got a job playing at a little bar in Nashville on weekends. It just came out of the blue. Jimmy can't do it, because his daddy's real bad off, but Will Ed and L. J. and me could go. Their wives already said they could.'

'What makes you think I'll let you?' she said, teasing.

'You're going with me.'

'But I've got too much to do.' She set his boots on a carpet sample near the door to the porch. Cold air was coming through the crack around the facing. Cody had pieced part of the facing with a broken yardstick when he installed the door, but he had neglected to finish the job.

Cody said, 'It's just a little bar with a little stage and this great guy that runs it. He's got a motel next to it and we can stay free. Hey, we can live it up in Nashville! We can watch Home Box Office and everything.'

'How can I go? Late beans are coming in, and all them tomatoes.'

'This is my big chance! Don't you think I sing good?'

'You're as good as anybody on the "Grand Ole Opry".'

'Well, there you go,' he said confidently.

'Patty says those studio deals are rip-offs. She saw it on "Sixty Minutes".'

'I don't care. The most I can lose is five hundred dollars. And at least I'll have a record album. I'm going to frame the cover and put it in the den.'

In bed, they lay curled together, like sweet potatoes. Joann listened to Cody describe how they had made the album, laying down separate tracks and mixing the sound. Each little operation was done separately. They didn't just go into a studio and sing a song, Joann realised. They patched together layers of sound. She didn't mention the new song she had heard. She had put the tape back where she had found it. Now another of Cody's tapes was playing—'I'd Rather Die Young,' a love song that seemed to have pointless suffering in it. Softly, Cody sang along with his taped voice. This was called a backup vocal, Joann reminded herself, trying to be very careful, taking one step at a time. Still, the idea of his singing with himself made her think of something self-indulgent and private, like masturbation. But country music was always like that, so personal.

'I'm glad you're home,' she said, reaching for him.

'The muffler fell off about halfway home,' Cody said, with a sudden hoot of laughter that made the covers quiver. 'But we didn't get caught. I don't know why, though. It's as loud as a hundred amplifiers.'

'Hold still,' Joann said. 'You're just like a wiggle-worm in hot ashes.'

Cody was trying on his new outfit for the show, and Joann had the sewing machine out, to alter the pants. The pants resembled suede and had fringe.

'They feel tight in the crotch,' Cody said. 'But they didn't have the next size.'

'Are you going to tell me what you paid for them?'

'I didn't pay for them. I charged them at Penney's.'

Joann turned the hem up and jerked it forward so that it fell against his boot. 'Is that too short?' she asked.

'Just a little longer.'

Joann pulled the hem down about a quarter inch and pinned it. 'Turn around,' she said.

The pants were tan with dark-brown stitching. The vest was embroidered with butterflies. Cody turned around and around, examining himself in the long mirror.

'You look wonderful,' she said.

He said, 'We may get deeper in debt before it's over with, but one thing I've learned: You can't live with regret. You have to get on with your life. I know it's a big risk I'm taking, but I don't want to go around feeling sorry for myself because I've wasted so much time. And if I fail, at least I will have tried.'

He sat on the bed and pulled his boots and then his pants off. The pants were too tight, but the seams were narrow, and there was no way Joann could let them out.

'You'll have to do something about that beer gut,' she said.

The Bluebird Lounge looked as innocent as someone's kitchen: all new inside, with a country decor—old lanterns, gingham curtains, and a wagon wheel on the ceiling. It seemed odd to Joann that Cody had said he didn't want to live with regret, because his theme was country memories. He opened with 'Walking the Floor Over You', then eased into 'Your Cheatin' Heart', 'The Wild Side of Life', and 'I'd Rather Die Young'. He didn't sing the new song she had heard on the tape, and she decided that he must be embarrassed by it. She liked his new Marty Robbins medley, a tribute to the late singer, though she had always detested the song 'El Paso'. In the pleasant atmosphere of the bar, Cody's voice sounded professional, more real there, somehow, than at home. Joann felt proud. She laughed when Will Ed and L. J. goofed around onstage, tripping over their electric cords and repeating things they had heard on 'Hee Haw'. L. J. had been kidding Joann, saying, 'You better come to Nashville with us to keep the girls from falling all over Cody.' Now Joann noticed the women, in twos and threes, sitting close to the stage, and she remembered the time she went across the county line and heard Cody sing. He still looked boyish, and he didn't have a single grey hair. She had cut his bangs too short, she realised now.

'They're really good,' the cocktail waitress, Debbie, a slim, pretty woman in an embroidered cowboy shirt, said to Joann. 'Most of the bands they get in here are so bad they really bum me out, but these guys are good.'

'Cody just cut an album,' Joann said proudly.

Debbie was friendly, and Joann felt comfortable with her, even though Debbie was only a little older than Patty. By the second night, Joann and Debbie were confiding in each other and trading notes on their hair. Joann's permanent was growing out strangely, and she was afraid getting a new permanent so soon would damage her hair, but Debbie got a permanent every three months and her hair stayed soft and manageable. In the rest room, Debbie fluffed her hair with her fingers and said, looking into the mirror, 'I reckon I better put on some lipstick to keep the mortician away.'

During the intermission, Debbie brought Joann a free Tequila Sunrise at her corner table. Cody was drinking beer at the bar with some musicians he had met.

'You've got a good-looking guy,' Debbie said.

'He knows it, too,' said Joann.

'He'd be blind if he didn't. It must be hard to be married to a guy like that.'

'It wasn't so hard till he lost his job and got this notion that he has to get on the "Grand Ole Opry".'

'Well, he just might do it. He's good.' Debbie told her about a man who had been in the bar once. He turned out to be a talent scout from a record company. 'I wish I could remember his name,' she said.

'I wish Cody would sing his Elvis songs,' Joann said. 'He can curl his lip exactly like Elvis, but he says he respects the memory of Elvis too much to do an Elvis act like everybody's doing. It would be exploitation.'

'Cody sure is full of sad, lonesome songs,' Debbie said. 'You can tell he's a guy who's been through a lot. I always study people's faces. I'm fascinated by human nature.'

'He went through a bad divorce,' Joann said. 'But right now he's acting like a kid.'

'Men are such little boys,' Debbie said knowingly.

Joann saw Cody talking with the men. Their behaviour was easygoing, full of laughter. Women were so intense together. Joann could feel Cody's jubilation all the way across the room. It showed in the energetic way he sang the mournful music of all the old hillbilly singers.

Debbie said, 'Making music must make you feel free. If I could make music, I'd feel that life was one big jam session.'

Coming home on Sunday was disorienting. The cat looked impatient with them. The weather was changing, and the flowers were dying. Joann had meant to take the potted plants into the basement for the winter. There had been a cold snap, but not a killing frost. The garden was still producing, languidly, after a spurt of growth during the last spell of warm weather. After work, during the week, Joann gathered in lima beans and squash and dozens of new green tomatoes. She picked handfuls of dried Kentucky Wonder pole beans to save for seed. Burrs clung to the cuffs of her jeans. Her father used to fight the burdock, knowing that one plant could soon take over a field.

Cody stayed indoors, listening to tapes and playing his guitar. He collected his unemployment cheque, but when someone called about a job opening, he didn't go. As she worked in the garden, Joann tried to take out her anger on the dying plants that she pulled from the soil. She felt she had to hurry. Fall weather always filled her with a sense of urgency.

Patty stopped by in her new Lynx. She had come out ahead on the insurance deal. Cody paraded around the car, admiring it, stroking the fenders.

'When's your album coming out, Cody?' Patty asked.

'Any day now.'

'I asked at the store if they could get it, but they said it would have to be nationally distributed for them to carry it.'

'Do you want a mess of lima beans, Patty?' Joann asked. 'There's not enough for a canning, so I'll let you have them.'

'No, this bunch won't eat any beans but jelly beans.' Patty turned to Cody, who was peering under the hood of her car. 'I told all the girls at work about your album, Cody. We can't wait to hear it. What's on it?'

'It's a surprise,' he said, looking up. 'They swore I'd have it by Christmas. The assistant manager of the studio said he thought it was going to be big. He told that to the Oak Ridge Boys and he was right.'

'Wow,' said Patty.

When Cody patted the pinch of snuff under his lip, she said, 'I think snuff's kind of sexy.'

Joann hauled the baby out of the car seat and bounced him playfully on her shoulder. 'Who's precious?' she asked the baby.

*

In the van on the way to Nashville that Friday, they sang gospel songs, changing the words crazily. 'Swing Low, Sweet Chariot' became 'Sweet 'n Low, Mr Coffee pot, perking for to hurry my heart'. Cody drove, and Joann sat in the back, where she could manage the food. She passed out beer and the sandwiches she had made before work that morning. She had been looking forward to the weekend, hoping to talk things over with Debbie.

Will Ed sat in the back with Joann, complaining about his wife, who was taking an interior-decorating course by correspondence. 'She could come with us, but instead she wants to stay home and rearrange the furniture. I'm afraid to go home in the dark. I don't know where to walk.' He added with a laugh, 'And I don't know *who* I might stumble over.'

'Joyce wouldn't cheat on you,' said Joann.

'What do you think all these songs we sing are about?' he asked.

At that moment, Cody was humming 'Pop a Top', a song about a wandering wife. He reached back for another beer, and Joann pulled the tab off for him. Cody set the can between his legs and said, 'Poor Joann here's afraid we're going to get corrupted. She thinks I ought to be home spreading manure and milking cows.'

'Don't "poor Joann" me. I can take care of myself.'

Cody laughed. 'If men weren't tied down by women, what do you reckon they'd do with themselves? If they didn't have kids, a house, instalments to pay?'

'Men want to marry and have a home just as much as women do, or they wouldn't do it,' Joann said.

'Tell him, Joann,' said L. J.

'Listen to this,' said Will Ed. 'I asked Joyce what was for supper? And she says, "*I'm* having a hamburger. What are *you* going to have?" I mean you can't say a word now without 'em jumping on you.'

'Y'all shut up,' said Joann. 'Let's sing another song. Let's sing "The Old Rugged Cross".'

'The old rugged cross' turned into 'an old Chevrolet,' a forlorn image, it seemed to Joann, like something of quality lost in the past. She imagined a handsome 1957 Chevrolet, its fins slashed by silver arrows, standing splendidly on top of a mountain.

'This is better than showing up at the plant with a lunch box!' Cody cried. 'Ain't it, boys?' He blasted the horn twice at the empty highway and broke into joyous song.

At the Bluebird, Joann drank the Tequila Sunrises Debbie brought her. The drink was pretty, with an orange slice—a rising sun—on the rim of the glass. Between customers, Debbie sat with Joann and they talked about life. Debbie knew a lot about human nature, though Joann wasn't sure Debbie was right about Cody being a man who suffered. 'If he's suffering, it's because I'm bringing in the pay cheque,' she said. 'But instead of looking for work, he's singing songs.'

'He's going through the change,' Debbie said. 'Men go through it, too. He's afraid he's missed out on life. I've seen a lot of guys like that.'

'I don't understand what's happening to people, the way they can't hold together anymore,' Joann said. 'My daughter's divorced, and I think it's just now hitting me that I got divorced too. In my first marriage, I got shafted—eighteen years with a man, working my fingers to the bone, raising three kids—but I didn't make a federal case out of it. I was lucky Cody came along. Cody says don't live with regret, but it's awful hard to look forward when there's so little you can depend on.'

Debbie jumped up to get a draft beer for a man who signalled her. When she returned, she suddenly confessed to

Joann, 'I had my tubes tied—but I was such an idiot! And now I've met this new guy, and he doesn't know. I think I'm serious about him, but I haven't got the heart to tell him what I did.'

'When did you have it done?' Joann cried, horrified.

'Last spring.' She lit a cigarette and exhaled smoke furiously. 'You know why I got my tubes tied? Because I hate to be categorised. My ex-husband thought I had to have supper on the table at six on the dot, when he came home. I was working too, and I got home about five-thirty. I had to do all the shopping and cleaning and cooking. I hate it when people *assume* things like that—that I'm the one to make supper because I've got reproductive organs.'

'I never thought of it that way exactly.'

'I was going to add kids to those responsibilities? Like hell.' Debbie punched holes in a cocktail napkin with her ballpoint pen. The napkin had jokes printed on it, and she punched out the jokes. 'It's the little things,' she said. 'I don't care about equal pay as much as I care about people judging me by the way I keep house. It's nobody's damn business how I keep house.'

Joann had never heard of anything like what Debbie had done. She hadn't known a woman would go that far to make a point to a man. Later, Debbie said, 'You don't know what problems are till you go through tubal litigation.' Joann had a feeling that that was the wrong term, but she didn't want to mention it.

'I hate to see you so upset,' Joann said. 'What can I do?'

'Tell them to stop playing those lovesick songs. All these country songs are so stupid. They tell you to stand by your man, but then they say he's just going to use you somehow.'

Joann thought she understood how Debbie felt about telling her new boyfriend what she had done. It seemed like a dreadful secret. Debbie had had her tubes tied rather than tell her husband in plain English to treat her better. The country songs were open and confessional, but in reality people kept things to themselves. The songs were an invasion of privacy. Debbie must have felt something like that about her housekeeping and her husband's demands. Debbie should have sung a song about it, instead of getting herself butchered, Joann thought. But maybe Debbie couldn't sing. Joann was getting drunk.

The next afternoon, at the motel, Cody said to Joann, 'They want us to play five nights a week at the bar. They've guaranteed me six months.' He was smiling and slamming things around happily. He had just brought in some Cokes and Big Macs. 'Will Ed and L. J. have to stay home and work, but I can get some backup men from here, easy. We could get a little apartment down here and put the house up for sale.'

'I don't want to sell Daddy's place.' Joann's stomach was churning.

'Well, we ain't doing nothing with it.'

'They say they're going to hire again at the plant in the spring,' Joann said.

'To hell with the plant. I gave 'em nineteen years and six months of my life and they cut me off without a pension. Screw *them*.'

Joann placed the Big Macs and Cokes on a tray. She and Cody sat on one of the two beds to eat. She nibbled at her hamburger. 'You're telling me to quit my job,' she said.

'You could find something in Nashville.'

'And be a cocktail waitress like Debbie? No, thanks. That's a rough life. I like my job and I'm lucky to have it.'

On TV, a preacher was blabbing about reservations for heaven. Cody got up and flipped the dial, testing all the channels. 'Just look how many TV channels we could get if we lived down here,' he said.

*

'Don't do it, Joann,' Debbie said flatly that evening.

'Cody and I haven't been together that long,' Joann said. 'Sometimes I feel I don't even know him. We're still in that stage where I ought to be giving him encouragement, the way you should do when you're starting out with somebody.' She added, sarcastically, 'Stand by your man.'

'We're always caught in one cliché or another,' Debbie said. 'But you've got to think about yourself, Joann.'

'I should give him more of a chance. He's got his heart set on this, and I'm being so contrary.'

'But look what he's asking you to do, girl! Look what-all you've worked for. You've got your daddy's homeplace and that good job. You don't want to lose all that.'

'We wouldn't come out ahead, after we pay off the mortgage. Maybe he wants to move to Nashville because there's ninety-nine TV stations to choose from. Well, the cable's coming down our road next year, and we'll have ten channels. That's enough television for anybody. They're bidding on the franchise now.'

'I never watch television,' Debbie said. 'I can't stand watching stuff that's straight out of my own life.'

At home, Cody was restless, full of nervous energy. He repaired some fences, as if getting the place ready to sell, but Joann hadn't agreed to anything. In the den one evening, after 'Dynasty' had ended, Cody turned the sound down and said, 'Let's talk, Jo.' She waited while he opened a beer. He had been drinking beer after beer, methodically. 'I've been thinking a lot about the way things are going, and I feel bad about how I used to treat my first wife, Charlene. I'm afraid I'm doing you the same way.'

'You don't treat me bad,' Joann said.

'I've taken advantage of you, letting you pay all the bills. I know I should get a job, but damn it, there's got to be more to life than punching a time clock. I think I always expected a lot more out of life than most people. I used to be a real hell-raiser. I thought I could get away with anything because people always gave me things. All my life, people gave me things.'

'What things?' Joann was sitting on the couch, and Cody was in the easy chair. The only light came from the television.

'In grade school, I'd get more valentines than anybody, and the valentines would have candy in them, little hearts with messages like "Be Mine" and "Cutie" and things like that. When I graduated from high school, all the storekeepers in town gave me stuff and took me in their backrooms and gave me whiskey. I had my first drink in the pharmacy in the back of the Rexall. I just breezed through life, letting people give me things, and it didn't dawn on me for a long time that people wanted something back. They expected something from me and I never gave it to them. I didn't live up to their expectations. Somehow, I want to give something back.'

'People always admired you, Cody. You're so good-natured. Isn't that giving something?'

Cody belched loudly and laughed. 'When I was about twelve, a man gave me five dollars to jack him off in the alley behind the old A and P.'

'Did you do it?'

'Yep. And I didn't think a thing about it. I just did it. Five bucks was five bucks.'

'Well, what do you owe *him*?' Joann said sharply.

'Nothing, I reckon, but the point is, I did a lot of stuff that wasn't right. Charlene was always thumping the Bible and hauling me off to church. I couldn't live with that. I treated her like dirt, the way I cheated on her. I always wanted what was free and available. It was what I was used to. I had a chance once, about fifteen years ago, to play in a little bar in Nashville, but the kids were little, and Charlene didn't want me to go. I've regretted that to this day. Don't you see why this chance means so much to me? I'm trying to *give* something of myself, instead of always taking. Just go along with me, Joann. Take this one risk with me.'

'What can I say when you put it that way?'

'A person has to follow his dream.'

'That sounds like some Elvis song,' she said, sounding unexpectedly sarcastic. She was thinking of Elvis's last few years, when he got fat and corrupted. She rearranged some pillows on the couch. The weather news was on TV. The radar was showing rain in their area. Slowly, her eyes on the flashing lines of the radar map, she said, 'What you want to do is be in the spotlight so people can adore you. That's the same thing as taking what's free.'

'That's not true. Maybe you think it's easy to be in the spotlight. But it's not. Look what happened to Elvis.'

'You're not Elvis. And selling the place is too extreme. Things can't be all one way or the other. There has to be some of both. That's what life is, when it's any good.' Joann felt drained, as though she had just had to figure out all of life, like doing a complicated maths problem in her head.

Cody turned the TV off, and the light vanished. In the dark, he said, 'I cheated on Charlene, but I never cheated on you.'

'I never said you did.'

'But you expect it,' he said.

Patty came over to ask Joann to keep the kids that weekend. She had a new boyfriend, who was taking her to St Louis.

'If I can take 'em to Nashville,' Joann told Patty. 'I have to go along to keep the girls away from Cody.' She looked meaningfully at Cody.

It was meant to be a casual, teasing remark, she thought, but it didn't come out that way. Cody glared at her, looking hurt.

'The kids will be in the way,' he said. 'You can't take them to the Bluebird Lounge.'

'We'll stay in the motel room,' Joann said. 'I wanted to watch *On Golden Pond* on HBO anyway. Nashville has so much more to offer. Remember?'

She realised that taking the children to Nashville was a bad idea, but she felt she had to go with Cody. She didn't know what might happen. She hoped that having the kids along would make her and Cody feel they had a family to be responsible for. Besides, Patty was neglecting the kids. Joann had kept them three nights in a row last week while Patty went out with her new boyfriend.

In the van on the way down, Rodney cried because he was teething, and L. J. gave him a piece of rawhide to chew on. Kristi played with a bucket of plastic toys. Will Ed practised the middle eight of a new song they had learned. It seemed pointless to Joann, since Cody planned to dump Will Ed and L. J. from his act. Will Ed played the passage over and over on his guitar, until Kristi screamed, 'Shut up!' Cody said little. L. J. was driving, because Joann didn't want Cody to drive and drink beer, with the children along.

Daylight saving time had ended, and the dark came early. The bright lights at the edge of Nashville reminded Joann of how soon Christmas was.

She liked being alone in the motel room with the kids. It made her think of when she'd had small children and her first husband had worked a night shift. She had always tried to be quiet around sleeping children, but nowadays children had more tolerance for noise. The TV didn't bother them. She sat in bed, propped against pillows. The children were asleep. In the large mirror facing the bed, she could see herself, watching

TV, with the sleeping bundles beside her. Joann felt expectant, as if some easy answers were waiting for her—from the movie, from the innocence of the children.

Suddenly Kristi sat straight up and shouted, 'Where's Mommy?'

'Hush, Kristi! Mommy's gone to St Louis. We'll see her Sunday.'

Kristi hurled herself out of bed and ran around the room. She looked in the closet and in the bathroom. Then she began to shriek. Joann grabbed her and whispered, 'Shush, you'll wake up your little brother!'

Kristi wiggled away from her and looked under the bed, but the bed was boxed in—a brilliant construction, Joann thought, so far as cleaning was concerned. Kristi bumped into a chair and fell down. She began bawling. Rodney stirred, and then he started to cry. Joann huddled both children in the centre of the bed and began singing to them. She couldn't think of anything to sing except the Kitty Wells song about honky-tonk angels. The song was an absurd one to sing to kids, but she sang it anyway. It was her life. She sang it like an innocent bystander, angry that that was the way women were, that they looked on approvingly while some man went out and either did something big or made a fool of himself trying.

When Cody came in later, she had fallen asleep with the children. She woke up and glanced at the travel alarm. It was three. The TV was still on. Cody was missing the Burt Reynolds movie he had wanted to watch. He stumbled into the bathroom and then fell into the other bed with all his clothes on.

'I was rehearsing with those new guys,' he said. 'And then we went out to eat something.' Joann heard his boots fall to the floor, and he said, 'I called home around ten-thirty, between shows, to wish Mama a happy birthday, and she told me Daddy's in the Memphis hospital.'

'Oh, what's wrong?' Joann sat up and pulled her pillow behind her. Cody's father, who was almost seventy-five, had always bragged about never being sick.

'It's cancer. He had some tests done. They never told me anything.' Cody flung his shirt to the foot of the bed. 'Lung cancer comes on sudden. They're going to operate next week.'

'I was *so* afraid of that,' Joann said. 'The way he smoked.'

Cody turned to face her across the aisle between the two beds. He reached over and searched for her hand. 'I'll have to go to Memphis tomorrow night after the show. Mama's going down tomorrow.'

Rodney squirmed beside Joann, and she pulled the covers around his shoulders. Then she crept into bed with Cody and lay close to him while he went on talking in a tone of disbelief about his father. 'It makes me mad that I forgot it was Mama's birthday. I thought of it during the first show, when I was singing "Blue Eyes Crying in the Rain". I don't know how it came to me to think of it then.'

'Do you want me to go to Memphis with you?'

'No. That's all right. You have to get the kids home. I'll take the bus and then come back here for the show Tuesday.' Cody drew her near him. 'Were you going to come back here with me?'

'I've been thinking about that. I don't want to quit my job or sell Daddy's place. That would be crazy.'

'Sometimes it's good to act a little crazy.'

'No. We have to reason things out, so we don't ruin anything between us.' She was half-whispering, trying not to wake the children, and her voice trembled as though she were having a chill. 'I think you should come down here by yourself first and see how it works out.'

'What if my album's a big hit and we make a million

dollars?' His eyes were on the TV. Burt Reynolds was speeding down an interstate.

'That would be different.'

'Would you move to Nashville if I got on the "Grand Ole Opry"?'

'Yes.'

'Is that a promise?'

'Yes.'

On Monday, Cody was still in Memphis. The operation was the next day, and Joann took off from work early in order to go down to be with Cody and his parents. She was ready to leave the house when the delivery truck brought the shipment of record albums. The driver brought two boxes, marked '1 of 3' and '2 of 3.'

'I'll bring the third box tomorrow,' the driver said. 'We're not allowed to bring three at once.'

'Why's that?' Joann asked, shivering in the open doorway to the porch.

'They want to keep us moving.'

'Well, I don't understand that one bit.'

Joann shoved the boxes across the threshold and closed the door. With a butcher knife, she ripped open one of the boxes and slipped out a record album. On the cover was a photograph of Cody and Will Ed and L. J. and Jimmy sitting on a bench. Above them, the title of the album was a red-and-blue neon sign: 'HUNKTOWN'. Cody and his friends were all wearing Hunktown T-shirts, cowboy boots, and cowboy hats. They had a casual, slouchy look, like the group called Alabama. It was a terrible picture. Looking at her husband, Joann thought no one would say he was really handsome. She held the cover up to the glass door to get a better light on his face. He looked old. His expression seemed serious and unforgiving, as though he expected the world to be ready for him, as though this were his revenge, not his gift. That face was now on a thousand albums.

But the picture was not really Cody at all, she thought. It was only his wild side, not the part she loved. Seeing it was something like identifying a dead body: it was so unfamiliar that death was somehow acceptable. She had to laugh. Cody had meant the album to be a surprise, but he would be surprised to see how he looked.

Joann heard a noise outside. She touched her nose to the door glass and left a smudge. On the porch, the impatiens in a hanging basket had died in the recent freeze. She had forgotten to bring the plant inside. Now she watched it sway and twist in a little whirl of wind.

Alice Munro
Fits

———

The two people who died were in their early sixties. They were both tall and well built, and carried a few pounds of extra weight. He was grey-haired, with a square, rather flat face. A broad nose kept him from looking perfectly dignified and handsome. Her hair was blond, a silvery blond that does not strike you as artificial anymore—though you know it is not natural—because so many women of that age have acquired it. On Boxing Day, when they dropped over to have a drink with Peg and Robert, she wore a pale-grey dress with a fine, shiny stripe in it, grey stockings, and grey shoes. She drank gin-and-tonic. He wore brown slacks and a cream-coloured sweater, and drank rye-and-water. They had recently come back from a trip to Mexico. He had tried parachute-riding. She hadn't wanted to. They had gone to see a place in Yucatán—it looked like a well—where virgins were supposed to have been flung down, in the hope of good harvests.

'Actually, though, that's just a nineteenth-century notion,' she said. 'That's just the nineteenth-century notion of being so preoccupied with virginity. The truth probably is that they threw people down sort of indiscriminately. Girls or men or old people or whoever they could get their hands on. So not being a virgin would be no guarantee of safety!'

Across the room, Peg's two sons—the older one, Clayton, who was a virgin, and the younger one, Kevin, who was not—watched this breezy-talking silvery-blond woman with stern, bored expressions. She had said that she used to be a high-school English teacher. Clayton remarked afterward that he knew the type.

Robert and Peg have been married for nearly five years. Robert was never married before, but Peg married for the first time when she was eighteen. Her two boys were born while she and her husband lived with his parents on a farm. Her husband had a job driving trucks of livestock to the Canada Packers Abattoir in Toronto. Other truck-driving jobs followed, taking him further and further away. Peg and the boys moved to Gilmore, and she got a job working in Kuiper's store, which was called the Gilmore Arcade. Her husband ended up in the Arctic, driving trucks to oil rigs across the frozen Beaufort Sea. She got a divorce.

Robert's family owned the Gilmore Arcade but had never lived in Gilmore. His mother and sisters would not have believed you could survive a week in such a place. Robert's father had bought the store, and two other stores in nearby towns, shortly after the Second World War. He hired local managers, and drove up from Toronto a few times during the year to see how things were getting on.

For a long time, Robert did not take much interest in his father's various businesses. He took a degree in civil engineering, and had some idea of doing work in underdeveloped countries. He got a job in Peru, travelled through South America, gave up engineering for a while to work on a ranch in British Columbia. When his father became ill, it was necessary for him to come back to Toronto. He worked for the Provincial Department of Highways, in an engineering job that was not a very good one for a man of his age. He was thinking of getting a teaching degree and maybe going up

North to teach Indians, changing his life completely, once his father died. He was getting close to forty then, and having his third major affair with a married woman.

Now and then, he drove up to Gilmore and the other towns to keep an eye on the stores. Once, he brought Lee with him, his third—and, as it turned out, his last—married woman. She brought a picnic lunch, drank Pimm's Number 1 in the car, and treated the whole trip as a merry excursion, a foray into hillbilly country. She had counted on making love in the open fields, and was incensed to find they were all full of cattle or uncomfortable cornstalks.

Robert's father died, and Robert did change his life, but instead of becoming a teacher and heading for the wilderness, he came to live in Gilmore to manage the stores himself. He married Peg.

It was entirely by accident that Peg was the one who found them.

On Sunday evening, the farm woman who sold the Kuipers their eggs knocked on the door.

'I hope you don't mind me bringing these tonight instead of tomorrow morning,' she said. 'I have to take my daughter-in-law to Kitchener to have her ultrasound. I brought the Weebles theirs, too, but I guess they're not home. I wonder if you'd mind if I left them here with you? I have to leave early in the morning. She was going to drive herself but I didn't think that was such a good idea. She's nearly five months but still vomiting. Tell them they can just pay me next time.'

'No problem,' said Robert. 'No trouble at all. We can just run over with them in the morning. No problem at all!' Robert is a stocky, athletic-looking man, with curly, greying hair and bright brown eyes. His friendliness and obligingness are often emphatic, so that people might get the feeling of being buffeted from all sides. This is a manner that serves him well in Gilmore, where assurances are supposed to be repeated, and in fact much of conversation is repetition, a sort of dance of good intentions, without surprises. Just occasionally, talking to people, he feels something else, an obstruction, and isn't sure what it is (malice, stubbornness?) but it's like a rock at the bottom of a river when you're swimming—the clear water lifts you over it.

For a Gilmore person, Peg is reserved. She came up to the woman and relieved her of the eggs she was holding, while Robert went on assuring her it was no trouble and asking about the daughter-in-law's pregnancy. Peg smiled as she would smile in the store when she gave you your change—a quick transactional smile, nothing personal. She is a small slim woman with a cap of soft brown hair, freckles, and a scrubbed, youthful look. She wears pleated skirts, fresh neat blouses buttoned to the throat, pale sweaters, sometimes a black ribbon tie. She moves gracefully and makes very little noise. Robert once told her he had never met anyone so self-contained as she was. (His women have usually been talkative, stylishly effective, though careless about some of the details, tense, lively, 'interesting'.)

Peg said she didn't know what he meant.

He started to explain what a self-contained person was like. At that time, he had a very faulty comprehension of Gilmore vocabulary—he could still make mistakes about it—and he took too seriously the limits that were usually observed in daily exchanges.

'I know what the words mean,' Peg said, smiling. 'I just don't understand how you mean it about me.'

Of course she knew what the words meant. Peg took courses, a different course each winter, choosing from what was offered at the local high school. She took a course on the History of

Art, one on Great Civilisations of the East, one on Discoveries and Explorations Through the Ages. She went to class one night a week, even if she was very tired or had a cold. She wrote tests and prepared papers. Sometimes Robert would find a page covered with her small neat handwriting on top of the refrigerator or the dresser in their room.

Therefore we see that the importance of Prince Henry the Navigator was in the inspiration and encouragement of other explorers for Portugal, even though he did not go on voyages himself.

He was moved by her earnest statements, her painfully careful small handwriting, and angry that she never got more than a B-plus for these papers she worked so hard at.

'I don't do it for the marks,' Peg said. Her cheekbones reddened under the freckles, as if she was making some kind of personal confession. 'I do it for the enjoyment.'

Robert was up before dawn on Monday morning, standing at the kitchen counter drinking his coffee, looking out at the fields covered with snow. The sky was clear, and the temperatures had dropped. It was going to be one of the bright, cold, hard January days that come after weeks of west wind, of blowing and falling snow. Creeks, rivers, ponds frozen over. Lake Huron frozen over as far as you could see. Perhaps all the way this year. That had happened, though rarely.

He had to drive to Keneally, to the Kuiper store there. Ice on the roof was causing water underneath to back up and leak through the ceiling. He would have to chop up the ice and get the roof clear. It would take him at least half the day.

All the repair work and upkeep on the store and on this house is done by Robert himself. He has learned to do plumbing and wiring. He enjoys the feeling that he can manage it. He enjoys the difficulty, and the difficulty of winter, here. Not much more than a hundred miles from Toronto, it is a differ-

ent country. The snow-belt. Coming up here to live was not
unlike heading into the wilderness, after all. Blizzards still isol-
ate the towns and villages. Winter comes down hard on the
country, settles down just the way the two-mile-high ice did
thousands of years ago. People live within the winter in a way
outsiders do not understand. They are watchful, provident,
fatigued, exhilarated.

A thing he likes about this house is the back view, over the
open country. That makes up for the straggling dead-end street
without trees or sidewalks. The street was opened up after the
war, when it was taken for granted that everybody would be
using cars, not walking anywhere. And so they did. The houses
are fairly close to the street and to each other, and when
everybody who lives in the houses is home, cars take up nearly
all the space where sidewalks, boulevards, shade trees might
have been.

Robert, of course, was willing to buy another house. He
assumed they would do that. There were—there are—fine old
houses for sale in Gilmore, at prices that are a joke, by city
standards. Peg said she couldn't see herself living in those
places. He offered to build her a new house in the subdivision
on the other side of town. She didn't want that either. She
wanted to stay in this house, which was the first house she and
the boys had lived in on their own. So Robert bought it—she
was only renting—and built on the master bedroom and another bathroom, and made a television room in the basement.
He got some help from Kevin, less from Clayton. The house
still looked, from the street, like the house he had parked in
front of the first time he drove Peg home from work. One and
a half stories high, with a steep roof and a living-room window
divided into square panes like the window on a Christmas
card. White aluminum siding, narrow black shutters, black
trim. Back in Toronto, he had thought of Peg living in this

house. He had thought of her patterned, limited, serious, and desirable life.

He noticed the Weebles' eggs sitting on the counter. He thought of taking them over. But it was too early. The door would be locked. He didn't want to wake them. Peg could take the eggs when she left to open up the store. He took the Magic Marker that was sitting on the ledge under her reminder pad, and wrote on a paper towel, *Don't forget eggs to W's. Love, Robert*. These eggs were no cheaper than the ones you bought at the supermarket. It was just that Robert liked getting them from a farm. And they were brown. Peg said city people all had a thing about brown eggs—they thought brown eggs were more natural somehow, like brown sugar.

When he backed his car out, he saw that the Weebles' car was in their carport. So they were home from wherever they had been last night. Then he saw that the snow thrown up across the front of their driveway by the town snowplough had not been cleared. The plough must have gone by during the night. But he himself hadn't had to shovel any snow; there hadn't been any fresh snow overnight and the plough hadn't been out. The snow was from yesterday. They couldn't have been out last night. Unless they were walking. The sidewalks were not cleared, except along the main street and the school streets, and it was difficult to walk along the narrowed streets with their banks of snow, but, being new to town, they might have set out not realising that.

He didn't look closely enough to see if there were footprints.

He pictured what happened. First from the constable's report, then from Peg's.

Peg came out of the house at about twenty after eight. Clayton had already gone off to school, and Kevin, getting over an ear infection, was down in the basement room playing a Billy Idol tape and watching a game show on television. Peg had not forgotten the eggs. She got into her car and turned on the engine to warm it up, then walked out to the street, stepped over the Weebles' uncleared snow, and went up their driveway to the side door. She was wearing her white knitted scarf and tam and her lilac-coloured, down-filled coat. Those coats made most of the women in Gilmore look like barrels, but Peg looked all right, being so slender.

The houses on the street were originally of only three designs. But by now most of them had been so altered, with new windows, porches, wings, and decks, that it was hard to find true mates anymore. The Weebles' house had been built as a mirror image of the Kuipers', but the front window had been changed, its Christmas-card panes taken out, and the roof had been lifted, so that there was a large upstairs window overlooking the street. The siding was pale green and the trim white, and there were no shutters.

The side door opened into a utility room, just as Peg's door did at home. She knocked lightly at first, thinking that they would be in the kitchen, which was only a few steps up from the utility room. She had noticed the car, of course, and wondered if they had got home late and were sleeping in. (She hadn't thought yet about the snow's not having been shovelled, and the fact that the plough hadn't been past in the night. That was something that occurred to her later on when she got into her own car and backed it out.) She knocked louder and louder. Her face was stinging already in the bright cold. She tried the door and found that it wasn't locked. She opened it and stepped into shelter and called.

The little room was dark. There was no light to speak of coming down from the kitchen, and there was a bamboo curtain over the side door. She set the eggs on the clothes dryer, and was going to leave them there. Then she thought she had better take them up into the kitchen, in case the Weebles wanted eggs for breakfast and had run out. They wouldn't think of looking in the utility room.

(This, in fact, was Robert's explanation to himself. She didn't say all that, but he forgot she didn't. She just said, 'I thought I might as well take them up to the kitchen.')

The kitchen had those same bamboo curtains over the sink window and over the breakfast-nook windows, which meant that though the room faced east, like the Kuipers' kitchen, and though the sun was fully up by this time, not much light could get in. The day hadn't begun here.

But the house was warm. Perhaps they'd got up a while ago and turned up the thermostat, then gone back to bed. Perhaps they left it up all night—though they had seemed to Peg to be thriftier than that. She set the eggs on the counter by the sink. The layout of the kitchen was almost exactly the same as her own. She noticed a few dishes stacked, rinsed, but not washed, as if they'd had something to eat before they went to bed.

She called again from the living-room doorway.

The living-room was perfectly tidy. It looked to Peg somehow too perfectly tidy, but that—as she said to Robert—was probably the way the living-room of a retired couple was bound to look to a woman used to having children around. Peg had never in her life had quite as much tidiness around her as she might have liked, having gone from a family home where there were six children to her in-laws' crowded farmhouse, which she crowded further with her own babies. She had told Robert a story about once asking for a beautiful bar of soap for Christmas, pink soap with a raised design of roses on it. She got it, and she used to hide it after every use so that it wouldn't get cracked and mouldy in the cracks, the way soap always did in that house. She was grown up at that time, or thought she was.

She had stamped the snow off her boots in the utility room. Nevertheless she hesitated to walk across the clean, pale-beige living-room carpet. She called again. She used the Weebles' first names, which she barely knew. Walter and Nora. They had moved in last April, and since then they had been away on two trips, so she didn't feel she knew them at all well, but it seemed silly to be calling, 'Mr and Mrs Weeble. Are you up yet, Mr and Mrs Weeble?'

No answer.

They had an open staircase going up from the living-room, just as Peg and Robert did. Peg walked now across the clean, pale carpet to the foot of the stairs, which were carpeted in the same material. She started to climb. She did not call again.

She must have known then or she would have called. It would be the normal thing to do, to keep calling the closer you got to where people might be sleeping. To warn them. They might be deeply asleep. Drunk. That wasn't the custom of the Weebles, so far as anybody knew, but nobody knew them that well. Retired people. Early retirement. He had been an accountant; she had been a teacher. They had lived in Hamilton. They had chosen Gilmore because Walter Weeble used to have an aunt and uncle here, whom he visited as a child. Both dead now, the aunt and uncle, but the place must have held pleasant memories for him. And it was cheap; this was surely a cheaper house than they could have afforded. They meant to spend their money travelling. No children.

She didn't call; she didn't halt again. She climbed the stairs and didn't look around as she came up; she faced straight ahead. Ahead was the bathroom, with the door open. It was clean and empty.

She turned at the top of the stairs toward the Weebles' bedroom. She had never been upstairs in this house before, but she knew where that would be. It would be the extended room at the front, with the wide window overlooking the street.

The door of that room was open.

Peg came downstairs and left the house by the kitchen, the utility room, the side door. Her footprints showed on the carpet and on the linoleum tiles, and outside on the snow. She closed the door after herself. Her car had been running all this time and was sitting in its own little cloud of steam. She got in and backed out and drove to the police station in the Town Hall.

'It's a bitter cold morning, Peg,' the constable said.

'Yes, it is.'

'So what can I do for you?'

Robert got more, from Karen.

Karen Adams was the clerk in the Gilmore Arcade. She was a young married woman, solidly built, usually good-humoured, alert without particularly seeming to be so, efficient without a lot of bustle. She got along well with the customers; she got along with Peg and Robert. She had known Peg longer, of course. She defended her against those people who said Peg had got her nose in the air since she married rich. Karen said Peg hadn't changed from what she always was. But after today she said, 'I always believed Peg and me to be friends, but now I'm not so sure.'

Karen started work at ten. She arrived a little before that and asked if there had been many customers in yet, and Peg said no, nobody.

'I don't wonder,' Karen said. 'It's too cold. If there was any wind, it'd be murder.'

Peg had made coffee. They had a new coffee maker, Robert's Christmas present to the store. They used to have to get take-outs from the bakery up the street.

'Isn't this thing marvellous?' Karen said as she got her coffee. Peg said yes. She was wiping up some marks on the floor.

'Oh-oh,' said Karen. 'Was that me or you?'

'I think it was me,' Peg said.

'So I didn't think anything of it,' Karen said later. 'I thought she must've tracked in some mud. I didn't stop to think, Where would you get down to mud with all this snow on the ground?'

After a while, a customer came in, and it was Celia Simms, and she had heard. Karen was at the cash, and Peg was at the back, checking some invoices. Celia told Karen. She didn't know much; she didn't know how it had been done or that Peg was involved.

Karen shouted to the back of the store. 'Peg! Peg! Something terrible has happened, and it's your next-door neighbours!'

Peg called back, 'I know.'

Celia lifted her eyebrows at Karen—she was one of those who didn't like Peg's attitude—and Karen loyally turned aside and waited till Celia went out of the store. Then she hurried to the back, making the hangers jingle on the racks.

'Both the Weebles are shot dead, Peg. Did you know that?'

Peg said, 'Yes. I found them.'

'You did! When did you?'

'This morning, just before I came in to work.'

'They were murdered!'

'It was a murder-suicide,' Peg said. 'He shot her and then he shot himself. That's what happened.'

'When she told me that,' Karen said, 'I started to shake. I shook all over and I couldn't stop myself.' Telling Robert this, she shook again, to demonstrate, and pushed her hands up inside the sleeves of her blue plush jogging suit.

'So I said, "What did you do when you found them," and

she said, "I went and told the police". I said, "Did you scream,
or what?" I said didn't her legs buckle, because I know mine
would've. I can't imagine how I would've got myself out of
there. She said she didn't remember much about getting out,
but she did remember closing the door, the outside door, and
thinking, Make sure that's closed in case some dog could get
in. Isn't that awful? She was right, but it's awful to think of.
Do you think she's in shock?'

'No,' Robert said. 'I think she's all right.'

This conversation was taking place at the back of the store
in the afternoon, when Peg had gone out to get a sandwich.

'She had not said one word to me. Nothing. I said, "How
come you never said a word about this, Peg," and she said, "I
knew you'd find out pretty soon." I said yes, but she could've
told me. "I'm sorry," she says. "I'm sorry." Just like she's apologising for some little thing like using my coffee mug. Only,
Peg would never do that.'

Robert had finished what he was doing at the Keneally store
around noon, and decided to drive back to Gilmore before
getting anything to eat. There was a highway diner just outside
of town, on the way in from Keneally, and he thought that he
would stop there. A few truckers and travellers were usually
eating in the diner, but most of the trade was local—farmers
on the way home, business and working men who had driven
out from town. Robert liked this place, and he had entered it
today with a feeling of buoyant expectation. He was hungry
from his work in the cold air, and aware of the brilliance of the
day, with the snow on the fields looking sculpted, dazzling, as
permanent as marble. He had the sense he had fairly often in
Gilmore, the sense of walking onto an informal stage, where a
rambling, agreeable play was in progress. And he knew his
lines—or knew, at least, that his improvisations would not fail.

His whole life in Gilmore sometimes seemed to have this quality, but if he ever tried to describe it that way, it would sound as if it was an artificial life, something contrived, not entirely serious. And the very opposite was true. So when he met somebody from his old life, as he sometimes did when he went to Toronto, and was asked how he liked living in Gilmore, he would say, 'I can't tell you how much I like it!' which was exactly the truth.

'Why didn't you get in touch with me?'

'You were up on the roof.'

'You could have called the store and told Ellie. She would have told me.'

'What good would that have done?'

'I could at least have come home.'

He had come straight from the diner to the store, without eating what he had ordered. He did not think he would find Peg in any state of collapse—he knew her well enough for that—but he did think she would want to go home, let him fix her a drink, spend some time telling him about it.

She didn't want that. She wanted to go up the street to the bakery to get her usual lunch—a roll with ham and cheese.

'I let Karen go out to eat, but I haven't had time. Should I bring one back for you? If you didn't eat at the diner, I might as well.'

When she brought him the sandwich, he sat and ate it at the desk where she had been doing invoices. She put fresh coffee and water into the coffee maker.

'I can't imagine how we got along without this thing.'

He looked at Peg's lilac-coloured coat hanging beside Karen's red coat on the washroom door. On the lilac coat there was a long crusty smear of reddish-brown paint, down to the hemline.

Of course that wasn't paint. But on her coat? How did she get blood on her coat? She must have brushed up against them in that room. She must have got close.

Then he remembered the talk in the diner, and realised she wouldn't have needed to get that close. She could have got blood from the door frame. The constable had been in the diner, and he said there was blood everywhere, and not just blood.

'He shouldn't ever have used a shotgun for that kind of business,' one of the men at the diner said.

Somebody else said, 'Maybe a shotgun was all he had.'

It was busy in the store most of the afternoon. People on the street, in the bakery and the café and the bank and the post office, talking. People wanted to talk face to face. They had to get out and do it, in spite of the cold. Talking on the phone was not enough.

What had gone on at first, Robert gathered, was that people had got on the phone, just phoned anybody they could think of who might not have heard. Karen had phoned her friend Shirley, who was at home in bed with the flu, and her mother, who was in the hospital with a broken hip. It turned out her mother knew already—the whole hospital knew. And Shirley said, 'My sister beat you to it.'

It was true that people valued and looked forward to the moment of breaking the news—Karen was annoyed at Shirley's sister, who didn't work and could get to the phone whenever she wanted to—but there was real kindness and consideration behind this impulse, as well. Robert thought so. 'I knew she wouldn't want not to know,' Karen said, and that was true. Nobody would want not to know. To go out into the street, not knowing. To go around doing all the usual daily things, not knowing. He himself felt troubled, even slightly humiliated, to think that he hadn't known; Peg hadn't let him know.

Talk ran backwards from the events of the morning. Where were the Weebles seen, and in what harmlessness and innocence, and how close to the moment when everything was changed?

She had stood in line at the Bank of Montreal on Friday afternoon.

He had got a haircut on Saturday morning.

They were together, buying groceries, in the IGA on Friday evening at about eight o'clock.

What did they buy? A good supply? Specials, advertised bargains, more than enough to last for a couple of days?

More than enough. A bag of potatoes, for one thing.

Then reasons. The talk turned to reasons. Naturally. There had been no theories put forward in the diner. Nobody knew the reason, nobody could imagine. But by the end of the afternoon there were too many explanations to choose from.

Financial problems. He had been mixed up in some bad investment scheme in Hamilton. Some wild money-making deal that had fallen through. All their money was gone and they would have to live out the rest of their lives on the old-age pension.

They had owed money on their income taxes. Being an accountant, he thought he know how to fix things, but he had been found out. He would be exposed, perhaps charged, shamed publicly, left poor. Even if it was only cheating the government, it would still be a disgrace when that kind of thing came out.

Was it a lot of money?

Certainly. A lot.

It was not money at all. They were ill. One of them or both of them. Cancer. Crippling arthritis. Alzheimer's disease.

Recurrent mental problems. It was health, not money. It was suffering and helplessness they feared, not poverty.

A division of opinion became evident between men and women. It was nearly always the men who believed and insisted that the trouble had been money, and it was the women who talked of illness. Who would kill themselves just because they were poor, said some women scornfully. Or even because they might go to jail? It was always a woman, too, who suggested unhappiness in the marriage, who hinted at the drama of a discovered infidelity or the memory of an old one.

Robert listened to all these explanations but did not believe any of them. Loss of money, cancer, Alzheimer's disease. Equally plausible, these seemed to him, equally hollow and useless. What happened was that he believed each of them for about five minutes, no longer. If he could have believed one of them, hung on to it, it would have been as if something had taken its claws out of his chest and permitted him to breathe.

('They weren't Gilmore people, not really,' a woman said to him in the bank. Then she looked embarrassed. 'I don't mean like you.')

Peg kept busy getting some children's sweaters, mitts, snowsuits ready for the January sale. People came up to her when she was marking the tags, and she said, 'Can I help you', so that they were placed right away in the position of being customers, and had to say that there was something they were looking for. The Arcade carried ladies' and children's clothes, sheets, towels, knitting wool, kitchenware, bulk candy, magazines, mugs, artificial flowers, and plenty of other things besides, so it was not hard to think of something.

What was it they were really looking for? Surely not much in the way of details, description. Very few people actually want that, or will admit they do, in a greedy and straightforward way. They want it, they don't want it. They start asking, they stop themselves. They listen and they back away. Perhaps they wanted from Peg just some kind of acknowledgment, some word or look that would send them away, saying, 'Peg Kuiper is absolutely shattered.' 'I saw Peg Kuiper. She didn't say much but you could tell she was absolutely shattered.'

Some people tried to talk to her, anyway.

'Wasn't that terrible what happened down by you?'

'Yes, it was.'

'You must have known them a little bit, living next door.'

'Not really. We hardly knew them at all.'

'You never noticed anything that would've led you to think this could've happened?'

'We never noticed anything at all.'

Robert pictured the Weebles getting into and out of their car in the driveway. That was where he had most often seen them. He recalled their Boxing Day visit. Her grey legs made him think of a nun. Her mention of virginity had embarrassed Peg and the boys. She reminded Robert a little of the kind of women he used to know. Her husband was less talkative, though not shy. They talked about Mexican food, which it seemed the husband had not liked. He did not like eating in restaurants.

Peg had said, 'Oh, men never do!'

That surprised Robert, who asked her afterward did that mean she wanted to eat out more often?

'I just said that to take her side. I thought he was glaring at her a bit.'

Was he glaring? Robert had not noticed. The man seemed too self-controlled to glare at his wife in public. Too well disposed, on the whole, perhaps in some way too indolent, to glare at anybody anywhere.

But it wasn't like Peg to exaggerate.

Bits of information kept arriving. The maiden name of Nora Weeble. Driscoll. Nora Driscoll. Someone knew a woman who had taught at the same school with her in Hamilton. Well-liked as a teacher, a fashionable dresser, she had some trouble keeping order. She had taken a French Conversation course, and a course in French cooking.

Some women here had asked her if she'd be interested in starting a book club, and she had said yes.

He had been more of a joiner in Hamilton than he was here. The Rotary Club. The Lions Club. Perhaps it had been for business reasons.

They were not churchgoers, as far as anybody knew, not in either place.

(Robert was right about the reasons. In Gilmore everything becomes known, sooner or later. Secrecy and confidentiality are seen to be against the public interest. There is a network of people who are married to or related to the people who work in the offices where all the records are kept.

There was no investment scheme, in Hamilton or anywhere else. No income-tax investigation. No problem about money. No cancer, tricky heart, high blood pressure. She had consulted the doctor about headaches, but the doctor did not think they were migraines, or anything serious.

At the funeral on Thursday, the United church minister, who usually took up the slack in the cases of no known af- filiation, spoke about the pressures and tensions of modern life but gave no more specific clues. Some people were disappointed, as if they expected him to do that—or thought that he might at least mention the dangers of falling away from faith and church membership, the sin of despair. Other people thought that saying anything more than he did say would have been in bad taste.)

*

Another person who thought Peg should have let him know was Kevin. He was waiting for them when they got home. He was still wearing his pajamas.

Why hadn't she come back to the house instead of driving to the police station? Why hadn't she called to him? She could have come back and phoned. Kevin could have phoned. At the very least, she could have called him from the store.

He had been down in the basement all morning, watching television. He hadn't heard the police come; he hadn't seen them go in or out. He had not known anything about what was going on until his girlfriend, Shanna, phoned him from school at lunch hour.

'She said they took the bodies out in garbage bags.'

'How would she know?' said Clayton. 'I thought she was at school.'

'Somebody told her.'

'She got that from television.'

'She *said* they took them out in garbage bags.'

'Shanna is a cretin. She is only good for one thing.'

'Some people aren't good for anything.'

Clayton was sixteen, Kevin fourteen. Two years apart in age but three years apart at school, because Clayton was accelerated and Kevin was not.

'Cut it out,' Peg said. She had brought up some spaghetti sauce from the freezer and was thawing it in the double boiler. 'Clayton. Kevin. Get busy and make me some salad.'

Kevin said, 'I'm sick. I might contaminate it.'

He picked up the tablecloth and wrapped it around his shoulders like a shawl.

'Do we have to eat off that?' Clayton said. 'Now he's got his crud on it?'

Peg said to Robert, 'Are we having wine?'

Saturday and Sunday nights they usually had wine, but

tonight Robert had not thought about it. He went down to the basement to get it. When he came back, Peg was sliding spaghetti into the cooker and Kevin had discarded the table-cloth. Clayton was making the salad. Clayton was small-boned, like his mother, and fiercely driven. A star runner, a demon examination writer.

Kevin was prowling around the kitchen, getting in the way, talking to Peg. Kevin was taller already than Clayton or Peg, perhaps taller than Robert. He had large shoulders and skinny legs and black hair that he wore in the nearest thing he dared to a Mohawk cut—Shanna cut it for him. His pale skin often broke out in pimples. Girls didn't seem to mind.

'So was there?' Kevin said. 'Was there blood and guck all over?'

'Ghoul,' said Clayton.

'Those were human beings, Kevin,' Robert said.

'Were,' said Kevin. 'I know they *were* human beings. I mixed their drinks on Boxing Day. She drank gin and he drank rye. They were human beings then, but all they are now is chemicals. Mom? What did you see first? Shanna said there was blood and guck even out in the hallway.'

'He's brutalised from all the TV he watches,' Clayton said. 'He thinks it was some video. He can't tell real blood from video blood.'

'Mom? Was it splashed?'

Robert has a rule about letting Peg deal with her sons unless she asks for his help. But this time he said, 'Kevin, you know it's about time you shut up.'

'He can't help it,' Clayton said. 'Being ghoulish.'

'You, too, Clayton. You, too.'

But after a moment Clayton said, 'Mom? Did you scream?'

'No,' said Peg thoughtfully. 'I didn't. I guess because there wasn't anybody to hear me. So I didn't.'

'I might have heard you,' said Kevin, cautiously trying a comeback.

'You had the television on.'

'I didn't have the sound on. I had my tape on. I might have heard you through the tape if you screamed loud enough.'

Peg lifted a strand of the spaghetti to try it. Robert was watching her, from time to time. He would have said he was watching to see if she was in any kind of trouble, if she seemed numb, or strange, or showed a quiver, if she dropped things or made the pots clatter. But in fact he was watching her just because there was no sign of such difficulty and because he knew there wouldn't be. She was preparing an ordinary meal, listening to the boys in her usual mildly censorious but unruffled way. The only thing more apparent than usual to Robert was her gracefulness, lightness, quickness, and ease around the kitchen.

Her tone to her sons, under its severity, seemed shockingly serene.

'Kevin, go and get some clothes on, if you want to eat at the table.'

'I can eat in my pajamas.'

'No.'

'I can eat in bed.'

'Not spaghetti, you can't.'

While they were washing up the pots and pans together—Clayton had gone for his run and Kevin was talking to Shanna on the phone—Peg told Robert her part of the story. He didn't ask her to, in so many words. He started off with 'So when you went over, the door wasn't locked?' and she began to tell him.

'You don't mind talking about it?' Robert said.

'I knew you'd want to know.'

She told him she knew what was wrong—at least, she knew that something was terribly wrong—before she started up the stairs.

'Were you frightened?'

'No. I didn't think about it like that—being frightened.'

'There could have been somebody up there with a gun.'

'No. I knew there wasn't. I knew there wasn't anybody but me alive in the house. Then I saw his leg, I saw his leg stretched out into the hall, and I knew then, but I had to go on in and make sure.'

Robert said, 'I understand that.'

'It wasn't the foot he had taken the shoe off that was out there. He took the shoe off his other foot, so he could use that foot to pull the trigger when he shot himself. That was how he did it.'

Robert knew all about that already, from the talk in the diner.

'So,' said Peg. 'That's really about all.'

She shook dishwater from her hands, dried them, and, with a critical look, began rubbing in lotion.

Clayton came in at the side door. He stamped the snow from his shoes and ran up the steps.

'You should see the cars,' he said. 'Stupid cars all crawling along this street. Then they have to turn around at the end and crawl back. I wish they'd get stuck. I stood out there and gave them dirty looks, but I started to freeze so I had to come in.'

'It's natural,' Robert said. 'It seems stupid but it's natural. They can't believe it, so they want to see where it happened.'

'I don't see their problem,' Clayton said. 'I don't see why they can't believe it. Mom could believe it all right. Mom wasn't surprised.'

'Well, of course I was,' Peg said, and this was the first time Robert had noticed any sort of edge to her voice. 'Of course I was surprised, Clayton. Just because I didn't break out screaming.'

'You weren't surprised they could do it.'

'I hardly knew them. We hardly knew the Weebles.'

'I guess they had a fight,' said Clayton.

'We don't know that,' Peg said, stubbornly working the lotion into her skin. 'We don't know if they had a fight, or what.'

'When you and Dad used to have those fights?' Clayton said. 'Remember, after we first moved to town? When he would be home? Over by the car wash? When you used to have those fights, you know what I used to think? I used to think one of you was going to come and kill me with a knife.'

'That's not true,' said Peg.

'It is true. I did.'

Peg sat down at the table and covered her mouth with her hands. Clayton's mouth twitched. He couldn't seem to stop it, so he turned it into a little, taunting, twitching smile.

'That's what I used to lie in bed and think.'

'Clayton. We would never either one of us ever have hurt you.'

Robert believed it was time that he said something.

'What this is like,' he said, 'it's like an earthquake or a volcano. It's that kind of happening. It's a kind of fit. People can take a fit like the earth takes a fit. But it only happens once in a long while. It's a freak occurrence.'

'Earthquakes and volcanoes aren't freaks,' said Clayton, with a certain dry pleasure. 'If you want to call that a fit, you'd have to call it a periodic fit. Such as people have, married people have.'

'We don't,' said Robert. He looked at Peg as if waiting for her to agree with him.

But Peg was looking at Clayton. She who always seemed

pale and silky and assenting, but hard to follow as a watermark in fine paper, looked dried out, chalky, her outlines fixed in steady, helpless, unapologetic pain.

'No,' said Clayton. 'No, not you.'

Robert told them that he was going for a walk. When he got outside, he saw that Clayton was right. There were cars nosing along the street, turning at the end, nosing their way back again. Getting a look. Inside those cars were just the same people, probably the very same people, he had been talking to during the afternoon. But now they seemed joined to their cars, making some new kind of monster that came poking around in a brutally curious way.

To avoid them, he went down a short dead-end street that branched off theirs. No houses had ever been built on this street, so it was not ploughed. But the snow was hard, and easy to walk on. He didn't notice how easy it was to walk on until he realised that he had gone beyond the end of the street and up a slope, which was not a slope of the land at all, but a drift of snow. The drift neatly covered the fence that usually separated the street from the field. He had walked over the fence without knowing what he was doing. The snow was that hard.

He walked here and there, testing. The crust took his weight without a whisper or a crack. It was the same everywhere. You could walk over the snowy fields as if you were walking on cement. (This morning, looking at the snow, hadn't he thought of marble?) But this paving was not flat. It rose and dipped in a way that had not much to do with the contours of the ground underneath. The snow created its own landscape, which was sweeping, in a grand and arbitrary style.

Instead of walking around on the ploughed streets of town, he could walk over the fields. He could cut across to the diner on the highway, which stayed open until midnight. He would have a cup of coffee there, turn around, and walk home.

One night, about six months before Robert married Peg, he and Lee were sitting drinking in his apartment. They were having an argument about whether it was permissible, or sickening, to have your family initial on your silverware. All of a sudden, the argument split open—Robert couldn't remember how, but it split open, and they found themselves saying the cruellest things to each other that they could imagine. Their voices changed from the raised pitch and speed of argument, and they spoke quietly with a subtle loathing.

'You always make me think of a dog,' Lee said. 'You always make me think of one of those dogs that push up on people and paw them, with their big disgusting tongues hanging out. You're so eager. All your friendliness and eagerness—that's really aggression. I'm not the only one who thinks this about you. A lot of people avoid you. They can't stand you. You'd be surprised. You push and paw in that eager pathetic way, but you have a calculating look. That's why I don't care if I hurt you.'

'Maybe I should tell you one of the things I don't like, then,' said Robert reasonably. 'It's the way you laugh. On the phone particularly. You laugh at the end of practically every sentence. I used to think it was a nervous tic, but it always really annoyed me. And I've figured out why. You're always telling somebody about what a raw deal you're getting somewhere or some unkind thing a person said to you—that's about two-thirds of your horrendously boring self-centred conversation. And then you laugh. Ha-ha, you can take it, you don't expect anything better. That laugh is sick.'

After some more of this, they started to laugh themselves, Robert and Lee, but it was not the laughter of a breakthrough into reconciliation; they did not fall upon each other in relief, crying, 'What rot, I didn't mean it, did you mean it?' ('No, of course not, of course I didn't mean it.') They laughed in recognition of their extremity, just as they might have laughed at another time, in the middle of quite different, astoundingly tender declarations. They trembled with murderous pleasure, with the excitement of saying what could never be retracted; they exulted in wounds inflicted but also in wounds received, and one or the other said at some point, 'This is the first time we've spoken the truth since we've known each other!' For even things that came to them more or less on the spur of the moment seemed the most urgent truths that had been hardening for a long time and pushing to get out.

It wasn't so far from laughing to making love, which they did, all with no retraction. Robert made barking noises, as a dog should, and nuzzled Lee in a bruising way, snapping with real appetite at her flesh. Afterward they were enormously and finally sick of each other but no longer disposed to blame.

'There are things I just absolutely and eternally want to forget about,' Robert had told Peg. He talked to her about cutting his losses, abandoning old bad habits, old deceptions and self-deceptions, mistaken notions about life, and about himself. He said that he had been an emotional spendthrift, had thrown himself into hopeless and painful entanglements as a way of avoiding anything that had normal possibilities. That was all experiment and posturing, rejection of the ordinary, decent contracts of life. So he said to her. Errors of avoidance, when he had thought he was running risks and getting intense experiences.

'Errors of avoidance that I mistook for errors of passion,' he said, then thought that he sounded pretentious when he was actually sweating with sincerity, with the effort and the relief.

In return, Peg gave him facts.

We lived with Dave's parents. There was never enough hot water for the baby's wash. Finally we got out and came to town and we lived beside the car wash. Dave was only with us weekends then. It was very noisy, especially at night. Then Dave got another job, he went up North, and I rented this place.

Errors of avoidance, errors of passion. She didn't say.

Dave had a kidney problem when he was little and he was out of school a whole winter. He read a book about the Arctic. It was probably the only book he ever read that he didn't have to. Anyway, he always dreamed about it; he wanted to go there. So finally he did.

A man doesn't just drive further and further away in his trucks until he disappears from his wife's view. Not even if he has always dreamed of the Arctic. Things happen before he goes. Marriage knots aren't going to slip apart painlessly, with the pull of distance. There's got to be some wrenching and slashing. But she didn't say, and he didn't ask, or even think much about that, till now.

He walked very quickly over the snow crust, and when he reached the diner he found that he didn't want to go in yet. He would cross the highway and walk a little further, then go into the diner to get warmed up on his way home.

By the time he was on his way home, the police car that was parked at the diner ought to be gone. The night constable was in there now, taking his break. This was not the same man Robert had seen and listened to when he dropped in on his way home from Keneally. This man would not have seen anything at first hand. He hadn't talked to Peg. Nevertheless he would be talking about it, everybody in the diner would be talking about it, going over the same scene and the same questions, the possibilities. No blame to them.

When they saw Robert, they would want to know how Peg was.

There was one thing he was going to ask her, just before Clayton came in. At least, he was turning the question over in his mind, wondering if it would be all right to ask her. A discrepancy, a detail, in the midst of so many abominable details.

And now he knew it wouldn't be all right; it would never be all right. It had nothing to do with him. One discrepancy, one detail—one lie—that would never have anything to do with him.

Walking on this magic surface, he did not grow tired. He grew lighter, if anything. He was taking himself further and further away from town, although for a while he didn't realise this. In the clear air, the lights of Gilmore were so bright they seemed only half a field away, instead of half a mile, then a mile and a half, then two miles. Very fine flakes of snow, fine as dust, and glittering, lay on the crust that held him. There was a glitter, too, around the branches of the trees and bushes that he was getting closer to. It wasn't like the casing around twigs and delicate branches that an ice storm leaves. It was as if the wood itself had altered and begun to sparkle.

This is the very weather in which noses and fingers are frozen. But nothing felt cold.

He was getting quite close to a large woodlot. He was crossing a long slanting shelf of snow, with the trees ahead and to one side of him. Over there, to the side, something caught his eye. There was a new kind of glitter under the trees. A congestion of shapes, with black holes in them, and unmatched arms or petals reaching up to the lower branches of the trees. He headed towards these shapes, but whatever they were did not become clear. They did not look like anything he knew. They did not look like anything, except perhaps a bit like armed giants half collapsed, frozen in combat, or like the jumbled towers of a crazy small-scale city—a space-age, small-scale city. He kept waiting for an explanation, and not getting one, until he got very close. He was so close he could almost have touched one of these monstrosities before he saw that they were just old cars. Old cars and trucks and even a school bus that had been pushed in under the trees and left. Some were completely overturned, and some were tipped over one another at odd angles. They were partly filled, partly covered, with snow. The black holes were their gutted insides. Twisted bits of chrome, fragments of headlights, were glittering.

He thought of himself telling Peg about this—how close he had to get before he saw that what amazed him and bewildered him so was nothing but old wrecks, and how he then felt disappointed, but also like laughing. They needed some new thing to talk about. Now he felt more like going home.

At noon, when the constable in the diner was giving his account, he had described how the force of the shot threw Walter Weeble backwards. 'It blasted him part ways out of the room. His head was laying out in the hall. What was left of it was laying out in the hall.'

Not a leg. Not the indicative leg, whole and decent in its trousers, the shod foot. That was not what anybody turning at the top of the stairs would see and would have to step over, step through, in order to go into the bedroom and look at the rest of what was there.

V. S. Pritchett
Blind Love

_____

'I'm beginning to be worried about Mr "Wolverhampton" Smith,' said Mr Armitage to Mrs Johnson, who was sitting in his study with her notebook on her knee and glancing from time to time at the window. She was watching the gardener's dog rooting in a flower bed. 'Would you read his letter again: the second paragraph about the question of a partnership?'

Since Mr Armitage was blind it was one of Mrs Johnson's duties to read his correspondence.

'He had the money—that is certain; but I can't make out on what conditions,' he said.

'I'd say he helped himself. He didn't put it into the business at Ealing—he used it to pay off the arrears on the place at Wolverhampton,' she said in her cheerful manner.

'I'm afraid you're right. It's his character I'm worried about,' said Mr Armitage.

'There isn't a single full stop in his letter—a full page on both sides. None. And all his words are joined together. It's like one word two pages long,' said Mrs Johnson.

'Is that so?' said Mr Armitage. 'I'm afraid he has an unpunctuated moral sense.'

Coming from a blind man whose open eyes and face had the fixed gleam of expression you might have seen on a piece of rock, the word 'unpunctuated' had a sarcasm unlike an ordinary sarcasm. It seemed, quite delusively, to come from a clearer knowledge than any available to the sighted.

'I think I'll go and smell out what he's like. Where is Leverton Grove? Isn't it on the way to the station? I'll drop in when I go up to London tomorrow morning,' said Mr Armitage.

The next morning he was driven in his Rolls-Royce to Mr Smith's house, one of two or three little villas that were part of a building speculation that had come to nothing fifty years before. The yellow-brick place was darkened by the firs that were thick in this district. Mrs Johnson, who had been brought up in London houses like this, winced at the sight of them. (Afterwards she said to Mr Armitage, 'It brings it back.' They were talking about her earlier life.) The chauffeur opened the car door, Mrs Johnson got out, saying 'No kerb', but Armitage waving her aside, stepped out unhelped and stood stiff with the sainted upward gaze of the blind; then, like an Army detail, the party made a sharp right turn, walked two paces, then a sharp left to the wooden gate, which the chauffeur opened, and went forward in step.

'Daffodils,' said Mrs Johnson, noting a flower bed. She was wearing blue to match her bold, practical eyes, and led the way up the short path to the door. It was opened before she rang by an elderly, sick-looking woman with swollen knuckles who half hid behind the door as she held it, to expose Smith standing with his grey jacket open, his hands in his pockets— the whole man an arrangement of soft smiles from his snowball head to his waistcoat, from his fly to his knees, sixteen stone of modest welcome with nothing to hide.

'It is good of you to come,' he said. He had a reverent voice.

'On my way to the station,' said Armitage.

Smith was not quite so welcoming to Mrs Johnson. He gave her a dismissive frown and glanced peremptorily at his wife.

'In here? said Mrs Johnson, briskly taking Armitage's arm in the narrow hall.

'Yes,' he said.

They all stood just inside the doorway of the front room. A fir tree darkened it. It had, Mrs Johnson recorded at once, two fenders in the fireplace, and two sets of fire-irons; then she saw two of everything—two clocks on the fireplace, two small sofas, a dining table folded up, even two carpets on the floor, for underneath the red one, there was the fringe of a worn yellow one.

Mr Smith saw that she noted this and, raising a grand chin and now unsmiling, said, 'We're sharing the 'ouse, the house, until we get into something bigger.'

And at this, Mrs Smith looked with the searching look of an agony in her eyes, begging Mrs Johnson for a word.

'Bigger,' echoed Mrs Smith and watched to see the word sink in. And then, putting her fingers over her face, she said, 'Much bigger,' and laughed.

'Perhaps,' said Mr Smith, who did not care for his wife's laugh, 'while we talk—er . . .'

'I'll wait outside in the car,' said the decisive Mrs Johnson, and when she was in the car she saw Mrs Smith's gaze of appeal from the step.

A half an hour later, the door opened and Mrs Johnson went to fetch Mr Armitage.

'At this time of the year the daffodils are wonderful round here,' said Armitage as he shook hands with Smith, to show that if he could not see there were a lot of things he knew. Mr Smith took the point and replaced his smiling voice with one of sportive yet friendly rebuke, putting Mr Armitage in his place.

'There is only one eye,' he stated as if reading aloud. 'The eye of God.'

Softly the Rolls drove off, with Mrs Smith looking at it fearfully from the edge of the window curtain.

'Very rum fellow,' said Armitage in the car. 'I'm afraid he's in a mess. The Inland Revenue are after him as well. He's quite happy because there's nothing to be got out of him. Remarkable. I'm afraid his friends have lost their money.'

Mrs Johnson was indignant.

'What's he going to do down here? He can't open up again.'

'He's come here,' Armitage said, 'because of the chalk in London water. The chalk, he says, gets into the system with the result that the whole of London is riddled with arthritis and nervous diseases. Or rather the whole of London is riddled with arthritis and nervous diseases because it believes in the reality of chalk. Now, chalk has no reality. We are not living on chalk or even on gravel: we dwell in God. Mr Smith explains that God led him to manage a chemist's shop in Wolverhampton, and to open one of his own in Ealing without capital. He now realises that he was following his own will, not the will of God. He is now doing God's work. Yesterday he had a cable from California. He showed it to me. "Mary's cancer cured gratitude cheque follows." He's a faith healer.'

'He ought to be in jail,' said Mrs Johnson.

'Oh, no. He's in heaven,' said Armitage. 'I'm glad I went to see him. I didn't know about his religion, but it's perfect: you get witnesses like him in court every day, always moving on to higher things.'

The Rolls arrived at the station and Mr Armitage picked up his white stick.

'Cancer today. Why not blindness tomorrow? Eh?' he said. Armitage gave one low laugh from a wide mouth. And though she enjoyed his dryness, his rare laugh gave a dangerous animal expression to a face that was usually closed. He got out of the car and she watched him walk into the booking hall and saw knots of people divide to make way for him on the platform.

In the damp town at the bottom of the hills, in the shops, at the railway station where twice a week the Rolls waited for him to come back from London, it was agreed that Armitage was a wonder. A gentleman, of course, they said; he's well-off, that helps. And there is that secretary-housekeeper, Mrs Johnson. That's how he can keep up his legal business. He takes his stick to London, but down here he never uses it. In London he has his lunch in his office or in his club, and can manage the club stairs which worry some of the members when they come out of the bar. He knows what's in the papers—ever had an argument with him?—of course Mrs Johnson reads them to him.

All true. His house stood, with a sudden flash of Edwardian prosperity, between two larch coppices on a hill five miles out and he could walk out on to the brick terrace and smell the lavender in its season and the grass of the lawns that went steeply down to his rose garden and the blue tiles of his swimming pool boxed in by yew.

'Fabian Tudor. Bernard Shaw used to come here—before our time, of course,' he would say, disparaging the high, panelled hall. He was really referring to his wife, who had left him when he was going blind twenty-two years ago. She had chosen and furnished the house. She liked leaded windows, brass, plain velvet curtains, Persian carpets, brick fireplaces and the expensive smell of wood smoke.

'All fake,' he would say, 'like me.'

You could see that pride made him like to embarrass. He seemed to know the effect of jokes from a dead face. But, in fact, if he had no animation—Mrs Johnson had soon perceived in her commonsensical way—this was because he was not affected, as people are, by the movements on other faces. Our faces, she had learned from Armitage, threw their lives away every minute. He stored his. She knew this because she stored hers. She did not put it like this, in fact what she said appeared to contradict it. She liked a joke.

'It's no good brooding. As Mother used to say, as long as you've got your legs you can give yourself an airing.'

Mrs Johnson had done this. She had fair hair, a good figure, and active legs, but usually turned her head aside when she was talking, as if to an imaginary friend. Mrs Johnson had needed an airing very badly when she came to work for Mr Armitage.

At their first interview—he met her in the panelled hall: 'You do realise, don't you, that I am totally blind. I have been blind for more than twenty years,' he said.

'Yes,' she said. 'I was told by Dr James.' She had been working for a doctor in London.

He held out his hand and she did not take it at once. It was not her habit to shake hands with people; now, as always, when she gave in she turned her head away. He held her hand for a long time and she knew he was feeling the bones. She had heard that the blind do this, and she took a breath as if to prevent her bones or her skin passing any knowledge of herself to him. But she could feel her dry hand coming to life and she drew it away. She was surprised that, at the touch, her nervousness had gone.

To her, Armitage's house was a wonderful place. The space, the light made friendly by the small panes of the tall leaded windows, charmed her.

'Not a bit like Peckham,' she said cheerfully.

Mr Armitage took her through the long sitting-room, where there were yellow roses in a bowl, into his study. He had been playing a record and put it off.

'Do you like music?' he said. 'That was Mozart.'

'I like a bit of a singsong,' she said. 'I can't honestly say I like the classical stuff.'

He took her round the house, stopped to point to a picture or two and, once more down in the long room, took her to a window and said, 'This is a bad day for it. The haze hasn't lifted. On a clear day you can see Sevenham Cathedral. It's twelve miles away. Do you like the country?'

'Frankly I've never tried it.'

'Are you a widow, Mrs Johnson?'

'No. I changed my name from Thompson to Johnson and not for the better. I divorced my husband,' said Mrs Johnson crisply.

'Will you read something to me—out of the paper?' he said. 'A court case.'

She read and read.

'Go on,' he said. 'Pick out something livelier.'

'Lonely monkeys at the zoo?'

'That will do.'

She read again and she laughed.

'Good,' he said.

'As Father used to say, "Speak up . . ." ' she began, but stopped. Mr Armitage did not want to hear what Father said.

'Will you allow me,' Armitage said, getting up from his desk, 'would you allow me to touch your face?'

Mrs Johnson had forgotten that the blind sometimes asked this.

She did not answer at once. She had been piqued from the beginning because he could not see her. She had been to the hairdresser's. She had bought a blouse with a high-frilled neck which was meant to set off the look of boyish impudence and frankness of her face. She had forgotten about touch. She feared he would have a pleading look, but she saw that the wish was part of an exercise for him. He clearly expected her to make no difficulty about it.

'All right,' she said, but she meant him to notice the pause, 'if you want to.'

She faced him and did not flinch as his hand lightly touched her brow and cheek and chin. He was, she thought, 'after her bones,' not her skin, and that, though she stiffened with resistance, was 'OK by her'. But when, for a second, the hand seemed about to rest on her jaw, she turned her head.

'I weigh eight stone,' she said in her bright way.

'I would have thought less,' he said. That was the nearest he came to a compliment. 'It was the first time,' she said afterwards to her friend Marge in the town, 'that I ever heard of a secretary being bought by weight.'

She had been his secretary and housekeeper for a long time now. She had understood him at once. The saintly look was nonsense. He was neither a saint nor a martyr. He was very vain; especially he was vain of never being deceived, though in fact his earlier secretaries had not been a success. There had been three or four before her. One of them— the cook told her—imagined him to be a martyr because she had a taste for martyrdom and drank to gratify it; another yearned to offer the compassion he hated, and muddled everything. One reckoning widow lasted only a month. Blatantly she had added up his property and wanted to marry him. The last, a 'lady', helped herself to the household money, behind a screen of wheezing grandeur and name-dropping.

Remembering the widow, the people who came to visit Mr Armitage when he gave a party were relieved after their meeting with Mrs Johnson.

'A good honest-to-God Cockney' or 'Such a cheery soul'. 'Down to earth,' they said. She said she had 'knocked about a bit.' 'Yes, sounds as if she had': they supposed they were denigrating. She was obviously not the kind of woman who would have any dangerous appeal to an injured man. And she, for her part, would go to the pictures when she had time off or simply flop down in a chair at the house of her friend Marge and say, 'Whew, Marge. His nibs has gone to London. Give me a strong cuppa. Let's relax.'

'You're too conscientious.'

'Oh, I don't mind the work. I like it. It occupies your mind. He has interesting cases. But sometimes I get keyed up.'

Mrs Johnson could not herself describe what 'keyed her up'—perhaps being on the watch? Her mind was stretched. She found herself translating the world to him and it took her time to realise that it did not matter that she was not 'educated up to it'. He obviously liked her version of the world, but it was a strain having versions. In the mornings she had to read his letters. This bothered her. She was very moral about privacy. She had to invent an impersonal, uninterested voice. His lack of privacy irked her; she liked gossip and news as much as any woman, but here it lacked the salt of the secret, the whispered, the found out. It was all information and statement. Armitage's life was an abstraction for him. He had to know what he could not see. What she liked best was reading legal documents to him.

He dressed very well and it was her duty to see that his clothes were right. For an orderly, practical mind like hers, the order in which he lived was a new pleasure. They lived under fixed laws: no chair or table, even no ashtray must be moved. Everything must be in its place. There must be no hazards. This was understandable: the ease with which he moved without accident in the house or garden depended on it. She did not believe when he said, 'I can hear things before I get to them. A wall can shout, you know.' When visitors came she noticed he stood in a fixed spot: he did not turn his head when people spoke to him and among all the head-turning and gesturing he was the still figure, the lawgiver. But he was very cunning. If someone described a film they had seen, he was soon talking as if he had been there. Mrs Johnson, who had duties when he had visitors, would smile to herself, at the surprise on the faces of people who had not noticed the quickness with which he collected every image or scene or character described. Sometimes, a lady would say to her, 'I do think he's absolutely marvellous', and, if he overheard this— and his hearing was acute—Mrs Johnson would notice a look of ugly boredom on his face. He was, she noted, particularly vain of his care of money and accounts. This pleased Mrs Johnson because she was quick to understand that here a blind man who had servants might be swindled. She was indignant about the delinquency of her predecessor. He must have known he was being swindled.

Once a month Mrs Johnson would go through the accounts with him. She would make out the cheques and take them to his study and put them on his desk.

The scene that followed always impressed her. She really admired him for this. How efficient and devious he was! He placed the cheque at a known point on his blotter. The blunt fingers of his hairless hands had the art of gliding and never groping, knowing the inches of distance; and then, as accurately as a geometrician, he signed. There might be a pause as the fingers secretly measured, a pause alarming to her in the early days, but now no longer alarming; sometimes she detected a shade of cruelty in this pause. He was listening for a small gasp of anxiety as she watched.

There was one experience which was decisive for her. It occurred in the first month of her employment and had the lasting stamp of a revelation. (Later on, she thought he had staged the incident in order to show her what his life was like and to fix in her mind the nature of his peculiar authority.) She came into the sitting-room one evening in the winter to find a newspaper and heard sharp, unbelievable sounds coming from his study. The door was open and the room was in darkness. She went to it, switched on the light, and saw he was sitting there typing in the darkness. Well, she could have done that if she had been put to it—but now she *saw* that for him there was no difference between darkness and light.

'Overtime, I see,' she said, careful not to show surprise.

This was when she saw that his mind was a store of maps and measured things; a store of sounds and touches and smells that became an enormous translated paraphernalia.

'You'd feel sorry for a man like that,' her friend Marge said.

'He'd half kill you if you showed you were sorry,' Mrs Johnson said. 'I don't feel sorry. I really don't.'

'Does he ever talk about his wife?'

'No.'

'A terrible thing to do to leave a man because he's blind.'

'She had a right to her life, hadn't she?' said Mrs Johnson flatly. 'Who would want to marry a blind man?'

'You are hard,' Marge said.

'It's not my business,' said Mrs Johnson. 'If you start pitying people you end up by hating them. I've seen it. I've been married, don't forget.'

'I just wish you had a more normal life, dear.'

'It suits me,' said Mrs Johnson.

'He ought to be very grateful to you.'

'Why should he be? I do my job. Gratitude doesn't come into it. Let's go and play tennis.'

The two women went out and played tennis in the park and Mrs Johnson kept her friend running from court to court.

'I smell tennis balls and grass,' said Mr Armitage when she returned.

In the March of her third year a bad thing happened. The

winter was late. There was a long spell of hard frost and you
could see the cathedral tower clearly over the low-lying woods
on most days. The frost coppered the lawns and scarcely faded
in the middle of the day. The hedges were spiked and white.
She had moved her typing table into the sitting-room close
to the window to be near a radiator and when she changed a page
she would glance out at the garden. Mr Armitage was out there
somewhere and she had got into the habit of being on the
watch. Now she saw him walk down the three lawns and find
the brick steps that led to the swimming pool. It was enclosed
by a yew hedge and was frozen over. She could see Armitage
at the far side of it pulling at a small fallen branch that had been
caught by the ice. His foot had struck it. On the other side of
the hedge, the gardener was cutting cabbage in the kitchen
garden and his dog was snuffling about. Suddenly a rabbit ran
out, ears down, and the dog was yelping after it. The rabbit ran
through the hedge and almost over Armitage's feet with the
dog nearly on it. The gardener shouted. The next moment
Armitage, who was squatting, had the dog under his legs, lost
his balance, and fell full length through the ice into the pool.
Mrs Johnson saw this. She saw the gardener drop his knife and
run to the gap in the hedge to help Armitage out. He was
clambering over the side. She saw him wave the gardener's
hand away and shout at him and the gardener step away as
Armitage got out. He stood clawing weed off his face, out of
his hair, wringing his sleeves and brushing ice off his shirt as he
marched back fast up the garden. He banged the garden door
in a rage as he came in.

'That bloody man. I'll have that dog shot,' shouted Armitage. She hurried to meet him. He had pulled off his jacket and
thrown it on a chair. Water ran off his trousers and sucked in
his shoes. Mrs Johnson was appalled.

'Go and change your things quickly,' she said. And she easily raced him to the stairs to the landing and to his room. By the time he got there she had opened several drawers, looking for underclothes, and had pulled out a suit from his cupboard. Which suit? She pulled out another. He came squelching after her into the room.

'Towel,' she cried. 'Get it all off. You'll get pneumonia.'

'Get out. Leave me alone,' shouted Armitage, who had been tugging his shirt over his head as he came upstairs.

She saw then that she had done a terrible thing. By opening drawers and putting clothes on the bed, she had destroyed one of his systems. She saw him grope. She had never seen him do this before. His bare white arms stretched out in a helpless way and his brown hands pitiably closed on air. The action was slow and his fingers frightened her.

'I told you to leave me alone,' he shouted.

She saw she had humiliated him. She had broken one of the laws. For the first time she had been incompetent.

Mrs Johnson went out and quietly shut the door. She walked across the landing to the passage in the wing where her own room was, looking at the wet marks of his muddy shoes on the carpet, each one accusing her. She sat down on the edge of her bed. How could she have been such a fool! How could she have forgotten his rule? Half naked to the waist, hairy on the chest and arms, he shocked because the rage seemed to be not in his mind but in his body like an animal's. The rage had the pathos of an animal's. Perhaps when he was alone he often groped; perhaps the drilled man she was used to, who came out of his bedroom or his study, was the expert survival of a dozen concealed disasters?

Mrs Johnson sat on her bed listening. She had never known Armitage to be angry; he was a monotonously considerate man. The shout abashed her and there was a strange pleasure in being abashed; but her mistake was not a mere mistake. She saw that it struck at the foundation of his life and was so gross that the surface of her own confidence was cracked. She was a woman who could reckon on herself, but now her mind was scattered. Useless to say to herself, 'What a fuss about nothing,' or 'Keep calm.' Or, about him, 'Nasty temper.' His shout, 'Get out. I told you to leave me alone,' had, without reason (except that a trivial shame is a spark that sets fire to a long string of greater shames), burned out all the security of her present life.

She had heard those words, almost exactly those words, before. Her husband had said them. A week after their wedding.

Well, *he* had had something to shout about, poor devil. She admitted it. Something a lot more serious than falling into a pool and having someone commit the crime of being kind to you and hurting your silly little pride.

She got up from the bed and turned on the tap of the washbasin to cool down her hot face and wash her hands of the dirt of the jacket she had brought upstairs. She took off her blouse and as she sluiced her face she looked through the water at herself in the mirror. There was a small birthmark the size of a red leaf which many people noticed and which, as it showed over the neck of the high blouses she usually wore, had the enticement of some signal or fancy of the blood; but under it, and invisible to them, were two smaller ones and then a great spreading ragged liver-coloured island of skin which spread under the tape of her slip and crossed her breast and seemed to end in a curdle of skin below it. She was stamped with an ineradicable bloody insult. It might have been an attempt to impose another woman on her. She was used to seeing it, but she carried it about with her under her clothes, hiding it and yet vaunting.

Now she was reaching for a towel and inside the towel, as she dried herself, she was talking to Armitage.

'If you want to know what shame and pride are, what about marrying a man who goes plain sick at the sight of your body and who says "You deceived me. You didn't tell me".'

She finished drying her face and put the towel on the warm rail and went to her dressing table. The hairbrush she picked up had been a wedding present and at each hard stroke of the brush on her lively fair hair, her face put up a fight, but it exhausted her. She brushed the image of Armitage away and she was left staring at the half-forgotten but never-forgotten self she had been.

How could she have been such a fool as to deceive her husband? It was not through wickedness. She had been blinded too—blinded by love; in a way, love had made her so full of herself that perhaps she had never seen *him*. And her deceptions: she could not stop herself smiling at them, but they were really pitiable because she was so afraid of losing him and to lose him would be to lose this new beautifully deluded self. She ought to have told him. There were chances. For example, in his flat with the grey sofa with the spring that bit your bottom going clang, clang at every kiss, when he used to carry on about her wearing dresses that a man couldn't get a hand into. He knew very well she had had affairs with men, but why, when they were both 'worked up', wouldn't she undress and go to the bedroom? The sofa was too short. She remembered how shocked his face looked when she pulled up her skirts and lay on the floor. She said she believed in sex before marriage, but she thought some things ought to wait: it would be wrong for him to see her naked before their wedding day. And to show him she was no prude—there was that time they pretended to be looking out of the window at a cricket match; or Fridays in his office when the staff was gone and the cleaners were only at the end of the passage.

'You've got a mole on your neck,' he said one day.

'Mother went mad with wanting plums when she was carrying me. It's a birthmark.'

'It's pretty,' he said and kissed it.

He kissed it. He kissed it. She clung to that when after the wedding they got to the hotel and she hid her face in his shoulder and let him pull down the zip of her dress. She stepped away, and pretending to be shy, she undressed under her slip. At last the slip came off over her head. They both looked at each other, she with brazen fear and he—she couldn't forget the shocked blank disgust on his face. From the neck over the left shoulder down to the breast and below, and spreading like a red tongue to the back was this ugly blob—dark as blood, like a ragged liver on a butcher's window, or some obscene island with ragged edges. It was as if a bucket of paint had been thrown over her.

'You didn't tell me,' he said. If only she had told him, but how could she have done? She knew she had been cursed.

'That's why you wouldn't undress, you little hypocrite.'

He himself was in his underpants with his trousers on the bed and with his cuff links in his hand, which made his words absurd and awful. His ridiculous look made him tragic and his hatred frightening. It was terrible that for two hours while they talked he did not undress and worse that he gave her a dressing gown to cover herself. She heard him going through the catalogue of her tricks.

'When ...' he began in a pathetic voice. And then she screamed at him.

'What do you think? Do you think I got it done, that I got myself tattooed in the Waterloo Road? I was born like it.'

'Ssh,' he said. 'You'll wake the people in the next room.'

'Let them hear. I'll go and show them,' she screamed. It was kind of him to put his arm round her. When she had recovered, she put on her fatal, sporty manner. 'Some men like it,' she said.

He hit her across the face. It was not then but in the following weeks when pity followed and pity turned to cruelty he had said, 'Get out. Leave me alone.'

Mrs Johnson went to her drawer and got out a clean blouse.

Her bedroom in Armitage's house was a pretty one, far prettier than any she had ever had. Up till now she had been used to bed-sitters since her marriage. But was it really the luxury of the house and the power she would have in it that had weighed with her when she had decided to take on this strange job? She understood now something else had moved her in the low state she had been in when she came. As a punished and self-hating person she was drawn to work with a punished man. It was a return to her girlhood: injury had led her to injury.

She looked out of the window at the garden. The diamond panes chopped up the sight of the frozen lawns and the firs that were frost-whiskered. She was used to the view. It was a view of the real world; that, after all, was her world, not his. She saw that gradually in three years she had drifted out of it and had taken to living in Armitage's filed memory. If he said, for example, 'That rambler is getting wild. It must be cut back,' because a thorn caught his jacket, or if he made his famous remark about seeing the cathedral on a clear day, the landscape limited itself to these things and in general reduced itself to the imposed topographical sketch in his mind. She had allowed him, as a matter of abnegation and duty, to impose his world on hers. Now this shock brought back a lost sense of the right to her own landscape; and then to the protest that this country was not hers at all. The country bored her. The fir trees bored her. The lanes bored her. The view from this window or the tame protected view of the country from the Rolls-Royce window bored her. She wanted to go back to London, to the streets, the buses and the crowds, to crowds of people with eyes in their heads. And—her spirits rising—'To hell with it, I want people who can *see* me.'

She went downstairs to give orders for the carpet to be brushed.

In the sitting-room she saw the top of Armitage's dark head. She had not heard him go down. He was sitting in what she called the cathedral chair facing the window and she was forced to smile when she saw a bit of green weed sticking to his hair. She also saw a heavy glass ashtray had fallen off the table beside him. 'Clumsy,' she said. She picked it up and lightly pulled off the piece of weed from his hair. He did not notice this.

'Mr Armitage,' she said in her decisive manner, 'I lost my head. I'm sorry.'

He was silent.

'I understand how you feel,' she said. For this (she had decided in her room) was the time for honesty and for having things out. The impersonality could not go on, as it had done for three years.

'I want to go back to London,' she said.

'Don't be a damn fool,' he said.

Well, she was not going to be sworn at. 'I'm not a damn fool,' she said. 'I understand your situation.' And then, before she could stop herself, her voice shaking and loud, she broke out with: 'I know what humiliation is.'

'Who is humiliated?' said Armitage. 'Sit down.'

'I am not speaking about you,' she said stiffly.

That surprised him, she saw, for he turned his head.

'I'm sorry, I lost my temper,' he said. 'But that stupid fellow and his dog . . .'

'I am speaking about myself,' she said. 'We have our pride, too.'

'Who is *we*?' he said, without curiosity.

'Women,' she said.

He got up from his chair, and she stepped back. He did not move and she saw that he really had not recovered from the fall in the pool, for he was uncertain. He was not sure where the table was.

'Here,' he said roughly, putting out a hand. 'Give me a hand out of this.'

She obediently took him by the arm and stood him clear of the table.

'Listen to me. You couldn't help what happened and neither could I. There's nothing to apologise for. You're not leaving. We get on very well. Take my advice. Don't be hard on yourself.'

'It is better to be hard,' she said. 'Where would you have been if you had not been hard? I'm not a girl. I'm thirty-nine.' He moved towards her and put his hand on her right shoulder and she quickly turned her head. He laughed and said, 'You've brushed your hair back.' He knew. He always knew.

She watched him make for his study and saw him take the wrong course, brush against the sofa by the fireplace, and then a yard or two further, he shouldered the wall.

'Damn,' he said.

At dinner, conversation was difficult. He offered her a glass of wine which she refused. He poured himself a second glass and as he sat down he grimaced with pain.

'Did you hurt your back this afternoon?' she asked.

'No,' he said. 'I was thinking about my wife.'

Mrs Johnson blushed. He had scarcely ever mentioned his wife. She knew only what Marge Brook had told her of the town gossip: how his wife could not stand his blindness and had gone off with someone and that he had given her a lot of money. Someone said, ten thousand pounds. What madness!

In the dining-room Mrs Johnson often thought of all those notes flying about over the table and out of the window. He was too rich. Ten thousand pounds of hatred and rage, or love, or madness. In the first place, she wouldn't have touched it.

'She made me build the pool,' he said.

'A good idea,' she said.

'I don't know why. I never thought of throwing her into it,' he said.

Mrs Johnson said, 'Shall I read the paper?' She did not want to hear more about his wife.

Mrs Johnson went off to bed early. Switching on the radio in her room and then switching it off because it was playing classical music, she said to herself, 'Well, funny things bring things back. What a day!' and stepped yawning out of her skirt. Soon she was in bed and asleep.

An hour later she woke up, hearing her name.

'Mrs Johnson. The water got into my watch, would you set it for me?' He was standing there in his dressing gown.

'Yes,' she said. She was a woman who woke up alert and clear-headed.

'I'm sorry. I thought you were listening to a programme. I didn't know you were in bed,' he said. He was holding the watch to his ear.

'Would you set it for me and put my alarm right?' He had the habit of giving orders. They were orders spoken into space—and she was the space, nonexistent. He gave her the watch and went off. She put on her dressing gown and followed him to his room. He had switched on the light for her. She went to the bedside table and bent down to wind the clock. Suddenly she felt his arms round her, pulling her upright, and he was kissing her head. The alarm went off suddenly and she dropped the clock. It went on screeching on the floor at her feet.

'Mr Armitage,' she said in a low angry voice, but not struggling. He turned her round and he was trying to kiss her on the lips. At this she did struggle. She twisted her head this way and that to stop him, so that it was her head rather than her body that was resisting him. Her blue eyes fought with all their light, but his eyes were dead as stone.

'Really, Mr Armitage. Stop it,' she managed to mutter. 'The door is open. Cook will hear.'

She was angry at being kissed by a man who could not see her face, but she felt the shamed insulted woman in her, that blotched inhabitant, blaze up in her skin.

The bell of the alarm clock was weakening and then choked to a stop and in her pettish struggle she stepped on it; her slipper had come off.

'I've hurt my foot.' Distracted by the pain she stopped struggling, and Armitage took his opportunity and kissed her on the lips. She looked with pain into his sightless eyes. There was no help there. She was terrified of being drawn into the dark where he lived. And then the kiss seemed to go down her throat and spread into her shoulders, into her breasts and branch into all the veins and arteries of her body and it was the tongue of the shamed woman who had sprung up in her that touched his.

'What are you doing?' she was trying to say, but could only groan the words. When he touched the stained breast she struck back violently, saying, 'No, no.'

'Come to bed with me,' he said.

'Please let me go. I've hurt my foot.'

The surprising thing was that he did let her go, and as she sat panting and white in the face on the bed to look at her foot, she looked mockingly at him. She forgot that he could not see her mockery. He sat beside her but did not touch her and he was silent. There was no scratch on her foot. She picked up the clock and put it back on the table.

Mrs Johnson was proud of the adroitness with which she had kept men away from her since her marriage. It was a war with the inhabitant of the ragged island on her body. That creature craved for the furtive, for the hand that slipped under a skirt, for the scuffle in the back seat of a car, for a five-minute disappearance into a locked office.

But the other Mrs Johnson, the cheerful one, was virtuous. She took advantage of his silence and got quickly up to get away; she dodged past him, but he was quick too. He was at the closed door. For a moment she was wily. It would be easy for her to dodge him in the room. And then she saw once more the sight she could not bear that melted her more certainly than the kisses which had filled her mouth and throat: she saw his hands begin to open and search and grope in the air as he came towards the sound of her breathing. She could not move. His hand caught her. The woman inside her seemed to shout, 'Why not? You're all right. He cannot see.' In her struggle she had not thought of that. In three years he had made her forget that blindness meant not seeing.

'All right,' she said, and the virtue in Mrs Johnson pouted. She gently tapped his chest with her fingers and said with the sullenness of desire, 'I'll be back in a minute.'

It was a revenge: that was the pleasure.

'Dick,' she called to her husband, 'look at this,' when the man was on top of her. Revenge was the only pleasure and his excitement was soon over. To please him she patted him on the head as he lay beside her and said, 'You've got long legs.' And she nearly said, 'You are a naughty boy' and 'Do you feel better?' but she stopped herself and her mind went off on to what she had to do in the morning; she listened and wondered how long it would be before he would fall asleep and she could stealthily get away. Revenge astonished by its quickness.

She slyly moved. He knew at once and held her. She waited. She wondered where Dick was now. She wished she could tell him. But presently this blind man in the bed leaned up and put both his hands on her face and head and carefully followed the round of her forehead, the line of her brow, her nose and lips and chin, to the line of her throat and then to her nape and shoulders. She trembled, for after his hands had passed, what had been touched seemed to be new. She winced as his hand passed over the stained shoulder and breast and he paused, knowing that she winced, and she gave a groan of pleasure to deceive him; but he went on, as if he were modelling her, feeling the pit under the arms, the space of ribs and belly and the waist of which she was proud, measuring them, feeling their depth, the roundness of her legs, the bone in her knees until, throwing all clothes back, he was holding her ankle, the arch of her foot, and her toes. Her skin and her bones became alive. His hands knew her body as she had never known it. In her brief love affairs, which had excited her because of the risk of being caught, the first touch of a man stirred her at once and afterwards left her looking demurely at him; but she had let no one know her with a pedantry like his. She suddenly sat up and put her arms round him, and now she went wild. It was not a revenge now; it was a triumph. She lifted the sad breast to his lips. And when they lay back she kissed his chest and then— with daring—she kissed his eyes.

It was six o'clock before she left him, and when she got to her room the stained woman seemed to bloom like a flower. It was only after she had slept and saw her room in day-light again that she realised that once more she had deceived a man.

It was late. She looked out of the window and saw Armitage in his city clothes talking to the chauffeur in the garden. She watched them walk to the garage.

'OK,' she said dryly to defend herself. 'It was a rape.' During the day there would be moments when she could feel his hands moving over her skin. Her legs tingled. She posed as if she were a new-made statue. But as the day went on she hardened and instead of waiting for him to return she went into the town to see Marge.

'You've put your hair up,' Marge said.

'Do you like it?'

'I don't know. It's different. It makes you look severe. No, not severe. Something. Restless.'

'I am not going back to dinner this evening,' she said. 'I want a change. Leonard's gone to London.'

'Leonard!' said Marge.

Mrs Johnson wanted to confide in Marge, but Marge bored her. They ate a meal together and she ate fast. To Marge's astonishment she said, 'I must fly.'

'You *are* in a mood,' Marge said.

Mrs Johnson was unable to control a longing to see Armitage. When she got back to the house and saw him sitting by the fire she wanted him to get up and at least put his arms round her; but he did not move, he was listening to music. It was always the signal that he wanted to be alone.

'It is just ending,' said Armitage.

The music ended in a roll of drums.

'Do you want something, Helen?' he said.

She tried to be mocking, but her voice could not mock and she said seriously, 'About last night. It must not happen again. I don't want to be in a false position. I could not go on living in the house.'

She did not intend to say this; her voice, between rebuke and tenderness, betrayed this.

'Sit down.'

She did not move.

'I have been very happy here,' she said. 'I don't want to spoil it.'

'You are angry,' he said.

'No, I'm not,' she said.

'Yes, you are; that is why you were not here when I got back,' he said.

'You did not wait for me this morning,' she said. 'I was glad you didn't. I don't want it to go on.'

He came nearer to her and put his hand on her hair.

'I like the way your hair shows your ears,' he said. And he kissed them.

'Now, please,' she said.

'I love you,' he said and kissed her on the forehead and she did not turn her head.

'Do you? I'm glad you said that. I don't think you do. When something has been good, don't spoil it. I don't like love affairs,' she said.

And then she changed. 'It was a party. Good night.'

'You made me happy,' he said, holding on to her hand.

'Were you thinking about it a long time?' she said in another voice, lingering for one more word.

'Yes,' he said.

'It is very nice of you to say that. It is what you ought to say. But I mean what I said. Now, really, good night. And,' giving a pat to his arm, she said, 'keep your watch wound up.'

Two nights later he called to her loudly and curtly from the stairs: 'Mrs Johnson, where are you?' and when she came into the hall he said quietly, 'Helen.'

She liked that. They slept together again. They did not talk. Their life went on as if nothing had happened. She began to be vain of the stain on her body and could not resist silently displaying, almost taunting him, when she undressed, with what he could not see. She liked the play of deceiving him like this; she was paying him out for not being able to see her; and when she was ashamed of doing this the shame itself would rouse her desire: two women uniting in her. And fear roused her too; she was afraid of his blindness. Sometimes the fear was that the blind can see into the mind. It often terrified her at the height of her pleasure that she was being carried into the dark where he lived. She knew she was not but she could not resist the excitement of imagining it. Afterwards she would turn her back to him, ashamed of her fancies, and as his finger followed the bow of her spine she would drive away the cynical thought that he was just filing this affair away in one of the systems of his memory.

Yet she liked these doubts. How dead her life had been in its practical certainties. She liked the tenderness and violence of sexual love, the simple kindness of the skin. She once said to him, 'My skin is your skin.' But she stuck to it that she did not love him and that he did not love her. She wanted to be simply a body: a woman like Marge who was always talking about love seemed to her a fool. She liked it that she and Armitage were linked to each other only by signs. And she became vain of her disfigurement, and looking at it, even thought of it as the lure.

I know what would happen to me if I got drunk, she thought at one of Armitage's cocktail parties, I'm the sort of woman who would start taking her clothes off. When she was a young woman she had once started doing so, and someone, thank God, stopped her.

But these fancies were bravado.

They were intended to stop her from telling him.

On Sundays Mrs Johnson went to church in the village near the house. She had made a habit of it from the beginning, because she thought it the proper thing to do: to go to church had made her feel she need not reproach herself for impropriety in living in the same house as a man. It was a practical matter: before her love affair the tragic words of the service had spoken to her evil. If God had done this to her, He must put up with the sight of her in His house. She was not a religious woman; going to church was an assertion that she had as much right to fair play as anyone else. It also stopped her from being 'such a fool' as to fall to the temptation of destroying her new wholeness by telling him. It was 'normal' to go to church and normality had been her craving ever since her girlhood. She had always taken her body, not her mind, to church.

Armitage teased her about her churchgoing when she first came to work for him; but lately his teasing became sharper: 'Going to listen to Dearly Beloved Brethren?' he would say.

'Oh, leave him alone,' she said.

He had made up a tale about her being in love with the vicar; at first it was a joke, but now there was a sharp edge to it. 'A very respectable man,' he said.

When the church bells rang on Sunday evening he said, 'He's calling to you.' She began to see that this joke had the grit of jealousy in it; not of the vicar, of course, but a jealousy of many things in her life.

'Why do you go there? I'd like to understand, seriously,' he said.

'I like to get out,' she said.

She saw pain on his face. There was never much movement in it beyond the deepening of two lines at the corners of his mouth; but when his face went really dead, it was as sullen as earth in the garden. In her sense, she knew, he never went out. He lived in a system of tunnels. She had to admit that when she saw the grey church she was glad, because it was not his house. She knew from gossip that neither he nor his wife had ever been to it.

There was something else in this new life; now he had freed her they were both more watchful of each other. One Sunday in April she saw his jealousy in the open. She had come in from church and she was telling him about the people who were there. She was sitting on the sofa beside him.

'How many lovers have you had?' he said. 'That doctor you worked for, now?'

'Indeed not,' she said. 'I was married.'

'I know you were married. But when you were working for those people in Manchester? And in Canada after the war?'

'No one else. That was just a trip.'

'I don't believe you.'

'Honestly, it's true.'

'In court I never believe a witness who says "Honestly".'

She blushed, for she had had three or four lovers, but she was defending herself. They were no business of his.

The subject became darker.

'Your husband,' he said. 'He saw you. They all saw you.'

She knew what he meant, and this scared her.

'My husband. Of course he saw me. Only my husband.'

'Ah, so there were others.'

'Only my husband saw me,' she said. 'I told you about it. How he walked out of the hotel after a week.'

This was a moment when she could have told him, but to see his jealousy destroy the happiness he had restored to her made her indignant.

'He couldn't bear the sight of me. He had wanted,' she invented, 'to marry another woman. He told me on the first night of our marriage. In the hotel. Please don't talk about it.'

'Which hotel was this?' he said.

The triviality of the question confused her. 'In Kensington.'

'What was the name?'

'Oh, I forget, the something Royal . . .'

'You don't forget.'

'I do honestly . . .'

'Honestly!' he said.

He was in a rage of jealousy. He kept questioning her about the hotel, the length of their marriage. He pestered for addresses, for dates, and tried to confuse her by putting his questions again and again.

'So he didn't leave you at the hotel!' he said.

'Look,' she said. 'I can't stand jealous men and I'm not going to be questioned like one of your clients.'

He did not move or shout. Her husband had shouted and paced up and down, waving his arms. This man sat bolt upright and still, and spoke in a dry, exacting voice.

'I'm sorry,' he said.

She took his hand, the hand that groped like a helpless tentacle and that had modelled her; it was the most disturbing and living thing about him.

'Are you still in love with your husband?'

'Certainly not.'

'He saw you and I have never seen you.' He circled again to his obsession.

'It is just as well. I'm not a beautiful woman,' she laughed. 'My legs are too short, my bottom is too big. You be grateful—my husband couldn't stand the sight of me.'

'You have a skin like an apple,' he said.

She pushed his hand away and said, 'Your hands know too much.'

'*He* had hands. And he had eyes,' he said in a voice grinding with violence.

'I'm very tired. I am going to bed,' she said. 'Good night.'

'You see,' he said. 'There is no answer.'

He picked up a Braille book and his hand moved fast over the sheets.

She went to her room and kicked off her shoes and stepped out of her dress.

I've been living in a dream, she thought. Just like Marge, who always thinks her husband's coming back every time the gate goes. It is a mistake, she thought, living in the same house.

The jealous fit seemed to pass. It was a fire, she understood, that flared up just as her shame used to flare, but two Sundays later the fit came on again. He must hate God, she thought, and pitied him. Perhaps the music that usually consoled him had tormented him. At any rate, he stopped it when she came in and put her prayer book on the table. There was a red begonia, which came from the greenhouse, on the table beside the sofa where he was sitting very upright, as if he had been waiting impatiently for her to come back.

'Come and sit down,' he said and began kindly enough. 'What was church like? Did they tell you what to do?'

'I was nearly asleep,' she said. 'After last night. Do you know what time it was?' She took his hand and laughed.

He thought about this for a while. Then he said, 'Give me your hands. No. Both of them. That's right. Now spit on them.'

'Spit!'

'Yes, that is what the church tells you.'

'What *are* you talking about?' she said, trying to get her hands away.

'Spit on them.' And he forced her hands, though not roughly, to her lips.

'What are you doing?' She laughed nervously and spat on her fingers.

'Now—rub the spittle on my eyes.'

'Oh, no,' she said.

He let go of her wrist.

'Do as I tell you. It's what your Jesus Christ did when he cured the blind man.'

He sat there waiting and she waited.

'He put dust or earth or something on them,' he said. 'Get some.'

'No,' she said.

'There's some here. Put your fingers in it,' he said shortly. She was frightened of him.

'In the pot,' he insisted as he held one of her wrists so that she could not get away. She dabbed her wet fingers in the earth of the begonia pot.

'Put it on my eyes.'

'I can't do that. I really can't,' she said.

'Put it on my eyes,' he said.

'It will hurt them.'

'They are hurt already,' he said. 'Do as I tell you.' She bent to him and, with disgust, she put her dirty fingers on the wet eyeballs. The sensation was horrible, and when she saw the dirty patches on his eyes, like two filthy smudges, she thought he looked like an ape.

'That is what you are supposed to do,' he said. Jealousy had made him mad.

I can't stay with a mad man, she thought. He's malicious. She did not know what to do, but he solved that for her. He reached for his Braille book. She got up and left him there. The next day he went to London.

His habits changed. He went several times into the nearby town on his own and she was relieved that he came back in a silent mood which seemed happy. The horrible scene went out of her mind. She had gone so far as to lock her bedroom door for several nights after that scene, but now she unlocked it. He had brought her a bracelet from London; she drifted into unguarded happiness. She knew so well how torment comes and goes.

It was full undreaming June, the leaves in the garden still undarkened, and for several days people were surprised when day after day the sun was up and hot and unclouded. Mrs Johnson went down to the pool. Armitage and his guests often tried to persuade her to go in but she always refused.

'They once tried to get me to go down to Peckham Baths when I was a kid, but I screamed,' she said.

The guests left her alone. They were snobbish about Peckham Baths.

But Mrs Johnson decided to become a secret bather. One afternoon when Armitage was in London and the cook and gardener had their day off, she went down with the gardener's dog. She wore a black bathing suit that covered her body and lowered herself by the steps into the water. Then she splashed at the shallow end of the pool and hung on to the rail while the dog barked at her. He stopped barking when she got out and sniffed round the hedge where she pulled down her bathing dress to her waist and lay down to get sun-drunk on her towel.

She was displaying herself to the sun, the sky and the trees. The air was like hands that played on her as Armitage did and she lay listening to the snuffles of the dog and the humming of the bees in the yew hedge. She had been there an hour when the dog barked at the hedge. She quickly picked up a towel and covered herself and called to the dog: 'What is it?'

He went on barking and then gave up and came to her. She sat down. Suddenly the dog barked again. Mrs Johnson stood up and tried to look through one of the thinner places in the hedge. A man who must have been close to the pool and who must have passed along the footpath from the lane, a path used only by the gardener, was walking up the lawns towards the house carrying a trilby hat in his hand. He was not the gardener. He stopped twice to get his breath and turned to look at the view. She recognised the smiling grey suit, the wide figure and snowball head: it was 'Wolverhampton' Smith. She waited and saw him go on to the house and ring a bell. Then he disappeared round the corner and went to the front of the house. Mrs Johnson quickly dressed. Presently he came back to look into the windows of the sitting-room. He found the door and for a minute or two went into the house and then came out.

'The cheek,' she said. She finished dressing and went up the lawn to him.

'Ah, there you are,' he said. 'What a sweet place this is. I was looking for Mr Armitage.'

'He's in London.'

'I thought he might be in the pool,' he said. Mr Smith looked rich with arch, smiling insinuation.

'When will he be back?'

'About six. Is there anything I can do?'

'No, no, no,' said Mr Smith in a variety of genial notes, waving a hand. 'I was out for a walk.'

'A long walk—seven miles.'

'I came,' said Mr Smith, modestly lowering his eyes in financial confession, 'by bus.'

'The best way. Can I give you a drink?'

'I never touch it,' Mr Smith said, putting up an austere hand. 'Well, a glass of water perhaps. As the Americans say, "I'm mighty thirsty." My wife and I came down here for the water, you know. London water is chalky. It was very bad for my wife's arthritis. It's bad for everyone, really. There's a significant increase in neuralgia, neuritis, arthritis in a city like London. The chalky water does it. People don't realise it'—and here Mr Smith stopped smiling and put on a stern excommunicating air—'If you believe that man's life is ruled by water. I personally don't.'

'Not by water only, anyway,' said Mrs Johnson.

'I mean,' said Mr Smith gravely, 'if you believe that the material body exists.' And when he said this, the whole sixteen stone of him looked scornfully at the landscape which, no doubt, concealed thousands of people who believed they had bodies. He expanded: he seemed to threaten to vanish.

Mrs Johnson fetched a glass of water. 'I'm glad to see you're still there,' she laughed when she came back.

Mr Smith was resting on the garden seat. 'I was just thinking—thank you—there's a lot of upkeep in a place like this,' he said.

'There is.'

'And yet—what is upkeep? Money—so it seems. And if we believe in the body, we believe in money, we believe in upkeep, and so it goes on,' said Mr Smith sunnily, waving his glass at the garden. And then sharply and loftily, free of this evil: 'It gives employment.' Firmly telling her she was employed. 'But,' he added, in warm contemplation, putting down his glass and opening his arms, gathering in the landscape, 'but there is only one employer.'

'There are a hell of a lot of employers.'

Mr Smith raised an eyebrow at the word 'hell' and said, 'Let me correct you there. I happen to believe that God is the only employer.'

'I'm employed by Mr Armitage,' she said. 'Mr Armitage loves this place. You don't have to see to love a garden.'

'It's a sweet place,' said Mr Smith. He got up and took a deep breath. 'Pine trees. Wonderful. The smell! My wife doesn't like pine trees. She is depressed by them. It's all in the mind,' said Mr Smith. 'As Shakespeare says. By the way, I suppose the water's warming up in the pool? June—it would be. That's what I should like—a swim.'

He *did* see me! thought Mrs Johnson.

'You should ask Mr Armitage,' she said coldly.

'Oh, no, no,' said Mr Smith. 'I just *feel* that to swim and have a sunbathe would be the right idea. I should like a place with a swimming pool. And a view like this. I feel it would suit me. And, by the way,' he became stern again, 'don't let me hear you say again that Mr Armitage enjoys this place although he doesn't see it. Don't tie his blindness on him. You'll hold him back. He *does* see it. He reflects all-seeing God. I told him so on Wednesday.'

'On Wednesday?'

'Yes,' he said. 'When he came for treatment. I managed to fit him in. Good godfathers, look at the time! I've to get the bus back. I'm sorry to miss Mr Armitage. Just tell him I called. I just had a thought to give him, that's all. He'll appreciate it.'

'And now,' Mr Smith said sportively, 'I must try and avoid taking a dive into that pool as I go by, mustn't I?'

She watched his stout marching figure go off down the path. For treatment! What on earth did Mr Smith mean? She knew the rest when Armitage came home.

'He came for his cheque,' he said. 'Would you make out a cheque for a hundred and twenty pounds—'

'A hundred and twenty pounds!' she exclaimed.

'For Mr Smith,' he repeated. 'He is treating my eyes.'

'Your eyes! He's not an ophthalmic surgeon.'

'No,' said Armitage coldly. 'I have tried those.'

'You're not going to a faith healer!'

'I am.'

And so they moved into their second quarrel. It was baffling to quarrel with Armitage. He could hear the firm ring of your voice but he could not see your eyes blooming wider and bluer with obstinacy; for her, her eyes were herself. It was like quarrelling with a man who had no self, or perhaps with one that was always hidden.

'Your church goes in for it,' he said.

'Proper faith healing,' she said.

'What is proper?' he said.

She had a strong belief in propriety.

'A hundred and twenty pounds! You told me yourself Smith is a fraud. I mean, you refused his case. How can you go to a fraud?'

'I don't think I said fraud,' he said.

'You didn't like the way he got five thousand pounds out of that silly young man.'

'Two thousand,' he said.

'He's after your money,' she said. 'He's a swindler.'

In her heart, having been brought up poor, she thought it was a scandal that Armitage was well-off; it was even more scandalous to throw money away.

'Probably. At the end of his tether,' he said. He was conveying, she knew, that he was at the end of his tether too.

'And you fall for that? You can't possibly believe the nonsense he talks.'

'Don't you think God was a crook? When you think of what He's done?'

'No, I don't.' (But in fact the stained woman thought He was.)

'What did Smith talk about?'

'I was in the pool. I think he was spying on me. I forget what he was talking about—water, chalky water, was it?'

'He's odd about chalk!' Armitage laughed. Then he became grim again: 'You see—even Smith can see *you*. You see people, you see Smith, everyone sees everything, and so they can afford to throw away what they see and forget. But I have to remember everything. You know what it is like trying to

remember a dream. Smith is right, I'm dreaming a dream,'
Armitage added sardonically. 'He says that I'm only dreaming
I cannot see.'

She could not make out whether Armitage was serious.

'All right. I don't understand, but all right. What happens
next?'

'You can wake up.'

Mr Armitage gave one of his cruel smiles. 'I told you. When
I used to go to the courts I often listened to witnesses like
Smith. They were always bringing "God is my witness" into
it. I never knew a more religious lot of men than dishonest
witnesses. They were always bringing in a higher power.
Perhaps they were in contact with it.'

'You don't mean that. You are making fun of me,' she said.
And then vehemently: 'I hate to see you going to an ignorant
man like that. I thought you were too proud. What has
happened to you?'

She had never spoken her mind so forcibly to him before.

'If a man can't see,' he said, 'if *you* couldn't see, humiliation
is what you'd fear most. I thought I ought to accept it.'

He had never been so open with her.

'You couldn't go lower than Mr Smith,' she said.

'We're proud. That is our vice,' he said. 'Proud in the dark.
Everyone else has to put up with humiliation. You said you
knew what it was—I always remember that. Millions of people
are humiliated: perhaps it makes them stronger because they
forget it. I want to join them.'

'No, you don't,' she said.

They were lying in bed and leaning over him she put her
breast to his lips, but he lay lifeless. She could not bear it that
he had changed her and that she had stirred this profound
wretchedness in him. She hated confession: to her it was the
male weakness—self-love. She got out of bed.

'Come to that,' she said. 'It's you who are humiliating me. You are going to this quack man because we've slept together. I don't like the compliment.'

'And you say you don't love me,' he said.

'I admire you,' she said. She dreaded the word 'love'. She picked up her clothes and left the room. She hadn't the courage to say she hadn't the courage. She stuck to what she had felt since she was a child: that she was a body. He had healed it with his body.

Once more she thought, I shall have to go. I ought to have stuck to it and gone before. If I'd been living in the town and just been coming up for the day it would have been OK. Living in the house was your mistake, my girl. You'll have to go and get another job. But of course when she calmed down, she realised that all this was self-deception: she was afraid to tell him. She brusquely drove off the thought, and her mind went to the practical.

That hundred and twenty pounds! She was determined not to see him swindled. She went with him to Mr Smith's next time. The roof of the Rolls-Royce gleamed over the shrubbery of the uncut hedge of Mr Smith's house. A cat was sitting on the window sill. Waiting on the doorstep was the little man, wide-waisted and with his hands in his optimistic pockets, and changing his smile of welcome to a reminder of secret knowledge when he saw her. Behind the undressing smile of Mr Smith stood the kind, cringing figure of his wife, looking as they all walked into the narrow hall.

'Straight through?' said Mrs Johnson in her managing voice. 'And leave them to themselves, I suppose?'

'The back gets the sun. At the front it's all these trees,' said Mrs Smith, encouraged by Mrs Johnson's presence to speak out in a weak voice, as if it was all she did get. 'I was a London girl.'

'So am I,' said Mrs Johnson.

'But you've got a beautiful place up there. Have you got these pine trees too?'

'A few.'

'They give me the pip,' said Mrs Smith. 'Coffee? Shall I take your coat? My husband said you'd got pines.'

'No, thank you, I'll keep it,' said Mrs Johnson. 'Yes, we've got pines. I can't say they're my favourite trees. I like to see leaves come off. And I like a bit of traffic myself. I like to see a shop.'

'Oh, you would,' said Mrs Smith.

The two women looked with the shrewd London look at each other.

'I'm so busy up there I couldn't come before. I don't like Mr Armitage coming alone. I like to keep an eye on him,' said Mrs Johnson, set for attack.

'Oh, yes, an eye.'

'Frankly, I didn't know he was coming to see Mr Smith.'

But Mrs Johnson got nothing out of Mrs Smith. They were both half listening to the rumble of men's voices next door. Then the meeting was over and they went out to meet the men. In his jolly way Mr Smith said to Mrs Johnson as they left, 'Don't forget about that swim!'

Ostentatiously to show her command and to annoy Armitage, she armed him down the path.

'I hope you haven't invited that man to swim in the pool,' said Mrs Johnson to Mr Armitage on the way home.

'You've made an impression on Smith,' said Armitage.

'No, *I* haven't.'

'Poor Mrs Smith,' said Mrs Johnson.

Otherwise they were silent.

She went a second, then a third time to the Smiths' house. She sat each time in the kitchen talking and listening to the men's voices in the next room. Sometimes there were long silences.

'Is Mr Smith praying?' Mrs Johnson asked.

'I expect so,' said Mrs Smith. 'Or reading.'

'Because it *is* prayer, isn't it?' said Mrs Johnson.

Mrs Smith was afraid of this healthy downright woman and it was an effort for her to make a stand on what evidently for most of her married life had been poor ground.

'I suppose it is. Prayer, yes, that is what it would be. Dad . . .' —she changed her mind—'my husband has always had faith.' And with this, Mrs Smith looked nervously at being able loyally to put forward the incomprehensible.

'But what does he actually *do*? I thought he had a chemist's shop,' pursued Mrs Johnson.

Mrs Smith was a timid woman who wavered now between the relics of dignity and a secretive craving to impart.

'He has retired,' said Mrs Smith. 'When we closed the shop he took this up.' She said this, hoping to clutch a certainty.

Mrs Johnson gave a bustling laugh. 'No, you misunderstand me. What I mean is, what does he actually *do*? What is the treatment?'

Mrs Smith was lost. She nodded, as it were, to nothingness several times.

'Yes,' she said. 'I suppose you'd call it prayer. I don't really understand it.'

'Nor do I,' said Mrs Johnson. 'I expect you've got enough to do keeping house. I have my work cut out too.'

They still heard the men talking. Mrs Johnson nodded to the wall.

'Still at it,' said Mrs Johnson. 'I'll be frank with you, Mrs Smith. I am sure your husband does whatever he does do for the best . . .'

'Oh, yes, for the best,' nodded Mrs Smith. 'It's saved us. He had a writ out against him when Mr Armitage's cheque came in. I know he's grateful.'

'But I believe in being open . . .'

'Open,' nodded Mrs Smith.

'I've told him and I've told Mr Armitage that I just don't believe a man who has been blind for twenty-two years—'

'Terrible,' said Mrs Smith.

'—can be cured. Certainly not by—whatever this is. Do you believe it, Mrs Smith?'

Mrs Smith was cornered.

'Our Lord did it,' she said desperately. 'That is what my husband says . . .'

'I was a nurse during the war and I have worked for doctors,' said Mrs Johnson. 'I am sure it is impossible. I've knocked about a lot. You're a sensible woman, Mrs Smith. I don't want to offend you, but you don't believe it yourself, do you?'

Mrs Johnson's eyes grew larger and Mrs Smith's older eyes were helpless and small. She longed for a friend. She was hypnotised by Mrs Johnson, whose face and pretty neck grew firmly out of her frilled and high-necked blouse.

'I try to have faith . . .' said Mrs Smith, rallying to her husband. 'He says I hold him back. I don't know.'

'Some men need to be held back,' said Mrs Johnson, and she gave a fighting shake to her healthy head. All Mrs Smith could do in her panic was to watch every move of Mrs Johnson's, study her expensive shoes and stockings, her capable skirt, her painted nails. Now, at the shake of Mrs Johnson's head, she saw on the right side of the neck the small petal of the birthmark just above the frill of the collar.

'None of us are perfect,' said Mrs Smith slyly.

'I have been with Mr Armitage four years,' Mrs Johnson said.

'It is a lovely place up there,' said Mrs Smith, eager to

change the subject. 'It must be terrible to live in such a lovely place and never see it . . .'

'Don't you believe it,' said Mrs Johnson. 'He knows that place better than any of us, better than me.'

'No,' groaned Mrs Smith. 'We had a blind dog when I was a girl. It used to nip hold of my dress to hold me back if it heard a car coming when I was going to cross the road. It belonged to my aunt and she said "That dog can see. It's a miracle".'

'He heard the car coming,' said Mrs Johnson. 'It's common sense.'

The words struck Mrs Smith.

'Yes, it is, really,' she said. 'If you come to think of it.'

She got up and went to the gas stove to make more coffee and new courage came to her. We know why she doesn't want Mr Armitage to see again! She was thinking: the frightening Mrs Johnson was really weak. Housekeeper and secretary to a rich man, sitting very pretty up there, the best of everything. Plenty of money, staff, cook, gardener, chauffeur, Rolls-Royce —if he was cured where would her job be? Oh, she looks full of herself now, but she is afraid. I expect she's got round him to leave her a bit.

The coffee began to bubble up in the pot and that urgent noise put excitement into her and her old skin blushed.

'Up there with a man alone. As I said to Dad, a woman can tell! Where would she get another man with that spot spreading all over? She's artful. She's picked the right one.' She was telling the tale to herself.

The coffee boiled over and hissed on the stove and a sudden forgotten jealousy hissed up in Mrs Smith's uncertain mind. She took the pot to the table and poured out a boiling-hot cup and, as the steam clouded up from it, screening her daring stare at the figure of Mrs Johnson, Mrs Smith wanted to say: 'Lying there stark naked by that swimming pool right in the face of my husband. What was he doing up there anyway?'

She could not say it. There was not much pleasure in Mrs Smith's life; jealousy was the only one that enlivened her years with Mr Smith. She had flown at him when he came home and had told her that God had guided him, that prayer always uncovered evil and brought it to the surface; it had revealed to him that the Devil had put his mark on Mrs Johnson, and that he wouldn't be surprised if that was what was holding up the healing of Mr Armitage.

'What were you doing,' she screamed at him, 'looking at a woman?'

The steam cleared and Mrs Smith's nervousness returned as she saw that composed face. She was frightened now of her own imagination and of her husband's. She knew him. He was always up to something.

'Don't you dare say anything to Mr Armitage about this!' she had shouted at him.

But now she fell back on admiring Mrs Johnson again.

Settled for life, she sighed. She's young. She is only fighting for her own. She's a woman.

And Mrs Smith's pride was stirred. Her courage was fitful and weakened by what she had lived through. She had heard Mrs Johnson was divorced and it gave Mrs Smith strength as a woman who had 'stuck to her husband'. She had not gone round taking up with men as she guessed Mrs Johnson might have done. She was a respectable married woman.

Her voice trembled at first but became stronger.

'Dad wanted to be a doctor when he was a boy,' Mrs Smith was saying, 'but there wasn't the money so he worked in a chemist's but it was always church on Sundays. I wasn't much of a one for church myself. But you must have capital and being just behind the counter doesn't lead anywhere. Of course I tried to egg him on to get his diploma and he got the papers—but I used to watch him. He'd start his studying and then he'd get impatient. He's a very impatient man and he'd say "Amy, I'll try the ministry"—he's got a good voice—"church people have money".'

'And did he?'

'No, he always wanted to, but he couldn't seem to settle to a church—I mean a religion. I'll say this for him, he's a fighter. Nixon, his first guv'nor, thought the world of him: quick with the sales. Nixon's Cough Mixture—well, he didn't invent it, but he changed the bottles and the labels, made it look—fashionable, dear—you know? A lot of Wesleyans took it.'

Mrs Smith spread her hands over her face and laughed through her fingers.

'When Nixon died someone in the church put up some money, a very religious, good man. One day Dad said to me—I always remember it—"It's not medicine. It's faith does it." He's got faith. Faith is—well, faith.'

'In himself?' suggested Mrs Johnson.

'That's it! That's it!' cried Mrs Smith with excitement. Then she quietened and dabbed a tear from her cheek. 'I begged him not to come down here. But this Mrs Rogers, the lady who owns the house, she's deaf and on her own, he knew her. She believes in him. She calls him Daniel. He's treating her for deafness, she can't hear a word, so we brought our things down after we closed up in Ealing, that's why it's so crowded, two of everything, I have to laugh.'

'So you don't own the house?'

'Oh, no dear—oh, no,' Mrs Smith said, frightened of the idea. 'He wants something bigger. He wants space for his work.'

Mrs Smith hesitated and looked at the wall through which the sound of Mr Smith's voice was coming. And then, fearing she had been disloyal, she said, 'She's much better. She's very funny. She came down yesterday calling him. "Daniel. Daniel. I hear the cuckoo." Of course I didn't say anything: it was the man calling out "Coal". But she is better. She wouldn't have heard him at all when we came here.'

They were both silent.

'You can't live your life from A to Z,' Mrs Smith said, waking up. 'We all make mistakes. We've been married for forty-two years. I expect you have your troubles too, even in that lovely place.'

After the hour Mr Smith came into the kitchen to get Mrs Johnson.

'What a chatter!' he said to her. 'I never heard such a tittle-tattle in my life.'

'Yes, we had a fine chat, didn't we?'

'Oh, yes,' said Mrs Smith boldly.

'How is it going on?' said Mrs Johnson.

'Now, now,' Mr Smith corrected her. 'These cases seemingly take time. You have to get to the bottom of it. We don't intend to, but we keep people back by the thoughts we hold over them.'

And then, in direct attack on her—'I don't want you to hold no wrong thoughts over me. You have no power over divine love.' And he turned to his wife to silence her.

'And how would I do that?' said Mrs Johnson.

'Cast the mote out of thine own eye,' said Smith. 'Heal yourself. We all have to.' He smiled broadly at her.

'I don't know what all this talk about divine love is,' said Mrs Johnson. 'But I love Mr Armitage as he is.'

Smith did not answer.

Armitage had found his way to the door of the kitchen. He listened and said, 'Good-bye, Mrs Smith.' And to Mr Smith: 'Send me your bill. I'm having the footpath closed.'

*

They drove away.

'I love Mr Armitage as he is.' The words had been forced out of her by the detestable man. She hated that she had said to him what she could not say to Armitage. They surprised her. She hoped Armitage had not heard them.

He was silent in the car. He did not answer any of her questions.

'I'm having that path closed,' he repeated.

I know! she thought. Smith has said something about me. Surely not about 'it'!

When they got out of the car at the house he said to the chauffeur, 'Did you see Mr Smith when he came up here three weeks ago? It was a Thursday. Were you down at the pool?'

'It's my afternoon off, sir.'

'I know that. I asked whether you were anywhere near the pool. Or in the garden?'

'No, sir.'

Oh, God, Mrs Johnson groaned. Now he's turned on Jim.

'Jim went off on his motorbike. I saw him,' said Mrs Johnson.

They went into the house.

'You don't know whom you can trust,' Armitage said and went across to the stairs and started up. But instead of putting his hand to the rail which was on the right, he put it out to the left, and not finding it, stood bewildered. Mrs Johnson quietly went to that side of him and nudged him in the right direction.

When he came down to lunch he sat in silence before the cutlets on his plate.

'After all these years! I know the rail is on the right and I put out my left hand.'

'You just forgot,' she said. 'Why don't you try forgetting a few more things?'

She was cross about the questioning of the chauffeur.

'Say, one thing a day,' she said.

He listened and this was one of those days when he cruelly paused a long time before replying. A minute went by and she started to eat.

'Like this?' he said, and he deliberately knocked his glass of water over. The water spread over the cloth towards her plate.

'What's this silly temper?' she said, and lifting her plate away, she lifted the cloth and started mopping with her table napkin and picked up the glass.

'I'm fed up with you blind people,' she said angrily. 'All jealousy and malice, just childish. You're so clever, aren't you? What happened? Didn't that good Mr Smith do the magic trick? I don't wonder your wife walked out on you. Pity the poor blind! What about other people? I've had enough. You have an easy life; you sail down in your Rolls and think you can buy God from Mr Smith just because—I don't know why—but if he's a fraud you're a fraud.' Suddenly the wronged inhabitant inside her started to shout: 'I'll tell you something about that Peeping Jesus: he saw the lot. Oh, yes, I hadn't a stitch on. The lot!' she was shouting. And then she started to unzip her dress and pull it down over her shoulder and drag her arm out of it. 'You can't see it, you silly fool. The whole bloody Hebrides, the whole plate of liver.'

And she went to his place, got him by the shoulder and rubbed her stained shoulder and breast against his face.

'Do you want to see more?' she shouted. 'It made my husband sick. That's what you've been sleeping with. And'— she got away as he tried to grip her and laughed—'you didn't know! *He* did.'

She sat down and cried hysterically with her head and arms on the table.

Armitage stumbled in the direction of her crying and put his hand on her bare shoulder.

'Don't touch me! I hate your hands.' And she got up, dodged round him to the door and ran out sobbing; slower than she was, he was too late to hear her steps. He found his way back to the serving hatch and called to the cook.

'Go up to Mrs Johnson. She's in her room. She's ill,' he said.

He stood in the hall waiting; the cook came downstairs and went into the sitting-room.

'She's not there. She must have gone into the garden.' And then she said at the window, 'She's down by the pool.'

'Go and talk to her,' he said.

The cook went out of the garden door and on to the terrace. She was a thin round-shouldered woman. She saw Mrs Johnson move back to the near side of the pool; she seemed to be staring at something in the water. Then the cook stopped and came shouting back to the house.

'She's fallen in. With all her clothes on. She can't swim. I know she can't swim.' And then the cook called out, 'Jim! Jim!' and ran down the lawns.

Armitage stood helpless.

'Where's the door?' he called. There was no one there.

Armitage made an effort to recover his system, but it was lost. He found himself blocked by a chair, but he had forgotten which chair. He waited to sense the movement of air in order to detect where the door was, but a window was half open and he found himself against glass. He made his way feeling along the wall, but he was travelling away from the door. He stood still again, and smelling a kitchen smell he made his way back across the centre of the long room and at last found the first door and then the door to the garden. He stepped out, but he was exhausted and his will had gone. He could only stand in the breeze, the disorderly scent of the flowers and the grass mocking him. A jeering bird flew up. He heard the gardener's dog barking below and a voice, the gardener's voice, shouting

'Quiet!' Then he heard voices coming slowly nearer up the lawn.

'Helen,' called Armitage, but they pushed past him. He felt her wet dress brush his hand and her foot struck his leg; the gardener was carrying her.

'Marge,' Armitage heard her voice as she choked and was sick.

'Upstairs. I'll get her clothes off,' said the cook.

'No,' said Armitage.

'Be quiet,' said the cook.

'In my room,' said Armitage.

'What an idea!' said the cook. 'Stay where you are. Mind you don't slip on all this wet.'

He stood, left behind in the hall, listening, helpless. Only when the doctor came did he go up.

She was sitting up in bed and Armitage held her hand.

'I'm sorry,' she said. 'You'd better fill that pool up. It hasn't brought you any luck.'

Armitage and Mrs Johnson are in Italy now; for how long it is hard to say. They themselves don't know. Some people call her Mrs Armitage, some call her Mrs Johnson; this uncertainty pleases her. She has always had a secret and she is too old, she says, to give up the habit now. It still pleases Armitage to baffle people. It is impossible for her to deny that she loves Armitage, because he heard what she said to Smith; she has had to give in about that. And she does love him because his system has broken down completely in Italy. 'You are my eyes,' he says. 'Everything sounds different here.' 'I like a bit of noise,' she says.

Pictures in churches and galleries he is mad about and he likes listening to her descriptions of them and often laughs at some of her remarks, and she is beginning, she says, to get 'a kick out of the classical stuff' herself.

There was an awkward moment before they set off for Italy when he made her write out a cheque for Smith and she tried to stop him.

'No,' he said. 'He got it out of you. I owe you to him.'

She was fighting the humiliating suspicion that in his nasty prying way Smith had told Armitage about her before *she* had told him. But Armitage said, 'I knew all the time. From the beginning. I knew everything about you.'

She still does not know whether to believe him or not. When she does believe, she is more awed than shamed; when she does not believe she feels carelessly happy. He depends on her entirely here. One afternoon, standing at the window of their room and looking at the people walking in the lemonish light across the square, she suddenly said, 'I love you. I feel gaudy!' She notices that the only thing he doesn't like is to hear a man talk to her.

A. S. Byatt
Precipice-Encurled

What's this then, which proves good yet seems untrue?
Is fiction, which makes fact alive, fact too?
The somehow may be thishow.

ROBERT BROWNING

I

The woman sits in the window. Beneath her is the stink of the canal and on the skyline is a steel-grey sheet of cloud and an unswallowed setting sun. She watches the long lines of dark green seaweed moving on the thick surface of the water, and the strong sweeping gulls, fugitives from storms in the Adriatic. She is a plump woman in a tea gown. She wears a pretty lace cap and pearls. These things are known, are highly probable. She has fine features fleshed—a compressed, drooping little mouth, a sharp nose, sad eyes, an indefinable air of disappointment, a double chin. This we can read from portraits, more than one, tallying, still in existence. She has spent the afternoon in bed; her health is poor, but she rallies for parties, for outings, for occasions. There she sits, or might be supposed to sit, any autumn day on any of several years at the end of the last century. She commands the devoted services of three gondoliers, a handyman, a cook, a maid and a kitchen-maid.

Also an accountant-housekeeper. She has a daughter, young and marriageable, and a husband, mysteriously ill in Paris, from whom she is estranged but not divorced. Her daughter is out on a party of pleasure, perhaps, and has been adjured to take her new umbrella, the one with the prettily carved crickets and butterflies on its handle. She has an eye for the execution of delicate objects: it has been said of her that she would exchange a Tintoretto for a cabinet of tiny gilded glasses. She has an eye for fashion: in this year where clothes are festooned with dead humming birds and more startling creatures, mice, moths, beetles and lizards, she will give a dance where everyone must wear flights of birds pasted on ribbons—'awfully chic'— or streamers of butterflies. The room in which she sits is full of mother-of-pearl cabinets full of intricate little artefacts. She is the author of an unpublished and authoritative history of Venetian naval architecture. Also of some completely undistinguished poems. She is the central character in no story, but peripheral in many, where she may appear reduced to two or three bold identifying marks. She has a passion for pug dogs and for miniature Chinese spaniels: at her feet, on this gloomy day, lie, shall we say, Contenta, Trolley, Yahabibi and Thisbe, snoring a little as such dogs do, replete. She also has a passion for peppermint creams; do the dogs enjoy these too, or are they disciplined? One account of her gives three characteristics only: plump, pug dogs, peppermint creams. Henry James, it is said, had the idea of making her the central character of a merely projected novel—did he mean to tackle the mysteriously absent husband, make of him one of those electric Jamesian force-fields of unspecific significance? He did, it is also said, write her into *The Aspern Papers*, in a purely subordinate and structural role, the type of the well-to-do American woman friend of the narrator, an authorial device, what James called a *ficelle*, economically connecting us, the readers, to the necessary people and the developing drama. She lent the narrator her gondola. She was a generous woman. She is an enthusiast: she collects locks of hair, snipped from great poetic temples, which she enshrines in lockets of onyx. She is waiting for Robert Browning. She has done and will do this in many years. She has supervised and will supervise the excellent provision of sheets and bathroom facilities for his Venetian visits. She chides him for not recognising that servants know their place and are happy in it. She sends him quires of hand-made Venetian paper which he distributes to artists and poets of his acquaintance. She selects brass salvers for him. She records his considered and unconsidered responses to scenery and atmosphere. She looks at the gulls with interest he has instilled. 'I do not know why I never see in descriptions of Venice any mention of the seagulls; to me they are even more interesting than the doves of St Mark.' He said that, and she recorded it. She recorded that occasionally he would allow her daughter to give him a cup of tea 'to our great delight'. 'As a rule, he abstained from what he considered a somewhat un-hygienic beverage if taken before dinner.'

II

Dear dead women, the scholar thinks, peering into the traces on the hooded green plane of the microfilm reader, or perhaps turning over browned packets of polite notes of gratitude, acceptance, anticipation, preserved perhaps in one of those fine boxes of which in her lifetime she had so many, containing delicate cigarettes on inlaid pearly octagonal tables, or precious fragments of verses copied out for autograph books. He has gleaned her words from Kansas and Cambridge, Florence, Venice and Oxford, he has read her essay on lace and her

tributes to the condescension of genius, he has heard the
flitting of young skirts at long-vanished festivities. He has
stood, more or less, on the spot where she stood with the poet
in Asolo in 1889, looking back to Browning's first contemplation of the place in 1838, looking back to the internecine
passions of Guelphs and Ghibellines, listening to the chirrup of
the contumacious grasshopper. He has seen her blood colour
the cheeks of her noble Italian grand-daughter who has opened
to him those houses where the poet dined, recited, conversed,
teased, reminisced. He likes her, partly because he now knows
her, has pieced her together. Resuscitated, Browning might
have said, did say, roundly, of his Roman murderers and
biassed lawyers, child-wife, wise moribund Pope and gallant
priest he found or invented in his dead and lively Yellow
Book. A good scholar may permissibly invent, he may have a
hypothesis, but fiction is barred. This scholar believes, plaus-
ibly, that his assiduous and fragile subject is the hidden heroine
of a love story, the inapprehensive object, at the age of fifty-
four, of a dormant passion in a handsome seventy-seven-year-
old poet. He records the physical vigour, the beautiful hands
and fine white head of hair of his hero. He records the
probable feelings of his heroine, which stop short at exalted
hero-worship, the touch of talismanic mementos, not living
flesh. He adduces a poem, 'Inapprehensiveness', in which the
poetic speaker reproves the inapprehensive stare of a companion intent on Ruskin's hypothetical observation of the waving
form of certain weed-growths on a ravaged wall, who ignores
'the dormant passion needing but a look To burst into immense life'. The scholar's story combs the facts this way. They
have a subtle, not too dramatic shape, lifelike in that. He
scrutinises the microfilm, the yellowing letters, for little bright
nuggets and filaments of fact to add to his mosaic. In 1882 the
poet was in the Alps, with a visit to Venice in prospect after a

proposed visit to another English family in Italy. She waited for him. In terms of this story she waited in vain. An 'incident' elsewhere, an 'unfortunate accident' the scholar wrote, following his thread, coupled with torrential rain in Bologna, caused the poet to return to London. He was in danger of allowing the friendship to cool, the scholar writes, perhaps anxious on her behalf, perhaps on the poet's, perhaps on his own.

III

A man, he always thought, was more himself alone in an hotel room. Unless, of course, he vanished altogether without the support of others' consciousness of him, and the solidity of his taste and his history in his possessions. To be itinerant suited and sharpened him. He liked this room. It was quiet, on the second floor, the last in a long corridor, its balcony face to face with a great, bristling primeval glacier. The hotel, he wrote, sitting at the table listening to the silent snow and the fraternising tinkle of unseen cattle, was 'quite perfect, with every comfort desirable, and no drawback of any kind'. The journey up had been rough— two hours carriage-drive, and then seven continued hours of clambering and crawling on mule-back. He wrote letters partly out of courtesy to his large circle of solicitous friends and admirers, but more in order to pick up the pen, to see the pothooks and spider-traces form, containing the world, the hotel, the mules, the paradise of coolness and quiet. The hotel was not absolutely perfect. 'My very handwriting is affected by the lumpy ink and the skewery pen.' Tomorrow he would walk. Four or five hours along the mountainside. Not bad for an old man, a hale old man. The mule-jolting had played havoc with his hips and the long muscles in his back. At my age, he thought, you listen to every small hurt as though it may be the beginning of the last and worst hurt, which will come. So the two things continued in his consciousness side by side, a solicitous attention to twinges, and the waiting to be reinvested by his private self. Which was like a cloak, a cloak of invisibility that fell into comfortable warm folds around him, or like a disturbed well, whose inky waters chopped and swayed and settled into blackly reflecting lucidity. Or like a brilliant baroque chapel at the centre of a decorous and unremarkable house.

He liked his public self well enough. He was surprised, to tell the truth, that he had one that worked so well, was so thoroughgoing, so at home in the world, so like other public selves. As a very young man, in strictly non-conformist South London, erudite and indulged within the four walls of a Camberwell bibliomaniac's home, he had supposed that this would be denied him, the dining-out, the gossip, the world. He wanted the world, because it was there, and he wanted everything. He had described his father, whom he loved, as a man of vast knowledge, reading and memory—totally ignorant of the world. (This ignorance had extended to his having had to leave England perpetually, as an aged widower, on account of a breach of promise action brought, with cause, against him.) His father had with consummate idealism freed him for art. My father wished me to do what I liked, he had explained, adding: I should not so bring up a son.

French novelists, he claimed, were ignorant of the habits of the English upper classes, who kept themselves to themselves. He had seen and noted them. 'I seem to know a good many—for some reason or other. Perhaps because I never had any occupation.' Nevertheless, he desired his son to have an occupation, and the boy, amiable and feckless, brooded over by his own irreducible large shadow, showed little sign of vocation or application. He amused himself as a matter of course in the world in which the father dined out and visited, so assiduously, with a perpetually renewed surprise at his own facility. He was aware that Elizabeth would have wished it otherwise. Elizabeth had been a great poet, a captive princess liberated and turned wife, a moral force, silly over some things, such as her growing boy's long curls and the flimsy promises and fake visions of the séance. She too had not known this world that was so important. *One such intimate knowledge as I have had with many a person would have taught her*, he confided once, unguarded, had she been inclined to learn. Though I doubt if she would have dirtied her hands for any scientific purpose. His public self had a scientific purpose, and if his hands were dirty, he could wash them clean in a minute before he saw her, as he trusted to do. He had his reasonable doubts about this event, too, though he wrote bravely of it, the step from this world to that other world, the fog in the throat, the mist in the face, the snows, the blasts, the pain and then the peace out of pain and the loving arms. It was not a time of certainties, however he might assert them from time to time. It was a time of doubt, doubt was a man's business. But it was also hard to imagine all this tenacious sense of self, all this complexity of knowledge and battling, force and curiosity becoming nothing. What is a man, what is a man's soul?

Descartes believed, he noted down, that the seat of the soul is the pineal gland. The reason for this is a pretty reason—all else in our apparatus for apprehending the world is double, *viz.* two ears, two eyes, etc. and two lobes of our brain moreover; Descartes requires that somewhere in our body all our diverse, our dual impressions must be unified before reaching the soul, which is one. He had thought often of writing a poem about Descartes, dreaming in his stove of sages and blasted churches, reducing all to the tenacity of the observing thinker, *cogito ergo sum*. A man can inhabit another man's mind, or body, or senses, or history, can jerk it into a kind of life, as galvanism moves frogs: a good poet could inhabit Descartes, the bric-à-brac of stove and ill-health and wooden bowls of onion soup, perhaps, and one of those pork knuckles, and the melon offered to the philosopher by the sage in his feverish dream, all this paraphernalia spinning round the naked cogito as the planets spin in an orrery. The best part of my life, he told himself, the life I have lived most intensely, has been the fitting, the infiltrating, the inventing the self of another man or woman, explored and sleekly filled out, as fingers swell a glove. I have been webbed Caliban lying in the primeval ooze, I have been madman and saint, murderer and sensual prelate, inspired David and the cringing medium, Sludge, to whom I gave David's name, with what compulsion of irony or equivocation, David Sludge? The rooms in which his solitary self sat buzzed with other selves, crying for blood as the shades cried at the pit dug by Odysseus in his need to interrogate, to revive the dead. His father's encyclopaedias were the banks of such blood-pits, bulging with paper lives and circumstances, no two the same, none insignificant. A set of views, a time-confined philosophy, a history of wounds and weaknesses, flowers, clothing, food and drink, light on Mont Blanc's horns of silver, fangs of crystal; these coalesce to make one self in one place. Then decompose. I catch them, he thought, I hold them together, I give them coherence and vitality, I. And what am I? Just such another concatenation, a language and its rhythms, a limited stock of learning, derived from my father's consumed books and a few experiments in life, my desires, my venture in dragon-slaying, my love, my loathings also, the peculiar colours of the world through my two eyes, the blind tenacity of the small, the single driving centre, soul or self.

What he had written down, with the scratchy pen, were one or two ideas for Descartes and his metaphorical orrery:

meaningless scraps. And this writing brought to life in him a kind of joy in greed. He would procure, he would soak in, he would comb his way through the Discourse on Method, and the Passions of the Soul: he would investigate Flemish stoves. His private self was now roused from its dormant state to furious activity. He felt the white hairs lift on his neck and his breath quickened. A bounded man, he had once written, may so project his surplusage of soul in search of body, so add self to self . . . so find, so fill full, so appropriate forms . . . In such a state a man became pure curiosity, pure interest in whatever presented itself of the creation, lovely or freakish, pusillanimous, wise or vile. Those of his creatures he most loved or most approved moved with such delighted and indifferent interest through the world. There was the tragic Duchess, destroyed by the cold egotism of a Duke who could not bear her equable pleasure in everything, a sunset, a bough of cherries, a white mule, his favour at her breast. There was Karshish the Arab physician, the not-incurious in God's handiwork, who noticed lynx and blue-flowering borage and recorded the acts of the risen Lazarus. There was David, seeing the whole earth shine with significance after soothing the passionate self-doubt of Saul; there was Christopher Smart, whose mad work of genius, his Song to David, a baroque chapel in a dull house, had recorded the particularity of the world, the whale's bulk in the waste of brine, the feather-tufts of Wild Virgin's Bower, the habits of the polyanthus. There was the risen Lazarus himself, who had briefly been in the presence of God and inhabited eternity, and to whose resuscitated life he had been able to give no other characteristics than these, the lively, indifferent interest in everything, a mule with gourds, a child's death, the flowers of the field, some trifling fact at which he will gaze 'rapt with stupor at its very littleness'.

*

He felt for his idea of what was behind all this diversity, all this interest. *At the back* was an intricate and extravagantly prolific maker. Sometimes, listening to silence, alone with himself, he heard the irregular but endlessly repeated crash of waves on a pebbled shore. His body was a porcelain-fine arched shell, sculpted who knew how, containing this roar and plash. And the drag of the moon, and the elliptical course of the planets. More often, a madly ingenious inner eye magnified small motions of flesh and blood. The twinge had become a tugging and raking in what he now feared, prophetically it turned out, was his liver. Livers were used for augury, the shining liver, the smoking liver, the Babylonians thought, was the seat of the soul: his own lay athwart him and was intimately and mysteriously connected with the lumpy pothooks. And with the inner eye which might or might not be seated in that pineal gland where Descartes located the soul. A man has no more measured the mysteries of his internal whistlings and flowings, he thought, than he has measured the foundations of the earth or of the whirlwind. It was his covert principle to give true opinions to great liars, and to that other fraudulent resuscitator of dead souls, and filler of mobile gloves, David Sludge the Medium, he had given a vision of the minutiae of intelligence which was near enough his own. 'We find great things are made of little things,' he had made Sludge say, 'And little things go lessening till at last Comes God behind them.'

'The Name comes close behind a stomach-cyst
The simplest of creations, just a sac
That's mouth, heart, legs and belly at once, yet lives
And feels and could do neither, we conclude
If simplified still further one degree.'

'But go back and back, as you please, *at* the back, as Mr Sludge is made to insist,' he had written, 'you find (*my* faith is as constant) creative intelligence, acting as matter but not resulting from it. Once set the balls rolling and ball may hit ball and send any number in any direction over the table; but I believe in the cue pushed by a hand.' All the world speaks the Name, as the true David truly saw: even the uneasy inflamed cells of my twinges. *At* the back, is something simple, undifferentiated, indifferently intelligent, live.

My best times are those when I approximate most closely to that state.

She put her hand on the knob of his door, and pushed it open without knocking. It was dark, a light, smoky dark; the window curtains were not drawn and the windows were a couple of vague, star-lighted apertures. She saw things, a rug thrown over a chair, a valise, a dim shape hunched and silver-topped, which turned out to be her brother, back towards her, at the writing-table. 'Oh, if you're busy,' she said, 'I won't disturb you.' And then, 'You can't write in the dark, Robert, it is bad for your eyes.' He shook himself, like a great seal coming up from the depths, and his eyes, dark spaces under craggy brows, turned unseeing in her direction. 'I don't want to disturb you,' she said again, patiently waiting for his return to the land of the living. 'You don't,' he said, 'dear Sarianna. I was only thinking about Descartes. And it must be more than time for dinner.' 'There is a woman here,' Sarianna confided, as they walked down the corridor, past a servant carrying candles, 'with an aviary on her head, who is an admirer of your poems and wishes to join the Browning society.' 'Il me semble que ce genre de chose frise le ridicule,' he said, growlingly, and she smiled to herself, for she knew that when he was introduced to the formidable Mrs Miller he would be everything that was agreeable and interested.

*

And the next day, on the hotel terrace, he was quite charming to his corseted and bustled admirer, who begged him to write in her birthday book, already graced by Lord Leighton and Thomas Trollope, who was indulgent when he professed not to remember on which of two days he had been born—was it May 7th or May 9th, he never could be certain, he said, appealing to Sarianna, who could. He had found some better ink, and copied out, as he occasionally did, in microscopic handwriting, 'All that I know of a certain star', adding with a bluff smile, 'I always end up writing the same thing; I vary only the size. I should be more inventive.' Mrs Miller protested that his eyesight must be exquisitely fine, closing the scented leather over the hand-painted wreaths of pansies that encircled the precious script. Her hat was monumental, a circle of wings; the poet admired it, and asked detailed questions about its composition, owls, hawks, jays, swallows, encircling an entire dove. He showed considerable familiarity with Paris prints and the vagaries of modistes. His public self had its own version of the indiscriminate interest in everything which was the virtue of the last Duchess, Karshish, Lazarus and Smart. He could not know how much this trait was to irritate Henry James, who labelled it bourgeois, whose fictional alter ego confessed to feeling a despair at his 'way of liking one subject—so far as I could tell—precisely as much as another'. He addressed himself to women exactly as he addressed himself to men, this af-fronted narrator complained; he gossiped to all men alike, talking no better to clever folk than to dull. He was loud and cheerful and copious. His opinions were sound and second-rate, and of his perceptions it was too mystifying to think. He seemed quite happy in the company of the insistent Mrs Miller, telling her about the projected visit to the Fishwick family, who had a house in the Apennines. Mrs Miller nodded vigorously under the wings of the dove, and leapt into vibrant recitation. 'What I love best in all the world Is a castle, precipice-encurled In a gash of the wind-grieved Apennines.' 'Exactly so,' said the benign old man, sipping his port, looking at the distant mountains, watched by Sarianna, who knew that he was braced against the Apennines as a test, that he had never since her death ventured so near the city in which he had been happy with his wife, in which he was never to set foot again. The Fishwicks' villa was in a remote village unvisited in that earlier time. He meant to attempt that climb, as he had attempted this. He needed to be undaunted. It was his idea of himself that he was undaunted. And so he was, Sarianna thought, with love. 'Then we may proceed to Venice,' said the poet to the lady in the hat, 'where we have very kind friends and many fond memories. I should not be averse to dying in Venice. When my time comes.'

IV

'What will he make of us?' Miss Juliana Fishwick enquired, speaking of the imminent Robert Browning, and in fact more concerned with what her companion, Mr Joshua Riddell, did make of them, of the Fishwick family and way of life, of the Villa Colomba, perched in its coign of cliff, with its rough lawn and paved rooms and heavy ancient furnishings. She was perhaps the only person in the company to care greatly what anybody made of anybody; the others were all either too old and easygoing or too young and intent on their journeys of discovery and complicated games. Joshua Riddell replied truthfully that he found them all enchanting, and the place too, and was sure that Mr Browning would be enchanted. He was a friend of Juliana's brother, Tom. They were at Balliol College, reading Greats. Joshua's father was a Canon of St Paul's.

Joshua lived a regular and circumspect life at home, where he was an only child, of whom much was expected. He expected very much of himself, too, though not in the line of his parents' hopes, the Bar, the House of Commons, the judiciary. He meant to be a great painter. He meant to do something quite new, which would have authority. He knew he should recognise this, when he had learned what it was, and how to do it. For the time being, living in its necessarily vague yet brilliant presence was both urgent and thwarting. He described it to no one; certainly not to Tom, with whom he was able, surprisingly, to share ordinary jokes and japes. He was entirely unused to the degree of playfulness and informality of Tom's family.

He was sketching Juliana. She was sitting, in her pink muslin, on the edge of the fountain basin. The fountain bubbled in an endless chuckling waterfall out of a cleft in the rockside. This was the lower fountain, furthest from the house, on a rough lawn on which stood an ancient stone table and chairs. Above the fountain someone had carved a round, sun-like face, flat and calmly beaming, with two uplifted, flat-palmed hands pushing through, or poised on, the rock face beside it. No one knew how old or new it was. In the upper garden, where there were flowerbeds and a slower, lead-piped fountain, was a pillar or herm surmounted with a head which, Solomon Fishwick had pointed out, was exactly the same as the heads on the covers of the hominiform Etruscan funerary urns. Joshua had made several drawings of these carvings. Juliana's living face, under her straw hat, was a different challenge. It was a face composed of softness and the smooth solid texture of young flesh, without pronounced bones, hard to capture. The blonde eyebrows did not stand out; the eyes were not emphasised by long lashes, only by a silver-white fringe which caught the sunlight here and there. The upper lip sloped upwards; the mouth was always slightly parted, the expression gently questioning, not insisting on an answer. It was an extremely pleasant face, with no salient characteristics. How to draw softness, and youth, and sheer *pleasantness?* Her arms should be full of an abundance of something; apples, rosebuds, a cascade of corn. She held her little hands awkwardly, clasping and unclasping them over her pink skirts.

Juliana was more used to looking than to being looked at. She supposed she was not pretty, though passable, not by any means grotesque. She had an unfortunate body for this year's narrow styles, which required height, an imposing bosom, a flat stomach, an upright carriage. She was round and short, though she had a good enough waist; corseting did violence to her, and in the summer heat in Italy was impossible. So she was conscious of rolls and half-moons and sausages of flesh which she would dearly have wished otherwise. She had pretty ankles and wrists, she knew, and had stockings of a lovely rose pink with butterfly-shells embroidered on them. Her elder sister, Annabel, visiting in Venice, was a beauty, much courted, much consulted about dashing little hats. Juliana supposed she might herself have trouble in finding a husband. She was not remarkable. She was afraid she might simply pass from being a shepherding elder sister to being a useful aunt. She was marvellous with the little ones. She played and tumbled and comforted and cleaned and sympathised, and wanted something of her own, some place, some thought, some silence that should be hers only. She did not expect to find it. She had a practical nature and liked comfort. She had been invaluable in helping to bestow the family goods and chattels in the two heavy carriages which had made their way up the hill, from the heat of Florence to this airy and sunny garden state. Everything had had to go in: baths and fish-kettles, bolsters and jelly-moulds, cats, dogs, birdcage and dolls' house. She had sat in the nursery carriage, with Nanny and Nurse and the restive little ones: Tom and Joshua had gone ahead with her parents and the household staff, English and Italian, had come behind. On the hot leather seat, she was impinged upon by Nurse's starched petticoats on one side, and the entwined, struggling limbs of Arthur and Gwendolen battling for space, for air on the other. When the climb became steep spare mules were attached, called *trapeli*, each with its attendant groom, groaning and coughing on the steeper and steeper turns, whilst the men went at strolling pace and the horses skidded and lay back in their collars leaving the toiling to the mules. She found their patient effort exemplary: she had given them all apples when they arrived.

She was in awe of Joshua, though not of Tom. Tom teased her, as he always had, amiably. Joshua spoke courteously to her as though she was as knowledgeable as Tom about Horace and Ruskin; this was probably because he had no experience of sisters and only a limited experience of young women. Her father had taught her a little Latin and Greek; her governess had taught her French, Italian, needlework, drawing and the use of the globes, accomplishments she was now imparting to Gwendolen, and Arthur and little Edith. They seemed useless, not because they were uninteresting but because they were like feathers stitched on to a hat, dead decorations, not life. They were life to Joshua; she could see that. His manner was fastidious and aloof, but he had been visibly shaken, before the peregrination to the Villa Colomba, by the outing they had made from Florence to Vallombrosa, with its sweeping inclines and steep declivities all clothed with the chestnut trees, dark green shades 'high overarched indeed, exactly,' Joshua had said, and had added, 'You can see that these leaves, being deciduous, will strow the brooks, thickly, like the dead souls in Virgil and Milton's fallen angels.' She had looked at the chestnut trees, suddenly seeing them, because he asked her to. They clothed the mountains here, too. The peasants lived off chestnuts: their cottages had chestnut-drying lofts, their women ground chestnut flour in stone mortars.

When they had first rushed into the Villa Colomba, chirruping children and pinch-mouthed, disapproving cook, and had found nothing but echoing, cool space between the thick walls with their barred slit windows, she had looked to Joshua in alarm, whilst the children cried out, 'Where are the chairs and tables?' He had found an immense hour glass, in a niche over the huge cavernous hearth, and said, smilingly, 'We are indeed in another time, a Saturnine time.' Civilisation, it turned out, existed upstairs, though cook complained mightily of ageing rusty iron pots and a ratcheted spit like a diabolical instrument of torture. Everything was massive and ancient: oak tables on a forest of oak pillars, huge leather-backed thrones, beds with heavy gilded hangings, chests ingeniously carved on clawed feet, too heavy to lift, tombs, Tom said, for curious girls. 'A house for giants,' Joshua said to Juliana, seeing her intrigue and anxiety both clearly. He drew her attention to the huge wrought-iron handles of the keys. 'We are out of the nineteenth century entirely,' he said. The walls of the *salone* were furnished with a series of portraits, silver-wigged and dark-eyed and rigid. Joshua's bedroom had a fearful and appalling painting of fruits and flowers so arranged as to form a kind of human form, bristling with pineapple spines, curvaceous with melons, staring through passion-flower eyes. '*That*,' said Juliana, 'is bound to appeal to Mr Browning, who is interested in the grotesque.' Tom said he would not make much of the family portraits, which were so similar as to argue a significant want of skill in the painter. 'Either that, or a striking family resemblance,' said Joshua. 'Or a painter whose efforts all turn out to resemble his own appearance. I have known one or two portraiture painters like that.' Sitting now on the rim of the fountain trough, watching him frown over his drawing, look up, correct, frown and scribble, she wondered if by some extraordinary process her undistinguished features might be brought to resemble his keen and handsome ones. He was gipsyish in colouring, and well-groomed by habit, a kind of contradiction. Here in the mountains he wore a loose jacket and a silk scarf knotted at his neck, but knotted too neatly. He was smaller and thinner than Tom.

Joshua worked on the mouth corner. He had chosen a very soft, silvery pencil for this very soft skin: he did not want to draw a caricature in a few sparing lines, he wanted somehow to convey the nature of the solidity of the flesh of cheek and chin. He had mapped in the rounds and ovals, of the whole head and the hat brim, and the descending curve of the looped plait in the nape of Juliana's neck, and the spot where her ear came, and parts of the calm wide forehead. The shadow cast on the flesh by the circumference of the hat was another pleasant problem in tone and shading. He worked in little, circling movements, feeling out little clefts with the stub of his pencil, isolating tiny white patches of light that shone on the ledge of the lip or the point of the chin, leaving this untouched paper to glitter by contrast with his working. He filled out the plump underthroat with love; *so* it gave a little, *so* it was taut.

'I wish I could see,' said Juliana, 'what you are doing.'

'When it is done.'

It was almost as if he was touching the face, watching its grey shape swim into existence out of a spider web of marks. His hand hovered over where the nose would be, curled a nostril, dented its flare. If anywhere he put dark marks where light should be, it was ruined. No two artists' marks are the same, no more than their thumbprints. Behind Juliana's head he did the edge, no more, of the flat stony texture of the solar face.

Juliana kept still. Her anxieties about Mr Browning and the massive awkwardness of their temporary home were calmed. Joshua's tentative pencil began to explore the area of the eyes. The eyes were difficult. They must first be modelled—the life was conferred by the pinpoint of dark and the flecks of white light, and the exact distances between them. He had studied the amazing eyes created by Rembrandt van Rijn, a precise little bristling, fine, hair-like movement of the brush, a spot of crimson here, a thread of carmine there, a spider-web paste of colour out of which a soul suddenly stared. 'Please look at me,' he said to Juliana, 'please look at me—yes, like that—and don't move.' His pencil point hovered, thinking, and Juliana's pupils contracted in the greenish halo of the iris, as she looked into the light, and blinked, involuntarily. She did not want to stare at him; it was unnatural, though his considering gaze, measuring, drawing back, turning to one side and the other, seemed natural enough. A flood of colour moved darkly up her throat, along her chin, into the planes and convexities of her cheeks. Tears collected, unbidden, without cause. Joshua noted the deepening of colour, and then the glisten, and ceased to caress the paper with the pencil. Their eyes met. What a complicated thing is this meeting of eyes, which disturbs the air between two still faces, which has its effects on the heartbeat, the hair on the wrists, the flow of blood. You can understand, Joshua thought, why poets talk of arrows, or of hooks thrown. He said, 'How odd it is to look at someone, after all, and to see their soul looking back again. How can a pencil catch that? How do we know we see each other?'

Juliana said nothing, only blushed, rosier and rosier, flooded by moving blood under her hat, and one large tear brimmed over the line of lower lashes, with their wet silkiness which Joshua had been trying to render.

'Ah, Juliana. There is no need to cry. Please, don't. I'll stop.'

'No. I am being silly. I—I am not used to be looked at so intently.'

'You are beautiful to look at,' said Joshua, comparing the flowing colours with the placid silver-grey of his attempt to feel out her face. He put down his drawing, and touched at her cheek with a clean handkerchief. The garden hummed with insect song and bubbled with water; he was somehow inside it, as he was when he was drawing; he looked down and there, under the tight pink muslin, was the generous round of a breast. It was all the same, all alive, the warm stone, the water, the rough grass, the swirl of pink muslin, the troubled young face. He put his two hands round the little ones that turned in her lap, stilling them like trapped birds.

'I have alarmed you, Juliana. I didn't mean that. I'm sorry.'

'I don't want you to be sorry.' Small but clear.

'Look at me again.' It was said for him; it was what came next; they no sooner looked but they loved, a voice told him; the trouble was delightful, compelling, alarming. 'Please look at me, Juliana. How often do we really look at each other?'

She had looked at him before, when he was not looking. Now she could not. And so it seemed natural for him to put his arms along the soft round shoulders, to push his face, briefly, briefly, under the brim of the hat, to rest his warm lips on the mouth corner his pencil had touched in its distance. Juliana could hear the sea, or her own life, swirling.

'Juliana,' he said, 'Juliana, Juliana.' And then, prompted by some little local daemon of the grass plot and the carved smiler, 'Juliana is the name of the lady in one of the poems I most love. Do you know it? It is by Andrew Marvell; it is the complaint of the mower, Damon.'

Juliana said she did not know it. She would like to hear it.
He recited.

> 'My mind was once the true survey
> Of all these meadows fresh and gay;
> And in the greenness of the grass
> Did see my thoughts as in a glass
> 'Til Juliana came, and she,
> What I do to the grass, did to my thoughts and me.'

'She was not very kind,' said Juliana.

'We do not know what she was,' said Joshua. 'Only the
effect she had upon the Mower.'

He gripped the little fingers. The fingers gripped back. And
then the children came bursting down the pathway under the
trees, announcing an expedition to the village.

Juliana was in no doubt about what had happened. It was love.
Love had blossomed, or struck, like lightning, like a hawk, as
it was clearly seen to do in novels and poems, as it took no
time to do, voracious or sunny, in the stories she lived on, the
scenes her imagination and more, her moral expectations,
naturally inhabited. Love visited all who were not ridiculous
or religious. Simply, she had always supposed her own, when it
came, would be unrequited and lowering, was unprepared for
kisses and poetry. She went to bed that night and turned on her
dusty bolster among her coarse sheets, all vaguely aflame, dif-
fusely desirous, terribly unused to violent personal happiness.

Joshua was less sure of what had happened. He too burned
that night, less vaguely, more locally, making a turmoil of his
coverings and tormented by aches and tensions. He recognised
the old cherub for what he was, and gave him his true name,
the name Juliana gave him, honourably, not wriggling into

demeaning her or himself by thinking simply of lust. He went over and over every detail with reverent pleasure, the pink muslin, the trusting tear-filled eyes, the flutter of a pulse, the soft mouth, the revelations of his questing pencil. But, unlike Juliana, he was already under the rule of another daemon or cherub; he was used to accommodating his body and mind to the currents of the dictates of another imperative; he felt a responsibility also to the empty greenness that had existed in his primitive innocence, before. He wanted, he loved; but did he want enough, did he love enough? Had he inadvertently behaved dishonourably to this young creature, certainly to-night the dearest to him in the world, certainly haloed with light and warm with charm and promise of affection? He was twenty years old. He had no experience and was confused. He finally promised himself that tomorrow he would do as he had already promised himself he would do, set off early and alone of the mountain-side, to do some sketching—even painting. He would look at the land beyond habitation. He would explain to her: she would immediately understand all, since what he should say would be no more than the serious and honourable truth; that he must go away.

He rose very early, and went into the kitchen to beg sandwiches, and a flask of wine, from cook. Gianni was sent off to saddle his mule, to take him as far as the village, Lucchio, which could be seen clinging to the face of the mountain opposite. It was barely dawn, but Juliana was up, too; he encountered her in the dark corridor.

'I am going up the cliff, to paint,' he said. 'That was what I had intended to do, before.'

'We must think a little,' he said. 'I must go up there, and think. You do understand? You will talk to me again—we will speak to each other—when I return?'

She could have said: it is nothing to me whether you go up the mountain or remain here. But she was honest.

'I shall look out for you coming back.'

'Juliana,' he said, 'ah, Juliana.'

The mule skidded on the stones. The road was paved, after a fashion, but the stones were upended, like rows of jagged teeth. Gianni walked stolidly and silently behind. The road circled the hill, under chestnuts, then out onto the craggier ascent. It twisted and the sun rose; the mule passed from cold shadow to whitish glare and back again. Hot stone was very hot, Joshua thought, and cold stone very cold. He could smell stone of both kinds, as well as the warm hairy sweating mule and the glossy rubbed ancient leather. He looked backwards and forwards, along the snaking line of the river that cut its way about and about between the great cones of the Apennines. The sky had a white clearness and emptiness, not yet gleaming, which was essentially Italian. He knew the mountains round: the Libro Aperto, or open book, the Prato Fiorito, velvety and enamelled with flowers, the Monte Pellegrino, covered with silvery edible thistles and inhabited, once, by hermits whose diet they were. He thought about the mountains, with reverence and curiosity, and his thoughts on the mountains, like those of many of his contemporaries, were in large part the thoughts of John Ruskin, who had seen them clearly, as no one else, it seemed, had ever seen them, and had declared that this clarity of vision was the essence of truth, virtue, and good art, which were, in this, one. Mountains are the bones of the earth, he had written. 'But there is this difference between the action of the earth, and that of a living creature; that while the exerted limb marks its bones and tendons through the flesh, the excited earth casts off the flesh altogether, and its bones come out from beneath.' Joshua thought about this, and looked at the working knobs of bone at the base of the mule-neck, under their thin layer of skin, and remembered, formally and then excitedly, the search for Juliana's bone under the round cheek. Ruskin was a geologist. His ideals of painting were founded on an intricate and analytical knowledge of how the movement of water shaped and unmade and shifted the eternal hills, of how clefts were formed, and precipices sheered. It had been a revelation to the young Joshua to read in *Modern Painters* how very young was man's interest in these ancient forms. The Greeks had seen them merely as threats or aids to the adventures of gods and heroes; mediaeval man had on the whole disliked anything wild or savage, preferring order and cultivation, trellised gardens and bowers to wild woods or louring cliffs. John Ruskin would have delighted in the mediaeval names of the hills through which he now travelled: the Open Book, the Flowery Meadow, the Pilgrim's Mount came straight out of Dante into the nineteenth century. Ruskin had characterised modern art, with some disparagement, as the 'service of clouds'. The mediaeval mind had taken pleasure in the steady, the definite, the luminous, but the moderns rejoiced in the dark, the sombre. Our time, Ruskin had said, and Joshua had joyfully learned, was the true Dark Ages, devoted to smokiness and burnt umber. Joshua had not understood about the necessity of brightness and colour until he came south this first time, until he saw the light, although intellectually he had been fired by Ruskin's diatribes against Victorian darkness and ugliness in all things, in dress, in manners, in machines and chimneys, in storm-clouds and grottoes.

Only, in Paris, he had seen something which changed, not the desire for brightness, but the ideas about the steady, the definite, the luminous. Something which should have helped him with the soft expanse of Juliana's pink dress, which he remembered, turning a corner and seeing the village again, clutching the cliff like thornbushes with half their roots in air. It was to do with the flesh and the muslin, the tones in common, the tones that were not shared, a blue in the pink cloth . . . you could pick up in the vein or the eyelid, the wrist, a shimmer, a thread . . . The hot saddle shifted beneath him: the mule sighed: the man sighed. Gianni said, 'Lucchio, una mezz'ora.' The white air was also blue and the blue white light.

When they got there, there was something alarming about this tenacious and vertiginous assembly of buildings, peacefully white in the mounting heat, chill in their dark aspects, all blindly shuttered, their dark life inside their doors. Houses stood where they were planted, where a level floor, or floors, could be found for them—often they were different heights on different sides. Many had tiny gardens fronting the empty air, and Gianni pointed out to Joshua, in two different instances, a toddling child, stiff-skirted, bonneted, tethered at the waist by a length of linen to a hook in the door posts. Even the church bells were grounded, caged in iron frames outside the church door, safe, Joshua could only suppose, from vibrating unstably against the overhanging rock-shelf.

Here Joshua parted from Gianni and the mules; they would meet again near the bells on the roadway, an hour or so from sunset. He took the path that curved up out of the village, which passed the ancient fountain where the girls came and went barefoot, carrying great copper vessels on their heads, swaying. At the fountain he replenished his water bottle, and moistened his face and neck. Then he went on up. Above the village was a ruined and much decayed castle, its thick outer wall continuous with the rock face, its courtyard littered with shattered building blocks. He thought of stopping here to draw the ancient masonry, but after reflection went on up. He had a need to study the wholly inhuman. His path, a branching, vertiginous sheep track, now wound between whitish sheer pillars of stone; his feet dislodged rubble and a powdery dust. He liked the feeling of the difficult going-up, and his step was springy. If he got far enough up and round he would have a downwards vantage point for sketching the improbable village. He thought alternately about Ruskin and about Juliana.

Ruskin disliked the Apennines: he found their limestone monotonous in hue, grey and toneless, utterly melancholy. He had expended several pages of exact lyrical prose on this gloomy colouring, pointing out that it was the colouring Dante gave to his Evil-pits in the Inferno, malignant grey, he gleefully recorded, akin to the robes of the purgatorial angel which were of the colour of ashes, or earth dug dry. Ashes, to an Italian mind, wrote Ruskin beside his London coals, necessarily meant *wood-ashes*—very pale—analogous to the hue seen on the sunny side of Italian hills, produced by the scorching of the ground, a dusty and lifeless whitish grey, utterly painful and oppressive. He preferred the strenuous, masculine, mossy and complicated Alps, awesome and sublime. Joshua had not really seen the Alps, but he found these smaller mountains beautiful, not oppressive, and their chalky paleness interesting, not dulling. Ruskin believed the great artists were those who had never despised anything, however small, of God's making. If he was prepared to treat the Apennine rocks as though they had been created perhaps only by a minor daemon or demi-urge, Joshua, on Ruskin's own principles, was not. If he could find a means of recording the effects of these ashy whitenesses, of the reddish iron-stains in the stone, of the way one block stood against another, of the root-systems of the odd, wind-sculpted trees, he would be content. He would, if he could find his vantage, 'do' the view of the village. He would also, for that love of the true forms of things desiderated by his master, do studies of the stones as they were, of the scrubby things that grew.

He found his perch, in time; a wideish ledge, in a cleft with a high triangular shadow bisecting it, diminishing as the sun climbed. He thought of it as his eyrie. From it he would see the village, a little lower, winding round the conical form of the mountain like a clinging wreath, crowned by a fantastic cluster of crags all sky-pointing like huge hot inverted icicles, white on the white-blue sky. These forms were paradoxical, strong yet aerial and delicate like needles, reminding him of the lightness of lace on the emptiness, yet stone of earth. He took out his sketching-glass and filled it, arranged his paints and his chalks and his pencils, became wholly involved in the conversion of estimated distances to perceived relative sizes and tones. The problem was to convey this blanched, bony world with shadows which should, by contrast, form and display its dazzle. He tried both with pencil and with washes of colour. Ruskin said: 'Here we are, then, with white paper for our highest light, and visible illuminated surface for our deepest shadow, set to run the gauntlet against nature, with the sun for her light, and vacuity for her gloom.' Joshua wrestled with these limitations, in a glare which made it hard for him to judge the brightness even of his own paper-surface. He was very miserable; his efforts took shape and solidified into failures of vision. He was supremely happy; unaware of himself and wholly aware of rock formations, sunlight and visible empty air, of which he became part, moment by moment and then timelessly, the notation of things seen being no more than the flow of his blood, necessary for continuance in this state.

At some point he became quite suddenly hungry, and took out of his knapsack his oily but agreeable packages of bread, meat, eggs, cheese. He devoured all, exhausted, as though his life was in danger, and put away his chicken bones and egg-shells, for had not Ruskin himself complained that modern man came to the mountains not to fast but to feast, leaving glaciers covered with bones and eggshells. He had an idea of himself tearing at his food like a young bird on its ledge. Wiping his fingers, pouring more water for his work, he remembered Juliana, confusedly and from a distance, a softness in the corner of his consciousness, a warmth to which he would return when he returned to himself. He could never hurt Juliana, never. Behind the stone he had chosen for his seat were the bleached remains of some other creature's meal; skeletal pinions and claws, a triangular pointed skull, a few snail shells, wrecked and pierced. He made a quick water-colour sketch of these, interested in the different whites and creams and greys of bone, shell and stone. And shadow. He was particularly pleased with his rendering of a snail shell, the arch of its entrance intact, the dome of the cavern behind shattered to reveal the pearly interior involution. These small things occupied as much space on the paper as the mountains. Their shadows were as intricate, though different.

When he came to look out at the land again, the air had changed, Near, it danced; farther away, on the horizon, white cloud was piling itself up and throwing out long arms from peak to peak; under the arms were horizontal bars of black shadow which seemed impossible where the sky had been so bright, so even. He set himself to draw this advance, watching the cloud hang along the precipices, waiting to stoop, and then engulf them. A wind began to blow, fitfully, rattling his sketch-book. The river-bed darkened: sounds were stilled that he had hardly noticed, insect songs and the odd bird call.

The thing that he had seen in Paris, the thing that he knew would change his ideas about painting, was a large canvas by

Monsieur Monet, a painting precisely of mist and fog, *Vétheuil in the Fog*. It had been rejected by its prospective purchaser because it had not enough paint on the canvas. It was not clear and definite. It was vague, it painted little more than the swirl and shimmer of light on the curtain of white water particles through which the shapes of the small town were barely visible, a slaty upright stroke here, a pearly faint triangle of possible roof or spire there. You could see, miraculously, that if you could see the town, which you could not, it would be reflected in the expanse of river at the foot of the canvas, which you could also not see. Monsieur Monet had found a solution to the problem posed by Ruskin, of how to paint light, with the small range of colours available: he had trapped light in his surface, light itself was his subject. His paint was light. He had painted, not the thing seen, but the act of seeing. So now, Joshua thought, as the first thin films of mist began to approach his eyrie, I want to note down these shifting, these vanishing veils. Through them, in the valley on the other side, he could see a perpendicular race of falling arrows dark and glistening, the hailstorm sweeping. The speed of its approach was beautiful. He made a kind of pattern on his paper of the verticals and the fleeciness, the different thickness and thinness of the vapour infiltrating his own ledge. He must be ready to pack up fast when it descended or his work would be ruined. When it came, it came in one fierce onslaught, a blast in his face, an impenetrable white darkness. He staggered a little, under the blows of the ice-bullets, put up an arm, took a false step, still thinking of Ruskin and Monet, and fell. And it was all over. Except for one or two unimaginable moments, a clutch at life, a gasp of useless air, a rush of adrenalin, a shattering of bone and brain, the vanishing between instants of all that warmth and intelligence and aspiration.

*

Down at the Villa Colomba they had been grateful for their thick walls and windows. The garden had been whipped and the flowers flattened, the white dark impenetrable. It lasted only ten minutes, maybe a quarter of an hour. Afterwards the children went out and came back crying that it was like Aladdin's palace. Everywhere, in the courtyard, was a glittering mass of green and shining stones, chestnut leaves bright with wet and shredded, hailstones as large as hazelnuts. Arthur and Gwendolen ran here and there gathering handfuls of these, tossing them, crying, 'Look at my diamonds.' The solid, the enduring, the familiar landscape smiled again in the washed sunlight. Juliana went out with the children, looked up at the still shrouded peaks, and filled her hands too with the jewels, cold, wet, gleaming, running away between her outstretched fingers.

Sarianna Browning received a letter, and wrote a letter. It took time for both these letters to reach their destinations, for the weather had deteriorated rapidly after those first storms, the mules could travel neither down from the Villa Colomba nor up to the paradise of coolness and quiet. Whips of rain flung themselves around the smiling tops; lightning cracked; tracks were rivers; Robert complained of the deep grinding of the pain that might be rheumatism and might be his liver. The envelope when she opened it was damp and pliant. Phrases stood out: 'terrible accident . . . taken from us at the height of his powers . . . we trust, with his Maker . . . our terrible responsibility to his father and mother . . . Villa Colomba unbearable to us now . . . we trust you will understand, and accept our deepest apologies and regrets . . . we know Mr Browning would not probably desire to visit us in Florence, though of course . . .'

Sarianna wrote to Mrs Bronson. 'Terrible accident . . . we

trust, with his Maker . . . Robert not at his best . . . weather unsettled . . . hope to make our way now to Venice, since Florence is out of the question . . .'

The sky was like slate. The poet was trapped in the pleasant room. Sheets of water ran down his windows and collected on his balcony. He thought of other deaths. Five years ago he had been planning to ascend another mountain with another woman; going to rouse her, after his morning swim, full of life, he had come round her balcony and looked through her window to see her kneeling, composed and unnatural, head bowed to the ground. She had been still warm when he went in and released her from this posture. Remembering this, he went through the shock of her dead warmth again, and shuddered. He had gone up the mountain, all the same, alone, and had made a poem of it, a poem which clambered with difficulty around the topic of what if anything survived, of which hands, if any, moulded or received us. He had been half-ashamed of his assertion of his own liveliness and vigour, half-exalted by height and oxygen and achievement, as he had meant to be. This dead young man was unknown to him. For a moment his imagination reached after him, and imagined him, in his turn, as it was his nature to imagine, reaching after the unattainable, up there. Man's reach must exceed his grasp. Or what's a Heaven for? Perhaps the young man was a very conventional and unambitious young man: he did not know: it was his idea, that height went with reaching, even if defeated, as we all are, and must be. Over dinner, Mrs Miller asked him if he would write a poem on the tragedy; this might, she suggested, bring comfort to the bereaved parents. No, he said. No, he would not. And elaborated, for good manners' sake. Even the greatest tragedies in his life had rarely stirred him directly to composition. They left him mute. He should hate any mechanical attempt to do what would only acquire worth from being a spontaneous outflow. Poems arose like birds setting off from stray twigs of facts to flights of more or less distance, unpredictably and often after many years. This was not to say that this tragedy, any tragedy, did not affect his whole mind and have its influence, more or less remarkably, on what he wrote. As he explained, his attention elsewhere, what he had explained before and would explain again, say, when Miss Teena Rochfort set fire to her skirts with a spark in her sewing-basket, in 1883, he thought of the young painter, now dead, and of his son, whose nude sculptures had been objects of moral opprobrium to ladies like Mrs Miller, and of Mrs Miller's hat. There was a poem in that, in her stolid and disagreeable presence, bedizened with murdered innocents, and the naked life of art and love. Lines came into his head.

> What
> (Excuse the interruption) clings
> Half-savage-like around your hat?
> Ah, do they please you? Wild-bird wings . . .

Yes. 'Clothed with murder.' That would do. A black irritability was assuaged. He smiled with polite enthusiasm.

The lady sits in the window. The scholar, turning the browned pages, discovers the letter that she will receive. At first, in the story that he is reading and constructing this letter appears to be hopeful. The poet and his sister will not go further south. They will set their steps towards Venice. But it is not to be. Further letters are exchanged. Torrential rain in Bologna . . . Robert's pains worse . . . medical opinion advisable . . . roads impassable . . . deeply regret disappointing you and even more our own disappointment . . . return to London. An opportunity has been missed. A tentative love has not flowered. Next year, however, is better. The poet returns to Venice, meets in the lady's drawing-room the Pretender to the French and Spanish thrones, discusses with him the identity of the Man in the Iron Mask, exposes himself, undaunted, on the Lido, to sea-fret and Adriatic gust, reads tombstones, kisses hands, and remarks on the seagulls.

Aunt Juliana kept, pressed in the family Bible, a curious portrait of a young girl, who looked out of one live eye and one blank, unseeing one, oval like those of angels on monumental sculpture.

Virginia Woolf
The Legacy

'For Sissy Miller.' Gilbert Clandon, taking up the pearl brooch that lay among a litter of rings and brooches on a little table in his wife's drawing-room, read the inscription: 'For Sissy Miller, with my love.'

It was like Angela to have remembered even Sissy Miller, her secretary. Yet how strange it was, Gilbert Clandon thought once more, that she had left everything in such order—a little gift of some sort for every one of her friends. It was as if she had foreseen her death. Yet she had been in perfect health when she left the house that morning, six weeks ago; when she stepped off the kerb in Piccadilly and the car had killed her.

He was waiting for Sissy Miller. He had asked her to come; he owed her, he felt, after all the years she had been with them, this token of consideration. Yes, he went on, as he sat there waiting, it was strange that Angela had left everything in such order. Every friend had been left some little token of her affection. Every ring, every necklace, every little Chinese box—she had a passion for little boxes—had a name on it. And each had some memory for him. This he had given her; this—the enamel dolphin with the ruby eyes—she had pounced upon one day in a back street in Venice. He could remember her little cry of delight. To him, of course, she had left nothing in particular, unless it were her diary. Fifteen little volumes, bound in green leather, stood behind him on her writing table. Ever since they were married, she had kept a diary. Some of their very few—he could not call them quarrels, say tiffs—had been about that diary. When he came in and found her writing, she always shut it or put her hand over it. 'No, no, no,' he could hear her say, 'After I'm dead—perhaps.' So she had left it him, as her legacy. It was the only thing they had not shared when she was alive. But he had always taken it for granted that she would outlive him. If only she had stopped one moment, and had thought what she was doing, she would be alive now. But she had stepped straight off the kerb, the driver of the car had said at the inquest. She had given him no chance to pull up . . . Here the sound of voices in the hall interrupted him.

'Miss Miller, Sir,' said the maid.

She came in. He had never seen her alone in his life, nor, of course, in tears. She was terribly distressed, and no wonder. Angela had been much more to her than an employer. She had been a friend. To himself, he thought, as he pushed a chair for her and asked her to sit down, she was scarcely distinguishable from any other woman of her kind. There were thousands of Sissy Millers—drab little women in black carrying attaché cases. But Angela, with her genius for sympathy, had discovered all sorts of qualities in Sissy Miller. She was the soul of discretion, so silent; so trustworthy, one could tell her anything, and so on.

Miss Miller could not speak at first. She sat there dabbing her eyes with her pocket handkerchief. Then she made an effort.

'Pardon me, Mr Clandon,' she said.

He murmured. Of course he understood. It was only natural. He could guess what his wife had meant to her.

'I've been so happy here,' she said, looking round. Her eyes rested on the writing table behind him. It was here they had worked—she and Angela. For Angela had her share of the duties that fall to the lot of the wife of a prominent politician. She had been the greatest help to him in his career. He had often seen her and Sissy sitting at that table—Sissy at the typewriter, taking down letters from her dictation. No doubt Miss Miller was thinking of that, too. Now all he had to do was to give her the brooch his wife had left her. A rather incongruous gift it seemed. It might have been better to have left her a sum of money, or even the typewriter. But there it was—'For Sissy Miller, with my love.' And, taking the brooch, he gave it her with the little speech that he had prepared. He knew, he said, that she would value it. His wife had often worn it . . . And she replied, as she took it, almost as if she too had prepared a speech, that it would always be a treasured possession . . . She had, he supposed, other clothes upon which a pearl brooch would not look quite so incongruous. She was wearing the little black coat and skirt that seemed the uniform of her profession. Then he remembered—she was in mourning, of course. She too had had her tragedy—a brother, to whom she was devoted, had died only a week or two before Angela. In some accident was it? He could remember only Angela telling him; Angela, with her genius for sympathy, had been terribly upset. Meanwhile Sissy Miller had risen. She was putting on her gloves. Evidently she felt that she ought not to intrude. But he could not let her go without saying something about her future. What were her plans? Was there any way in which he could help her?

She was gazing at the table, where she had sat at her typewriter, where the diary lay. And, lost in her memories of Angela, she did not at once answer his suggestion that he should help her. She seemed for a moment not to understand. So he repeated:

'What are your plans, Miss Miller?'

'My plans? Oh, that's all right, Mr Clandon,' she exclaimed. 'Please don't bother yourself about me.'

He took her to mean that she was in no need of financial assistance. It would be better, he realised, to make any suggestion of that kind in a letter. All he could do now was to say as he pressed her hand, 'Remember, Miss Miller, if there's any way in which I can help you, it will be a pleasure . . .' Then he opened the door. For a moment, on the threshold, as if a sudden thought had struck her, she stopped.

'Mr Clandon,' she said, looking straight at him for the first time, and for the first time he was struck by the expression, sympathetic yet searching, in her eyes. 'If at any time,' [she] was saying, 'there's anything I can do to help you, remember, I shall feel it, for your wife's sake, a pleasure . . .'

With that she was gone. Her words and the look that went with them were unexpected. It was almost as if she believed, or hoped, that he would have need of her. A curious, perhaps a fantastic idea occurred to him as he returned to his chair. Could it be, that during all those years when he had scarcely noticed her, she, as the novelists say, had entertained a passion for him? He caught his own reflection in the glass as he passed. He was over fifty; but he could not help admitting that he was still, as the looking-glass showed him, a very distinguished-looking man.

'Poor Sissy Miller!' he said, half laughing. How he would have liked to share that joke with his wife! He turned instinctively to her diary. 'Gilbert,' he read, opening it at random, 'looked so wonderful . . .' It was as if she had answered his question. Of course[,] she seemed to say, you're very attractive to women. Of course Sissy Miller felt that too. He read on. 'How proud I am to be his wife!' And he had always been very proud to be her husband. How often when they dined out somewhere he had looked at her across the table and said to himself, She is the loveliest woman here! He read on. That first year he had been standing for Parliament. They had toured his constituency. 'When Gilbert sat down the applause was terrific. The whole audience rose and sang: "For he's a jolly good fellow." I was quite overcome.' He remembered that, too. She had been sitting on the platform beside him. He could still see the glance she cast at him, and how she had tears in her eyes. And then? He turned the pages. They had gone to Venice. He recalled that happy holiday after the election. 'We had ices at Florians.' He smiled—she was still such a child, she loved ices. 'Gilbert gave me a most interesting account of the history of Venice. He told me that the Doges . . .' she had written it all out in her schoolgirl hand. One of the delights of travelling with Angela had been that she was so eager to learn. She was so terribly ignorant, she used to say, as if that were not one of her charms. And then—he opened the next volume—they had come back to London. 'I was so anxious to make a good impression. I wore my wedding dress.' He could see her now sitting next old Sir Edward; and making a conquest of that formidable old man, his chief. He read on rapidly, filling in scene after scene from her scrappy fragments. 'Dined at the House of Commons . . . To an evening party at the Lovegroves. Did I realise my responsibility, Lady L. asked me, as Gilbert's wife?' Then as the years passed—he took another volume from the writing table—he had become more and more absorbed in his work. And she, of course, was more often alone. It had been a great grief to her, apparently, that they had had no children. 'How I wish,' one entry read, 'that Gilbert had a son!' Oddly enough he had never much regretted that himself. Life had been so full, so rich as it was. That year he had been given a minor post in the government. A minor post only, but her comment was: 'I am quite certain now that he will be Prime Minister!' Well, if things had gone differently, it might have been so. He paused here to speculate upon what might have been. Politics was a gamble, he reflected; but the game wasn't over yet. Not at fifty. He cast his eyes rapidly over more pages, full of the little trifles, the insignificant, happy, daily trifles that had made up her life.

He took up another volume and opened it at random. 'What a coward I am! I let the chance slip again. But it seemed selfish to bother him about my own affairs, when he has so much to think about. And we so seldom have an evening alone.' What was the meaning of that? Oh here was the explanation—it referred to her work in the East End. 'I plucked up courage and talked to Gilbert at last. He was so kind, so good. He made no objection.' He remembered that conversation. She had told him that she felt so idle, so useless. She wished to have some work of her own. She wanted to do something—she had blushed so prettily, he remembered, as she said it sitting in that very chair—to help others. He had bantered her a little. Hadn't she enough to do looking after him, after her home? Still if it amused her of course he had no objection. What was it? Some district? Some committee? Only she must promise not to make herself ill. So it seemed that every Wednesday she went to Whitechapel. He remembered how he hated the clothes she wore on those occasions. But she had taken it very seriously it seemed. The diary was full of references like this: 'Saw Mrs Jones . . . She has ten children . . . Husband lost his arm in an accident . . . Did my best to find a job for Lily.' He skipped on. His own name occurred less frequently. His interest slackened. Some of the entries conveyed nothing to him. For example: 'Had a heated argument about socialism with B. M.' Who was B. M.? He could not fill in the initials; some woman[,] he supposed[,] that she had met on one of her committees. 'B. M. made a violent attack upon the upper classes . . . I walked back after the meeting with B. M. and tried to convince him. But he is so narrow-minded.' So B. M. was a man—no doubt one of those 'intellectuals' as they call themselves, who are so violent, as Angela said, and so narrow-minded. She had invited him to come and see her apparently. 'B. M. came to dinner. He shook hands with Minnie!' That note of exclamation gave another twist to his mental picture. B. M. it seemed wasn't used to parlourmaids; he had shaken hands with Minnie. Presumably he was one of those tame working men who air their views in ladies' drawing-rooms. Gilbert knew the type, and had no liking for this particular specimen, whoever B. M. might be. Here he was again. 'Went with B. M. to the Tower of London . . . He said revolution is bound to come . . . He said we live in a Fool's Paradise.' That was just the kind of thing B. M. would say—Gilbert could hear him. He could also see him quite distinctly—a stubby little man, with a rough beard, red tie, dressed as they always did in tweeds, who had never done an honest day's work in his life. Surely Angela had the sense to see through him? He read on. 'B. M. said some very disagreeable things about . . .' The name was carefully scratched out. 'I told him I would not listen to any more abuse of . . .' Again the name was obliterated. Could it have been his own name? Was that why Angela covered the page so quickly when he came in? The thought added to his growing dislike of B. M. He had had the impertinence to discuss him in this very room. Why had Angela never told him? It was very unlike her to conceal anything; she had been the soul of candour. He turned the pages, picking out every reference to B. M. 'B. M. told me the story of his childhood. His mother went out charring . . . When I think of it, I can hardly bear to go on living in such luxury . . . Three guineas for one hat!' If only she had discussed the matter with him, instead of puzzling her poor little head about questions that were much too difficult for her to understand! He had lent her books. Karl Marx. 'The Coming Revolution.' The initials B. M., B. M., B. M., recurred repeatedly. But why never the full name? There was an informality, an intimacy in the use of initials that was very unlike Angela. Had she called him B. M. to his face? He read on. 'B. M. came unexpectedly after dinner. Luckily, I was alone.' That was only a year ago. 'Luckily'—why luckily?—'I was alone.' Where had he been that night? He checked the date in his engagement book. It had been the night of the Mansion House dinner. And B. M. and Angela had spent the evening alone! He tried to recall that evening. Was she waiting up for him when he came back? Had the room looked just as usual? Were there glasses on the table? Were the chairs drawn close together? He could remember nothing—nothing whatever, nothing except his own speech at the Mansion House dinner. It became more and more inexplicable to him—the whole situation: his wife receiving an unknown man alone. Perhaps the next volume would explain. Hastily he reached for the last of the diaries—the one she had left unfinished when she died. There on the very first page was that cursed fellow again. 'Dined alone with B. M. . . . He became very agitated. He said it was time we understood each other . . . I tried to make him listen. But he would not. He threatened that if I did not . . .' the rest of the page was scored over. She had written 'Egypt. Egypt. Egypt.' over the whole page. He could not make out a single word; but there could be only one interpretation: the scoundrel had asked her to become his mistress. Alone in his room! The blood rushed to Gilbert Clandon's face. He turned the pages rapidly. What had been her answer? Initials had ceased. It was simply 'he' now. 'He came again. I told him I could not come to any decision . . . I implored him to leave me.' He had forced himself upon her in this very house? But why hadn't she told him? How could she have hesitated for an instant? Then: 'I wrote him a letter.' Then pages were left blank. Then there was this: 'No answer to my letter.' Then more blank pages; and then this.

'He has done what he threatened.' After that—what came after that? He turned page after page. All were blank. But there[,] on the very day before her death[,] was this entry: 'Have I the courage to do it too?' That was the end.

Gilbert Clandon let the book slide to the floor. He could see her in front of him. She was standing on the kerb in Piccadilly. Her eyes stared; her fists were clenched. Here came the car . . .

He could not bear it. He must know the truth. He strode to the telephone.

'Miss Miller!' There was silence. Then he heard someone moving in the room.

'Sissy Miller speaking'—her voice at last answered him.

'Who,' he thundered, 'is B. M.?'

He could hear the cheap clock ticking on her mantelpiece; then a long drawn sigh. Then at last she said:

'He was my brother.'

He *was* her brother; her brother who had killed himself.

'Is there,' he heard Sissy Miller asking, 'anything that I can explain?'

'Nothing!' he cried. 'Nothing!'

He had received his legacy. She had told him the truth. She had stepped off the kerb to rejoin her lover. She had stepped off the kerb to escape from him.

Ivan Klima
The Tightrope Walkers

It was a rather overcast, blustery early evening in July when I arrived at Ota's wooden weekend cottage on my ancient Eska bicycle. The cottage stood in the bend of a river which at that moment looked like a tranquil little stream. The water lapped against the stony banks and the aspen leaves rustled softly. The spot was so full of peace and ease that it conjured up the images of my dead friends. Here I was listening to those gentle sounds, while they had long been enveloped in silence.

Perhaps it was the result of my wartime experiences or of a self-pity typical of my age, but I had never quite been able to surrender to pleasure or joy, or to relax. As if I never ceased to be aware of the connection between happiness and despair, freedom and anxiety, life and ruin. My feelings were probably those of a tightrope walker on his high wire. No matter how fixedly I was looking upwards I was still conscious of the drop below me.

I had only once in my life seen tightrope walkers. That was less than a year after the war. They'd come in four horse-drawn caravans, and on the open ground in our street—that is where the town actually ended then, because beyond there were only cemeteries and army training grounds—they'd put up three masts. One of them was so high I felt giddy merely looking up at it from the ground. Between the two lower ones they stretched the wire, and below that they suspended a net.

On the upper platforms of the masts they then laid out a lot of props: various bicycles, a two-legged table and one-legged chairs, an umbrella, a hoop and those long balancing poles that tightrope walkers use.

I couldn't wait for the performance to start and so I was one of the first to arrive. I chose a spot on a hard-trampled heap of clay, from where, I assumed, there'd be the best view, and peered up. I was aware of a vibration of the wire, the tall mast was visibly swaying from side to side. Then the gigantic searchlights were turned on and the loudspeakers came hoarsely to life. A moment later a girl in glittering blue clothes, with hair as dark as coal and a heart-stoppingly beautiful face, stepped up to me and held out a little collecting-box. I gave her a ten-crown note and she smiled charmingly at me: with her lips, her face and her eyes. Then she flicked her head back so that the band in her hair flashed for a moment as if it was on fire, and tore off a ticket for me. I watched her moving lithely through the spectators and quite forgot to look forward to the performance. After a little while it began. Two tall young men rode and jumped along the high wire, passed one another, about-turned, juggled, and even turned somersaults, but I still wasn't so gripped that my eyes wouldn't from time to time sweep the crowd of spectators in search of that gorgeous creature. But I'd lost sight of her, all I saw was a sea of faces turned skyward. Then the two chaps came off the wire, there was a drum roll from below and at last I saw her, the beautiful girl, now in a short, silvery skirt and a close-fitting, sleeveless, silvery top, climbing up that third mast, the highest one, under which there was no safety net and which towered like a huge spike ready to be thrust into the black sky. Everyone around me slowly raised their heads as, together with me, they watched the silvery tightrope walker ascend, captured in a circle of light.

When she stood at the top she bowed, reached out for something, fastened something invisible, abandoned the one solid point under her feet and was suddenly in mid-air. Along with everybody else I gasped in horror, expecting a terrible crash, but she must have been holding on to a rope or perhaps a bar, so thin it couldn't be made out from the ground, though it seemed to me that the acrobat was being kept in the air by some miracle or perhaps by the lightness of her body being carried by puffs of wind. In the monstrous silence which had fallen nobody dared make a move or take an audible breath, and in that silence the acrobat up there was turning ever wilder somersaults, doing handstands, standing on her head and pulling her body through loops made by her own limbs, rising like an angel, like a fiery phoenix, she was magnificent and admirable in her skill and her strength. But, while I admired her, I also felt uneasy, terrified that she might fall, and it seemed to me that this was not just my own unease, an understandable vertigo at the thought of someone else falling, but that I was experiencing her unease, that I was gripped by her vertigo, and I felt like screaming. I had to shut my eyes. I opened them only when the drums came to life again. I just caught a glimpse of her flying through a totally blank void and catching an invisible rope. Then she slid down.

The tumblers performed in our street for four days running, and during that time I watched every single performance.

My savings were swallowed up to the last cent but I had no regrets. The moments when I came face to face with her, when the clinging gaze of her dark eyes rested on me, as I offered her a ten-crown note, and from her long strong fingers accepted the tiny slip of paper, flooded me with a happiness that lasted me for the rest of the day. I dreamed of speaking to her, of telling her how I admired her, how I shared in her vertigo. Needless to say, I never summoned up enough courage.

On the fifth day I saw the men cram the masts and their equipment into the caravans and harness the horses. I knew that I should ask them where they were making for, but at the same time I realised that their answer would have been no use to me. I had no money left to pay for admission to another performance, and I lacked the skills and the courage to offer to travel with them. There wasn't a single drop of circus blood in me and quite certainly not the slightest talent for tightrope walking. So I just took up my place on the heap of clay and waited in case she looked out of a window. I was determined to wave to her. Or even to blow her a kiss. But the caravans drove off and I didn't see her again.

I kept thinking about her for a long time.

What, I wondered, did she dream of as she climbed up the mast for her *pièce de résistance*? Of a solid net under her? Of a mast so low that one might safely jump down at the moment of fatal vertigo? Or of having wings?

But who'd get excited about acrobatic acts on a stunted mast? Who'd be interested in a girl acrobat with wings? If she began to dream about wings she'd only be dreaming of her ruin. That's when I saw the connection between heights and vertigo, ecstasy and ruin, soaring and falling.

Ota and I had been classmates ever since the third form. After finishing school he studied engineering and I philosophy, and so we drifted apart. But at school we'd been friends, and the last year at school we'd shared a bench. Our temperaments and gifts were suitably complementary: I tended to be melancholic, agonising over such problems as life after death and the existence of God, and also over how to build a better world, but he was not disturbed by any such things. He was sure that one day man would work everything out mathematically, including how the world began and how it should be arranged to make life on it better straight away. He got me to correct his essays and copied my Latin compositions, while I cribbed his physics homework and science tests.

Anyway, he'd invited me to this cottage many times but I had never taken up his invitation. This year he'd sent me a card again urging me to come. Under his signature there had been a note in a strange hand: 'Be sure to come, I'm looking forward to it a lot, Dana.'

How could someone be looking forward to my coming if they'd never seen me in their lives?

I leaned my bike against the rim of the well. It felt odd being here: in front of a strange house in an unfamiliar countryside. I have always been anxious not to be a burden to anybody. And on top of it all he had his girl here.

So why had they invited me?

I pulled the string, and at the far end of it something rang. Inwardly I hoped they wouldn't be at home so I could quickly ride away again.

The door was opened by a thin girl with black hair and dark eyes in an unseasonably pale face. From the face, a long sorcerer's nose projected expressively. For a moment she looked at me in astonishment, then she smiled: why of course, she knew me from a photograph and from Ota's account. Besides, ever since this morning she'd had a feeling I would come this very day.

How could she have had a feeling someone would come whom she'd never seen in her life?

Ota and I took a walk along the river while his girl friend promised to get a meal ready for us.

The whole way he talked about her. She was younger than us, had only just finished school, but it seemed to him as if it was the other way about, by her side he felt uneducated, uninteresting and immature—maybe also because she'd been through a lot of ghastly things in her life or because there was in her something he couldn't put a name to. The nearest word he could think of was 'clairvoyant'. Maybe I'd be interested to know she also wrote poetry. It was very odd. I probably remembered he never thought much of poetry, but her poems, he had to admit, seemed to him interesting.

I asked what ghastly things she'd been through.

During the war both her parents had been executed and she herself had been dangerously ill. No, by then the war had been over, that had been recently. Meningitis—that's why she was so pale and wasn't allowed out in the sun. If I asked her, maybe she'd show me her poems. He'd be interested to know what I thought of them.

When we got back she was standing by the cooker frying potato pancakes. The table was perfectly laid: cutlery, plates, glasses and napkins.

We sat down and she began to bring in the food. Her cheeks were now flushed and whenever she passed by me I thought I could feel the glow that was emanating from her. We praised the food and she smiled at me and Ota, but when she looked at him it was a different kind of smile: with an inner light to it, a smile full of kisses.

I couldn't get rid of the feeling that I was in the way. I stuck out like a sore thumb, like a boulder in a field. No one here needed me. If only I had had a girl to bring along.

Why was I always alone? Was I not worthy of attention or love? Surely there had been times when I felt exceptional, destined for some glorious, unrepeatable achievement: countless ideas, incidents, destinies and images were chasing one another in my mind. But who would suspect it of me? I'd never been able to overcome my shyness, not even in my writing. Those few stories which I'd so far had published revealed nothing of all the grand goings-on inside my mind.

Perhaps she noticed my taciturnity because she suggested we might go outside and light a fire.

The wind had dropped almost completely, the night sky was clear, except over the river where there still hung some narrow half-transparent streaks of mist. We collected some wood and the fire was soon going well. The flame illuminated the branches of the trees from below, and also those two as they sat side by side, happy to be close to each other. How many similar fires were at that moment burning in the furthest corners of the earth—harmless, friendly fires? But one day they might fuse together into one single, searing, white flame that would run across the earth in a single flash, melting the rocks and turning the air red-hot. What would be left then?

I felt sorry for the world, and also for myself at the thought of melting in that fierce heat, of not being able to escape, no, I wouldn't succeed a second time. I was aware that, in spite of the heat from the fire, there was again the chill breath of death at my back. If I turned my head I might perhaps catch sight of it. I suspected that it bore no resemblance to that skeletal monster with empty eye-sockets and a scythe over its shoulder: it had a starry face and its wings, even at the slightest trembling, would block out the sun like a thick cloud. Through its mouth flowed a river that had neither beginning nor end, it was a river I would like to sail down, gazing at its banks, but it was a river I would be sailing till the end of time and whose banks I wouldn't see again.

I was aware that she was watching me.

'Let's sing something?' she suggested.

Ota got up to fetch his guitar and the two of us were left alone. She asked if something had happened to me.

No, nothing at all.

What had I been thinking of?

That I couldn't say. I really couldn't.

Had I been thinking of somebody, of somebody close?

No, I hadn't been thinking of anybody. Not of anybody in particular.

Had I been thinking about death?

What made her say that?

She wouldn't want me to think of such things. At least not that evening.

Was she really clairvoyant? I didn't know what to say. I rose to my feet and chucked some more logs on the fire. A column of sparks shot skyward and quickly died away like falling stars.

She would like me to feel happy here. Was there anything I'd like her to do for me?

No, I was entirely content.

I was merely trying to make her believe that. Why didn't I tell her what I wanted most of all at that moment.

I was silent.

But I must answer spontaneously.

No, I couldn't do that!

Why not?

I couldn't say it out loud.

By why not? She, for instance, would like to be able to love someone. Completely and without reservation.

But wouldn't she like even more for someone to love her?

She shook her head. A person who accepted love was like a passenger. Maybe on a boat, at night, on some vast lake. Whichever way you looked there was nothing but calm black water. It was true that the water might rise and swamp you. But to love someone meant to fly, to rise above the earth yourself. So high that you could see everything. Even if the world looked different from that height, even if it looked changed, even if what on the ground seemed important was transformed into insignificance. She'd say, moreover, that you could always get out of a boat and go ashore, but from that height you could only crash.

When we went inside again I asked her for her poems and

she lent me an exercise book. They'd put me up in a tiny room which contained only a hat-stand, a bed, a little table and a candlestick with a candle.

I lit the candle and read for a while from her exercise book. Her poems abounded in images that were difficult to understand: timid violets, cobalt depths, glances of mournful souls, stars that had died and the healing nature of friendly lakes. Now and again between the pages I found a pressed flower with a pungent fragrance.

The next morning, immediately after breakfast, I thanked them for their hospitality and said goodbye. She squeezed my hand. She was glad she'd made my acquaintance and she hoped we'd meet again soon.

I mounted my bicycle. They were standing in front of their little cottage, holding hands and seeing me off like a happy, loving married couple.

About two months later she dropped in on me.

She was wearing a suit, her hair was carefully groomed and she was wearing lipstick. She blushed when she saw me. Her dark-brown eyes looked at me mournfully.

She happened to be walking past, returning from Ota's, and she suddenly thought she might drop in.

I couldn't understand why she'd visited me. Had anything happened to Ota?

No, nothing. Nothing at all. She'd been walking past and she just thought she'd look to see if I really lived here. And now she'd be off again.

I asked her in but she refused to enter my flat. Her cheeks were flushed as if she were feverish.

'You're sure nothing's happened?'

She shook her head. Ota was great. He was the best person she could imagine. But she had to go now.

I said at least I'd see her to the tram.

She wasn't taking the tram, she only lived a short distance away, by the park behind the water tower.

I walked with her down a narrow little street between villas. Dusk was beginning to fall, a cloudless September evening, the gardens fragrant with foliage and with roses past their peak.

I learned that she was living with a distant aunt here in Prague. But she had been brought up by her grandmother. Her grandmother had looked after her from the time they'd taken her parents away, and she'd looked after her better than anyone else could possibly have done. But last summer she'd died. Soon afterwards she herself had caught virus encephalitis and it had really seemed as if she'd follow her family, but that wasn't to be yet. Ota had been marvellous during that time. When she'd been a bit better he'd sat with her in the garden and read to her, because she was forbidden to read. If the doctors had had their way they'd have forbidden her to think too, because thoughts were sometimes painful, and hers were continually drifting over to the other side, into the darkness, where her dear ones were. Or else to the divide, to the edge, to the moment when everything collapsed. She kept imagining the moment when they were called by name, when they were led in perfect health down a corridor into a room where there was nothing except tiles, and then a machine for . . .

Her voice shook. She wouldn't talk about it any more. She knew from Ota that I'd been there too. That I'd been through something similar. She'd wanted to ask me about it but she wasn't sure she wouldn't be hurting me, because it must be terrible to think back to those days, and no doubt I'd much rather forget all about it and it was silly of her to hark back to it.

I said I wasn't trying either to remember or to forget; I believed that even the most terrible experiences, provided a person got over them, could in retrospect become their very opposite.

And if a person didn't survive them?

I did not understand her question.

Weren't the souls of those people marked permanently by their frightful experiences?

I gasped. No such question had ever occurred to me. Which was odd, considering I often reflected on the existence of the human soul, and considering so many of my relations and friends had come to a similar end, standing—how did she put it?—at the divide, on the edge from which they hurtled down, who could tell where.

I said that death, surely, was always a fall and that violence was always done to the body of him who died. But if we believed in the immortality of the soul then it followed that we also believed in its ability to free itself from suffering, from the fall of the body.

And did I believe in that immortality? After everything I'd been through? That's what she wanted to know—if, after all that, it was still possible to believe.

I shrugged. I dared not say No.

And the people back there—she wouldn't say any more after that—had they believed, had they been able to believe?

I replied that some of them had—in as much as anyone could know that sort of thing about somebody else. But I remembered that at the *sukkoth* festival they had collected brushwood and built a tabernacle in the barracks yard. I also remembered a dark room in the attic where the men had met for prayers, there had been so many I thought I'd suffocate in the crowd. And I had a friend, my own age, he was dead now, we used to talk about it, and he maintained that man was in the hands of the All-Highest, that everything was happening by His will and decision, and therefore had a purpose, except that man often did not understand it and therefore questioned it and even rebelled, yes, he'd certainly believed in it all even at the moment when, as she had put it, he stood at the divide.

She said she was grateful to me.

I accompanied her to the little park at the edge of which she lived; it was only a few blocks away from Ota's. The street-lamps were coming on and an evening mist was descending.

Was I sure I wasn't angry with her for delaying me so? She'd really meant to ask me what I did, what I was writing, and she'd also wanted to tell me about a book by Dos Passos which she'd just finished: she liked it, it seemed to her to be interestingly written, but she didn't want to make me even later, she hoped I didn't mind. She might bring me that book some time, or else she'd get Ota to give it to me.

As I was falling asleep and once more went over that unexpected visit in my mind, I realised that the house where I lived was quite definitely not on the way from her flat to Ota's.

About a week later I caught sight of her from my window. She was walking up and down the pavement opposite. I ran out to meet her. When she saw me she smiled at me and blushed. Her hair was curled into shiny black ringlets—clearly the hairdresser had been at work on them very recently.

She'd brought me the Dos Passos book but she'd been afraid she might be disturbing me. Perhaps I'd been writing?

She handed me the book.

Again we walked down the same little street of villas. I asked about her health.

She was feeling excellent. As recently as the summer, when I visited them, she used to get tired towards evening and find it difficult to control her thoughts; they'd be drifting through her head like clouds and at night they'd enter her dreams, such ugly dreams, but now she could control them and she seldom had any dreams now, at least not those bad ones. When they'd discharged her from hospital in the summer they'd advised her to postpone her studies for a year, but now she thought that mightn't be necessary. She'd try to attend lectures. Her grandmother agreed with her. Anyway she believed one shouldn't give up without trying and one shouldn't make things too easy for oneself. Ota, on the other hand, wanted her to take care of herself and not to study. Sometimes she had the feeling that he was jealous—jealous of anything that was not somehow connected with him. She wasn't saying this as if she was complaining about him—she'd never complain about him even if she had good cause to do so, which she hadn't, he really was the best human being she knew, but no doubt he'd change in that respect too as he matured more fully.

What did she mean? Surely he was older than her.

That wasn't the point. The real point was how a person was able completely to accept whatever life brought him. And stop making excuses. To himself and to others. But who could claim to be able to do just that? Ota was loving, perceptive and attentive. When she was ill he'd sent her flowers every day, and always different ones. What flowers did I like?

Flowers, unfortunately, were something I'd never understood. Once, it must have been in the fifth form, Ota and I had bought a guide to the local flora and had set out to the Prokopské valley. We'd succeeded in identifying a euphorbia and a tall buttercup which, however, might also have been a golden-yellow buttercup, depending on whether one regarded the stem as smooth or hairy. We couldn't agree and finally we picked the plant and showed it to our botany master, who informed us that it was a helianthemum. Since then I hadn't done any flower guessing.

Ota also spoke of me and our schooldays, but he hadn't told her that incident.

How did he speak of me?

Approvingly, always approvingly. He didn't speak ill of

anybody, except that he'd warned her to be on her guard with me because I invariably tried to get off with any girl, but she was sure he didn't mean it nastily, he'd probably merely wanted to say that I had a knack with girls. She broke off abruptly and blushed.

I was stunned by my friend's statement. I said I hoped she didn't think anything of the sort.

Oh no, although she didn't really know me.

We stopped at the edge of the little park where she lived. She looked at me and I noticed the colour leaving her face.

Was anything wrong with her?

No, nothing!

Was she not feeling well?

She was perfectly well. She was better than she'd been for a long time.

I suggested that we might go for a longer walk some time and have a chat about books if she liked. If it was all right with her I'd wait for her at this spot on Sunday, straight after lunch. Unless one o'clock was too early?

I stood at the corner of the little park and watched her till she disappeared into her building. What had made me suggest that excursion? Surely I knew she was in love with someone else.

On Sunday she arrived on the dot. I asked her if she'd ever been to the Šárka Wilderness.

No, she hardly ever went walking with Ota, at most they'd go to the cinema or to a concert. That evening they were going to see *Umberto D*. Had I seen the film?

I hadn't. It was said to be good. But I had no one to go with.

We took a Number 11 tram to its terminus and set out towards the cliffs. Although September was nearing its end, it was a mild day and the warm yellow of the birch leaves lay poured out against a blue sky.

When I said I had no one to go to the cinema with, what did I mean?

Well, my friends all had their girls and my brother had different tastes.

She didn't want to be nosy but surely, if I wanted to, surely . . . I wouldn't have to be alone.

I'd probably not yet met a girl with whom I felt I'd want to spend my time, let alone my life.

Yes, she knew what I meant. She'd felt the same until she met Ota. When she first saw him she realised that he was that person, the right person, for her. Suddenly she blushed and added that at least she thought so at the time.

And didn't she think so any more?

She swallowed, looked at me, and shrugged. I understood her gesture. I had brought on that shrug. At that point I should have turned back, returned home, or at least been silent, or avoided talking about anything to do with emotions. But at the same time I was happy or at least pleased that she was interested in me. So we continued walking and I talked—that was the only thing I was reasonably good at then. Words and their secret power. I reflected on the advantages and disadvantages of loneliness and I knew that she would understand how I longed for love, I spoke about my wartime childhood, the lack of feeling in the world in which I had to live, and she understood that I was longing for tenderness.

She was a receptive listener. I watched my words dropping into her like some instantly sprouting seeds. Several times, as though by accident, she touched my hand. We also saw a late butterfly and rings of autumn crocuses and some shrub whose leaves were a bright fiery red. Then a small stream ran across our path. I jumped over to the far side and held out my hand to her. She gripped my fingers and jumped. She was standing so close to me that I only had to open my arms, and that's what

I did. She pressed herself against me and her lips enveloped my mouth: she was kissing me, I realised, not I kissing her. One passionate kiss, then she pushed me away. She was sorry, she was terribly sorry, she didn't know what had come over her. What was she to do now? How was she to explain it?

Whom did she have to explain anything to?

Her grandmother, of course.

But she'd said, or at least I'd understood, that she was on her own now, that her grandmother had died last summer.

Yes, but surely that didn't mean she couldn't still turn to her.

We said goodbye at the edge of the park again. She whispered not to be angry with her. She didn't understand anything, she'd had no idea anything like that might happen. Because she loved Ota. Anyway, she didn't quite know what to do, how she could go to the cinema with him that evening; she only knew she mustn't hurt him.

I proposed that I would wait for her there in the park in three days' time, at six in the evening.

She thanked me for the invitation but she wasn't sure if she'd come. Perhaps I understood, I was sure to understand. She made a movement with her head as if about to kiss me but she checked herself, turned and quickly walked away.

I followed her with my eyes. What did I actually feel? Happiness? Unease? Self-satisfaction? Should I break into a run to follow her or turn and escape?

In the morning there was an envelope in the letter box for me. I immediately recognised her small, neat handwriting.

It was a sheet of paper with eight lines of poetry:

> The shades now steal over the rocks,
> my heart constricts as in a dream
> and in my head an angels' team
> sounds the alarm, a fear now rocks

and chills my wildly shaking bones:
my body still lives in this world
like a birch rooted amid stones
but, oh, my soul is downward hurled.

I had written a number of poems myself, and some of them I'd dedicated to people, but I had never yet received from anybody a poem dedicated to me. Now that I was out of reach of her mournful gaze and only her words could reach me, as tokens of her favour, I surrendered totally to a sense of happiness. I was being loved!

For the rest of the day I couldn't tear my thoughts away from her. Towards evening I set out at random for the park by the water tower. It was getting dark but, because it was a fine day, mothers with pushchairs were still moving along the neat paths. I tried to look for her window but I didn't know which of the many third-floor windows was the right one. A floor higher a young woman stood on the window-ledge, sleeves rolled up, washing the window frames. I was seized by vertigo and quickly turned away. I sat down on a park bench and waited. I shut my eyes to give her an opportunity to appear unexpectedly. She did not appear, but the woman in the window disappeared and I was flooded by a sense of loneliness. This was how I would be all my life: lonely. I'd wait for a woman who had no idea I was waiting for her because I couldn't face up to addressing her and telling her that I wanted her to come. I walked home down the little street between the villas and I could see myself lying lonely on a bed in some cold, dingy room, dying. No one knew who I was, no one loved me, I was like a stray dog, except that I was a human being who, at that moment at least, longed for another living human being; and just then I caught sight of one. I saw an angel appearing out of the heavens and floating down to my bed: a delicate, slim, sharp-nosed angel.

Back home I wrote until it was nearly midnight. I did not put myself on the bed but her—or rather a strange girl student. She was incurably sick and had been bedridden for several months. Her parents had placed her bed by the window so she could watch the branches of a massive lime-tree. Through the branches shone the blue of the sky; on clear days the sun sank amidst a reddish haze in the west. The girl had a boy friend who was a student, too, though during the last few weeks he had done virtually no work but had sat by the sick girl for hours on end, talking in order to lessen the thickening gloom of her mind. He would tell her what had happened to him during the day and whom he had met, he re-enacted the plots of films, he reproduced conversations he'd happened to over-hear, and finally, when he had told her everything, he began to invent incidents and meetings, and because by then he'd become a good story-teller he invented such detail that not only she but even he himself was no longer able to tell what had really happened and what he'd dreamed up. And so he told her one day that he'd seen an angel, and that this had happened while he was walking home from her in the evening. The angel had floated up outside his window and there had been a glow coming from it.

She did not doubt the encounter, she merely said that the angel had probably visited him because he was so good to her, and he was glad she believed him: it is good for a dying person to believe in heavenly beings. After that he told her frequently of encounters with the angel. He described its appearance, its ability to turn up at any time. The angel never spoke but it inspired thoughts and filled him with a sense of bliss. She listened to him attentively, sometimes it seemed to her that she too was seeing this being, she saw it rising up above her bed or above the head of her lover, and whenever she saw the angel, she experienced a particular relief.

As the disease which consumed her spine was causing her more and more pain the girl yearned increasingly for this being. And indeed the angel would now always come to her as soon as her boy friend had left, and would spread a fine cloud of light before her, with brightly coloured reflections gyrating and spinning, merging into a continuous chain of pictures: landscapes never seen, the rise and fall of waves, the reflection of peacocks' feathers in lakes, mountain ranges, snowdrifts, or the shy eyes of animals. Such tranquillity emanated from the cloud that it quieted her suffering and all she was aware of was the calm passage of time.

Her condition worsened, the doctor held out hope for only a few more days of life and in his bag he had his morphia ampoules ready in case the pain should become unbearable. Surprisingly, however, the girl did not seem to suffer.

Then one evening, as the sun's disc was sinking behind the branches, the girl awoke feeling anxious and lonely. Her boy friend had gone a little while earlier, leaving his place to her unearthly comforter. Except that in the space between the window and the empty chair there was now no one and she looked around in vain into all the corners. And then she saw it. She gazed into starry eyes which stared from emptiness into emptiness and their glance pierced her with a chill. The girl softly cried out for her comforter. And at that moment she actually saw the angel in the window. The gentle, good, comforting being motioned with its head, and the movement was so eloquent that the girl, as though driven by some strange force, got up from her bed and with hesitant steps approached the window. When the angel saw her coming it opened its arms and stepped back a short distance. Now it no longer stood in the window but hung between heaven and earth, its translucent wings quivering in rainbow hues and its golden eyes looking at her. That glance lifted a great weight from her, she felt preternaturally light, so light she could fly. And, as she stood by the window, she opened her arms wide, rose to the narrow ledge and with a single small step pushed off upwards to follow the unearthly being into eternity, even though her body fell to the ground.

I was surprised by my own product. Until then I had written about things and about people who were either real or modelled on reality, but what was the meaning of this incident? It was nonsensical. Or did it carry a message? Had she planted it in me?

I did not know, but I managed to copy the text first thing the next morning, put it in an envelope and drop it into her letterbox.

I spent the day under the wing of my angel. I attended my lectures, somebody spoke to me and I even replied, then I walked through the city, got on a tram and got off again, but I didn't take any of this in. Only towards the evening did the world begin to get through to me the way I had become used to perceiving it: full of incident, struggle, great emotions and movements, a world of pain, passions and wars, a world whose dimensions surpassed the human mind's capacity for comprehension no matter how much we kept trying to comprehend it. And I, instead of endeavouring to discern at least its outline, had written down a crazy vision and, what was more, given it to a person whom I cared about to read. How could I now show my face to her without shame?

I had to wait for her for nearly half an hour. But she came. A little pale and with swollen eyes.

She realised she was late, it wasn't like her, but she'd wavered to the last moment about coming at all, about whether even seeing me wasn't already an act of betrayal vis-à-vis Ota. Except that she'd be thinking of me anyway. As a matter of fact, she'd been thinking of me from the moment she'd found in her letterbox the thing I had sent her; she wasn't sure what to call it, for her it was something like a parable. A parable about love and death.

We walked down little backstreets to the river. It was not yet really dark but the lamplighter with his long pole was already turning the streetlamps on. She went on talking about my story. She felt that it had come from the depths of my soul. Every single image and every sentence. She thought this was the only way one person could speak to another, touch another's soul.

Her words filled me with satisfaction. Perhaps I really had touched her, and what more could I have hoped for? You marvellous power of words, I invoke you, I conjure you up so that I may conjure with you!

I said that she'd helped me, without her I couldn't have written anything like it. She reminded me of an angel. There was in her something other-worldly and fragile. When I was vainly waiting for her that afternoon . . .

When had I been waiting for her? Yesterday afternoon? Yes, she'd been with Ota then but she couldn't get rid of a feeling that I was within a few steps of her, that if she turned her head I'd be there; she had to say goodbye to Ota, she even asked him to leave her alone and hurried home. She'd been looking for some message from me but didn't find one until this morning! Ever since, she'd been unable to cut herself loose, even though she knew she had to drive me out, at least out of her mind. For Ota's sake and for hers.

No, she didn't have to, I implored her. Surely we weren't doing anything wrong. And I felt at ease with her. She'd no idea what it meant to me to be walking with her like this and listening to her.

Was that true?

I wouldn't say so if it wasn't!

She was glad she could mean something to me. At least for a while.

Why only for a while?

Because I would slip away from her anyway. She could feel it.

We had come along Karlova Street to the stone bridge. The lamps were casting striking patches of light on the grimy features of the saints and the windows of the Little Quarter shone like the lights of some gigantic Christmas crib.

Did she like it here?

Very much. This was the first time she'd been here at night.

But it wasn't night yet.

She didn't even go out in the evening. Grandmother had always wanted her to get home before nightfall.

Even in winter?

But it wasn't winter now.

But she was older now than when her grandmother died.

But grandmother was still wanting it. She worried about her. More than ever during these past few days.

'Because of me?'

We went down the steps, past some abandoned market stalls, and got to the Sova Mills.

'Not because of you. Because of me.'

We leaned against the little stone wall above the weir. The water was low and quiet. A few ducklings scurried about the dark surface. There was a smell of rotten chestnuts. She said: 'Last night I dreamed that Ota came to me in tears. Begging me not to leave him. And you were sitting there, smiling. I wanted to ask you to go away but I couldn't move my lips. Then I noticed that grandmother was sitting there too. I waited for her to advise me what to do, but she kept silent as if she couldn't open her mouth either. When I woke up I wanted her to come to me, to whisper at least one word

to me—yes or no—but she kept silent. I'm sure she's angry
with me.'

'Or else she thinks you're old enough now! That you must
make your own decisions!'

'Yes,' she agreed, 'I realised that later. Now she'll never
appear to me again . . . Got to stand on my own feet now. I've
made my decision. That's why I am late; I didn't want to come
until I'd made my decision.' She pressed herself against me and
I could feel her lips passionately covering mine.

I was aware of a sense of almost exultant satisfaction. Simultaneously I felt some irritation that she should have made her
decision without me, that she hadn't even bothered to ask for
my consent. I also felt fear: fear of the fateful earnestness with
which she was entrusting herself to me.

It seemed as if she were concentrating into her kiss all her
love, her whole passionate being, as if she were preparing to
die very shortly, entrust herself to those wings that would not
bear her, and sink into the abyss. Then she stepped back from
me. 'We mustn't see each other again!' Her voice struck me as
painfully severe. 'If we were to see each other even once more
I just couldn't bear it. Please try to understand!'

'But I thought,' I attempted an objection, 'we'd just agreed
that we felt at ease together . . .'

'Please, please, don't say anything!'

'I thought,' and a wave of self-pity suddenly washed over
me, 'that at last I'd found a person close to me.'

There was only the faint light of a distant streetlamp but
nevertheless I thought I could see tears in her eyes.

'Perhaps some day, after a while,' she said. 'I shan't forget
you. I shall never forget you.'

I was silent. Across the low, stone wall I was gazing at the
river's surface on which a circular patch of moonlight was
rocking. All around me and within me silence was spreading.

Then suddenly, just by my legs, a heavy object hit the ground. It took me a moment to realise that it was she. She was lying on her back, arms flung out, eyes closed, a froth of saliva about her lips. I bent down over her and tried to lift her head. A horrible presentiment paralysed me. I had invoked death and now it had come. What was I to do now?

She drew a noisy breath and opened her eyes.

'What's wrong with you, what's wrong?'

She sat up and looked about her in surprise. I helped her to her feet.

'I don't know what happened. Did I fall?' She held on to me for support.

'Let's go home, you're tired!'

'I'm all right now. Please forgive me, dearest!' She clutched my hand frantically. 'Do believe that I can't act differently. Would you act differently? A person just can't carve up his soul.'

I led her to the nearest seat but I clearly didn't lead her carefully enough, for when she fell again I managed only to break her fall but not to catch her.

This time she remained motionless for longer, I was unable to guess for how long, and people started to come running up.

At last she came to, some stranger helped me lift her and offered to find a taxi.

At the hospital they took her in at once. They allowed me to sit on a white bench in an empty, half-lit corridor.

She came back after about half an hour, smiling absently. It wasn't anything, she'd probably been overdoing things, they'd given her an injection and she would be all right now. I found another taxi, we were both silent during the ride, and I thought she was sleeping. In the passing light of the streetlamps she looked as pale as in a dream. Her nose projected sharply from her face like the beak of a dead bird. Hard as I tried I was unable to suppress a sense of ugliness. As if I were still hearing that gurgling sound that had come from her mouth and still seeing the froth round her sick lips. With a sudden sense of relief I realised that this girl was a stranger, that she did not belong to me nor I to her, and that fortunately we had realised this in time, that she herself had realised it and made her decision, and that I had submitted to it.

The following evening Ota turned up at our flat. He rang the bell, waited for my mother to call me, did not return my greeting and only said: 'I want to talk to you. I'll wait for you downstairs!'

The thought struck me that she might be dying after all and I was seized by terror. I quickly changed and ran outside. He was waiting for me, leaning against the trunk of an acacia.

'How is she?' I blurted out.

He did not reply but merely motioned me to follow him. We walked down the little street along which I had so recently seen her home. How many times? It had all been so short-lived—it seemed hardly worth mentioning. Except how much time did a person need to step out on to a window ledge and entrust himself to wings that would not bear him?

'She's told me everything,' he spoke up suddenly. 'You behaved disgustingly. But what else can one expect from such a . . . such a . . .' He seemed unable to find the right word. But then he found it. 'If anything happens to her, you're a murderer.'

For the first time I entered the flat where she lived. We crossed a hall; at the far end of it he stopped me abruptly. He knocked and entered. From inside I could hear her voice but I couldn't make out the words. What did she want from me? How had she got him to bring me along? And why, if she didn't want to see me again?

At last he reappeared. 'You can go in!' He did not look at

me. He stepped aside and let me enter the room behind the glass door, while he himself remained in the hall.

It was a large room, with tall walls and a stucco ceiling.

She was lying in bed, a sickly pallor on her face, a red-and-white striped duvet drawn up to her chin.

She motioned me to come closer. There was a chair by the bedside and I sat down on it. 'How are you?'

'I am absolutely fine,' her voice sounded light, almost cheerful. 'It's only that he's ordered me to stay in bed. He worries about me. I wanted to come and see you myself but he forbade me to get up. Only I had to tell you that I shall get well again. So you don't worry; this isn't ever going to happen again.'

'I know you'll get well again.'

'It was all my own fault. I thought I could force myself to come to a decision and then I couldn't stand the strain. But I've come to realise that it would have been pointless anyway. I wanted you to know that I realise it now.'

I didn't understand her but before I could question her Ota walked in. 'Need anything, dear?'

'No,' she said, 'I don't want anything.'

'Got to take care of yourself, you know!' He turned to me. 'She was at death's door. The doctors said the slightest excitement could kill her. Except that some people think only of themselves. Of their own gratification.'

There was no point in defending myself. She held out her hand to me. When I took it she responded with a long and frantic squeeze. Then Ota opened the door for me and I walked out.

About three days later, as I was coming home from a lecture, I found a letter from her in our letterbox. The envelope, without a stamp or address, had only my name on it.

I tore it open as I went upstairs.

There was such a lot she wanted to say to me, she wrote,

she'd wanted to do so when I visited her but there hadn't been an opportunity, so she'd tried at least to convey to me the most important thing but she wasn't now sure what she'd actually managed to say to me during that brief moment and what she'd said to me only in her mind—because she was continuously talking to me in her mind, both day and night.

She was also afraid that I might think her fickle, that I might regard her as someone who kept changing her mind. But it had all been difficult for her because she knew how much Ota loved her, and because she too regarded him highly, as a splendid, kind-hearted and self-sacrificing person. But something had occurred that she hadn't been able to imagine beforehand: she had drifted away from him, she no longer loved him. At first she'd refused to admit it to herself, she'd tried to save their relationship somehow, but then she'd come to realise that it was hopeless; love was either total or miserable, and why should she reward someone she admired, someone who had been good to her, with a love that was miserable? Why should she commit violence against herself and believe that by doing so she could make someone happy? She'd said all this to Ota, and it had been difficult for both of them because they had already been preparing for a life together, but she thought he'd understood her and agreed with her decision. She didn't know what would happen now—I read with growing unease—but she felt that something had happened between the two of us, maybe beside that fire some spark had leapt across between us and lit a flame which, provided we were sufficiently wise, might burn for us always and we might spend a life together in love. She believed that we were both capable of doing so. Now she could see me in her mind's eye, my sad thoughtful eyes, my smile, beneath which she could always feel pain, and now she was waiting, waiting for my answer.

I folded the letter again and put it back in the envelope. If only I could put it back completely, put back everything that had happened, put time back.

The telephone rang. I picked up the receiver but there was silence at the other end, and all I could hear was weak breathing. I realised that she wanted to know if I'd got back home and found her message. From this moment my count-down started.

If only her letter hadn't been so totally urgent or her offer so unconditional. Did I even have the right to reject her after what I'd caused? But what feelings did I have for her? Did I have any feelings of the kind she wrote about?

Everything had happened so quickly. I wasn't able to sort out my own feelings. Maybe I could at least explain this to her. I didn't want to lose her, I was sure I'd *manage* to be fond of her, but I just wasn't ready for anything of the sort. Suppose I disappointed her? Hadn't she better reflect on whether her decision was not precipitate?

I was gripped by a fever. I had to talk to her as soon as possible. Go over it all, gain time.

I slipped on my coat and hurried along the little streets through which I'd recently walked with her. I'd yet to reach the little park, the spot where we used to say goodbye, when scraps of fairground music drifted over to me and suddenly the sky ahead was lit up by an unaccustomed glow. Then the unexpected point of a mast appeared, swaying, above the rooftops.

They had erected the masts at the edge of the little park, the high wire stretching directly above the now empty children's sandpit.

The performance was in full swing and high up I saw a spectral figure in a gleaming leotard balancing on a tall cycle, and all of a sudden I experienced that old excitement, as though I were stepping out of the damp autumn day, and I mingled with the crowd of spectators as though I had suddenly forgotten my purpose.

Was it possible that she was still with them, that for all those years, evening after evening, right to this day, my acrobat had turned her somersaults up there without crashing down?

The tightrope walker now put his bicycle aside, fetched a little table and a chair, and sat down. From the other end of the wire his girl companion approached, dressed as a waitress, a tray stacked with plates on her flat palm. I tried to make out her features but she was too high up above me. Even if she had been closer, and even if it was really her, would I still recognise her?

She was laying the plates on the little table and I was still trying to make out her features, just as though, if it were her, she might offer me some kind of salvation, just as though she might bring me some message or even some hope.

The number came to an end, the two artistes put away their props, then the man picked up a loud-hailer and turned to the spectators, inviting us to approach; he announced that he'd carry anyone among us safely on his back from one end of the wire to the other. Then he was joined by his girl companion, she too was coaxing us up on to the wire, and from her height she looked down into our dark ranks, and it seemed to me that she was looking for somebody amongst us, somebody with courage. Suddenly I realised that she was looking for me. I could feel vertigo flooding me. Yes, who else but me should go up the mast? Only what kind of figure would I cut up there, ridiculous and helpless on someone else's back? In my giddiness, would I not bring myself and my carrier down off the wire?

I looked around at the others, to see if they too had noticed that it was I who was being addressed, but they were all calmly

looking upwards in the expectation of new thrills, the appe-
did not concern them, they weren't even interested in whom
they concerned. My feet were growing heavy. Would I even
manage to climb that swinging rope-ladder up the mast?

The alluring voice appealed again to me, cut a path to me
through the darkness.

I began to move in its direction but just then I caught sight
of some chap in a chequered cap agilely climbing up the
ladder. He'd reached the top now and was getting on to the
back of the artiste in the glittering leotard.

As the two staggered across the rope there was a drum roll
and I saw a slim, white figure climbing to the top of the highest
mast. But it wasn't her, it wasn't a woman at all; some strange
man had climbed up to the spot that had belonged to her,
bowed and immediately done a handstand so that it looked as
if he were trying in vain to stride across the darkness of the vast
heavens.

I was watching the high-wire acrobatics, wondering if another person's anxiety and vertigo would rack me as they had
once done, but I felt nothing. Either that tumbler meant
nothing to me or else I was too much taken up with myself,
with my own emotions. As I was standing there in the crowd,
gazing up at the celestial acrobat who, high above our heads,
above the dark void, was invoking that vaster one with the
starry face, it seemed to me that I was beginning to understand
something of the secret of life, that I would be able to see
clearly what until then I had been helplessly groping for. I felt
that life was a perpetual temptation of death, one continual
performance above the abyss, that in it man must aim for the
opposite mast even though, from sheer vertigo, he might not
even see it, that he must go forward, not look behind, not look
down, not allow himself to be tempted by those who were
standing comfortably on firm ground, who were mere spectators.

also felt that I had to walk my own tightrope, that I must myself sling it between two masts as those tumblers had done, and venture out on it, not wait for someone to invite me up and offer to carry me across on his back. I must begin my own performance, my grand unrepeatable performance. And I felt that I could do it, that I had sufficient strength in me to do it. At that moment somebody touched my shoulder. It gave me such a start I nearly cried out. But then the collecting box tinkled and before me I saw the all but forgotten, familiar stranger's face of the beautiful girl of long ago. Hurriedly I produced some coins from my pocket and gave them to her. She smiled, her teeth flashed at me in the dark and I almost felt the hot, liberating touch of her lips.

When the performance was over and the crowd had dispersed I hung about for a while in the suddenly deserted, dark, open space. Whom or what was I still waiting for?

A short distance away the eyes of a caravan shone dim yellow. Inside someone was playing a guitar and now and again a child cried noisily. I listened to this blend of sounds for a while, then I turned back home through the little streets with their gardens.

Not until the following evening did I resolve to reply: her letter had moved and surprised me, and indeed stunned me. I feared that she might have made her decision precipitately. Certainly we should meet (I was looking forward to seeing her) and talk everything over. I suggested a date, time and place (as usual, the little park outside her building). The next morning I dropped the letter in her letterbox.

It was raining on the day I had fixed. Nevertheless I got to the appointed spot a few minutes early. The tightrope walkers had gone; small heaps of disturbed soil marked the spots where their masts had stood.

I sheltered under a tall spruce, listened to the rustle of the rain in the autumn branches and watched her building; there was a light in one of the third-floor windows but I wasn't sure if it was really hers. I stared at it in the hope that I might catch some movement, the flapping of a wing, the flash of a soothing, understanding glance, but the window glowed emptily and without a sign of life, as though some will-o'-the-wisp were burning behind it.

My recent resolution evaporated. Suppose I spent my whole life just waiting, waiting for the moment when at last I saw that starry face? It would turn its glance on me and say: You've been incapable of accepting life, dear friend, so you'd better come with me! Or, on the other hand, it might say: You've done well because you knew how to bear your solitude at a great height, because you were able to do without consolation in order not to do without hope!

What would it really say?

At that moment I could not tell.

Antonio Tabucchi
Cinema

I

The small station was almost deserted. It was the station of a town on the Riviera, with palms and agaves growing near the wooden benches on the platform. At one end, behind a wrought-iron gate, a street led to the centre of the town; at the other a stone stairway went down to the shore.

The stationmaster came out of the glass-walled control room and walked under the overhanging roof to the tracks. He was a short, stout man with a moustache; he lit a cigarette, looked doubtfully at the cloudy sky, stuck out a hand beyond the roof to see if it was raining, then wheeled around and with a thoughtful air put his hands in his pockets. The two workmen waiting for the train on a bench under the sign bearing the station's name greeted him briefly and he nodded his head in reply. On the other bench there was an old woman, dressed in black, with a suitcase fastened with a rope. The stationmaster peered up and down the tracks then, as the bell announcing a train's arrival began to ring, went back into his glass-walled office.

At this moment the girl came through the gate. She was wearing a polka-dotted dress, shoes laced at the ankles, and a pale blue sweater. She was walking quickly, as if she were cold, and a mass of blonde hair floated under the scarf tied around

her head. She was carrying a small suitcase and a straw ha.
bag. One of the workmen followed her with his eyes ar
nudged his apparently distracted companion. The girl stared
indifferently at the ground, then went into the waiting room,
closing the door behind her. The room was empty. There was
a large cast-iron stove in one corner and she moved towards it,
perhaps in the hope that the fire inside was lighted. She
touched it, disappointedly, and then laid her straw handbag on
top. Then she sat down on a bench and shivered, holding her
face between her hands. For a long time she remained in this
position, as if she were crying. She was good-looking, with
delicate features and slender ankles. She took off her scarf
and rearranged her hair, moving her head from one side to
the other. Her gaze wandered over the walls of the room as
if she were looking for something. There were threatening
signs on the walls addressed to the citizenry by the Occupation Forces and notices of 'wanted' persons, displaying their
photographs. She looked around in confusion, then took the
handbag she had left on the stove and laid it at her feet as if to
shield it with her legs. She hunched her shoulders and raised
her jacket collar. Her hands were restless; she was obviously
nervous.

The door was flung open and a man came in. He was tall and
thin, wearing a belted tan trenchcoat and a felt hat pulled down
over his forehead. The girl leaped to her feet and shouted, with
a gurgle in her throat: 'Eddie!'

He held a finger to his lips, walked towards her, and,
smiling, took her into his arms. She hugged him, leaning her
head on his chest. 'Oh, Eddie!' she murmured finally, drawing
back, 'Eddie!'

He made her sit down and went back to the door, looking
furtively outside. Then he sat down beside her and drew some
folded papers from his pocket.

You're to deliver them directly to the English major,' he
id. 'Later I'll tell you how, more exactly.'

She took the papers and slipped them into the opening of
her sweater. She seemed fearful, and there were tears in her
eyes.

'And what about you?' she asked.

He made a gesture signifying annoyance. Just then there was
a rumbling sound and a goods train was visible through the
door's glass panel. He pulled his hat further down over his
forehead and buried his head in a newspaper.

'Go and see what's up.'

The girl went to the door and peered out. 'A goods train,'
she said. 'The two workmen sitting on the bench climbed
aboard.'

'Any Germans?'

'No.'

The stationmaster blew his whistle and the train pulled
away. The girl went back to the man and took his hands into
hers.

'What about you?' she repeated.

He folded the newspaper and stuffed it into his pocket.

'This is no time to think about me,' he said. 'Now tell me,
what's your company's schedule?'

'Tomorrow we'll be in Nice, for three evening performances. Saturday and Sunday we play in Marseille, then Montpel-
lier and Narbonne, one day each, in short, all along the coast.'

'On Sunday you'll be in Marseille,' said the man. 'After the
show you'll receive admirers in your dressing room. Let them
in one at a time. Many of them will bring flowers; some will
be German spies, but others will be our people. Be sure to read
the card that comes with the flowers, in the visitor's presence,
every time, because I can't tell you what the contact will look
like.' She listened attentively; the man lit a cigarette and went

on: 'On one of the cards you'll read: *Fleurs pour une fleur.* Hand over the papers to that man. He'll be the major.'

The bell began to ring again, and the girl looked at her watch.

'Our train will be here in a minute. Eddie, please . . .'

He wouldn't let her finish.

'Tell me about the show,' he interrupted. 'On Sunday night I'll try to imagine it.'

'It's done by all the girls in the company,' she said unenthusiastically. 'Each one of us plays a well-known actress of today or of the past. That's all there is to it.'

'What's the title?' he asked, smiling.

'Cinema Cinema.'

'Sounds promising.'

'It's a disaster,' she said earnestly. 'The choreography is by Saverio, just imagine that, and I play Francesca Bertini, dancing in a dress so long that I trip on it.'

'Watch out!' he exclaimed jokingly. 'Great tragic actresses simply mustn't fall.'

Again she hid her face in her arms and started to cry. She was prettier than ever with tear marks on her face.

'Come away, Eddie, please, come away,' she murmured.

He wiped her tears away gently enough, but his voice hardened, as if in an effort to disguise his feelings.

'Don't, Elsa,' he said. 'Try to understand.' And, in a playful tone, he added: 'How should I get through? Dressed like a dancer, perhaps, with a blond wig?'

The bell had stopped ringing and the incoming train could be heard in the distance. The man got up and put his hands in his pockets.

'I'll put you aboard,' he said.

'No,' she said, shaking her head resolutely. 'You mustn't do that; it's dangerous.'

'I'm doing it anyhow.'

'Please!'

'One last thing,' he said; 'I know the major's a ladies' man. Don't smile at him too much.'

She looked at him supplicatingly. 'Oh, Eddie!' she exclaimed with emotion, offering him her lips.

He seemed nonplussed for a moment, as if in embarrassment or because he didn't have the courage to kiss her. Finally he deposited a fatherly kiss on her cheek.

'Stop!' called out the clapperboy. 'A break!'

'Not like that!' The director's voice roared through the megaphone. 'The last bit has to be done again.' He was a bearded young man with a long scarf wound around his neck. Now he got down from the seat on the boom next to the camera and came to meet them. 'Not like that,' he repeated disappointedly. 'It must be a passionate kiss, old-fashioned style, the way it was in the original film.' He threw an arm around the actress's waist, bending her backwards. 'Lean over her and put some passion into it,' he said to the actor.

Then looking around him, he added, 'Take a break!'

II

The actors invaded the station's shabby café, jostling one another in the direction of the bar. She lingered at the door, uncertain what to do, while he disappeared in the crowd. Soon he came back, precariously carrying two cups of coffee, and beckoned to her with his head to join him outside. Behind the café there was a rocky courtyard, under a vine-covered arbour, which served also for storage. Besides cases of empty bottles, there were some misshapen chairs, and on two of these they sat down, using a third one as a table.

'We're winding up,' he observed.

'He insisted on doing the last scene last,' she answered. 'I don't know why.'

'That's *modern*.' he said emphatically. 'Straight out of the *Cahiers du Cinema* . . . look out, that coffee's boiling hot.'

'I still don't know why.'

'Do they do things differently in America?' he asked.

'They certainly do!' she said with assurance. 'They're less pretentious, less . . . intellectual.'

'This fellow's good, though.'

'It's only that, once upon a time, things weren't handled this way.'

They were silent, enjoying their coffee. It was eleven in the morning, and the sea was sparkling, visible through a privet hedge around the courtyard. The vine leaves of the pergola were flaming red and the sun made shifting puddles of light on the gravel.

'A gorgeous autumn,' he said, looking up at the leaves. And he added, half to himself. ' "Once upon a time" . . . Hearing you say those words had an effect on me.'

She did not answer, but hugged her knees, which she had drawn up against her chest. She, too, seemed distracted, as if she had only just thought about the meaning of what she had said.

'Why did you agree to play in this film?' she asked.

'Why did *you*?'

'I don't know, but I asked you first.'

'Because of an illusion,' he said; 'the idea of re-living . . . something like that, I suppose. I don't really know. And you?'

'I don't really know, either; with the same idea, I suppose.'

The director emerged from the path which ran around the café, in good spirits and carrying a tankard of beer.

'So here are my stars!' he exclaimed, sinking into one of the misshapen chairs, with a sigh of satisfaction.

'Please spare us your speech on the beauties of direct takes,' she said. 'You've lectured us quite enough.'

The director did not take offence at this remark and fell into casual conversation. He spoke of the film, of the importance of this new version, of why he had taken on the same actors so many years later and why he was underlining the fact that it was a remake. Things he had said many times before, as was clear from his hearers' indifference. But he enjoyed the repetition, it was almost as if he were talking to himself. He finished his beer and got up.

'Here's hoping it rains,' he said as he left. 'It would be too bad to shoot the last scenes with pumps.' And, before turning the corner, he threw back: 'Half an hour before we start shooting again.'

She looked questioningly at her companion, who shook his head and shrugged his shoulders.

'It did pour during the last scene,' he said, 'and I was left standing in the rain.'

She laughed and laid a hand on his shoulder as if to signify that she remembered.

'Do they still show it in America?' he asked with a stolid expression on his face.

'Hasn't the director projected it for our benefit exactly eleven times?' she countered, laughing. 'Anyhow, in America it's shown to film clubs and other groups from time to time.'

'It's the same thing here,' he said. And then, abruptly: 'How's the major?'

She looked at him questioningly.

'I mean Howard,' he specified. 'I told you not to smile at him too much, but obviously you didn't follow my advice, even if the scene isn't included in the film.' And, after a moment of reflection: 'I still don't understand why you married him.'

'Neither do I,' she said in a childlike manner. 'I was very

young.' Her expression relaxed, as if she had put mistrust aside and given up lying. 'I wanted to get even with you,' she said calmly. 'That was the real reason, although perhaps I wasn't aware of it. And then I wanted to go to America.'

'What about Howard?' he insisted.

'Our marriage didn't last long. He wasn't right for me, really, and I wasn't cut out to be an actress.'

'You disappeared completely. Why did you give up acting?'

'I couldn't get anywhere with it. After all, I'd been in just one hit, and that because of winning an audition. In America they're real pros. Once I made a series of films for television, but they were a disaster. They cast me as a disagreeable rich woman, not exactly my type, was it?'

'I think not. You look like a happy woman. Are you happy?'

'No,' she said, smiling. 'But I've a lot going for me.'

'For instance?'

'For instance a daughter. A delightful creature, in her third university year, and we're very close.'

He stared at her incredulously.

'Twenty years have gone by,' she reminded him. 'Nearly a lifetime.'

'You're still beautiful.'

'That's make-up. I have wrinkles. And I could be a grand-mother.'

For some time they were silent. Voices from the café drifted out to them, and someone started up the jukebox. He looked as if he were going to speak, but stared at the ground, seemingly at a loss for words.

'I want you to tell me about your life,' he said at last. 'All through the filming I've wanted to ask you, but I've got around to it only now.'

'Certainly,' she said, spiritedly. 'And I'd like to hear you talk about yours.'

At this juncture the production secretary appeared in the doorway, a thin, homely, plaintive young woman with her hair in a ponytail and a pair of glasses on her nose.

'Make-up time!' she called out. 'We start shooting in ten minutes.'

III

The bell stopped ringing and the incoming train could be heard in the distance. The man got up and put his hands in his pockets.

'I'll put you aboard,' he said.

'No,' she said, shaking her head resolutely. 'You mustn't do that, it's dangerous.'

'I'm doing it anyhow.'

'Please!'

'One last thing,' he said, 'I know the major's a ladies' man. Don't smile at him too much.'

She looked at him supplicatingly. 'Oh, Eddie!' she exclaimed with emotion, offering him her lips.

He put his arm around her waist, bending her backwards. Looking into her eyes, he slowly advanced his mouth towards her and gave her a passionate kiss, a long, intense kiss, which aroused an approving murmur and some catcalls.

'Stop!' called the clapperboy. 'End of scene.'

'Lunchtime,' the director announced through the megaphone. 'Back at four o'clock.'

The actors dispersed in various directions, some to the café, others to caravans parked in front of the station. He took off his trenchcoat and hung it over his arm. They were the last to arrive on the street, where they set out towards the sea. A 'blade of sunlight struck the row of pink houses along the harbour, and the sea was of a celestial, almost diaphanous blue. A woman with a tub under her arm appeared on a balcony and began to hang up clothes to dry. Then she grasped a pulley and the clothes slid along a line from one house to another, fluttering like flags. The houses formed the arches of a portico and underneath there were stalls, covered during the midday break with oilcloth. Some bore painted blue anchors and a sign saying *Fresh Fish*.

'There used to be a pizzeria here,' he said, 'I remember it perfectly, it was called *Da Pezzi*.'

She looked at the paving-stones and did not speak.

'You *must* remember,' he continued. 'There was a sign "Pizza to take away", and I said to you: "Let's purchase a pizza from Pezzi," and you laughed.'

They went down the steps of a narrow alley with windows joined by an arch above them. The echo of their footsteps on the shiny paving-stones conveyed a feeling of winter, with the crackling tone that sounds acquire in cold air. Actually there was a warm breeze and the fragrance of mock-orange. The shops on the waterfront were closed and café chairs were stacked up around empty tables.

'We're out of season,' she observed.

He shot her a surreptitious look, wondering if the remark had a double meaning, then let it go.

'There's a restaurant that's open,' he said, gesturing with his head. 'What do you say?'

The restaurant was called *L'Arsella*; it was a wood and glass construction resting on piles set into the beach next to the blue bathhouses. Two gently rocking boats were tied to the piles. Some windows had blinds drawn over them; lamps were lit on the tables in spite of the bright daylight. There were few customers: a couple of silent, middle-aged Germans, two intellectual-looking young men, a woman with a dog, the last holiday-makers. They sat down at a corner table, far from the others. Perhaps the waiter recognised them; he came quickly but with an embarrassed and would-be confidential air. They ordered grilled sole and champagne and looked out at the horizon, which changed colour as wind pushed the clouds around. Now there was a hint of indigo on the line separating sea and sky, and the promontory that closed the bay was silvery green like a block of ice.

'Incredible,' she said after a minute or two, 'only three weeks to shoot a film, ridiculous, I call it. We've done some scenes only once.'

'That's avant-garde,' he said, smiling. 'Fake realism, *cinéma-vérité*, they call it. Today's production costs are high, so they do everything in a hurry.' He was making bread crumbs into little balls and lining them up in front of his plate. 'Anghelo-poulos,' he said ironically. 'He'd like to do a film like *O Thiassos*, a play within a play, with us acting ourselves. Period songs and accessories and transitional sequences, all very well, but what's to take the place of myth and tragedy?'

The waiter brought on the champagne and uncorked the bottle. She raised her glass as if in a toast. Her eyes were malicious and shiny, full of reflections.

'Melodrama,' she said, 'Melodrama, that's what.' She took short sips and broke into a smile. 'That's why he wanted the acting overdone. We had to be caricatures of ourselves.'

He raised his glass in return. 'Then hurrah for melodrama!' he said. 'Sophocles, Shakespeare, Racine, they all go in for it. That's what I've been up to myself all these years.'

'Talk to me about yourself,' she said.

'Do you mean it?'

'I do.'

'I have a farm in Provence, and I go there when I can. The

countryside is just hilly enough, people are welcoming, and I like horses.'

He made more bread-crumb balls, two circles of them around a glass, and then he moved one behind the other as if he were playing patience.

'That's not what I meant,' she said.

He called the waiter and ordered another bottle of champagne.

'I teach at the Academy of Dramatic Arts,' he said. 'My life's made up of Creon, Macbeth, Henry VIII.' He gave a guilty smile. 'Hardhearted fellows, all.'

She looked at him intently, with a concentrated, almost anxious air.

'What about films?' she asked.

'Five years ago I was in a mystery story. I played an American private detective, just three scenes, and then they bumped me off in an elevator. But in the titles they ran my name in capital letters . . . "With the participation of . . ." '

'You're a myth,' she said emphatically.

'A leftover,' he demurred. 'I'm this butt between my lips, see . . .' He put on a hard, desperate expression and let the smoke from the cigarette hanging between his lips cover his face.

'Don't play Eddie!' she said, laughing.

'But I *am* Eddie,' he muttered, pulling an imaginary hat over his eyes. He refilled the glasses and raised his.

'To films and filmmaking!'

'If we go on like this we'll be drunk when we go back to the set, *Eddie*.' She stressed the name, and there was a malicious glint in her eyes.

He took off the imaginary hat and laid it over his heart.

'Better that way. We'll be more melodramatic.'

For a sweet they had ordered ice-cream with hot chocolate

sauce. The waiter arrived with a triumphal air, bearing a tray with ice-creams in one hand and the steaming chocolate sauce in the other. While serving them he asked, timidly but coyly, if they would honour him with their autographs on a menu and shot them a gratified smile when they assented.

The ice-cream was in the shape of a flower, with deep red cherries at the centre of the corolla. He picked one of these up with his fingers and carried it to his mouth.

'Look here,' he said. 'Let's change the ending.'

She looked at him, seemingly perplexed, but perhaps her look signified that she knew what he was driving at and was merely awaiting confirmation.

'Don't go,' he said. 'Stay here with me.'

She lowered her eyes to her plate as if in embarrassment.

'Please,' she said, 'please.'

'You're talking the way you do in the film,' he said. 'That's the exact line.'

'We're not in a film now,' she said, almost resentfully. 'Stop playing your part; you're overdoing it.'

He made a gesture that seemed to signify dropping the whole thing.

'But I love you,' he said in a low voice.

She put on a teasing tone.

'Of course,' she said, in slightly haughty fashion, 'in the film.'

'It's the same thing,' he said. 'It's all a film.'

'All what's a film?'

'Everything.' He stretched his hand across the table and squeezed hers. 'Let's run the film backwards and go back to the beginning.'

She looked at him as if she didn't have the courage to reply. She let him stroke her hand and stroked his in return.

'You've forgotten the title of the film,' she said, trying for a quick retort. ' "Point of No Return." '

The waiter arrived, beaming and waving a menu for them to autograph.

IV

'You're mad!' she said laughing, but letting him pull her along. 'They'll be furious.'

He pulled her onto the pier and quickened his steps.

'Let them be furious,' he said. 'Let that cock-of-the-walk wait. Waiting makes for inspiration.'

There were no more than a dozen people on the boat, scattered on the benches in the cabin and on the iron seats, painted white, at the stern. Their dress and casual behaviour marked them as local people, used to this crossing. Three women were carrying plastic bags bearing the name of a well-known shop. Plainly they had come from villages on the perimeter of the bay to make purchases in the town. The employee who punched the tickets was wearing blue trousers and a white shirt with the company seal sewed onto it. The actor asked how long it would take to make the round trip. The ticket-collector made a sweeping gesture and enumerated the villages where they would be stopping. He was a young man with a blond moustache and a strong local accent.

'About an hour and a half,' he said, 'but if you're in a hurry, there's a larger boat which returns to the mainland from our first stop, just after we arrive, and will bring you back in forty minutes.'

He pointed to the first village on the north side of the bay.

She still seemed undecided, torn between doubt and temptation.

'They'll be furious,' she repeated. 'They wanted to wrap it up by evening.'

He shrugged his shoulders and threw up his hands.

'If we don't finish today we'll finish tomorrow,' he countered. 'We're paid for the job, not by the hour, so we can surely take an extra half-day.'

'I've a plane for New York tomorrow,' she said. 'I made a reservation, and my daughter will be waiting for me.'

'Lady, make up your mind,' said the ticket-collector. 'We have to push off.'

A whistle blew twice and a sailor started to release the mooring rope. The ticket-collector pulled out his pad and tore off two tickets.

'You'll be better off at the bow,' he remarked. 'There's a bit of breeze, but you won't feel the rolling.'

The seats were all free, but they leaned on the low railing and looked at the scene around them. The boat drew away from the pier and gathered speed. From a slight distance the town revealed its exact layout, with the old houses falling into an unexpected and graceful geometrical pattern.

'It's more beautiful viewed from the sea,' she observed. She held down her windblown hair with one hand, and red spots had appeared on her cheekbones.

'You're the beauty,' he said, 'at sea, on land, and wherever.'

She laughed and searched her bag for a scarf.

'You've turned very gallant,' she said. 'Once upon a time you weren't like that at all.'

'Once upon a time I was stupid, stupid and childish.'

'Actually, you seem more childish to me now than then. Forgive me for saying so, but that's what I think.'

'You're wrong, though. I'm older, that's all.' He shot her a worried glance. 'Now don't tell me I'm old.'

'No, you're not old. But that's not the only thing that matters.'

She took a tortoiseshell case out of her bag and extracted a cigarette. He cupped his hands around hers to protect the match from the wind. The sky was very blue, although there was a black streak on the horizon and the sea had darkened. The first village was rapidly approaching. They could see a pink bell tower and a bulging spire as white as meringue. A flight of pigeons rose up from the houses and took off, describing a wide curve towards the sea.

'Life must be wonderful there,' he said, 'and very simple.'

She nodded and smiled.

'Perhaps because it's not ours.'

The boat they were to meet was tied up at the pier, an old boat looking like a tug. For the benefit of the new arrival it whistled three times in greeting. Several people were standing on the pier, perhaps waiting to go aboard. A little girl in a yellow dress, holding a woman's hand, was jumping up and down like a bird.

'That's what I'd like,' he said inconsequentially. 'To live a life other than ours.'

From her expression he saw that this meaning was not clear and corrected himself.

'I mean a happy life rather than ours, like the one we imagine they lead in this village.'

He grasped her hands and made her meet his eyes, looking at her very hard.

She gently freed herself, giving him a rapid kiss.

'Eddie,' she said tenderly, 'dear Eddie.' Slipping her arm into his she pulled him towards the gangplank. 'You're a great actor,' she said, 'a truly great actor.' She was happy and brimming over with life.

'But it's what I feel,' he protested feebly, letting her pull him along.

'Of course,' she said, 'like a true actor.'

V

The train came to a sudden stop, with the wheels screeching and puffs of smoke rising from the engine. A compartment opened and five girls stuck out their heads. Some of them were peroxide blondes, with curls falling over their shoulders and on their foreheads. They started to laugh and chat, calling out: 'Elsa! Elsa!' A showy redhead, wearing a green ribbon in her hair, shouted to the others: 'There she is!' and leaned even further out to wave her hands in greeting. Elsa quickened her step and came close to the window, touching the gaily outstretched hands.

'Corinna!' she exclaimed, looking at the redhead, 'What's this get-up?'

'Saverio says it's attractive,' Corinna called back, winking and pointing her head towards the inside of the compartment. 'Come on aboard,' she added in a falsetto voice; 'you don't want to be stuck in a place like this, do you?' Then, suddenly, she screamed: 'Look girls, there's a Rudolph Valentino!'

The girls waved madly to catch the man's attention. Eddie had come out from behind the arrivals and departures board; he advanced slowly along the platform, with his hat pulled over his eyes. At that same moment, two German soldiers came through the gate and went towards the stationmaster's office. After a few moments the stationmaster came out with his red flag under his arm and walked towards the engine, with rapid steps, which accentuated the awkwardness of his chubby body. The soldiers stood in front of the office door, as if they were on guard. The girls fell silent and watched the scene looking worried. Elsa set down her suitcase and looked confusedly at Eddie, who motioned with his head that she should go on. Then he sat down on a bench, under a tourist poster, took the newspaper out of his pocket and buried his face in it. Corinna seemed to understand what was up.

'Come on, dearie!' she shouted. 'Come aboard!'

With one hand she waved at the two staring soldiers an'
gave them a dazzling smile. Meanwhile the stationmaster was
coming back with the flag now rolled up under his arm.
Corinna asked him what was going on.

'Don't ask me,' he answered, shrugging his shoulders. 'It
seems we have to wait for a quarter of an hour. It's orders,
that's all I know.'

'Then we can get out and stretch our legs, girls,' Corinna
chirped. 'Climb aboard,' she whispered as she passed Elsa.
'We'll take care of them.'

The little group moved in the direction opposite to where
Eddie was seated, passing in front of the soldiers. 'Isn't there
anywhere to eat in this station?' Corinna asked in a loud voice,
looking around. She was superb at drawing attention to herself, swinging her hips and also the bag she had taken off her
shoulder. She had on a clinging flowered dress and sandals with
cork soles.

'The sea, girls!' she shouted. 'Look at that sea and tell me if
it isn't divine!' She leaned theatrically against the first lamp-
post and raised her hand to her mouth, putting on a childish
manner. 'If I had my bathing suit with me, I'd dive, never
mind the autumn weather,' she said, tossing her head and
causing her red curls to ripple over her shoulders.

The two soldiers were stunned and couldn't take their eyes
off her. Then she had a stroke of genius, due to the lamp-post,
perhaps, or to the necessity of resolving an impossible situation. She let her blouse slip down off her shoulders, leaned
against the lamp-post, stretched out her arms and addressed an
imaginary public, winking as if the whole scene were in
cahoots with her.

'It's a song they sing the world over,' she shouted, 'even
our enemies!' And, turning to the other girls, she clapped

hands. It must have been part of the show, because they fell into line, raising their legs in marching time but without moving an inch, their hands at their foreheads in a military salute. Corinna clung to the lamp-post with one hand and, using it as a pivot, wheeled gracefully around it, while her skirt, fluttering in the breeze, displayed her legs to advantage.

> '*Vor der Kaserne vor dem grossen Tor,*
> *Stand eine Laterne, und steht sie noch davor . . .*
> *So wollen wir uns da wiedersehen,*
> *Bei der Laterne wollen wir stehen,*
> *Wie einst Lili Marlene, wie einst Lili Marlene.*'

The girls applauded and one of the soldiers whistled. Corinna thanked them with a mock bow and went to the fountain near the hedge. She passed a wet finger over her forehead while looking down at the street below; then, trailed by the other girls, she started to reboard the train.

'Goodbye, boys!' she shouted to the soldiers. 'We're going to snatch some rest. We've a long tour ahead of us.'

Elsa was waiting in the corridor and threw her arms around her.

'You're an angel, Corinna,' she said, giving her a kiss.

'Think nothing of it,' said Corinna, starting to cry like a baby.

The two soldiers had come close to the waiting train; they looked up at the girls and tried to exchange words; one of them knew some Italian. Just then there was the sound of a motor, and a black car came through the gate and travelled the length of the platform until it stopped at the front, just behind the engine. The girls tried to fathom what was happening, but there was a curve in the tracks and they couldn't see very well around it. Eddie hadn't moved from the bench. Apparently was immersed in the newspaper that shielded his face.

'What's up?' asked Elsa, trying to seem indifferent as she stowed her things in the luggage net.

'Nothing,' one of the girls answered. 'It must be a big shot who arrived in the car. He's in civilian clothes and travelling first-class.'

'Is he alone?' Elsa asked.

'It seems so. The soldiers are standing to attention and not boarding the train.'

Elsa peered out the window. The soldiers had turned around and were walking towards the road leading into the town. The stationmaster came back, dragging the red flag behind him and looking down at his shoes.

'The train's leaving,' he said in a philosophical, knowing manner, and waved the flag. The engine whistled. The girls returned to their seats, only Elsa stayed at the window. She had combed her hair off her forehead and her eyes were still gleaming. At this moment Eddie came up and stood directly under the window.

'Goodbye, Eddie,' Elsa murmured, stretching out her hand.

'Shall we meet in another film?' he asked.

'What the devil is he saying?' shouted the director from behind him. 'What the devil?'

'Shall I hold?' asked the cameraman.

'No,' said the director. 'It's going to be dubbed anyhow.' And he shouted into the megaphone. 'Walk, man, the train's moving, move faster, follow it along the platform, hold her hand.'

The train had, indeed, started, and Eddie obeyed orders, quickening his pace and keeping up as long as he could. The train picked up speed and went around the curve and through a switch on the other side. Eddie wheeled about and took a

w steps before stopping to light a cigarette and then walk
lowly on into camera. The director made gestures to regulate
his pace, as if he were manipulating him with strings.

'Insert a heart attack,' said Eddie imploringly.

'What do you mean?'

'A heart attack,' Eddie repeated. 'Here, on the bench. I'll
look exhausted, sink onto the bench and lay my hand on my
heart like Dr Zhivago. Make me die.'

The clapperboy looked at the director, waiting for instruc-
tions.

The director moved his fingers like scissors to signify that
he'd cut later, but meanwhile the shooting must go on.

'What do you mean by a heart attack?' he said to Eddie. 'Do
you think you look like a man about to have a heart attack?
Pull your hat over your eyes, like a good Eddie, don't make
me start all over.' And he signalled to the crew to put the
pumps into action. 'Come on, move! It's starting to rain.
You're Eddie, remember, not a poor lovelorn creature . . . Put
your hands in your pockets, shrug your shoulders, that's it,
good boy, come towards us . . . your cigarette hanging from
your lips . . . perfect! . . . eyes on the ground.'

He turned to the cameraman and shouted: 'Pull back—
tracking shot; pull back!'

Angela Carter
Puss-in-Boots

Figaro here; Figaro, there, I tell you! Figaro upstairs, Figaro downstairs and—oh, my goodness me, this little Figaro can slip into my lady's chamber smart as you like at any time whatsoever that he takes the fancy for, don't you know, he's a cat of the world, cosmopolitan, sophisticated; he can tell when a furry friend is the Missus' best company. For what lady in all the world could say 'no' to the passionate yet toujours discret advances of a fine marmalade cat? (Unless it be her eyes incontinently overflow at the slightest whiff of fur, which happened once, as you shall hear.)

A tom, sirs, a ginger tom and proud of it. Proud of his fine, white shirtfront that dazzles harmoniously against his orange and tangerine tessellations (oh! what a fiery suit of lights have I); proud of his bird-entrancing eye and more than military whiskers; proud, to a fault, some say, of his fine, musical voice. All the windows in the square fly open when I break into impromptu song at the spectacle of the moon above Bergamo. If the poor players in the square, the sullen rout of ragged trash that haunts the provinces, are rewarded with a hail of pennies when they set up their makeshift stage and start their raucous choruses, then how much more liberally do the citizens deluge me with pails of the freshest water, vegetables hardly spoiled and, occasionally, slippers, shoes and boots.

Do you see these fine, high, shining leather boots of mine?

A young cavalry officer made me the tribute of, first, one; then, after I celebrate his generosity with a fresh obbligato, the moon no fuller than my heart—whoops! I nimbly spring aside—down comes the other. Their high heels will click like castanets when Puss takes his promenade upon the tiles, for my song recalls flamenco, all cats have a Spanish tinge although Puss himself elegantly lubricates his virile, muscular, native Bergamasque with French, since that is the only language in which you can purr.

'Merrrrrrrrrrrrci!'

Instanter I draw my new boots on over the natty white stockings that terminate my hinder legs. That young man, observing with curiosity by moonlight the use to which I put his footwear, calls out: 'Hey, Puss! Puss, there!'

'At your service, sir!'

'Up to my balcony, young Puss!'

He leans out, in his nightshirt, offering encouragement as I swing succinctly up the façade, forepaws on a curly cherub's pate, hindpaws on a stucco wreath, bring them up to meet your forepaws while, first paw forward, hup! on to the stone nymph's tit; left paw down a bit, the satyr's bum should do the trick. Nothing to it, once you know how, rococo's no problem. Acrobatics? Born to them; Puss can perform a back somersault whilst holding aloft a glass of vino in his right paw and *never spill a drop*.

But, to my shame, the famous death-defying triple somersault en plein air, that is, in middle air, that is, unsupported and without a safety net, I, Puss, have never yet attempted though often I have dashingly brought off the double tour, to the applause of all.

'You strike me as a cat of parts,' says this young man when I'm arrived at his window-sill. I made him a handsome genuflection, rump out, tail up, head down, to facilitate his friendly

chuck under my chin; and, as involuntary free gift, my natu
my habitual smile.

For all cats have this particularity, each and every one, from
the meanest alley sneaker to the proudest, whitest she that ever
graced a pontiff's pillow—we have our smiles, as it were,
painted on. Those small, cool, quiet Mona Lisa smiles that
smile we must, no matter whether it's been fun or it's been
not. So all cats have a politician's air; we smile and smile and
so they think we're villains. But, I note, this young man is
something of a smiler hisself.

'A sandwich,' he offers. 'And, perhaps, a snifter of brandy.'

His lodgings are poor, though he's handsome enough and
even en déshabillé, nightcap and all, there's a neat, smart,
dandified air about him. Here is one who knows what's what,
thinks I; a man who keeps up appearances in the bedchamber
can never embarrass you out of it. And excellent beef sandwiches; I relish a lean slice of roast beef and early learned a taste
for spirits, since I started life as a wine-shop cat, hunting cellar
rats for my keep, before the world sharpened my wits enough
to let me live by them.

And the upshot of this midnight interview? I'm engaged, on
the spot, as Sir's valet. valet de chambre and, from time to
time, his body servant, for, when funds are running low, as
they must do for every gallant officer when the pickings fall
off, he pawns the quilt, doesn't he. Then faithful Puss curls up
on his chest to keep him warm at nights. And if he don't like
me to knead his nipples, which, out of the purest affection and
the desire—ouch! he says—to try the retractability of my
claws, I do in moments of absence of mind, then what other
valet could slip into a young girl's sacred privacy and deliver
her a billet-doux at the very moment when she's reading her
prayerbook with her sainted mother? A task I once or twice
perform for him, to his infinite gratitude.

...nd, as you will hear, brought him at last to the best of ...rtunes for us all.

So Puss got his post at the same time as his boots and I dare say the Master and I have much in common for he's proud as the devil, touchy as tin-tacks, lecherous as liquorice and, though I say it as loves him, as quick-witted a rascal as ever put on clean linen.

When times were hard, I'd pilfer the market for breakfast—a herring, an orange, a loaf; we never went hungry. Puss served him well in the gaming salons, too, for a cat may move from lap to lap with impunity and cast his eye over any hand of cards. A cat can jump on the dice—he can't resist to see it roll! poor thing, mistook it for a bird; and, after I've been, limp-spined, stiff-legged, playing the silly buggers, scooped up to be chastised, who can remember how the dice fell in the first place?

And we had, besides, less . . . gentlemanly means of maintenance when they closed the tables to us, as, churlishly, they sometimes did. I'd perform my little Spanish dance while he went round with his hat: *olé!* But he only put my loyalty and affection to the test of this humiliation when the cupboard was as bare as his backside; after, in fact, he'd sunk so low as to pawn his drawers.

So all went right as ninepence and you never saw such boon companions as Puss and his master; until the man must needs go fall in love.

'Head over heels, Puss.'

I went about my ablutions, tonguing my arsehole with the impeccable hygienic integrity of cats, one leg stuck in the air like a ham bone; I choose to remain silent. Love? What has my rakish master, for whom I've jumped through the window of every brothel in the city, besides haunting the virginal back garden of the convent and god knows what other goatish errands, to do with the tender passion?

'And she. A princess in a tower. Remote and shinin.
Aldebaran. Chained to a dolt and dragon-guarded.'

I withdrew my head from my privates and fixed him wit.
my most satiric smile; I dare him warble on in *that* strain.

'All cats are cynics,' he opines, quailing beneath my yellow
glare.

It is the hazard of it draws him, see.

There is a lady sits in a window for one hour and one hour
only, at the tenderest time of dusk. You can scarcely see her
features, the curtains almost hide her; shrouded like a holy
image, she looks out at the piazza as the shops shut up, the stalls
go down, the night comes on. And that is all the world she
ever sees. Never a girl in all Bergamo so secluded except, on
Sundays, they let her go to Mass, bundled up in black, with a
veil on. And then she is in the company of an aged hag, her
keeper, who grumps along grim as a prison dinner.

How did he see that secret face? Who else but Puss revealed it?

Back we come from the tables so late, so very late at night
we found, to our emergent surprise, that all at once it was early
in the morning. His pockets were heavy with silver and both
our guts sweetly a-gurgle with champagne; Lady Luck had sat
with us, what fine spirits were we in! Winter and cold weather.
The pious trot to church already with little lanterns through
the chill fog as we go ungodly rolling home.

See, a black barque, like a state funeral; and Puss takes it into
his bubbly-addled brain to board her. Tacking obliquely to her
side, I rub my marmalade pate against her shin; how could any
duenna, be she never so stern, take offence at such attentions
to her chargeling from a little cat? (As it turns out, this one:
attishooo! does.) A white hand fragrant as Arabia descends from
the black cloak and reciprocally rubs behind his ears at just the
ecstatic spot. Puss lets rip a roaring purr, rears briefly on his
high-heeled boots; jig with joy and pirouette with glee—she

...ns to see and draws her veil aside. Puss glimpses high
...ove, as it were, an alabaster lamp lit behind by dawn's first
...ush: her face.

And she smiling.

For a moment, just that moment, you would have thought
it was May morning.

'Come along! Come! Don't dawdle over the nasty beast!'
snaps the old hag, with the one tooth in her mouth, and warts;
she sneezes.

The veil comes down; so cold it is, and dark, again.

It was not I alone who saw her; with that smile he swears she
stole his heart.

Love.

I've sat inscrutably by and washed my face and sparkling
dicky with my clever paw while he made the beast with two
backs with every harlot in the city, besides a number of good
wives, dutiful daughters, rosy country girls come to sell celery
and endive on the corner, and the chambermaid who strips the
bed, what's more. The Mayor's wife, even, shed her diamond
earrings for him and the wife of the notary unshuffled her
petticoats and, if I could, I would blush to remember how her
daughter shook out her flaxen plaits and jumped in bed between them and she not sixteen years old. But never the word,
'love', has fallen from his lips, nor in nor out of any of these
transports, until my master saw the wife of Signor Panteleone
as she went walking out to Mass, and she lifted up her veil
though not for him.

And now he is half sick with it and will go to the tables no
more for lack of heart and never even pats the bustling rump
of the chambermaid in his new-found, maudlin celibacy, so we
get our slops left festering for days and the sheets filthy and the
wench goes banging about bad-temperedly with her broom
enough to fetch the plaster off the walls.

I'll swear he lives for Sunday morning, though never before was he a religious man. Saturday nights, he bathes himself punctiliously, even, I'm glad to see, washes behind his ears, perfumes himself, presses his uniform so you'd think he had a right to wear it. So much in love he very rarely panders to the pleasures, even of Onan, as he lies tossing on his couch, for he cannot sleep for fear he miss the summoning bell. Then out into the cold morning, harking after that black, vague shape, hapless fisherman for this sealed oyster with such a pearl in it. He creeps behind her across the square; how can so amorous bear to be so inconspicuous? And yet, he must; though, sometimes, the old hag sneezes and says she swears there is a cat about.

He will insinuate himself into the pew behind milady and sometimes contrive to touch the hem of her garment, when they all kneel, and never a thought to his orisons; she is the divinity he's come to worship. Then sits silent, in a dream, till bed-time; what pleasure is his company for me?

He won't eat, either. I brought him a fine pigeon from the inn kitchen, fresh off the spit, parfumé avec tarragon, but he wouldn't touch it so I crunched it up, bones and all. Performing, as ever after meals, my meditative toilette, I pondered thus: one, he is in a fair way to ruining us both by neglecting his business; two, love is desire sustained by unfulfilment. If I lead him to her bedchamber and there he takes his fill of her lily-white, he'll be right as rain in two shakes and next day tricks as usual.

Then Master and his Puss will soon be solvent once again.

Which, at the moment, very much not, sir.

This Signor Panteleone employs, his only servant but the hag, a kitchen cat, a sleek, spry tabby whom I accost. Grasping the slack of her neck firmly between my teeth, I gave her the customary tribute of a few firm thrusts of my striped loins and, when she got her breath back, she assured me in the friendliest fashion the old man was a fool and a miser who kept herself on short commons for the sake of the mousing and the young lady a soft-hearted creature who smuggled breast of chicken and sometimes, when the hag-dragon-governess napped at midday, snatched this pretty kitty out of the hearth and into her bedroom to play with reels of silk and run after trailed handkerchiefs, when she and she had as much fun together as two Cinderellas at an all-girls' ball.

Poor, lonely lady, married so young to an old dodderer with his bald pate and his goggle eyes and his limp, his avarice, his gore belly, his rheumaticks, and his flag hangs all the time at half-mast indeed; and jealous as he is impotent, tabby declares—he'd put a stop to all the rutting in the world, if he had his way, just to certify his young wife don't get from another what she can't get from him.

'Then shall we hatch a plot to antler him, my precious?'

Nothing loath, she tells me the best time for this accomplishment should be the one day in all the week he forsakes his wife and his counting-house to ride off into the country to extort most grasping rents from starveling tenant farmers. And she's left all alone, then, behind so many bolts and bars you wouldn't believe; all alone—but for the hag!

Aha! This hag turns out to be the biggest snag; an iron-plated, copper-bottomed, sworn man-hater of some sixty bitter winters who—as ill luck would have it—shatters, clatters, erupts into paroxysms of the *sneeze* at the very glimpse of a cat's whisker. No chance of Puss worming his winsome way into *that* one's affections, nor for my tabby, neither! But, oh my dear, I say; see how my ingenuity rises to this challenge . . . So we resume the sweetest part of our conversation in the dusty convenience of the coalhole and she promises me, least she can do, to see the fair, hitherto-inaccessible one gets a

letter safe if I slip it to her and slip it to her forthwith I do
though somewhat discommoded by my boots.

He spent three hours over his letter, did my master, as long
as it takes me to lick the coaldust off my dicky. He tears up half
a quire of paper, splays five pen-nibs with the force of his
adoration: 'Look not for any peace, my heart; having become
a slave to this beauty's tyranny, dazzled am I by this sun's rays
and my torments cannot be assuaged.' *That's* not the high road
to the rumpling of the bedcovers; she's got *one* ninny between
them already!

'Speak from the heart,' I finally exhort. 'And all good
women have a missionary streak, sir; convince her her orifice
will be your salvation and she's yours.'

'When I want your advice, Puss, I'll ask for it,' he says, all at
once hoity-toity. But at last he manages to pen ten pages; a
rake, a profligate, a card-sharper, a cashiered officer well on
the way to rack and ruin when first he saw, as if it were a
glimpse of grace, her face . . . his angel, his good angel, who
will lead him from perdition.

Oh, what a masterpiece he penned!

'Such tears she wept at his addresses!' says my tabby friend.
'Oh, Tabs, she sobs—for she calls me "Tabs" —I never meant
to wreak such havoc with a pure heart when I smiled to see a
booted cat! And put his paper next to her heart and swore, it
was a good soul that sent her his vows and she was too much
in love with virtue to withstand him. If, she adds, for she's a
sensible girl, he's neither old as the hills nor ugly as sin, that is.'

An admirable little note the lady's sent him in return, per
Figaro here and there; she adopts a responsive yet uncom-
promising tone. For, says she, how can she usefully discuss his
passion further without a glimpse of his person?

He kisses her letter once, twice, a thousand times; she must
and will see me! I shall serenade her this very evening!

So, when dusk falls, off we trot to the piazza, he with an old guitar he pawned his sword to buy and most, if I may say so, outlandishly rigged out in some kind of vagabond mountebank's outfit he bartered his gold-braided waistcoat with poor Pierrot braying in the square for, moonstruck zany, lovelorn loon he was himself and even plastered his face with flour to make it white, poor fool, and so ram home his heartsick state.

There she is, the evening star with the clouds around her; but such a creaking of carts in the square, such a clatter and crash as they dismantle the stalls, such an ululation of ballad-singers and oration of nostrum-peddlers and perturbation of errand boys that though he wails out his heart to her: 'Oh, my beloved!', why she, all in a dream, sits with her gaze in the middle distance, where there's a crescent moon stuck on the sky behind the cathedral pretty as a painted stage, and so is she.

Does she hear him?

Not a grace-note.

Does she see him?

Never a glance.

'Up you go, Puss; tell her to look my way!'

If rococo's a piece of cake, that chaste, tasteful, early Palladian stumped many a better cat than I in its time. Agility's not in it, when it comes to Palladian; daring alone will carry the day and, though the first storey's graced with a hefty caryatid whose bulbous loincloth and tremendous pects facilitate the first ascent, the Doric column on her head proves a horse of a different colour, I can tell you. Had I not seen my precious Tabby crouched in the gutter above me keening encouragement, I, even I, might never have braved that flying, upward leap that brought me, as if Harlequin himself on wires, in one bound to her window-sill.

'Dear god!' the lady says, and jumps. I see she, too, ah, sentimental thing! clutches a well-thumbed letter. 'Puss in boots!'

I bow her with a courtly flourish. What luck to hear no snit or sneeze; where's hag? A sudden flux sped her to the privy— not a moment to lose.

'Cast your eye below,' I hiss. 'Him you know of lurks below, in white with the big hat, ready to sing you an evening ditty.'

The bedroom door creaks open, then, and: whee! through the air Puss goes, discretion is the better part. And, for both their sweet sakes I did it, the sight of both their bright eyes inspired me to the never-before-attempted, by me or any other cat, in boots or out of them—the death-defying triple somersault!

And a three-storey drop to ground, what's more; a grand descent.

Only the merest trifle winded, I'm proud to say, I neatly land on all my fours and Tabs goes wild, huzzah! But has my master witnessed my triumph? Has he, my arse. He's tuning up that old mandolin and breaks, as down I come, again into his song.

I would never have said, in the normal course of things, his voice would charm the birds out of the trees, like mine; and yet the bustle died for him, the homeward-turning costers paused in their tracks to hearken, the preening street girls forgot their hard-edged smiles as they turned to him and some of the old ones wept, they did.

Tabs, up on the roof there, prick up your ears! For by its power I know my heart is in his voice.

And now the lady lowers her eyes to him and smiles, as once she smiled at me.

Then, bang! a stern hand pulls the shutters to. And it was as if all the violets in all the baskets of all the flower-sellers drooped and faded at once; and spring stopped dead in its tracks and might, this time, not come at all; and the bustle and

the business of the square, that had so magically quieted for his
song, now rose up again with the harsh clamour of the loss of
love.

And we trudge drearily off to dirty sheets and a mean supper
of bread and cheese, all I can steal him, but at least the poor
soul manifests a hearty appetite now she knows he's in the
world and not the ugliest of mortals; for the first time since that
fateful morning, sleeps sound. But sleep comes hard to Puss
tonight. He takes a midnight stroll across the square, soon
comfortably discusses a choice morsel of salt cod his tabby
friend found among the ashes on the hearth before our con-
verse turns to other matters.

'Rats!' she says. 'And take your boots off, you uncouth
bugger; those three-inch heels wreak havoc with the soft flesh
of my under-belly!'

When we'd recovered ourselves a little, I ask her what she
means by those 'rats' of hers and she proposes her scheme to
me. How my master must pose as a *rat-catcher* and I, his
ambulant marmalade rat-trap. How we will then go kill the rats
that ravage milady's bedchamber, the day the old fool goes to
fetch his rents, and she can have her will of the lad at leisure
for, if there is one thing the hag fears more than a cat, it is a rat
and she'll cower in a cupboard till the last rat is off the premises
before she comes out. Oh, this tabby one, sharp as a tack is she!
I congratulate her ingenuity with a few affectionate cuffs
round the head and home again, for breakfast, ubiquitous Puss,
here, there and everywhere, who's your Figaro?

Master applauds the rat ploy; but, as to the rats themselves,
how are they to arrive in the house in the first place? he
queries.

'Nothing easier, sir; my accomplice, a witty soubrette who
lives among the cinders, dedicated as she is to the young lady's
happiness, will personally strew a large number of dead and

dying rats she has herself collected about the bedroom of the said ingénue's duenna, and, most particularly, that of the said ingénue herself. This to be done tomorrow morning, as soon as Sir Pantaloon rides out to fetch his rents. By good fortune, down in the square, plying for hire, a rat-catcher! Since our hag cannot abide either a rat or a cat, it falls to milady to escort the rat-catcher, none other than yourself, sir, and his intrepid hunter, myself, to the site of the infestation.

'Once you're in her bedroom, sir, if *you* don't know what to do, then I can't help you.'

'Keep your foul thoughts to yourself, Puss.'

Some things, I see, are sacrosanct from humour.

Sure enough, prompt at five in the bleak next morning, I observe with my own eyes the lovely lady's lubbery husband hump off on his horse like a sack of potatoes to rake in his dues. We're ready with our sign: SIGNOR FURIOSO, THE LIVING DEATH OF RATS; and in the leathers he's borrowed from the porter, I hardly recognise him myself, not with the false moustache. He coaxes the chambermaid with a few kisses— poor, deceived girl! love knows no shame—and so we install ourselves under a certain shuttered window with the great pile of traps she's lent us, the sign of our profession, Puss perched atop them bearing the humble yet determined look of a sworn enemy of vermin.

We've not waited more than fifteen minutes—and just as well, so many rat-plagued Bergamots approach us already and are not easily dissuaded from employing us—when the front door flies open on a lusty scream. The hag, aghast, flings her arms round flinching Furioso; how fortuitous to find him! But, at the whiff of me, she's sneezing so valiantly, her eyes awash, the vertical gutters of her nostrils as will with snot, she barely can depict the scenes inside, rattus domesticus dead in her bed and all; and worse! in the Missus' room.

So Signor Furioso and his questing Puss are ushered into the very sanctuary of the goddess, our presence announced by a fanfare from her keeper on the noseharp. *Attishhoooo ! ! !*

Sweet and pleasant in a morning gown of loose linen, our ingénue jumps at the tattoo of my boot heels but recovers instantly and the wheezing, hawking hag is in no state to sniffle more than: 'Ain't I seen that cat before?'

'Not a chance,' says my master. 'Why, he's come but yesterday with me from Milano.'

So she has to make do with that.

My Tabs has lined the very stairs with rats; she's made a morgue of the hag's room but something more lively of the lady's. For some of her prey she's very cleverly not killed but crippled; a big black beastie weaves its way towards us over the turkey carpet, Puss, pounce! Between screaming and sneezing, the hag's in a fine state, I can tell you, though milady exhibits a most praiseworthy and collected presence of mind, being, I guess, a young woman of no small grasp so, perhaps, she has a sniff of the plot, already.

My master goes down hands and knees under the bed.

'My god!' he cries. 'There's the biggest hole, here in the wainscoting, I ever saw in all my professional career! And there's an army of black rats gathering behind it, ready to storm through! To arms!'

But, for all her terror, the hag's loath to leave the Master and me alone to deal with the rats; she casts her eye on a silver-backed hair-brush, a coral rosary, twitters, hovers, screeches, mutters until milady assures her, amidst scenes of rising pandemonium:

'I shall stay here myself and see that Signor Furioso doesn't make off with my trinkets. You go and recover yourself with an infusion of friar's balsam and don't come back until I call.'

The hag departs; quick as a flash, la belle turns the key in the door on her and softly laughs, the naughty one.

Dusting the slut–fluff from his knees, Signor Furioso now stands slowly upright; swiftly, he removes his false moustache, for no element of the farcical must mar this first, delirious encounter of these lovers, must it. (Poor soul, how his hands tremble!)

Accustomed as I am to the splendid, feline nakedness of my kind, that offers no concealment of that soul made manifest in the flesh of lovers, I am always a little moved by the poignant reticence with which humanity shyly hesitates to divest itself of its clutter of concealing rags in the presence of desire. So, first, these two smile, a little, as if to say: 'How strange to meet you here!', uncertain of a loving welcome, still. And do I deceive myself, or do I see a tear a-twinkle in the corner of his eye? But who is it steps towards the other first? Why, she; women, I think, are, of the two sexes, the more keenly tuned to the sweet music of their bodies. (A penny for my foul thoughts, indeed! Does she, that wise, grave personage in the négligé, think you've staged this grand charade merely in order to kiss her hand?) But, then—oh, what a pretty blush! steps back; now it's his turn to take two steps forward in the saraband of Eros.

I could wish, though, they'd dance a little faster; the hag will soon recover from her spasms and shall she find them in flagrante?

His hand, then, trembling, upon her bosom; hers, initially more hesitant, sequentially more purposeful, upon his breeches. Then their strange trance breaks; that sentimental havering done, I never saw two fall to it with such appetite. As if the whirlwind got into their fingers, they strip each other bare in a twinkling and she falls back on the bed, shows him the target, he displays the dart, scores an instant bullseye. Bravo! Never can that old bed have shook with such a storm before. And their sweet, choked mutterings, poor things: 'I never . . . ' 'My darling . . .' 'More . . .' And etc. etc. Enough to melt the thorniest heart.

He rises up on his elbows once and gasps at me: 'Mimic the murder of the rats, Puss! Mask the music of Venus with the clamour of Diana!'

A-hunting we shall go! Loyal to the last, I play catch as catch can with Tab's dead rats, giving the dying the coup de grâce and baying with resonant vigour to drown the extravagant screeches that break forth from that (who would have suspected?) more passionate young woman as she comes off in fine style. (Full marks, Master.)

At that, the old hag comes battering at the door. What's going on? Whyfor the racket? And the door rattles on its hinges.

'Peace!' cries Signor Furioso. 'Haven't I just now blocked the great hole?'

But milady's in no hurry to don her smock again, she takes her lovely time about it; so full of pleasure gratified her languorous limbs you'd think her very navel smiled. She pecks my master prettily thank-you on the cheek, wets the gum on his false moustache with the tip of her strawberry tongue and sticks it back on his upper lip for him, then lets her wardress into the scene of the faux carnage with the most modest and irreproachable air in the world.

'See! Puss has slaughtered all the rats.'

I rush, purring proud, to greet the hag; instantly, her eyes o'erflow.

'Why the bedclothes so disordered?' she squeaks, not quite blinded, yet, by phlegm and chosen for her post from all the other applicants on account of her suspicious mind, even (oh, dutiful) when in grande peur des rats.

'Puss had a mighty battle with the biggest beast you ever saw upon this very bed; can't you see the bloodstains on the sheets?

And now, what do we owe you, Signor Furioso, for this singular service?'

'A hundred ducats,' says I, quick as a flash, for I know my master, left to himself, would, like an honourable fool, take nothing.

'That's the entire household expenses for a month!' wails avarice's well-chosen accomplice.

'And worth every penny! For those rats would have eaten us out of house and home.' I see the glimmerings of sturdy backbone in this little lady. 'Go, pay them from your private savings that I know of, that you've skimmed off the house-keeping.'

Muttering and moaning but nothing for it except do as she is bid; and the furious Sir and I take off a laundry basket full of dead rats as souvenir—we drop it, plop! in the nearest sewer. And sit down to one dinner honestly paid for, for a wonder.

But the young fool is off his feed, again. Pushes his plate aside, laughs, weeps, buries his head in his hands and, time and time again, goes to the window to stare at the shutters behind which his sweetheart scrubs the blood away and my dear Tabs rests from her supreme exertions. He sits, for a while, and scribbles; rips the page in four, hurls it aside. I spear a falling fragment with a claw. Dear God, he's took to writing poetry.

'I must and will have her for ever,' he exclaims.

I see my plan has come to nothing. Satisfaction has not satisfied him; that soul they both saw in one another's bodies has such insatiable hunger no single meal could ever appease it. I fall to the toilette of my hinder parts, my favourite stance when contemplating the ways of the world.

'How can I live without her?'

You did so for twenty-seven years, sir, and never missed her for a moment.

'I'm burning with the fever of love!'

Then we're spared the expense of fires.

'I shall steal her away from her husband to live with me.'

'What do you propose to live on, sir?'

'Kisses,' he said distractedly. 'Embraces.'

'Well, you won't grow fat on that, sir; though *she* will. And then, more mouths to feed.'

'I'm sick and tired of your foul-mouthed barbs, Puss,' he snaps. And yet my heart is moved, for now he speaks the plain, clear, foolish rhetoric of love and who is there cunning enough to help him to happiness but I? Scheme, loyal Puss, scheme!

My wash completed, I step out across the square to visit that charming she who's wormed her way directly into my own hitherto-untrammelled heart with her sharp wits and her pretty ways. She exhibits warm emotion to see me; and, oh! what news she has to tell me! News of a rapt and personal nature, that turns my mind to thoughts of the future, and, yes, domestic plans of most familial nature. She's saved me a pig's trotter, a whole, entire pig's trotter the Missus smuggled to her with a wink. A feast! Masticating, I muse.

'Recapitulate,' I suggest, 'the daily motions of Sir Pantaloon when he's at home.'

They set the cathedral clock by him, so rigid and so regular his habits. Up at the crack, he meagrely breakfasts off yesterday's crusts and a cup of cold water, to spare the expense of heating it up. Down to his counting-house, counting out his money, until a bowl of well-watered gruel at midday. The afternoon he devotes to usury, bankrupting, here, a small tradesman, there, a weeping widow, for fun and profit. Dinner's luxurious, at four; soup, with a bit of rancid beef or a tough bird in it—he's an arrangement with the butcher, takes unsold stock off his hands in return for a shut mouth about a pie that had a finger in it. From four-thirty until five-thirty, he unlocks the shutters and lets his wife look out, oh, don't I

know! while hag sits beside her to make sure she doesn't sm▓
(Oh, that blessed flux, those precious loose minutes that set t▓
game in motion!)

And while she breathes the air of evening, why, he checks
up on his chest of gems, his bales of silk, all those treasures he
loves too much to share with daylight and if he wastes a candle
when he so indulges himself, why, any man is entitled to one
little extravagance. Another draught of Adam's ale healthfully
concludes the day; up he tucks besides Missus and, since she is
his prize possession, consents to finger her a little. He palpitates
her hide and slaps her flanks: 'What a good bargain!' Alack, can
do no more, not wishing to profligate his natural essence. And
so drifts off to sinless slumber amid the prospects of tomorrow's gold.

'How rich is he?'

'Croesus.'

'Enough to keep two loving couples?'

'Sumptuous.'

Early in the uncandled morning, groping to the privy
bleared with sleep, were the old man to place his foot upon the
subfusc yet volatile fur of a shadow-camouflaged young tabby
cat—

'You read my thoughts, my love.'

I say to my master: 'Now, you get yourself a doctor's gown
impedimenta all complete or I'm done with you.'

'What's this, Puss?'

'Do as I say and never mind the reason! The less you know
of why, the better.'

So he expends a few of the hag's ducats on a black gown
with a white collar and his skull cap and his black bag and,
under my direction, makes himself another sign that announces,
with all due porc osity, how he is Il Famed Dottore: *Aches
cured, pains averted, bones set, graduate of Bologna, physician*

traordinary. He demands to know, is she to play the invalid to give him further access to her bedroom?

'I'll clasp her in my arms and jump out of the window; we too shall both perform the triple somersault of love.'

'You just mind your own business, sir, and let me mind it for you after my own fashion.'

Another raw and misty morning! Here in the hills, will the weather ever change? So bleak it is, and dreary; but there he stands, grave as a sermon in his black gown and half the market people come with coughs and boils and broken heads and I dispense the plasters and the vials of coloured water I'd fore-thoughtfully stowed in his bag, he too *agitato* to sell for himself. (And, who knows, might we not have stumbled on a profitable profession for future pursuit, if my present plans miscarry?)

Until dawn shoots his little yet how flaming arrow past the cathedral on which the clock strikes six. At the last stroke, that famous door flies open once again and—*eeeeeeeeeeeeech!* the hag lets rip.

'Oh, Doctor, oh, Doctor, come quick as you can; our good man's taken a sorry tumble!'

And weeping fit to float a smack, she is, so doesn't see the doctor's apprentice is most colourfully and completely furred and whiskered.

The old booby's flat out at the foot of the stair, his head at an acute angle that might turn chronic and a big bunch of keys, still, gripped in his right hand as if they were the keys to heaven marked: *Wanted on voyage*. And Missus, in her wrap, bends over him with a pretty air of concern.

'A fall—' she begins when she sees the doctor but stops short when she sees your servant, Puss, looking as suitably down-in-the-mouth as his chronic smile will let him, humping his master's stock-in-trade and hawing like a sawbones. 'You, again,' she says, and can't forbear to giggle. But the dragon too blubbered to hear.

My master puts his ear to the old man's chest and shakes his head dolefully; then takes the mirror from his pocket and puts it to the old man's mouth. Not a breath clouds it. Oh, sad! Oh, sorrowful!

'Dead, is he?' sobs the hag. 'Broke his neck, has he?'

And she slyly makes a little grab for the keys, in spite of her well-orchestrated distress; but Missus slaps her hand and she gives over.

'Let's get him to a softer bed,' says Master.

He ups the corpse, carries it aloft to the room we know full well, bumps Pantaloon down, twitches an eyelid, taps a knee-cap, feels a pulse.

'Dead as a doornail,' he pronounces. 'It's not a doctor you want, it's an undertaker.'

Missus has a handkerchief very dutifully and correctly to her eyes.

'You just run along and get one,' she says to hag. 'And then I'll read the will. Because don't think he's forgotten you, thou faithful servant. Oh, my goodness, no.'

So off goes hag; you never saw a woman of her accumulated Christmases sprint so fast. As soon as they are left alone, no trifling, this time; they're at it, hammer and tongs, down on the carpet since the bed is occupé. Up and down, up and down his arse; in and out, in and out her legs. Then she heaves him up and throws him on his back, her turn at the grind, now, and you'd think she'll never stop.

Toujours discret, Puss occupies himself in unfastening the shutters and throwing the windows open to the beautiful beginnings of morning in whose lively yet fragrant air his sensitive nostrils catch the first and vernal hint of spring. In a few moments, my dear friend joins me. I notice already—or is only my fond imagination?—a charming new *portliness* in her gait, hitherto so elastic, so spring-heeled. And there we sit upon the window-sill, like the two genii and protectors of the house; ah, Puss, your rambling days are over. I shall become a hearthrug cat, a fat and cosy cushion cat, sing to the moon no more, settle at last amid the sedentary joys of a domesticity we two, she and I, have so richly earned.

Their cries of rapture rouse me from this pleasant revery.

The hag chooses, *naturellement*, this tender if outrageous moment to return with the undertaker in his chiffoned topper, plus a brace of mutes black as beetles, glum as bailiffs, bearing the elm box between them to take the corpse away in. But they cheer up something wonderful at the unexpected spectacle before them and he and she conclude their amorous interlude amidst roars of approbation and torrents of applause.

But what a racket the hag makes! Police, murder, thieves! Until the Master chucks her purseful of gold back again, for a gratuity. (Meanwhile, I note that sensible young woman, mother-naked as she is, has yet the presence of mind to catch hold of her husband's keyring and sharply tug it from his sere, cold grip. Once she's got the keys secure, she's in charge of all.)

'Now, no more of your nonsense!' she snaps to hag. 'If I hereby give you the sack, you'll get a handsome gift to go along with you for now'—flourishing the keys—'I am a rich widow and here'—indicating to all my bare yet blissful master—'is the young man who'll be my second husband.'

When the governess found Signor Panteleone had indeed remembered her in his will, left her a keepsake of the cup he drank his morning water from, she made not a squeak more, pocketed a fat sum with thanks and, sneezing, took herself off with no more cries of 'murder', neither. The old buffoon briskly bundled in his coffin and buried; Master comes into a great fortune and Missus rounding out already and they as happy as pigs in plunk.

But my Tabs beat her to it, since cats don't take much time about engendering; three fine, new-minted ginger kittens, all complete with snowy socks and shirtfronts, tumble in the cream and tangle Missus's knitting and put a smile on every face, not just their mother's and proud father's for Tabs and I smile all day long and, these days, we put our hearts in it.

So may all your wives, if you need them, be rich and pretty; and all your husbands, if you want them, be young and virile; and all your cats as wily, perspicacious and resourceful as:

PUSS-IN-BOOTS.

Also available in Vintage

A.S.Byatt

THE MATISSE STORIES

'It is exhilarating to watch Byatt claim so large a territory in these short stories. Her natural, buoyant art makes Matisse an appropriate touchstone for the collection'
Helen Dunmore, *Observer*

'*The Matisse Stories* will be prized by those who like their reading matter to be "analogous to a good armchair", and who are neither threatened nor harrassed by unusual affinities'
Anita Brookner, *Spectator*

'Quite beautifully done...Lucid, sensuous, generous and intelligent...A miniature worthy of being set beside Matisse's own work'
Allan Massie, *Scotsman*

'Classier you could hardly hope to get than this delectable slim volume...Byatt is adept at rendering disintegration in a series of more or less macabre, violent and comical set-pieces'
Hilary Spurling, *Daily Telegraph*

V

VINTAGE

A SELECTED LIST OF CONTEMPORARY FICTION
ALSO AVAILABLE IN VINTAGE

☐ THE HANDMAID'S TALE	Margaret Atwood	£6.99
☐ DANCING GIRLS	Margaret Atwood	£6.99
☐ THE MATISSE STORIES	A.S.Byatt	£4.99
☐ SUGAR AND OTHER STORIES	A.S.Byatt	£5.99
☐ BURNING YOUR BOATS: COMPLETE		
SHORT STORIES	Angela Carter	£8.99
☐ WISE CHILDREN	Angela Carter	£5.99
☐ BIRDSONG	Sebastian Faulks	£5.99
☐ THE FRENCH LIEUTENANT'S WOMAN	John Fowles	£6.99
☐ A MAGGOT	John Fowles	£6.99
☐ PEOPLE FOR LUNCH/SPOILT	Georgina Hammick	£6.99
☐ SUNRISE WITH SEA MONSTER	Neil Jordan	£5.99
☐ THE AUTOBIOGRAPHY OF MY MOTHER	Jamaica Kincaid	£7.99
☐ JUDGE ON TRIAL	Ivan Klíma	£6.99
☐ LOVE LIFE	Bobbie Ann Mason	£4.99
☐ SPENCE + LILA	Bobbie Ann Mason	£4.99
☐ FEATHER CROWNS	Bobbie Ann Mason	£5.99
☐ FRIEND OF MY YOUTH	Alice Munro	£5.99
☐ THE PROGRESS OF LOVE	Alice Munro	£5.99
☐ OPEN SECRETS	Alice Munro	£5.99
☐ NOBODY'S FOOL	Richard Russo	£5.99
☐ LADDER OF YEARS	Anne Tyler	£5.99
☐ THE ACCIDENTAL TOURIST	Anne Tyler	£5.99
☐ ORANGES ARE NOT THE ONLY FRUIT	Jeanette Winterson	£5.99
☐ THE PASSION	Jeanette Winterson	£5.99

- All Vintage books are available through mail order or from your local bookshop.

- Please send cheque/eurocheque/postal order (sterling only), Access, Visa or Mastercard:

☐☐☐☐☐☐☐☐☐☐☐☐☐☐☐☐

Expiry Date:_____Signature:_____

Please allow 75 pence per book for post and packing U.K.
Overseas customers please allow £1.00 per copy for post and packing.

ALL ORDERS TO:
Vintage Books, Book Service by Post, P.O.Box 29, Douglas, Isle of Man, IM99 1BQ.
Tel: 01624 675137 • Fax: 01624 670923

NAME:_____

ADDRESS:_____

_____

_____

Please allow 28 days for delivery. Please tick box if you do not   ☐
wish to receive any additional information
Prices and availability subject to change without notice.